KU-317-689

# THE CHILD THEY DIDN'T EXPECT

BY
YVONNE LINDSAY

MILLS &
BOON

Published in Great Britain 2014
by Mills & Boon, an imprint of Harlequin (UK) Limited,
Eton House, 18-24 Paradise Road, Richmond, Surrey, TW9 1SR

© 2014 Dolce Vita Trust

ISBN: 978-0-263-91482-5

51-1014

Harlequin (UK) Limited's policy is to use papers that are natural, renewable and recyclable products and made from wood grown in sustainable forests. The logging and manufacturing processes conform to the legal environmental regulations of the country of origin.

Printed and bound in Spain
by Blackprint CPI, Barcelona

New Zealand born, to Dutch immigrant parents, **Yvonne Lindsay** became an avid romance reader at the age of thirteen. Now married to her "blind date" and with two fabulous children, she remains a firm believer in the power of romance. Yvonne feels privileged to be able to bring to her readers the stories of her heart. In her spare time, when not writing, she can be found with her nose firmly in a book, reliving the power of love in all walks of life. She can be contacted via her website, www.yvonnelindsay.com.

I'm always very grateful to the generous hearts and minds that help me with the finer details of my books and this one is no different. This book I dedicate to Ashwini Singh with sincere thanks. Any errors relating to newborn intensive care are completely my own.

# One

Ronin lay wide awake in the darkness, his body sated and relaxed, yet hyperaware of the woman sleeping in his arms—of the softness of her curves pressed against his skin, of the sound of her gentle rhythmic breathing. Her lush dark brown hair tickled his sensitized flesh but he didn't want to move from this place, lost as he still was in the intensity of their lovemaking.

He didn't do one-night stands. Not ever. Well, not until tonight. But there had been something about this woman—a fellow New Zealander—that had struck him from the moment he'd brushed past her in the beachfront restaurant of their hotel complex. An instant responsiveness he had never experienced before had stirred in him. Something that saw him agree to the restaurant hostess's suggestion that Ali join him at his reserved table after she was turned away due to overbooking.

The same something that had seen them go on to

dancing after dinner, and then to a walk on the moon-lit sands of Waikiki Beach. And finally, they had made love in her hotel room with a spontaneity and passion he'd never permitted himself to indulge in before.

His friends would be shocked if they ever heard that he—the king of all that was analytical and organized—had fallen into bed with a virtual stranger, purely based on *feelings* and the impulse of the moment. It wasn't his way, not at all. It flew in direct contrast to his talent for deductive reasoning, to his clinical efficiency in being able to take a problem apart and put it back together, to his ability to fix all things falling apart through logic and rationality. There had been nothing logical or ratio-nal about the night he had spent with this woman. And yet, it had been…magical. Yes, that was the only word he could think of to describe it—a word too ephemeral for his charts and numbers world.

Ali sighed and turned on her side, shifting away from him. He was about to reach for her, to pull her back and wake her so they could build on what they'd already savored together, when the discreet but persistent buzz of his cell phone from the pocket of his trousers, some-where on the floor, dragged his attention away.

He flicked a glance at the time on the digital dis-play across the room as he felt around for his trousers in the dark. 5:10 a.m. It definitely wouldn't be his client here in Waikiki who was calling. That only left home—New Zealand. His mind swiftly made the calculation. That would make it 4:10 a.m. tomorrow there, which was hardly a typical time for anyone to call. It was ei-ther a wrong number…or an emergency. He swept the phone into his hand, identifying his father's photo and number on the screen, and moved quickly to the hotel room bathroom.

Pulling the door closed behind him, he answered the phone. His father's anguished voice filled his ear.

"Dad, Dad, slow down. I can barely understand you."

"It's CeeCee, Ronin. She's dead. And R.J., too."

The horrifying words came through loud and clear. An icy cold sensation flooded through his veins. Surely this was some kind of nightmare. His beautiful and vibrant baby sister—dead? It couldn't be true. She'd been the picture of good health, blooming in late pregnancy, when he'd left home three days before. Ronin's brother-in-law had teased him about potentially missing the birth of his first niece or nephew because he'd been called to troubleshoot for an overseas client, yet again.

"How, Dad? When?" Shock made his lips stiff and uncooperative as he tried to form the words. "Tell me what happened."

"She went into labor. R.J. was driving her to the birthing unit. A drunk driver went through a red light. He hit them broadside, pushed them into a pole. They didn't stand a chance."

His father's voice cracked with emotion. The enormity of what had happened overwhelmed Ronin, and he felt his eyes burn with tears. As much as his brain screamed at him that this wasn't happening, logic dictated that this was real, actual, true. And here he was, in Hawaii, far from his family when they needed him most.

"The baby?" he managed to ask through a throat constricted by the clutch of raw grief.

"He was born by emergency caesarian. He nearly didn't make it. CeeCee died during the operation. Her injuries were too great for the doctors to save them both."

Amid excoriating pain that threatened to drive him to his knees, Ronin processed the news that he had a nephew and forced himself to grapple with the knowledge that the much-loved, much-anticipated baby was now an orphan. He dragged his thoughts together. "Is Mum all right?"

"She's in shock. We both are. I'm worried, Ronin. This isn't good for her heart. We need you, son."

"I'll be there as soon as I can. I promise."

He took some details from his father and then, telling him he'd be in touch as soon as he had flight information, he reluctantly severed the call. Leaning against the cool tile of the wall, he took in several deep breaths. Calm. He needed to be calm and organized and all those things that usually came to him as second nature. It was a tall order when all he wanted to do was weep for the senseless loss his family had just suffered. For the dreams his sister and her husband would never see fulfilled. For the child who would grow up without his parents.

When he felt he had himself under control, he slipped back into the hotel room and silently gathered his clothing from where he'd scattered it so mindlessly on the floor only a few hours before. He dressed as quickly and quietly as he could and then let himself out of the room with one thing and one thing only on his mind. He had to get home.

The flight back to New Zealand, via Brisbane in Australia, had been undeniably long. He could have waited for a shorter, more direct flight later that day, but he needed to be home *now* and this was the flight that would get him there first. Ronin had filled the time by making lists of what needed to be done when he arrived home, of people who would need to be contacted, the arrangements made. Through it all his heart ached with a pain that was not as easily compartmentalized as the lists and instructions he'd so assiduously written.

Finally, after fifteen-plus hours of travel and transit, he was back where he belonged—where he was needed most. He spotted his father's pale face in the Arrivals Hall the moment he stepped through from Customs. Strong, familiar arms clapped around him in a gesture that reminded him so much of when he was younger. And then he felt the shudder that passed through his father's body and knew the older man now needed his comfort far, far more than he'd ever needed his father's.

"I'm so glad you're back, son. So glad." His father's voice trembled, sounding a hundred years older than he'd been only a few short days before.

"Me too, Dad. Me too."

It was late, after midnight, when they drove from the airport to his parents' Mission Bay apartment. As they carefully traversed the rain-slicked roads, his father hesitating that extra few seconds as each red light turned to green, Ronin turned his thoughts back to the woman he'd left behind in Hawaii. He'd have to contact the hotel, to leave a message explaining where he'd gone. He'd been so focused on the task of getting home as quickly as possible it hadn't occurred to him until right now that he'd completely abandoned her.

When had she said she was traveling home again? He racked his memory but grief and exhaustion proved a barrier to his usually highly proficient brain. He made a mental note to get a message to her as soon as possible. But right now, he thought as they pulled into the underground parking at his parents' apartment building on Auckland's waterfront, his family—what was left of it—came first.

\* \* \*

A touch of jet lag still weighed on her as Ali pulled up outside her business, Best for Baby. She knew she'd made the right decision to go to Hawaii for a vacation—it had been on her bucket list for years and she'd finally been able to tick it off. But she promised herself she'd be finding an airline carrier that offered direct flights at a more reasonable hour the next time she took the trip—cost be damned.

Of course it would have been more fun to share the vacation with someone else, but, in lieu of company, Ali had enjoyed the luxury of taking things at her own pace and being at her own beck and call for a change. Establishing her baby-planning business had taken everything out of her these past three years. She was proud of everything she'd accomplished, but it had taken a toll. She'd more than earned her holiday.

She should have returned reenergized and full of vigor. Instead, she was nursing emotional bruises that, logically, she knew shouldn't hurt quite as much as they did. It had been one night only. A handful of hours at best. She'd gone into it with no expectations, and yet she felt cheated, as if something potentially special had slipped from her grasp.

It was ridiculous, she knew. The confused pain she was experiencing was nothing like the pain she'd felt five years before, when her husband had admitted he didn't love her anymore, or even when he'd admitted to having an affair with the decorator he'd commissioned to redo his offices and to now loving *her*. But still, it left a sting when a guy sneaked out on a girl after the date night that, for Ali at least, had been the most excellent of all date nights—and especially when she'd broken every single rule in her book by sleeping with him. It had been an unpleasant shock to wake up alone. If he hadn't planned to see her again, why had he suggested they have breakfast in the morning and then spend her last full day in Hawaii together? Would it have killed him to leave her a message? Anything?

She gave herself a sharp mental shake. *Let it go, Ali,* she censured silently. *Let it go.* She'd suffered far worse and survived. This was a blip on her personal radar—no more, no less—and it was about time she treated it as such. She had to be practical about it. She didn't want another relationship—ever. Her business now filled the hole in her life that her broken marriage had left behind. Romance wasn't in the cards for her again. And she was fine with that. She should have known better than to let a little moonlight and a handsome stranger confuse matters. The entire experience now proved to her that she should never break her own rules about getting close to another guy, no matter how strongly she was attracted to him.

Satisfied she had her head on straight, Ali walked through the front door and called out to her assistant and good friend, Deb, at the front desk. "Good morning! Did you miss me?"

"Oh my God, yes. I've been flat off my feet. I have so much to tell you, but first you must tell me about Hawaii. Is it as beautiful as it looks in pictures?"

"It certainly is beautiful," she said with a smile. "Especially the sunsets. Here, let me show you."

Ali retrieved her cell phone from her satchel and opened the picture gallery. Together they oohed and ahhed over the shots she'd taken during the past week. "Are you sure you didn't just photograph a postcard or something?" Deb asked dubiously as they lingered over a shot of the beach at sunset.

Ali looked at the screen of her phone, at the shades of apricot through to pink and purple that stained the sky and at the ubiquitous palm trees forming perfect silhouettes against it. That had been the night she'd met Ronin. The night she'd taken the plunge, thrown inhibitions to the wind and indulged in…well…*him*—the only man she'd ever slept with aside from her ex.

She vividly remembered everything about him from the first moment they'd brushed against one another. She'd just been turned away because the restaurant was fully booked, and as she was starting to leave, without looking where she was going, they had connected. She didn't so much *see* him, as get a series of *impressions* of him. The first, being his size. Not just his height exactly, but his bulk and presence. It was almost as if he wore his masculinity like a coat of armor, his strength and power as much a part of him as the cells that made up his body. The second impression was his scent. With the tangle of fragrances and aromas in the air the hint of his cologne had been a subtle contrast. Almost like the sea breeze that blew up the beach, yet with a cool freshness that tantalized and teased her senses.

Their arms had grazed one another with the lightest of touches, and her breath had caught in her chest. It had been so long since her body had reacted in that way—that buzz, that zing of total awareness—that she'd almost forgotten what attraction felt like, especially attraction on such a visceral level. She'd felt feminine in every sense of the word.

His voice had been deep and resonant as he'd excused himself and stepped away. Ali had remained silent, too stunned by her physical reaction to his touch to do any more than nod her acknowledgment of his apology. It wasn't until he was well past her that she'd realized his accent was just like her own—from New Zealand. She'd looked back over her shoulder and seen the hostess smile at him and pick up a menu before showing him through to his table. Beachfront. For one. And then she'd been invited to join him.

She shook off the flash of memory before her ever-astute friend saw too much on her face. Ali forced a laugh.

"Yes, I'm sure."

"And did you meet any hot guys? Please tell me you met someone."

She managed to summon a smile from somewhere. "I didn't go there to meet someone. I went there for a vacation, and that's exactly what I had. Now, tell me about what's kept you so busy while I was away," she finished, deflecting Deb's attention as effectively as she could.

Deb spent a good twenty minutes giving Ali the abridged version of what had been going on in her absence. Best for Baby, if requested, provided a range of services to expectant families, from baby showers to nursery shopping to interviewing and providing a shortlist of nannies, when needed. She'd had a slow start when she'd opened their doors three years prior, but over the past twelve months, referrals had begun to bring business with increasing frequency.

It was bittersweet work for a woman who knew she'd never bear a child of her own, but it was rewarding in its own way to create the perfect world for a new family.

A perfect world she'd never believed she wouldn't have.

As a child she'd been a little mother for all her toys. She loved children, and had always been eager to raise a house full of them—a dream that she had shared with her high school sweetheart, who had become her husband. They'd hoped to start building their family right away after their wedding…but it wasn't meant to be. Discovering she lacked the essential female ability to have a baby of her own had been a massive blow—one she'd believed she'd overcome with Richard at her side. But she'd discovered she was too flawed for him. So flawed that he'd stopped loving her—and eventually left her for another woman.

Over the past few years she'd become adept at hiding the pain her inadequacies caused her. As the youngest of four sisters, all of whom had children and had remained happily together with their spouses, it hadn't been easy, but she'd gotten there. Best for Baby had given her a sorely needed sense of purpose, and had gotten her through the worst of it.

"The Holden baby shower went really well. They loved the games, and the cupcakes," Deb said, pulling Ali's focus to the here and now.

"Did you send flowers to the bakery with our thank-you note? The way they pulled that together on such short notice really saved us," Ali said, remembering how, on the day of her departure to Hawaii, their usual catering supplier had let them down at the last minute.

"I certainly did. The owner called to say she'd be happy to continue to work with us in the future. Oh, and yesterday we got a new contract."

"Don't you mean a lead?"

"Nope. A bright, shiny new contract. Signed and everything."

"What? Just like that?" Ali asked in disbelief.

"Yup, just like that." Deb looked smug.

Usually there was a process—meetings with clients, presentations of proposals, acceptance of ideas and terms, etc. You didn't *just* get a new contract straightaway like that. Or at least she hadn't, up until now. Her incredulity must have shown on her face.

"Yes, I know. I was surprised, too, but there's some urgency involved as the baby has already been born," Deb said. "Because of complications he's still in hospital. The client wants the nursery completed before the baby is released to the family. And wait, there's more."

"How much more?" Ali asked, doubtful about this sudden good fortune.

"You have carte blanche on the nursery. Your design, your budget."

"No! Seriously? Are you certain this is legit?"

"Sure am. I emailed the contract to the client and it arrived back, fully completed and in duplicate, by courier the same day. Even better, the deposit landed in our bank account overnight."

Ali accepted the clipped papers that Deb handed to her and quickly perused them. Everything seemed to be in order. She looked at the bold signature at the bottom of the agreement. She couldn't make out the name, but it appeared a company rather than an individual had contracted Best for Baby's services. She hadn't heard of REM Consulting before, but that didn't mean anything.

"Well," she said on a slow exhalation of breath. "It certainly looks genuine."

"They want you to go around to the house, today if possible, and start putting things in motion. It doesn't sound like they have the vaguest idea of what they want, which is a bit weird, but they need the job done quickly. I told them you'd be there at three this afternoon."

Ali groaned inwardly. She'd hoped to spend all day in the office, catching up on email and correspondence, but it looked like some of that would have to wait until tonight. Oh well, it wasn't as if she had any grand plans for her evening, anyway. Work had been her constant companion in the past three years, so why should it be any different now?

"Okay, then. I'd better at least attempt to get up-to-date before I head out, hadn't I?"

"Lucky for you I left you a few things to do," Deb said with a cheeky smile. "I'll put the coffee on while you go through your email."

"Thanks, Deb. You're a lifesaver."

The morning passed quickly. Ali ate her lunch at her desk while checking job sheets for clients before heading out to her appointment. She'd made steady progress today, with Deb fielding her calls for her. With taking work home, by tomorrow afternoon, she'd be fully back on deck and up-to-date. She looked up at Deb as she came into her office.

"I called the client to confirm the meeting and I've checked the traffic report. The southern motorway is slow, so you might want to head out soon if you're going to make it to Whitford on time."

Ali glanced at her watch. "Thanks. I'll head out now."

It took nearly an hour for Ali to reach her destination, and she sent a silent message of thanks to Deb for giving her the heads-up to start driving early. She prided herself on punctuality but was prone to getting wrapped up in a project, so she sometimes needed that extra nudge. Once she left the motorway and headed into the green and rolling hills of the rural area on the fringe of the city, she felt herself begin to get excited about the task ahead.

This was the first time she had carte blanche to create everything from the floorboards up. Usually clients had pretty strong ideas already about what they wanted by the time they came to her, so it was a little odd that the parents didn't seem to have any preferences. But, she rationalized, if the baby was scheduled to remain in the hospital for another few days then he was likely premature. The parents might have thought they'd have more time to make a final decision. And now, maybe they were simply too busy with their new arrival to want to even think about such matters.

She wondered what business the baby's parents were in that they could afford both to live out here and to commission a job that would command a very high figure from Best for Baby. Well, whatever they did, Ali was committed to providing an exemplary nursery. Her GPS alerted her to the turnoff coming ahead and Ali slowed her car to take a right into the driveway. At the entrance she announced herself to the console and drove through as the verdigris iron gates gracefully swung open.

The driveway itself was long, more like a private road, she thought as she drove along it. Cows grazed in fields on either side of the gentle rise and she caught a glimpse of a couple of ponds with a few ducks floating happily on the surface. This really was idyllic. The child who grew up here would be lucky, indeed. The driveway curved up the rise to reveal the home she was visiting. It was difficult not to feel a pang of envy for the owners of the beautiful property that spread out before her. Constructed with a steeply sloping gray slate roof, the cream-toned brick house was both imposing and graciously subtle at the same time. She'd barely noticed it from the roadside, and yet from up here, it magnificently commanded an uninterrupted sweeping view right out over the Waitemata Harbor and out to the Hauraki Gulf.

*Get with the program,* she reminded herself as she parked her car near the front door. *You're not here to admire the scenery. You're here to do a job.* She gathered her things and got out of her car. An uncharacteristically nervous tremor passed through her at the prospect of meeting her new clients. Ali chalked it up to the unusual circumstances of the job as she rang the doorbell and then stood waiting in the portico, looking out at the expansive rural scene that spread before her.

Normally she'd have met with her clients at least twice before coming to their home. She liked to gauge how well they'd work together through preliminary meetings at her office before any contracts were signed. In a couple of cases, she'd even refused contracts because she'd known she wouldn't be able to get along with the people involved. This was such a personal business, everyone needed to be on the same page from the get-go. Would she get along with this couple? She hoped so. Her imagination fired to life as she waited, the natural setting and water beyond it already stimulating ideas for the nursery. It would be profoundly disappointing, and not just from a financial perspective, if she found she couldn't work with these clients.

Hearing the front door open behind her, she turned with a smile on her face. A smile that instantly froze in place as her eyes and her brain identified the person framed in the imposing entrance in front of her. As she recognized the stubbly jaw, the spikey dark blond hair, the intense blue gaze.

Ronin Marshall. Her one-night lover.

The last man on earth she'd ever expected, or now wanted, to see again.

# Two

Ronin did a swift double take before his brain and his mouth kicked into gear.

"Ali?"

He'd heard the voice on the intercom at the gate but he'd been distracted, not really listening. Ali stood before him looking as poleaxed as he himself felt, but she seemed to gather herself together a moment later. Dressed in a salmon-pink rolled-collar blouse and pale gray pencil skirt, she was the epitome of professional chic. The color of her blouse did amazing things to her gently sun-kissed skin and made the soft gray-blue of her eyes stand out. Strange, he hadn't noticed what color her eyes were. Well, not so strange when he considered they'd met at night and most of what they'd done together after that had been by candlelight or no light at all.

"There must be some mistake," she said hesitantly. "*You* contracted our services?"

"Yes. Well, technically, my P.A. organized it."

"But you want a nursery," she stated.

"Yes, yes. Please, come in." He stepped back and gestured for her to enter the foyer. "I had no idea it would be you," he said involuntarily.

"Does that make a difference?" Ali asked pointedly, almost with a hint of challenge.

There was a light in her eyes that implied she was angry about something. It confused him. What on earth did she have to be so mad about?

"Of course not. I'm sure you're very good at your job. I just never expected to see you again. I tried to leave a message for you at the hotel, but you'd already checked out."

She raised one perfectly plucked brow in response. It was clear she didn't believe him. He sighed. Believe him or not, they'd have to put their feelings aside. They had a job to do, and he badly needed her help.

The funeral that morning had been harrowing and his emotions were still raw, his thoughts uncommonly scattered. Seeing Ali here, in his home, compounded that confusion. It'd been a hell of a day so far and, judging by the expression on Ali's face, it wasn't going to get better any time soon.

"Look," he said. "I owe you an apology. Can we please start again?"

He put out his hand. She hesitated a moment before grasping it. The second she did, he was instantly struck by that jolt of awareness he'd felt the first time he'd met her. Despite everything that had transpired since he'd left her bed, the connection between them remained.

He wanted to cling to it, to her. The notion was both atypical of him and utterly compelling at the same time.

"Please don't worry," she said. She pulled free of his clasp with a jerk. "Now, shall we get down to business?"

"Business." He nodded. So that was how she wanted to play it. To act like they'd never met before. To pretend that they'd never touched or kissed. That he had never been buried so deep inside her body that he'd begun to lose all sense of himself, instead reveling in her glory. Was it really possible for her to forget all that? He knew full well it wouldn't be possible for him.

If he hadn't seen the telltale flush of color that bloomed at the opening of her blouse when they'd shaken hands, he might have thought she'd been unmoved by their physical contact. But that hint of color, that evidence of the heat that had burned between them, told him far more than her demeanor. He was the king of compartmentalizing things. Of course he could play it her way. That didn't mean he'd like it.

"Come this way." He led her over the foyer's parquet flooring and turned right down a short hall. He gestured for her to go ahead of him into the slightly less formal living room, where he spent much of his leisure time while at home. "Please, take a seat. Can I get you something? Tea, coffee? A cool drink?"

"Just water, thank you," she said as she settled herself into one of the comfortable fabric-covered chairs arranged conversationally around the large wooden coffee table.

It only took a moment to grab a bottle of mineral water from the fridge and a couple of tumblers. He returned to the living room and poured water for each of them.

"I appreciate you being able to come out at such short notice."

"We pride ourselves on our service, Mr. Marshall," she said primly as she unfolded the cover from a tablet. A light touch of her fingertip and he saw the device come to life, much like he had not so very long ago beneath that very same touch.

"Ronin," he corrected.

They'd been intimate together—so deeply intimate. They might be discussing business, but he refused to sit there and listen to her call him Mr. Marshall.

She inclined her head but still avoided using his name. "Now, what is it exactly that you need from us?"

"Everything," he said.

For a moment grief and helplessness surged to the forefront of his mind, but he resolutely pushed the feelings back. He had to keep control of himself…but his usual cool rationality had never been so hard to reach. CeeCee and R.J.'s funeral had been hell in every sense of the word. It had made everything so real, so final. His parents had gone directly from the wake to the hospital. He'd wanted to go, too, but this meeting took precedence. He couldn't bring the baby home until he had something to bring him home to.

A ripple of fear rolled through the back of his mind. What if he'd bitten off more than he could chew with the decision to raise his nephew himself? For the briefest second he considered what his cousin Julia had said to him after the funeral. Already a mother of two, she and her husband had offered to bring CeeCee's son up in their family. It made sense, she'd said. She was already geared up for small children, and with her, her husband and her two daughters—both in primary school—the baby would have a wonderfully stable home. As she'd pointed out, being the infant's guardian didn't mean he had to actually raise him. He could still make sure the little boy had the best of everything without having him directly under his roof. With his long working hours, frequent travel and lack of a wife or committed girlfriend to share the load, Julia had claimed that Ronin's life simply didn't have room for a baby in it.

But it had been clearly outlined in CeeCee's and R.J.'s wills that they had wanted him to care for any children of theirs should anything ever happen to them. Ronin raised a hand to his eyes and swiped at the burning sensation that stung them. He owed it to his sister to fulfill her wishes. Besides, he'd assessed this from every angle already, and he was committed to seeing it through. And, as with any issue he troubleshot, that meant getting the right people in to help with the job. People, who in this case, had turned out to be Ali Carter.

He continued, "Look, I don't have the first idea of what to do."

"Then it's a good thing you called Best for Baby," Ali said, oblivious to the turmoil that was churning inside him. "So, correct me if I'm wrong. You have absolutely nothing here in preparation for the baby."

"That's right," he confirmed. "CeeCee was fiercely superstitious about buying anything before the baby was born. And she forbade anyone else from buying things. There wasn't even a baby shower, at her insistence. We tried to persuade her otherwise, but she was nothing if not determined."

A small frown flittered across her face so swiftly he wasn't sure he'd seen it. She drew in a deep breath and let it go slowly.

"And when is the baby coming home?"

"He should be released in about ten days' time, if all goes well."

She typed a note on her tablet. Even though she hadn't commented on the short time frame she had to work with, he had the impression she disapproved somehow. He knew his request was unusual, but this had mostly been covered in the contract, so he couldn't believe she was surprised by it. But then what was the problem? Maybe she was still angry with him for walking out on her in Hawaii. He had never been one to leave issues to fester. This thing between them needed to be brought out into the open.

"Look, Ali, about that night—"

She looked up from her note-taking.

"That night? Oh, you mean *that* night. Let's not talk about it shall we." She gave him a smile that was no more than a mere upward twitch of the corners of her full lips, utterly devoid of warmth. "I'd prefer it if we could confine our discussion to the task at hand."

Well, he'd tried. She didn't want to talk about it. That was just fine. A pity though, he thought, as his gaze followed the chain of silver beads that slipped inside the neckline of her blouse. He had a feeling that getting to know Ms. Alison Carter all over again would have been a very interesting exercise.

Ali focused on the ten-inch screen she held in front of her, building a checklist of all the things she'd need to tackle if she took this job on. She gave herself a mental shake. Who was she kidding—*if*? Best for Baby wouldn't and couldn't turn down this job. Deb had shown her the signed contract. They were bound to work with this…this *man*!

A near overwhelming surge of fury threatened to

break past her carefully controlled professionalism. How dare he cheat on his pregnant wife with her? How dare he cheat on his wife, period! Having been victim to an unfaithful husband herself, an affair with a married man was the last thing on this entire earth she would ever have willingly embarked upon. She'd rather die than be the other woman, than be the cause of the kind of pain and grief she'd gone through. Betrayal, on any level, was cruel—but this went several levels deeper than that.

Ali reached for her glass of water and took a long slug of the crystal clear liquid in an effort to tamp down the fiery anger that vied with sickening disgust deep inside her. *What a bastard,* she told herself. Yes, he was attractive. Even now her body, traitor that it was, virtually hummed with recognition, remembering his touch as if it were an imprint on her skin.

She drained her glass and set it back on the table with a sharp clunk. Attractive meant nothing whatsoever if it didn't come packaged along with a few other necessities to make up the man. Necessities like integrity, honesty and reliability—just to name the basics. Ali briefly closed her eyes and searched deeply for the inner strength she needed to get through this meeting as quickly and efficiently as possible. It galled her to even have to breathe the same air he was.

She pitied his poor wife, and the baby as well. They both deserved better. Ali quietly resolved to get this contract over with fast. She didn't want to find herself face-to-face with the new mother, not with the guilt she was now forced to bear, hanging like a yoke around her shoulders.

"Right," she said as she opened her eyes again. "Perhaps you could show me the room that will be the baby's nursery so I can take some measurements."

"Sure," Ronin said, his eyes never leaving her face as he stood. "It's upstairs. Come with me."

Ali rose to her feet and followed him from the room. As he ascended the staircase in front of her, she tried not to let her gaze linger on how the finely woven fabric of his trousers skimmed his taut behind, or to notice how the crisp fresh scent of his cologne subtly trailed in his wake. Every breath of him reminded her of the one sinfully exquisite night they'd spent together. Night? No, it hadn't even been that. It had been no more than a few hours, she reminded herself. And she wasn't entitled to reflect on the memory of those hours now that she knew the truth behind his oh-so-alluring facade. Ronin Marshall was a married man and, therefore, completely off limits.

"There are several bedrooms upstairs. The nannies will have the guest suite at the far end at their disposal. It's fully equipped with two bedrooms, a bathroom, a sitting room and a kitchenette."

Ali just nodded. It wasn't unusual for her wealthier clients to employ a nanny, although it definitely sounded as if he was talking in terms of more than one.

Ronin continued down the hall and pushed open the door into a spacious and airy bedroom. "I thought this room next to the guest suite would be best as a nursery."

She looked around, taking in the high-quality furnishings that already filled the room. "Do you want to keep anything that's already in here? The bed, perhaps?"

"Will the baby need any of it?" he asked with a helpless expression in his eyes.

Ali fought back the urge to sigh. Hadn't he paid any attention during his wife's pregnancy? Surely he should know the very basics of what their own child required.

"Not right away, no," she said, controlling her voice

so her disapproval wouldn't shine through. "I'd like to keep the bureau in here." She ran a hand over the provincial French chest of drawers. "But the rest can go into storage. The sooner the better, so I can get painters and paper hangers in here within the next couple of days."

"You have people who can come in that quickly?"

She arched a brow. "There are always people who can come in that quickly when the price is right."

He nodded. "That's good. I'll see to it that the furniture is out of here tomorrow. Do what you have to do."

"That's what you're paying me for," she answered, digging into her bag for her laser tape measure.

It only took a moment to record the dimensions of the room and the window. Together with the ideas she'd begun to dream up as she'd waited in the front portico her mind was brimming with enthusiasm. If only the client wasn't such a dirty, rotten, philandering creep, she'd be relishing this job. Instead, she couldn't wait to get back to the office and hand it off to Deb.

"Right," she said, with a brightness she was far from feeling. "I think that's everything. We'll be in touch."

"That's it?" he asked.

"For today."

"Okay, then." For a minute he looked nonplussed, but then his brow cleared. "Will you stay a while? Talk with me about the steps you'll be taking? I know I'm off to a late start, but I want to understand the task ahead, and what I can do to help it along."

"Mr. Marshall—" she started.

"Ronin. At least you can call me Ronin."

She pressed her lips into a line and sharply shook her head. "I need to get back and get the ball rolling on this so we don't waste any time."

"Look, I'm sorry I didn't leave you a message straightaway. I shouldn't have—"

"Please, that's not necessary. I'll see myself out."

She couldn't stay there another minute and hear his empty platitudes or even ponder at the gall of him to make them. Nothing would change the truth. She'd done the unthinkable—slept with a married man—and he'd done the unforgivable in betraying his wife, and making Ali party to that betrayal. Ali moved quickly out of the room and down the stairs. Behind her, Ronin's heavier tread was muffled by the carpet. He beat her to the door. With one hand on the ornate brass handle he faced her and offered her the other.

"Thank you for coming out. I do really appreciate you taking this on. Right now we have too many other things to focus on."

"Yes, well, this is what we're good at, so you can rest assured the baby will get the best of everything possible."

She steeled herself to take his hand, determined to keep their physical contact to a minimum. It made no difference. Palm against palm, their touch all but sizzled. She quickly pulled away and walked through the open doorway to her car. He stepped out onto the portico and watched her leave—not moving back inside, she noted through the rearview mirror, until she was a good distance from the house.

It was so unfair, she thought as she drove through the iron gates and turned left onto Whitford-Maraetai Road. How could he have been so...so *everything* and so nothing all at the same time? Clearly she needed to hone her inner lie detector some more. First her husband, now this guy. What kind of message was she inadvertently transmitting to the universe that caused her to attract men for whom fidelity was a negotiable bond?

She might never know the answer to that, she told herself as she whipped along the road back toward the motorway interchange. But there was one thing she definitely knew—and that was that Ronin Marshall, and men like him, had no place in her life.

Ever.

# Three

Two days later Ronin pushed open the door to Best for Baby and decisively rang the silver-and-crystal bell at the abandoned reception desk. Abandoned, no doubt, because he'd been fobbed off with *the receptionist* while Alison Carter hid from him here at her office.

He rarely lost his temper. In fact, he was known for being cool under pressure. But this had made his blood boil and, as did everything involving Alison Carter from the moment he'd met her in Hawaii, it churned up emotions that were both unfamiliar and uncomfortable.

The soft noise of a door opening made him wheel around to face her. He didn't even give her a moment before he spoke.

"Why aren't you at my house?" he growled, fighting to keep his voice level.

For a split second she looked taken aback, but her

composure quickly settled back around her like an invisible cape.

"I sent my associate. Is there a problem?" she asked.

"Yes, there's a problem. Your lack of professionalism is the problem."

"My what? Are you complaining about the level of care my company is giving to your contract?" she answered, her face pale but resolute.

"I'm complaining that you're not doing the job yourself."

She squared her shoulders and lifted that dainty chin of hers a notch. "Deb has been with me since the firm opened, and she is equally capable of seeing to it that your nursery is completed on time."

"Deb's your receptionist, right?"

"Normally, yes," she answered, with obvious reluctance.

"And how many contracts has she undertaken that are as time-sensitive as this one?"

"This is her first, but I'm still supervi—"

"Not good enough."

"Your contract is with Best for Baby, not specifically with me," she pointed out in what was, to his way of thinking, a totally unreasonable *reasonable* voice.

But beneath her sangfroid, though, he heard the tremor of unease. It gave him power he wasn't afraid to use. Not when the ends justified the means. He wanted the best for his nephew, and that meant Ali Carter. If he had to make a stink to get her to handle his contract with her precious company personally, then a stink he'd darned well make.

"*You* will complete the contract with me, and only you."

*Or else* ominously remained unsaid.

"Are you threatening me?" she asked, her voice obviously unsteady now.

"Do I need to? Your firm promotes itself as doing what's best for baby. It's your name behind that promotion. If I'm not mistaken, doing what's best is the basis of your mission statement. Yes," he said in response to the look of surprise that flitted through her blue-gray eyes, "I've done my research."

"And your problem?"

Oh, she was good. He'd give her that. She'd pulled herself together, and if he hadn't already heard that weakness just a few moments before, he'd have thought she had the upper hand right now.

"My problem is that I contracted with your company with the expectation that I would receive the best, not the second best."

"I can assure you that Deb is as skilled and efficient as I am. In fact, she's probably better for this contract, as she has no reason on earth not to be. *She's* eager to work with you." She left the words "*I* am not" unsaid, but they echoed in the air around them nonetheless.

"So you admit that you're letting a personal issue stand in the way of your Best for Baby creed, as stated on your company website?"

"I…"

"Not terribly professional, is it?"

"I'm not compromising what my firm offers in any way by putting Deb on the contract."

"But she's not you. I want *you.*"

*In more ways than one,* he added silently. She picked up on the entendre, her cheeks draining of color before flushing pink once more.

"Well, we don't always get what we want, do we?" she snapped back.

"Give me one good reason why you won't work on this project yourself."

"A reason?" her voiced raised an octave. She let out a forced laugh that hung bitterly in the air between them.

"Is that so difficult?"

His words became the catalyst that broke the crucible of her control.

"Fine," she snapped. "You want my reason for not working directly with you, you can have it. Men like you who cheat on their wives and who expect the rest of the world to simply drop everything at their behest make me sick. Do you hear me? Sick! You're scum. You swan around an exotic location under the guise of work and you pick up stray needy women. You betray everything about yourself as a decent human being and all the promises you've made before heading home— without so much as a goodbye, I might add—to your perfect life and your perfect wife. *That's* why I won't work directly for you. Satisfied?"

A lesser man might have staggered under her onslaught. He was not that man.

"I'm not married," he said succinctly in the echoing silence that followed her unexpected tirade.

"Oh, and you think that makes it okay? Wife, partner—what difference does it make? You betrayed the mother of your child when you slept with me, which in my book makes you both a liar and a cheat."

Ronin tamped down his increasing anger, forcing his voice to remain calm. "I repeat. I am not married. Nor am I currently in any kind of romantic relationship. The baby is not my son. Legally, he's my ward."

"Your…your ward?"

Ali clutched at the lapels of her blouse with a shaking hand.

"He's my nephew. My dead sister's son." He sighed. Just saying the words ripped off the carefully layered mental dressing he'd been using to protect his emotional wounds. "Look, can we sit somewhere and discuss this like rational people?"

Ali let go of her blouse and gestured to the room behind her. "Please, come into my office."

Her heart raced as her mind played over the appalling way she'd just spoken to him. She never lost it like that, ever. Not to anyone, and especially not to a client. But this was just a little bit too raw for her. The first time since her divorce she'd trusted anyone enough to even consider kissing them, let alone sleeping with them, and this had happened. She could be forgiven for jumping to the wrong conclusion, but she couldn't be forgiven for the diatribe she'd just delivered. She'd be lucky if he didn't rip up their contract right now and throw it back in her face.

Two facts now echoed in her mind.

The baby wasn't his.

*He wasn't married.*

"Take a seat," she said, moving over to the carafe of iced water she kept on a credenza. She poured out two glasses and placed one on her desk in front of him. "Here. I know we both could probably do with something stronger, but it's all I have on hand."

"It's fine," he said. He reached for the glass and drained it with one long swallow.

"I apologize for jumping to conclusions, and for speaking to you like that," she said as calmly as she could. She settled behind her desk and looked at him directly. "And I'm deeply sorry for your loss."

Her eyes raked over him, taking in the shadows that

lingered under his eyes and the fine lines of strain that hadn't been on his face the first time she'd met him. She must have been too preoccupied to notice them when she'd seen him at his house the other day. He looked haggard, as if he'd been on the go non-stop.

"Thank you. It's why I had to leave you so suddenly the night we met. My father called to say my sister and her husband had been in a fatal accident. My nephew was born by emergency C-section immediately before his mother died. I left your room on autopilot. I wasn't really thinking clearly, I just knew I had to get home. By the time I realized how unfairly I'd treated you, I was already back here, and when I contacted the hotel, they said you'd checked out."

"I understand," she assured him, her heart breaking for the shock and pain he must have felt. She was close to her sisters and couldn't begin to imagine how she'd feel if the same thing had happened to one of them. "I would have done exactly the same thing."

He dipped his head in acknowledgment. "It's been hell this past week. So much to organize, so many people to see." He swiped a hand over his face. "And the baby. It would have helped if CeeCee hadn't been such a superstitious thing and had organized the nursery already. I could have simply transported everything to my house."

"Or stayed at theirs?"

"No," he shuddered. "That would have been too much. I couldn't."

"What about your parents? How are they coping?"

"They're devastated. The stress is playing havoc with my mother's heart condition."

Ali felt her heart break a little at the note of sheer anguish in his voice. She could tell he was holding on

by a thread. Had he even had the chance to begin griev-
ing himself?

"Oh, Ronin. I'm so sorry. If there's anything I can
do, just name it."

"There is," he said, pulling himself together before
her eyes. "Given the circumstances, you'll understand
why I need you to complete the nursery. I don't want any
mistakes or oversights. Everything has to be perfect."

She was about to point out that she wouldn't have put
Deb on the assignment—with Best for Baby's reputation
hanging on it—if she hadn't been confident that things
would be done to his satisfaction. Instead, completely
understanding how vital this all was to him, she murmured her assent.

"So you'll come back on the job?" he asked, lifting
his head and looking straight into her eyes.

She could see the worry behind them and his concern that everything be perfect.

"Yes, but better than that, you'll have two of us for
the price of one. Deb will continue to assist—for good
reason," she clarified when it looked as if he might protest. "There is a great deal to be done in a very short
time. Two heads will be better than one in this case.
She's already coordinating the work crews. I'll get
started on the nursery supplies and furniture tomorrow."

The tension that had gripped his frame from the moment she'd laid eyes on him seemed to slowly leach out.

"Good," he said on a harshly blown out breath.
"Good. You know, I always imagined that one day I'd
fill my house with a family. I just never thought for a
minute it would happen like this."

He got up to leave and Ali rose with him. At the
main door to her office he turned to her, composed
once again.

"I'll be working from my home office tomorrow. Will I see you?"

Ali ran through a mental checklist in her head before giving him an affirmative nod. "Probably after lunch time. I'll bring some curtain swatches just to make sure we've got the right match with the walls."

"Fine. I'll key you in to the biometric reader at the gate and the front door so you can come and go as you wish."

She blinked at that.

"You'd trust me with that?"

"Why not? You aren't going to steal the family silver, are you?"

"No, of course not," she laughed in response.

"Then what's the problem? It'll be more convenient while you're coming and going in the next few days."

And, no doubt, it would ensure that it was her and not Deb going to the house, Ali thought after he'd gone. The idea wasn't unappealing—now that she knew he wasn't a dirty cheater.

He wasn't married. As the thought came back to her, she couldn't help it—an ember of longing flickered to life deep inside her once more.

As soon as Deb returned to the office, Ali explained she'd be back on the nursery outfitting as well. Her friend seemed unfazed about the change in seniority.

"Many hands make light work, and there's certainly plenty of work on this job to go around," Deb said, cocking her head to study her friend. "I get the feeling, though, that there's something you're not telling me."

Ali tried to hold her gaze and refute the underlying question on Deb's face but in the end she gave in.

"Look, I don't want to go into details, but long story

short, I met Ronin once a little while ago and we kind of hit it off, but nothing eventuated. Of course, when we got this contract and I saw him again, I assumed the baby was his and that he had been married when we first met."

"Oh," Deb said on a long sigh of understanding. "I get it. You must have been pretty mad, huh?"

"You could say that," Ali responded. Her stomach twisted sickly with the memory of how she'd spoken to Ronin earlier that day.

"But it's all sorted now, right?"

"It looks that way."

"So are you going to, y'know, see him again? And don't get all coy on me and say that naturally you'll see him in the course of the job. That's not what I mean, and you know it." Deb smirked and crossed her arms.

Ali shook her head slightly. Deb knew her too well. That was exactly what she'd been about to say. "No. We won't start seeing each other like that. He's just been through the wringer with the loss of his sister and her husband, and he has the additional pressure of keeping an eye out for his parents—not to mention the worry of the baby."

"Sounds like he needs a bit of distraction then, wouldn't you agree?" Deb said with a slow wink.

"I think distraction is the last thing he needs right now," Ali replied firmly, determined to close the subject. "Now, tell me, how did the paint finish turn out?"

They discussed the dove gray walls with white trim that had been painted that morning, and Deb showed Ali a couple of photos she'd taken with her tablet. Ali gave an approving nod at the contractor's work.

"They're fast and they're good, aren't they? We should pay a little over their premium for doing the job on such short notice. There's a large enough buffer in the budget for that, isn't there?"

Deb agreed, and they went on to check the list of items Ali had planned for her shopping expedition in the morning. They divided the lists. Deb was to purchase a diaper bag and supplies along with car seats—one for Ronin and one for the nannies—as well as a stroller and a portable crib in case the baby overnighted with his grandparents when he was a little older. Ali took on the nursery furniture and final decorations for the room, as well as the clothing and feeding necessities. She made a mental note to ask Ronin to check with the hospital about which formula the infant was being fed so she could make sure there was a sufficient supply at the house for when the baby came home.

By the time their working day drew to a close, she was feeling excited. It was because she would deeply enjoy the tasks ahead, she told herself firmly as she locked up the office and headed for her tiny apartment in Mount Eden. It had nothing to do with seeing Ronin again the next day.

*Liar,* she admitted to herself with an illicit thrill. Dressing the nursery was a fun job, but it had nothing to do with the slow moving heat that was spreading through her veins at the thought of being near him again. For all the words she'd bandied in Deb's direction today, she couldn't help but wonder—what would it be like if she and Ronin had another chance? Ali dismissed the question almost as swiftly as she'd thought it. She'd made her decision to remain single after the devastation her marriage had caused her. She didn't want or need the complications that a relationship with a man like Ronin Marshall would bring. Not one little bit.

# Four

Ronin huffed in frustration as the doorbell rang for what felt like the hundredth time that morning. He'd had no idea how disruptive changing one room over for a tiny baby could be, but he was certainly finding out. He'd thought he could work quite comfortably at home but the steady stream of courier deliveries had negated that possibility. Now he had boxes strewn all over his foyer and no idea what was in them or where they needed to go.

"Feeling a bit under siege?" Ali asked with a sunny smile as he opened the door to her and she espied the stacks of boxes around him.

Relief seeped through him. Thank God she was there. *Now I might be able to put my focus where it belongs and get something done.*

"You could say that," he replied. "I could have done with you here from about ten this morning."

"I'm sorry. I came as quickly as I could." She hefted a book of curtain samples a little higher, and he swiftly reached out for the heavy item.

"Here, let me take that for you."

"Thanks. I have a couple more in the car."

"Seriously?"

She laughed at his obvious surprise and he felt his lips curl in response. "Yes, seriously. This is important."

She spun on a ridiculously delicate high heel and went straight to her car. Ronin followed and accepted the additional sample books from her, all the while trying to keep his gaze averted as the fabric of her neatly cut trousers pulled across the curves of her backside as she reached down into the trunk of her car. It occurred to him that nothing she wore stood out as particularly high fashion, yet everything still managed to deliver a punch when she put it on. He shifted his focus to the heavy books in his arms.

"All this for one set of curtains?" he asked.

"Oh, there were more," she answered with a sweet curve of her lips. "But they didn't have what I was looking for."

He followed her back into the house, where she paused in the foyer and inspected the labels on the various boxes that had accumulated there. She pulled her tablet out of her voluminous handbag and made some notes before stacking a couple of the smaller boxes in her arms.

"Shall we go upstairs? I'd like your opinion on the fabric swatches."

"Really, I know nothing about color. I usually left all that to…" His voice tailed off as that sweeping sense of loss tugged hard at his heart.

Decorating had been CeeCee's forte and her business, and she'd been exceptional at it. It was part of the reason he'd teased her so mercilessly about not doing anything for the baby's room. She'd never been superstitious growing up, which begged the question—had she had some intuition that something was going to go wrong? He shoved the idea from his mind before it could bloom into something further. He'd never held with that way of thinking and never would. To him intuition was, more accurately, picking up subconscious clues. No clue on earth could have predicted what would happen the night CeeCee and R.J. were killed.

He realized that Ali was waiting for him to finish his sentence. "To others who are far more adept at it than I am," he finished lamely.

"Well, if you're happy for me to make the final choice, I'm okay with that. I just thought that since it's your home we're working on you might like some input."

"I'll take these up for you and leave you to it. I have a conference call with a client in Vietnam shortly that should take about an hour. Please don't leave until I'm done. I really can't afford any delivery interruptions during the call, so if you could take care of opening the gate and getting the door, I would really appreciate it."

Ali smiled calmly. "No problem at all. I'll be here all afternoon. The furniture will be delivered by three, and I'd like to set it up as quickly as possible."

"Good, I'll get your fingerprint programmed into the biometric reader when I'm finished on the call."

They went upstairs and Ali pushed open the door to what was to be the nursery. Ronin was a little surprised at how much had already changed. He'd gotten his two part-time groundsmen to remove the furniture and store it in the loft above his multicar garage, together with the carpet square that had been in the room. Last time he'd looked in, the wooden plank floorboards had been covered with paint-spattered drop cloths and the walls had been a patchwork of the original off-white with an array of softer lemons, blues and grays. He was pleasantly surprised by the solid block of pale but warm gray that now covered the walls, offset by pristine white-painted trim on the deep skirting boards and the window frame.

"I wasn't sure what you'd decided on in here, but I have to say I like it," he said, laying the stack of curtain books on the floor.

"It looks great, doesn't it? Initially I'd thought to go with the pale blue on three walls and then to have a farm scene mural painted on one wall, but you only need to look out the window to appreciate that view more than anything that could be painted in place. Deb and I decided the gray was best and would work as baby grows older, too. Removable borders can provide features anyway, and they can be changed more easily, too."

Ronin tried to envision what she was talking about, but it all went right over his head. He was far more comfortable talking specifications and load-bearing structures than he was visualizing what was obviously so clear in her head.

Ali bent and rummaged through the fabric samples, extracting a sheer white gauze and then flipping back and forth through each of the other books. Their samples were, to his eye at least, much the same color as the nursery walls.

"Here," she said, holding one book open to a self-patterned fabric swatch a couple of shades darker than what was already on the wall. "Could you hold that up for me over by the window? I want to see how it works with the rest of the room."

He did as she bid and was surprised to see her shake her head vehemently. "What? Wrong color?"

"Totally," she muttered, digging back through the samples again. "Here, try this one."

To him they looked identical, but he dutifully held the sample up for her.

"Yes, that's better," she said, tilting her head slightly to one side and taking a step back. "In fact, I think that's perfect. We'll put the drapes against the window with the sheers on the bedroom side. That way the sheers will soften the effect on the whole room when the drapes are closed."

"I know what you're saying should make sense," he laughed. "But it sounds like a foreign language to me."

Her face broke into a wide smile and she gave him a cheeky wink. "Then it's a good job you hired Best for Baby, isn't it?"

She looked just as she had when they'd talked over the dinner table in Hawaii. He'd been reluctant, after a taxing day with a client, to share his solitude. But when the restaurant hostess had requested he allow someone she'd had to turn away to join him, and had pointed Ali out in the bar, he'd recognized her as the woman he'd brushed against in the crowded restaurant lobby. The woman who'd unwittingly triggered a startlingly visceral reaction. His initial resistance had been demolished and he'd said yes.

He wanted that again. That carefree easiness between them. That sense of being on a voyage of discovery together.

"Ali—" he started, taking a tentative step toward her. "Yes?"

God, he wanted nothing more than to take her in

his arms and kiss her. To revisit that exquisite oblivion they'd shared the night they met.

"I—" He broke off with a muttered expletive as his phone chirped in his trouser pocket. He identified the number of his office on the screen. "I'm sorry, but I need to get this."

"No problem. I'll be around here or downstairs if you need me."

She took the sample book from him, and as she moved away again he caught the fresh floral sweetness of her perfume. It was so subtle he was unsure he'd even smelled it at all, but it had a very immediate effect on his body. Need bloomed low in his groin. The phone in his hand continued to chirp. He forced his attention away from the woman who'd ensnared him and fought his libido under control. This kind of thing didn't happen in his normally rigidly structured world. Yes, he knew desire—what man didn't? But he'd never known it like this.

He barked a greeting into his phone. Walking from the nursery, he forced himself not to wonder why each step away from Ali felt as if it were a mile rather than a mere yard.

Well, that was intense, Ali thought as she watched Ronin leave the room. For a moment there she'd thought he was going to close the gap between them and kiss her. His eyes had darkened to a deep denim blue and fixed on her, as if the world had narrowed to only contain the two of them. Her heart still thumped in her chest, pumping blood to her extremities and heightening her awareness to a fever pitch.

She bit down on her lower lip. A lip that tingled in anticipation of his caress. A lip that mourned the caress that hadn't happened. Obviously their initial attraction was still there just as strongly as it had been an entire hemisphere away—their more recent contretemps notwithstanding.

She closed the sample books and stacked them on one side of the room. It was getting more difficult every time she saw him to remind herself she didn't want to go there again—that she was totally wrong for him. She had to stay professional. He was her client and she was contracted by him to do a job—a job that involved a helpless, parentless infant. Something deep inside her ached at the thought. What she wouldn't give to be that parent—to be that special someone to nurture and raise and love the child.

When she'd discovered she couldn't bear children of her own, she'd imagined that she and her husband would adopt, but he'd been opposed to the idea. She had thought he just needed a while to adjust to the idea of their dreams taking a different shape. She'd tried to give him space and time—space and time he'd used to go behind her back and fall in love with the woman he'd left her for. His lover had represented a new start for Richard, a second chance on the path to the life he'd planned...while Ali was clearly nothing more to him than a dead end.

It had been a painfully hard lesson to learn. Never in their years of courtship, or their marriage, had he even intimated that his love for her was contingent on her ability to produce and raise a family with him. That knowledge had been even more hurtful than the news that she was infertile.

Infertility was something they should have been able to deal with together. Thousands of couples the world over did every day. While she'd railed against the unfairness of it all—especially when faced consistently with evidence of her three sisters' abundant fertility and happy marriages—it had been her husband's rejection of *her*, and his twisted belief that it somehow reflected on him as a man, that had been her undoing. Those scars still ran deep—still made her feel vulnerable and inclined to withdraw from placing herself in that position a second time.

She reminded herself she was not, and probably never would be, ready to put herself out there again. There was no way she would run the risk of being rejected again. Hadn't she learned her lesson? She'd already felt dreadful when Ronin had seemingly abandoned her after their night together. What if they did get together and he did let her down again?

"Talk about getting ahead of yourself," she muttered to the empty space around her. "Very shortly he's going to be incredibly busy raising a child. He certainly won't have time for you. Nothing's happened and nothing will happen."

But there was a piece of her that *wanted* something to happen, that wanted Ronin Marshall with an ache that went deep down to her core.

Ali busied herself over the next few hours unpacking the boxes that had been stowed in the foyer. Some of the items needed assembly, so she retrieved her tool kit from her car before kicking off her heels and starting to put together the change station and the crib. After a short time, even without all the finishing touches, the nursery began to look like a baby's room. Just doing this, creating a safe and loving haven for someone else's unknown child, filled the echoing hollow inside her. Even if only briefly. It was why she loved doing what she did.

A sound at the door made her look up from where she was kneeling on the floor, reading the final instructions on the change station. Heat flushed her skin when she saw Ronin. She scrambled to her stocking feet, only to feel at a disadvantage as he towered over her.

"Is everything going okay here?" he asked, his eyes scanning the room.

"Pretty much," she said. "I just need a step ladder to put this mobile up over the crib. I can bring one out tomorrow, unless you have one here I can borrow?"

"There's one in the garage. I'll get it for you."

"Great. After that's up I'd best head off. I need to stop at the office and clear messages with Deb."

"Must you?" he asked, his brows pulling into a straight line. "I was wondering if you'd like to join me for an early dinner. I thought we could go down to Pine Harbor and eat there. There's a nice place overlooking the marina."

"Dinner?" she repeated, startled.

"Yes, you know, that meal people have in the evening some time before they go to bed?"

She laughed, but even so she felt her breath hitch just a little. Here it was. An overture. She should make it clear the only thing between them was a professional relationship, and turn his offer down. Really, she should. Hadn't she just been having a major internal discussion about this very issue? She'd say no, and that would be that. Simple.

"I'd love to," she said with a smile.

# Five

$A$li found the drive to the marina in Ronin's car too short and too long at the same time. She could barely keep her eyes from his long, capable fingers wrapped casually on the leather-covered steering wheel, nor push away the memories that flooded her mind of how those fingers had felt as they'd explored her body. Memories that left her breath shallow, an unignorable sensation tingling at her core.

When they pulled into the parking lot she dragged her eyes and her awareness to her surroundings and an involuntary exclamation of delight escaped her. The marina glowed in the early evening sun. The palm trees that bordered the road suddenly reminded her of another sunset, another dinner shared with this man…and what had come after.

"It's pretty here," she said, squirming a little in her seat.

"It is," he agreed, getting out of the car and coming around to open her door.

He offered her a hand and she took it automatically. Again she felt that electric sense of awareness at his touch. *Will this never stop?* she wondered. A part of her really didn't want it to, but then the other part, the fragile broken part of her mind and her heart, craved protection and set up a new caution in her mind.

Not letting go of her hand, he led her toward one of the buildings. They took a seat at the window, looking toward the ferry landing, where passengers—most of them from Auckland's city center, by the looks of it— were disembarking a vessel.

"This is such a lovely setting," she commented after the waitress took their drink orders and left them to peruse the menu. "I had no idea this place existed. Thank you for inviting me."

"Thank you for joining me."

She studied him a moment. "Why did you ask me to dinner?"

"Isn't it obvious?" he replied, his eyes doing that thing where they darkened to denim again.

Obvious? Did he feel the same attraction she felt? "Perhaps you need to explain."

Ronin leaned forward, one hand playing with the condensation on the side of his glass as he chose his words with obvious deliberation.

"I'm not normally an impulsive man, Ali. But there's something about you that makes me want to throw all my caution to the wind. To be with you."

"Oh," she uttered, her eyes widening in shock. Of all the things he could have said—the polite conversation she'd expected—that was probably what she'd least expected to hear.

"Too much?" he asked with a quick grin that crinkled the corners of his eyes and lifted most of the strain she'd become accustomed to seeing there.

"Maybe," she hedged. Even as she did so, her pulse leapt in response to the intensity reflected in his gaze.

"The way I see it is this. We jumped over several vital steps in the getting-to-know you stages of attraction when we met in Waikiki, and then I ran out on you without explanation. I figure we didn't really have the opportunity to get off to the right start, and I'd like to remedy that."

The waitress returned with their drinks, interrupting him for a moment.

"Are you ready to order?" the waitress asked brightly.

"Just a few more minutes, please," Ronin replied. The moment she was gone, he turned the intensity of his attention back to Ali. "I think we should start over. Get better acquainted. What do you think?"

"I…" Ali searched for the right words to say. Regret at her impulsive acceptance of his dinner offer pounded through her brain. Hadn't she just been telling herself she didn't want a relationship? It was time to draw a line in the sand. To make it clear to Ronin exactly where her boundaries were. "Look, please don't take this the wrong way, but I really don't think that's a good idea. What happened when we met, I'm not like that. I mean, I don't usually—"

"Me neither," he interrupted, picking up the glass of Central Otago Pinot Noir he'd ordered. "That's exactly my point. Clearly there's something here—something that made both of us willing to take a chance. Don't you think the chemistry we shared is worth exploring some more?"

"Look, Ronin, I—"

"Just think about it. A new beginning." He held his drink toward her in a toast. Automatically she lifted her lemon lime and bitters and allowed him to clink his glass against hers. This was wrong and yet so incredibly tempting at the same time. She already knew they struck sparks off one another—sparks that would make it far too difficult for her to keep a clear head. If she gave in to the attraction between them, she wouldn't be able to stay detached. She'd fall too hard, too fast and far too deep to be able to pull herself back out without pain. If she had an ounce of sense left in her mind she'd be hightailing it out of there as fast as she could.

Clearly that last ounce had departed.

Tomorrow she'd make it clear that theirs couldn't be any more than a client/contractor association. She just had to hope that would be soon enough.

They studied their menus. Ali asked Ronin for his recommendations, since he was a regular. When the waitress came back, they were ready. After she'd gone, Ali looked up to find Ronin watching her.

"What?" she asked. "Have I got lipstick on my teeth or something?"

"No," he laughed. "I was just calculating what the odds were of us meeting up again like we did."

"Pretty slim, I would have thought. It certainly wasn't a good thing that reintroduced us," she said, with a pang in her heart for the loss his family had undergone.

"No, it wasn't."

"Was your sister your only sibling?"

He nodded. "I still struggle to believe she's gone."

"How's the baby doing?" Ali asked, wishing suddenly that she hadn't chosen this track of conversation, but feeling committed now she'd started it.

"He's holding his own. Getting a little stronger every

day. They're trying to establish feeding so he can come home. We each try to spend time with him at the hospital, my mum and dad and I, so he'll be used to us when he comes out." A strangely bemused expression settled on his face.

"What is it?" Ali asked, concerned.

"Since he's been in the Newborn Intensive Care Unit, they've encouraged us to be there as much as possible, and to hold him even though he's been ventilated. Last night, when I went to see him, he was off the ventilator. The nurse told me about kangaroo cuddles."

"Kangaroo cuddles? I haven't heard of those."

"It's chest-to-chest, skin-to-skin contact. You sit in an easy chair and the nurse lays the baby on your bare skin." Ronin's eyes became unfocused for a moment, as if he was lost in the memory. "It's weird, but it's like he knows he's coming home to me. He was fussy when she first picked him up, but as soon as she laid him on me and covered him with a blanket, he gave this little sigh and settled right into my chest."

"That must have made you feel special," she said softly.

"Special? I don't know. He's so small. So dependent. It's kind of terrifying."

Ali felt tears sting her eyes. To hear this big, strong man admit his fear of caring for and raising his nephew tugged at her heart. "He's so lucky to have you."

His gaze returned to its usual sharpness. "He'd have been better off with his parents."

"I know, but at least he has you and your mum and dad, who care so much about him. What about his other grandparents. Are they around?"

"No, R.J.'s parents died some time ago apparently, and he was an only child."

"It must be hard for you all."

"It is, but we still have the baby. To have lost him too would have been the final blow for my mother, I think." He took another sip of his wine and looked out the window for a while before returning his gaze to her. "What about you? Brothers? Sisters? Parents still around?"

Ali latched on to the change in subject. "Oh, I have three sisters, all older than me. All married with families. Mum and Dad complain they never get a weekend to themselves because they're always having one lot of grandkids or another, but, just privately, I think they love it. They wouldn't have it any other way."

"Must make family gatherings fun," Ronin said, with another one of those heart-stopping grins.

"They're busy, that's for sure."

"And you? Is coming from a big family part of the reason you do what you do?"

Ali had been hoping the conversation would not lead in this direction, but she was well practiced at diversion. "Well, I certainly had plenty of experience helping my sisters prepare for my nieces and nephews," she said with a forced laugh. "But, I guess I was at a crossroads in my life and I figured there was a gap in the market here for something like that. I'd heard of party and other types of planners here, but when I heard about baby planners in the States, I decided that was what I wanted to do. After some research I did exactly that and started the company."

The summary didn't do justice to how hard she'd had to work to establish her business, or all she'd had to sacrifice. Most of the money she'd received in the settlement when her marriage had been dissolved—after their requisite two-year separation—had been poured into Best for Baby. She'd only kept back enough to pay for six months of living expenses and the lease on her apartment—against her parents' urging that she move back home with them until she was securely on her feet. She had trusted in her ability to earn enough to make the monthly payments and to live after those first six months.

There had been times when she'd wanted to crawl away from it all and to stay wrapped in the cocoon of safety her parents had offered. But with the failure of her marriage and her own perceived failure of herself as a woman still so sharply painful, she knew she had to reach out for herself, to rebuild her life, or give up all together.

"What about you?" she asked of Ronin, eager to turn the focus of their conversation back to him before he probed too deeply into her past. "What is REM Consulting?"

"We're a civil engineering company, and we consult on international projects. Mostly major building sites and complexes. My role is mainly as a troubleshooter. Generally I try to prevent the bad things from happening, handle risk management, that kind of thing. When things go wrong and solutions need to be found fast, I get called in to put everything right again."

She thought about how swiftly he must have had to move when he'd received the news about his sister and her husband. Having that background probably helped him remain calm and controlled in a situation that would most likely render others incapable of logical thoughts.

"Does your work take you away often?" she asked.

He nodded. "And usually at very short notice. It's why I'll need a rotation of nannies at the house. You got the brief on that, didn't you?"

"Yes, I did. I've got Deb compiling a list of suitable

applicants for initial interview. You mentioned you preferred nannies with nursing experience. Those skills
will come at quite a cost. You do realize that?"

He made a sweeping movement with one arm. "Cost
isn't an issue. My nephew's well-being is all that matters."

It struck Ali that while Ronin was doing all he could
both physically and materially for the newborn, she still
had questions about the baby's emotional support system. Ronin was clearly confident when it came to providing for his nephew, but was visibly nervous at the
thought of nurturing the baby. While her family life
had been loud and chaotic with six of them crowded
into a small three-bedroom bungalow in the suburbs,
her upbringing had been a happy one, with love and affection showered on Ali and her sisters by parents who
put their children first.

And then there was Ronin's work. With him being on
call for a wide range of clients all over the world, how
consistent would things be at home? It was impossible
for him to be a full-time father, with all the loving care
that should entail, even if he wanted to.

"When will you be available to interview the shortlist of nannies?" she asked, forcing her thoughts back
to her tasks.

"It'd probably be best if I see them in my office in
town. I'll check my diary and call you with dates in
the morning."

She'd have to be satisfied with that for now, she decided. No matter her own thoughts on the situation, the
baby's emotional care wasn't her responsibility, and besides, Ronin was doing his best to step up to his duty
to the baby. It wasn't her place to pry, beyond the scope
of her job.

Their meals arrived and they turned their attention to the food. As the sun lowered over the western horizon, their conversation drifted away from what were, for Ali at least, work-related matters, and onto more personal interests. By the time they finished coffee and dessert they'd found a mutual love of English crime novels and old black-and-white movies.

Ali flicked a glance at her watch and sighed regretfully. "As lovely as this has been, I'm really going to need to head home."

"You could stay with me," Ronin offered without hesitation. "I have several guest rooms. You're welcome to use one, if you prefer."

If she preferred? Her imagination set her synapses firing.

"Oh, no, I don't think that's a good idea, but thank you for the offer," she answered with a twist of her lips. As if she could sleep under the same roof as him and not replay in her mind over and over what they could be enjoying together. She had enough trouble in her own bed in her tiny apartment. "I need an early start at the office tomorrow before another round of shopping and then the preliminary interviews for your nannies."

If he was disappointed in her response, he hid it well.

"Will I see you out at the house tomorrow?" he asked.

"No, not tomorrow, but I'll be back first thing the day after."

"I'll make sure I'm home. We can do lunch together."

"I *am* supposed to be working when I'm at your house," she reminded him with a small frown. "I take my obligations seriously."

"As do I," he answered, his face an implacable mask all of a sudden. He leaned forward and took her hand.

"Besides, as your current employer, surely it's my duty to make sure you have all your breaks?"

She couldn't help but laugh. "Okay, lunch together sounds nice. Thank you."

Ronin studied the figures on the estimate for the new project in Southeast Asia. It was the third time he'd applied himself to the document today—or at least attempted to apply himself to it. But he couldn't make himself concentrate. Giving up in frustration, he pushed his executive chair back from his desk and swiveled around to face the sparkling Waitemata Harbor. Even so, he didn't notice the spectacular view. His thoughts were elsewhere, far away from his office.

It wouldn't take a rocket scientist to figure out why his thoughts were so fractured, why his legendary control was so off-balance.

Alison Carter. Just picturing her in his mind was distraction enough, let alone remembering the night they'd shared in Hawaii. That night before his world imploded. He raised a hand to rub wearily at his forehead. So much had happened in the past few weeks, and he'd had so little power over any of it. His life had changed, and even though he was holding on to whatever he could, with a grip that was becoming more tenacious every second, he felt as if he was losing self-control. He couldn't afford to fall apart, not with everyone depending on him—and sometimes the weight of keeping everything together bore down on him more heavily than it should.

But Ali? She was a beacon in the darkness. A reminder that life did go on. And for some reason just being around her calmed him. Well, he admitted with a rueful smile, maybe *calm* wasn't quite the word he was looking for, not when his body reacted the way it did at the simple thought of her. Normally, he'd have worried about the strength of his response to her, the way she could push all other thoughts out of his head. Even the most passionate of his relationships in the past had never made him feel the way Ali had in just one night. Feelings that intense, especially on such a short acquaintance, should have seen him stepping back. But he couldn't step back from Ali, not when just being around her was enough to make the weight of his grief and his responsibility fade. Surely there was no harm in indulging in that pleasure for just a little while longer.

He looked forward to seeing her again the next day, to treating her to lunch and getting to know her a little better outside of her efficient capacity as a baby planner.

His eyes focused on the harbor now, giving him an idea for what they could do for their lunch date. He spun his chair around and punched the speaker to talk to his P.A. in the office outside his.

"Maeve? Can you get me a list of restaurants on Waiheke that have helipads?" he asked.

"Restaurants. Waiheke. Helipads. I'll get back to you shortly, Mr. Marshall," his scarily efficient P.A. replied in a smooth tone.

His mother's age, Maeve was one of those miracles of efficiency who made his job and quite frankly his life much simpler—even if she was old-school enough to insist on calling him Mr. Marshall and not Ronin, as he'd asked. As good as her word, Maeve was in his office ten minutes later with a printed list of restaurant names, website links, phone numbers and addresses, together with GPS coordinates. A perfectionist himself, Ronin appreciated her attention to detail.

"Is that what you wanted?" she asked as he scanned

the list, his eyes alighting on the name he was looking for.

"Perfect," he said, looking up. "Thanks."

"Did you want me to make a booking for you?" Maeve began to turn to leave his office.

"No, I'll handle this myself."

Her step faltered on the carpeted floor. "Yourself?"

He looked up, meeting her surprised expression. "I do know how to make my own restaurant bookings," he said drily.

"You might know how, but you never do it. This isn't work-related—it's personal. You've met someone, haven't you?" she asked, her eyes alight now with curiosity.

Maeve had worked for him for five years, and they were a well-oiled machine. He'd never known her to ask an intimate question before. In fact, aside from the facts that she was unmarried and shared a rambling old Kauri villa in Epsom with her mother, he knew very little about her personal life, either. He raised an eyebrow at her and her expression sharpened.

"Don't bother giving me that look," she said sternly. "Everyone around here knows you eat, sleep and dream work in your downtime. If you even *have* downtime. I think it's good that you have something other than work to look forward to in your life. Especially now. Life..." She hesitated a second or two, as if trying to decide whether or not she should continue before taking a deep breath and forging on. "Life is too precious to waste a moment or to let it pass you by. Everyone needs balance. It's past time you found yours."

"You think I'm unbalanced?" he asked, deliberately misconstruing her comments.

She made a sound of irritation that made him feel

like nothing more than a difficult child. "Don't twist my words, Mr. Marshall. You know exactly what I mean."

Chastened, he gave her a half smile. "Yes, it is personal, and I'll handle the booking myself. Thank you for the information, Maeve, I appreciate it. Oh, and could you book the helicopter for me for three hours tomorrow afternoon from one o'clock?"

"Consider it done," she said, her smile making her look ten years younger. "And I meant what I said about not wasting a moment. If she's special, you make sure you don't let her pass you by."

"What makes you so sure a woman is involved?" he asked, testing her knowledge and insight into him just that little bit further.

"Oh, please. If it wasn't a woman, those estimates would be back on my desk by now, even with all you've been through these past two weeks," she replied archly. "It's a woman, all right."

Ronin watched in wonder as Maeve left his office, closing his door behind her. He weighed her words carefully. She was right, as she always was, he conceded.

Ali truly was a distraction from his work—a distraction that he never would have tolerated before. But somehow he couldn't bring himself to mind too much. With all he was handling, it might seem like now was the worst possible time for any diversions, but instead Ali was exactly what he needed—someone to pull him away from it all, to restore him for the challenges that still lay ahead. For once, he wouldn't focus on the big picture. He wouldn't make contingency plans, or find an exit strategy. He'd just take this unexpected source of pleasure that had fallen into his life right when he needed it most, and enjoy it while it lasted.

He ran his finger down the list of restaurants and

stopped on one, then lifted the handset of his phone to make the lunch booking.

When Ali arrived at Ronin's house, her car loaded with supplies for the nursery, he was waiting on the front porch for her.

"Looks like my bank account is getting a hammering," he commented as he helped her carry several bags and boxes from the car.

"Looking after a little one isn't cheap, and you did say you wanted the best of everything," she pointed out.

"I would never settle for anything less."

Upstairs, she exclaimed in delight as they entered the nursery. "Oh, the carpet square arrived. What do you think?"

"Am I supposed to think anything of it? It's carpet."

"That's such a male response." Ali chuckled as she slipped out of her shoes and let her stocking feet sink into the thick gray-and-white-patterned square she'd ordered for the room several days before. "Take your shoes off and feel it," she urged.

Throwing her a quizzical glance, Ronin did as she requested.

"Doesn't it feel divine?" she asked him.

"It feels like carpet." When she cast him a disparaging look, he shrugged. "I can't help it. I'm an engineer, not a decorator. That was more my sister's forte than mine. She did most of the house for me."

She'd done a lovely job of it, too, Ali thought. Even though the property could easily grace the pages of a home decorating magazine, it still had a homelike feel about it. As if you could just curl up on a couch in the living room and read a book without worrying about leaving marks on the furniture or flattening the cushions.

"She certainly had a knack for it," Ali commented. "Right, well, I need to unpack these things and put them away, and then I'll be ready for that lunch you promised."

"I hope you'll enjoy it. I've got something special planned," he said enigmatically as he left her to her own devices.

*What did he mean by that?* she wondered as she stacked packets of newborn diapers on the shelving in the cupboard. It was lunch, for heaven's sake. How complicated could that be? The only way she'd find out would be to finish her morning's tasks, she told herself, dragging her thoughts back to where they belonged. It was time to apply herself to the work in which she took so much pride.

Ali extracted a selection of babywear, which she'd hand-washed, from one of the carry bags she'd brought upstairs, and placed the clothing carefully into the chest of drawers against the wall. Once done, she looked around her. Her gaze alighted on the sheep mobile hanging above the crib, and she smiled. Aside from a few bits and bobs, there was only one thing still missing from the room, she thought as she tidied up the packaging and prepared to put it in the trash—that special baby smell and the infant who'd bring it. He'd be there all too soon, and then her work would be done. The thought was both reassuring and a little saddening at the same time.

It was the hardest part of her job, reaching the end of a contract. Knowing a new family was on the precipice of a shared journey that she'd never experience for herself. It was a feeling she'd become used to but that never made it hurt any less.

She picked up the pacifiers and airtight containers she'd bought for storing them in and took them downstairs to be sterilized. As she neared the bottom of the stairs she heard a door down the corridor to her left close.

"You're all finished?" Ronin asked as he strolled down the hall toward her.

"I just need to sterilize these and then I'm all yours."

"I like the sound of that," he answered. "And I hope you'll like the sound of what I've got planned for you."

"I'm intrigued," Ali admitted with a grin. "Any hints?"

"Be patient and you'll find out," Ronin answered with an enigmatic smile.

He took her through to the kitchen, where she extracted the sterilizing equipment from the bottom of a cupboard.

"Here," Ali said, gesturing to the items she'd collated on the benchtop. "I'll instruct, you do."

"Me? Won't the nannies be doing all that?" he asked, taking the pacifiers from her and staring at them as if they were something to be dissected and studied.

"Absolutely. But you should still know what to do, even if you have the nannies here around the clock. I think you should still be hands-on."

"My sister trusted me enough to put her son in my care, so I guess I owe it to her."

Together they went through the steps outlined on the packaging. They were just finishing up when Ali heard a beating rotor noise, which got louder and louder and then tapered away, like a helicopter being shut down.

"There's that clue you wanted," Ronin commented. "Hungry?"

"You're taking me to lunch in a helicopter?"

"Ever been in one before?"

Ali shook her head. She'd always wanted to ride in one, but the tour flights offered in the city were so expensive.

"Then you're in for a treat."

Ali got her things together quickly and followed Ronin out the big sliding glass doors that led out through the kitchen and family room. Sure enough, about fifty meters from the house sat a gleaming black helicopter with the words REM Consulting emblazoned in gold on its tail.

"This is *yours*?" she asked incredulously.

"Well, it's my company's, to be more precise. While we contract overseas a great deal, about forty percent of our work is here in New Zealand. Sometimes we need to get to places that commercial flights and hired cars can't get to quickly or easily."

Ali tried not to look overawed as Ronin introduced her to the pilot and then handed her up into the cabin, but she had a feeling she failed miserably. There, he showed her how to buckle her seat belt and adjust her headset before he climbed in next to her. Her stomach gave a delighted flip as the pilot completed preflight checks and the machine lifted into the sky. She'd already thought the view from Ronin's house toward the harbor was without par, but this bird's-eye view was truly amazing.

The rain from earlier in the morning had cleared and the sun shone on the rippled surface of the sea as they flew toward Waiheke Island. In far too short a time, they descended outside what looked like a vineyard with a restaurant. Ronin showed her into the restaurant build-ing, where a cheery fire burned in a fireplace in one wall. This early in autumn it wasn't strictly necessary, but it lent a delightful ambience to the dining room.

She couldn't remember ever having anyone pay her quite as much attention as Ronin did. She and Richard had known each other so long and had been so comfort-able together they'd lost touch with the little things that made a marriage sparkle like new again. It scared her that she was enjoying herself so much and that Ronin could make her feel so special and, with each linger-ing glance, wanted. She'd have to be made of stone not to respond.

"See anything you like?" he asked as they perused their menus.

Oh, she saw something she liked, all right. And it had nothing to do with the menu in her hand. It was some-thing more like forbidden fruit. A delight, once tasted, that remained forever on your tongue, inciting a crav-ing that was almost too hard to resist. *Almost.*

Ali dragged her gaze away from the man seated across the table and scanned the menu again.

"It's too hard to choose," she said on a huff of air. "There's so much on here that I love. Why don't you select something for me? I promise you, you can't go wrong."

"Whatever the lady wants," he replied, lifting his gaze to mesh with hers briefly.

Ali felt her whole body bloom under his attention, her senses coming to life like a neglected garden after a drenching rain. His unrelenting interest in her was both thrilling and terrifying in equal proportion. She wanted to take a step back, to create a sense of safety and space between them—a distance between right now and that night in Hawaii. But could she hold out against his allure? More importantly, did she really want to?

# Six

Ronin savored the rising tide of desire that ebbed and flowed through his veins as he watched Ali enjoy the food he'd chosen for her. He'd always considered it chauvinistic to order for a woman, but when Ali had surrendered the choice to him, he'd felt a sense of honor that she'd entrusted him with the job.

Her tongue swept her upper lip as she finished the last of the ripe camembert from the cheeseboard and crackers he'd selected as their dessert. He remembered, all too well, how that tongue had felt on his body, and he wanted to experience it again.

Softly, softly, he reminded himself. There was a wounded fragility about her that he'd discerned beneath the capable businesswoman who'd taken over the nursery at the house. He had a feeling it wouldn't take much to frighten her away, and that was very definitely the last thing he wanted to do.

"Good?" he asked, as she took a sip of the Pinot Gris he'd chosen to go with their meal and sighed.

"Perfect. Everything is perfect."

"I aim to please," he said lowly, letting her see in his eyes that he meant to please her in *all* things.

To his delight a flush of color highlighted her cheeks and she dropped her gaze, her dark lashes sweeping down to hide the expression in her eyes. But he could see the sudden flutter of her pulse at the base of the pale column of her throat. He ached to kiss her there again. Soon, he promised himself. Soon.

The other day she'd mentioned a time when she'd been at a crossroads in her life. The engineer in him wanted to pick what she'd said apart, to understand exactly what had happened to give her that air of fragility he saw when her guard was down. It was only after you pulled something apart and put it back together that you could fully understand a problem and begin to solve it.

But, while fixing problems was something he was very good at, he sensed she'd throw her barriers back up again if he attempted to pick her pain and her troubles apart. No, he had to go slowly, to let her come to him in her own time. Still, he considered as her eyes lifted to his again and he saw the warmth in them reflecting back at him, there was no harm in stepping up the pace just a little.

After lunch the helicopter returned to fly them back to the house. Before they did, Ronin asked his pilot to take them on a low-flying scenic journey of the inner harbor and its islands. Ali's excitement and pleasure in the flight was palpable, and he found himself smiling in response as she exclaimed over yet another feature she recognized beneath them.

At the house, after they'd disembarked from the

chopper and gone back inside, she turned to give him a beatific smile.

"That was, without doubt, the best lunch of my life," she gushed. "It was amazing, Ronin."

"I'm glad you enjoyed it. I did, too."

"I really don't know how to thank you properly."

He took a step closer to her, his hands reaching for her waist. "I do," he said firmly, and pulled her toward him.

Her lips were soft and lush as he claimed them, and he was hard-pressed to control the urge to take them fiercely, to plunder their sweetness. He'd meant to let her come to him of her own volition, and he'd taken a risk doing this, but a surge of exaltation washed through him as her lips parted against his and her tongue slid between his lips.

Her kiss was so giving, its effect so instantaneous, that a tremor of need shuddered through him. A groan escaped his mouth as her form molded to his, as she fitted herself against him, her softness absorbing all of him that was hard and aching. Fire lit in his groin, sending fingers of heat to scorch through his body and igniting a powerful passion. One that clouded rational behavior and grew stronger and more demanding every second they touched.

Ali's hands rose to his head, her fingers threading through his short hair and holding him close as their tongues met and retreated, only to meet again. He was starving for her, all of her. The pulse in his body made him harden even more as desire overcame thought and reason, making its demands clear. He pressed his hips against hers, groaning again as his erection nudged her pelvis.

Ali pulled her head away, her breath coming in rapid

gasps, her hands falling to his wrists where she gently forced him to let her go.

"Ronin, I—" she started.

He pressed a short kiss to her mouth, fighting the need to make it more persuasive. He knew he could. But that didn't mean she'd welcome it, or him—especially when she'd been the first to disengage from their embrace.

"Don't," he said gruffly. "No need for an explanation. It's okay."

They were difficult words to enunciate when every cell, every nerve, in his body clamored for their contact to resume. For each wet kiss, for each fervent touch, to progress to its natural conclusion. Ronin forced his recalcitrant libido back under control.

Ali dipped her head. "I'm sorry." The words were so quiet he wasn't even sure he'd heard right. "I'd better go."

"Don't be sorry. I'm not. You're a beautiful woman, Ali Carter—inside and out. I want to know you better, and I'm prepared to wait if that's what it takes."

How long he could continue to wait might be an issue, he thought as his flesh strained against the confines of his briefs. But then again, that's what punishing workouts at midnight in his home gym and icy cold showers were for, right?

She lifted her face and looked at him. "Where are we going with this, Ronin?"

He'd have thought that was obvious. "I'd like to think we're getting to know one another."

"You're my client."

"And I'd like to be more." *Much more.*

She shook her head. "No. Look, what I said before about Hawaii, about that not being me? I meant it. I'm not normally that person. That's not to say that I regret it—what we did together was, well, great. But that's all it was. A holiday fling. A one-off. I'm not in the market for anything else, Ronin. I've been hurt before. Badly hurt. I will not put myself through that again."

A primitive roar surged within him. He wanted to protect her, to wipe the slate clean of her past hurts, past regrets. He wanted to make her world right. But she had to let him. The ultimate control lay within her.

"I don't plan to hurt you, Ali. Anything, everything, but that."

She shook her head. "There are things about me you don't know. I've been married before, for starters."

"And you aren't now, which makes getting to know you a great deal simpler, wouldn't you say?"

She shook her head. "Don't joke about this, Ronin. It's not open to discussion."

"I'm sorry. I know firsthand how you feel about infidelity, and if it's any consolation, I feel the same way. But I'm not prepared to give up on you, Ali Carter. We first met by accident. We were lucky enough to meet again. Some might call it fate, but I don't believe in that. What I do believe in is what I know, what I can substantiate—that we potentially have something I've never had with anyone before. Give us a chance."

He studied her carefully. Her lips, still glistening with moisture, were softly swollen from his kiss. Her skin was flushed, her breathing shallow. A pulse leapt at the base of her throat. But her eyes made him draw in a breath and take a moment. While her body showed all the signs of arousal, her eyes still held shadows. Who was it, he thought, who had done such a number on her? Who had hurt her so badly that she could do what he was unable to and put mental strength before physical demand when it came to their fiery attraction?

She shook her head again, more emphatically this time. "Please respect me on this. Let's keep our relationship purely business. If you don't agree, I don't think I can continue to work for you."

He sighed and shoved his hands in his trouser pockets. "Okay. Business." *For now,* he added silently.

Ali had double-checked the supplies in the kitchen and triple-checked the nursery. Everything was perfect for the baby's homecoming today. The past few days since their lunch together had been...well, difficult. While Ronin hadn't put any pressure on her, she could still feel the hunger that rolled off him in waves every time they were together. A hunger that she had to admit she shared. Even though he'd spent more time at his office in the city, they'd still crossed paths a few times, and each time she'd felt every cell in her body go on alert. She didn't know what was worse. Anticipating their meetings or arriving at the house—like she had today—and finding he wasn't there.

At least her role was coming to an end. It was finally okay for the baby to come home, so Ronin had organized to collect his nephew, together with his parents, and bring them all back to his house this afternoon. For the first week the baby was home, Ronin and parents would care for him, and from next week, the rotation of nannies would begin. It had been a big job to pull together in the time they'd had, but it was done—and done to perfection, Ali thought as she swiped an imaginary speck of dust from the top rail of the baby's crib.

He wouldn't be sleeping there any time soon, though, she thought with a smile. While he was still small he'd be in the adorable bassinet she'd found online and had express-shipped here two days ago.

She hated to admit it, but this job had become a complete labor of love. She'd always managed to maintain a degree of separation during nursery fit outs before. It had been something she'd learned to do out of necessity. It was one thing to pour all your love and expectations for a child into your work—quite another when you got too invested and forgot that the children you worked to care for would never be your own. No, emotional distance was key. But with this job it had been different.

Maybe it was because of the circumstances of this infant's birth, or maybe it had more to do with the man who'd become the child's guardian. Either way, Ali had poured her heart into every last detail. The room was perfect. She took one last glance and then turned to put it, and Ronin Marshall, behind her.

She was at the top of the main stairs when she heard a car pull up outside. How had someone gotten through the main gates? She wasn't expecting any deliveries, and to spare herself the turmoil, she had planned to be gone before Ronin and his parents returned with the baby. So who could it be?

A car door closed, and, after a pause, another. She heard footsteps coming into the front portico. A few seconds later, the door opened to reveal an older, slightly shorter version of Ronin, carrying an infant car seat.

His face was gray and drawn, his faded blue eyes filled with anxiety.

"Oh, thank God you're here!" he said with vehement relief.

"Mr. Marshall?"

"Yes," he answered. "My wife, she collapsed at the hospital as we were leaving with the baby—they've taken her into the ER. I have to get back to her, but someone needs to care for my grandson, here."

"Ronin was called to fly out urgently just as we arrived at the hospital. He said he'd ring you and see if you could bring the start date forward for the nannies. That's what you're waiting here for, isn't it? For the nanny to arrive? Please say that's so."

Ronin had called her? Ali felt a clutch in her chest. She'd left her phone in her bag at the bottom of the stairs when she'd arrived. Being upstairs, she wouldn't have heard it ring. The house phone had sounded a few times, but with it not being her home she'd left it unanswered. None of that mattered right now, though, as Ronin's father appeared increasingly distraught.

"Don't worry, Mr. Marshall, I'll take care of things."

He thrust the baby carrier toward her.

"Thank you. I'd stay, but I really must get back. I just knew this would all be too much for Delia. We'd just gotten to the car when she collapsed. Before they took her into ER she made me promise I'd bring our grandson out here, to his new home. And anyway, I couldn't wait around the ER with him."

"I understand," Ali said soothingly, even though inside her nerves were jumping like water droplets on a hot skillet. "He'll be fine with me for now. You take care on the trip back to town, okay?"

He looked at her a moment, his eyes stricken. "I will. Thank you. I can see why Ronin speaks so highly of you, and why he was so certain you'd have things under control."

He did? A bloom of warmth filled her heart. Ali adjusted the weight of the car seat in her arms and looked down at the tiny life cocooned in there. Her heart flipped over. She'd wanted to avoid this—potentially falling in love with the tiny tot—but one glance and she was done for. Only a couple of weeks old and he'd already lost so much. She ached to cuddle him close and make him feel loved.

"I will take good care of him," she promised, her voice infused with all the assurance she was capable of.

"I'll be off then." He was already halfway down the front stairs when he realized he still had a bag filled with baby supplies on his shoulder. "I'd better leave this with you, too. It's some formula and clothes and other things that Delia put together for his homecoming, as well as the release notes from the hospital."

"Thank you. If you could leave it just inside I'll grab it once I've settled him in his bassinet."

Ronin's father's gaze lingered on his grandson. "Delia so wanted to be here when he came home. When Ronin had to leave us at the hospital and go straight out to the airport she was adamant that we carry on as planned. She didn't want the baby in the hospital a moment longer than he needed to be. Ronin doesn't even know his mother's ill. I hope she'll be okay." His voice broke on the words. "She's got to be."

"Mr. Marshall." Ali placed one hand on his trembling arm. "Your wife is in the best place possible. Don't you worry about a thing here. I have it all under control, okay? You go and be where you're most needed. Call the house if you want to check on us, or if you want to let me know how Mrs. Marshall is doing."

"I will," he said, and with a half-hearted attempt at a wave he walked swiftly toward his car.

It was only once he'd driven away that Ali realized that no one had told her the baby's name. Not once in the past week and a half with Ronin had he mentioned it, and she'd been too startled to find Ronin's father on the front steps just now to even think of asking him. What was she supposed to call him? Baby X? *Think,* she urged her sluggish brain. The solution presented itself almost immediately. Of course, his name would be on the release notes tucked in the diaper bag.

Ali closed the front door and looked again at the sleeping child. The enormity of what she'd just agreed to do settled over her like a lead cloak as anxiety coiled like a snake in the pit of her belly. It would only be for a few hours, max, she assured herself as she began to ascend the stairs. As soon as baby was settled, she'd be on the phone to the nanny service to see who would be able to start early.

Her stomach did a nervous flip as the infant squirmed a little—his tiny face screwing up, his mouth twisting—before, to her great relief, he settled again. What would she do if he cried? The logical side of her brain kicked into action. It wasn't difficult, she tried to assure herself. She knew the basics. Besides, if he was still at risk, they wouldn't have released him from the hospital today. She'd do whatever needed doing. She'd check his diaper, she'd feed him if he needed feeding, and if none of that worked, well, she'd just hold him.

*Hold him.* The thought in itself shouldn't have made her tremble with anxiety. She'd handled babies before. Her three older sisters had seven kids between them and Ali had been hands-on at every stage of her nieces' and nephews' lives. *This shouldn't be any different,* she assured herself as she carried the car seat upstairs to the nursery. *This shouldn't be any different at all.*

And yet, when it came to unbuckling the belt that secured him, she was all thumbs.

"This is ridiculous," she muttered to herself. "Get your act together."

Unsnapping the clip, she eased the straps away from the baby's tiny body and scooped her hands beneath him, taking extra care to support his head. He was so small, so light—like a doll almost. And yet he was strong and tenacious, as well. He'd fought through a tough delivery and against breathing difficulties to be well enough to get released from hospital. There was no need to be unduly concerned about him. All she needed to do until help arrived was provide him with a safe place to sleep and food to eat. She could do that.

Ali held his tiny body against her chest as she pulled back the cover on the bassinet. He nestled against her automatically, as if seeking that nurturing care that only a cuddle could bring. It was with great reluctance that she laid him on the pristine white sheet that covered the mattress. His little arms flung out as she released him, startling him awake. She looked for the first time into his blue eyes.

"There, there," she soothed, rubbing his chest until his eyes slid closed again.

Before she pulled the coverlet up, she saw the hospital ID tag that remained on his ankle. His name was right there. Although the surname had become obscured, his first name stood out clearly—Joshua. Tears stung her eyes and she drew in a deep breath to combat the painful wrench that pulled at her from deep inside. Joshua was the name she and Richard had chosen for their firstborn child, if he were to be a boy. Except their firstborn child had never even been conceived.

*It shouldn't hurt this much,* she told herself. Lots of little boys the world over were called Joshua. It was a lovely name, a great name—that's why she and her ex had chosen it themselves. But somehow, knowing this poor motherless child was named Joshua was her undoing.

First one tear, then another, slid down her face. She swallowed a gulp of grief for the baby boy she'd never have and forced herself to tuck Joshua into his bassinet, and then she left the room. Outside she leaned against the wall until she could get her emotions under control. This was too hard, too much. She needed to contact the agency and get the appropriate help so she could get out of here right now. She cursed the fact she hadn't received any of Ronin's calls and fervently wished she could speak to him right now, but if he was in the air already and on his way to Vietnam it would be hours before he'd land. Besides, even if she reached him, what would she say? That she didn't want to care for his nephew because the baby reminded her of all she couldn't have?

Instead she straightened slowly from the wall, squared her shoulders and silently stepped back into the nursery to check on Joshua. He was still exactly as she'd left him. She needlessly adjusted his covers then activated the baby monitor and left to go downstairs. In the kitchen she activated the monitor's partner unit and then she delved into her handbag for her phone. Three missed calls and one new message. She listened to the message—it was from Ronin, as she'd expected.

His warm, deep voice filled her ear, and she told herself it was ridiculous to feel a sense of relief at his tone. There was nothing he could do for her right now. He'd left on business secure in the knowledge that his nephew was being cared for—now it was up to her to make sure that happened. After explaining how long he'd probably be away and asking her to organize at least one of the nannies to start earlier to help his parents, he closed off with, "I'll call you as soon as I land in Hanoi."

Well, she had to be satisfied with that. There was nothing else she could do for now except leave a message on his phone and, given what the family had been through already, to assure him that she had everything under control. She said nothing of his mother's urgent admission to hospital. It wouldn't be fair to impart that kind of news in a message. He needed to hear that person-to-person. With a deep sigh, she scrolled through her contacts for the nanny service she'd used and pressed Call.

Sixty minutes of frustration later, Ali was forced to admit defeat. Ronin's initial brief on what he wanted in a nanny had been explicit. He wanted people with neonatal care experience and a proven track record as a private nanny in the bargain. He already had the four best candidates for the position lined up to work in rotating twelve-hour shifts, four days on, four days off—starting next week. Not a single one could start any earlier and, given their expertise and the demand for their skills, Ali wasn't all that surprised. And the backup candidates she'd considered had all accepted other placements.

Even calls to a private nursing agency had proven fruitless, and she already knew the other agencies she'd used from time to time currently had no one suitable and available on their books.

A squawk over the monitor had her heart pounding. Joshua was waking. He'd need attention, and there was no one else here but her to give it to him. She flew up the stairs and into the nursery, where his reedy cry built up in tempo. She scooped him up into her arms and began to rock from side to side, humming a tuneless sound in an attempt to soothe him.

Yes, she'd assured Ronin's dad that the baby would be all right and that she'd look after things, but that was when she'd thought she'd be able to hand over the responsibility to someone who was far more experienced and capable with an infant than she was herself. She wasn't in any way as qualified as the nannies Ronin had selected to care for this poor mother- and fatherless babe. *But right here, right now?* It was she who was left holding the baby.

Literally.

# Seven

Ronin disembarked from the plane and strode through the airport, getting through customs and immigration with the weary acceptance of a frequent long-distance traveler. It had never bothered him before, but after four frustratingly endless days it seemed to him that this game was most definitely for someone else. Someone, perhaps, who had less responsibility here at home.

He'd already called his dad the moment phone use had been permitted after landing. Thankfully his mother was steadily improving. She was as comfortable as could be expected after coronary bypass surgery, and his dad hoped she'd be home within the next couple of days.

Guilt for leaving town in the first place had battered him during the entire trip, especially once he'd belatedly received the news about his mother's condition. When his father called, Ronin had been stuck in Hanoi—bound by the strictures of the contract he'd agreed to with his client and bound to solve the issues that had arisen, as swiftly as possible. Besides, as his father had pointed out to him, his mother was receiving excellent care and making steady progress with her recovery. Him being there, or not, would make no difference at this stage.

And then there was Ali. She'd been singlehandedly taking care of Joshua for them. A role that was way above and beyond anything he could have anticipated or expected. He'd heard the weariness in her voice when he'd managed to speak with her before boarding in Hanoi more than seventeen hours ago. She'd assured him that Joshua was fine, and that a home care nurse had visited in a follow-up from the hospital, but there'd been a note of strain in her voice that worried him.

His dad had been out to the house a couple of times to help where he could, and he'd assured Ronin that Ali was coping well. Still, nothing would convince him that everything was all right until he could see it for himself.

The drive home from the airport took forever, but Ronin felt himself relaxing in increments as he headed out of the built-up zones and toward Whitford. He called Ali from the car when he was about twenty minutes from the house.

"Hello, Marshall residence," her voice replied, so very correctly.

"It's me," he said with a smile. "Is there anything you need me to pick up on the way through?"

As much as he didn't want to stop en route, he realized she'd been pretty much housebound in a place that wasn't her own home from the day he'd left.

"No, it's okay. Deb brought some things out to me and I've had groceries delivered."

*Just come home.* The message wasn't spoken, but it was there in the underlying tone of her voice. A tone that said, while she was coping, she really wasn't happy about the situation at all.

"Okay, I'll be there soon."

"I'll see you then."

He disconnected, but not before he heard her faint sigh over the car speakers. He thought again about the mammoth undertaking she'd accepted when she'd agreed to stay on at the house with his nephew. He had only intended her responsibilities to last a couple of hours, and yet they had stretched out into four, nearly five, days. He owed her—big time. He pressed his foot down a little more firmly on the accelerator, more eager than ever to cover the final miles to his home.

He'd always prided himself on his personal attention to a job and yet, in this most important role he'd ever agreed to take on, he'd been horribly remiss. Something had to change, and it needed to change right now. He'd also always prided himself on succession planning at work, on training up his second and third in charge to be able to step into the breach when necessary. But what good was succession planning if you didn't pass on responsibility to someone else when you needed to? When he'd agreed to take on the responsibility of his nephew's guardianship he hadn't thought beyond the immediate issues, but it was clear now that he hadn't considered every contingency. Things were going to be very different from now on. It would be an adjustment, but he'd figure out how to make it work—he was good at that.

Ali was in the front entrance as he drove his car up the drive. He felt that familiar sense of heat and desire pulling at him the moment he identified her standing there. Dressed in form-fitting jeans and a long-sleeved

T-shirt, she was certainly turned out more casually than he'd become used to seeing her, although she was no less attractive for it. Not even bothering to put his car in the garage, he parked and got out, walking straight over to her. His cases—hell, everything else—could wait.

He shortened the distance between them with long strides, fighting the urge to pull her into his arms the moment she was within reach. She was paler than usual, her eyes were more shadowed and her high cheekbones appeared more prominent. Had she lost weight?

"Ali, I can't begin to thank you—" he started.

"There's no need for thanks. Joshie needed someone to care for him and I was here. That's all there is to it."

Despite her reassurance, he could hear the note of strain in her voice. Clearly it hadn't been easy. Was there something wrong with the baby? Had he been unwell?

"Joshua? How is he?"

"He's doing great. I think the home care nurse was a bit surprised to find me caring for him, but I seem to have passed with full marks."

"I wouldn't have expected you to do anything less," he said, forcing a smile to his lips. If there was one thing among the many things he'd noticed about Alison Carter, it was that she was competent and capable. "Is he upstairs?"

They headed through the front door, and then Ronin turned toward the staircase.

"No, I have him downstairs. I ordered a second bassinet for down here so I could keep working while I watched him. I hope you don't mind, but I commandeered the kitchen dining table as a makeshift office and popped Joshua in the living room next door during the day."

A pang of guilt struck him. He'd been so absorbed

in doing what was right for his own business that he'd barely given any consideration to hers. The debt he owed her kept mounting.

"Of course I don't mind. I'm deeply grateful to you for stepping in when my family needed you most." *When I needed you most,* he added silently.

"I'm glad I could help."

She smiled, but it didn't quite reach her eyes. Eyes that were underscored by the purplish bruises of weariness and strain. He was sorely tempted to reach out and touch her, as if he could gently wipe away those traces of darkness. But his touch couldn't magically heal whatever hurt she carried with her—if she'd even accept his touch in the first place, he growled silently as he curled his hand into a fist in his pocket.

"It's been tough?" he asked.

Her lips pulled into a tight smile. "A little," she admitted. "But he's a beautiful baby. In fact I think he's quite stolen my heart."

"Yeah, he seems to have that effect on people. I've been looking forward to seeing him again."

A cry from inside the house made them both turn their heads.

Ali gave a short laugh. "And it sounds like he's heard your arrival and wants to see you, too."

They went through from the foyer and down the hall toward the family room as the baby's cries became more insistent. Ronin hesitated when he saw the bassinet over by the French doors.

"He's ready for a feed. Would you like to do it?" she asked.

"Sure," he said, still a little unsure about the precious bundle squirming and squalling in his bassinet.

Ali looked up at him. "You didn't feed him in the hospital?"

Ronin shook his head. "Mum did that, whenever our hospital visits coincided with mealtimes. Guess I've gotta learn sometime. Should I wash my hands first?"

Ali pointed over to the kitchen sink, where she'd obviously put a bottle of antiseptic hand wash. "You can do it there while I change his diaper."

She moved over to the baby and, seemingly unaffected by his cries, lifted him from his bassinet onto a folding change table she'd set up nearby. She was just fastening the sides on Joshua's clean diaper when he returned.

"I guess I'd better get some experience in that too, huh?" he said dubiously.

Ali cracked a smile. "You certainly will, but I've let you off the hook with this one."

"Thanks. So, feeding him. Do I sit down?"

"I usually sit over there," Ali said, gesturing to an easy chair set in the corner by the doors.

"Come on," Ali urged him. "Pick him up while I warm his bottle."

*Pick him up?* Ronin forced his feet in the direction of the change table, but he came to an abrupt halt when he saw the demanding red face above the blue-and-white striped onesie that encased his nephew.

"Don't be frightened," Ali said softly. "You handled him before at the hospital, right?"

"Kind of," Ronin said, suddenly feeling underprepared, a sensation he had never enjoyed. He'd thought he was ready for this, but it seemed that it was one thing to have the nurses lay Joshua in his arms, and quite another to pick him up himself.

"Here," Ali said, leaning over the change table and

deftly scooping the squalling infant up. She handed him to Ronin. "Hold him against you, like this." She guided one of his hands to the back of Joshua's head and the other to his bottom. "There. You're a natural."

Her words were reassuring, especially with Joshua's cries suddenly ceasing and his little face burrowing against the fine cotton of Ronin's shirtfront. Ali moved away from him to the kitchen, where she washed her hands, efficiently warmed some formula and then brought the small bottle over to Ronin.

"He can still be a bit fussy over the bottle, but just persevere and he'll get the message."

Fussy? What did she mean by that? Didn't babies just drink? He soon found out that just because Joshua was hungry, it didn't mean he was entirely happy to actually have to work at being fed.

"He's a bit of a rascal, but he's better now than he has been," Ali said from her vantage point beside him.

There was a wealth of things unsaid in her words. Again Ronin felt that pang of guilt over the burden he had left her to shoulder alone. He got a solid hint of what she meant as the baby took his own good time to latch on to the bottle. He found himself caught by Joshua's stare as he finally drank. He'd had nothing to do with babies before Joshie's birth. It had all seemed to be a great idea when CeeCee and R.J. had talked about his duties as uncle, but the reality of now being wholly responsible for this tiny life came crashing down onto him like a tidal wave.

It all rested on his shoulders now. Everything. Caring for this little person wasn't something he could chart on a spreadsheet. He couldn't draw up a diagram for satisfying all the baby's needs, nor could he calculate every possible risk. He would have to bear the load alone, a situation his usual methods would do nothing to resolve. Caring for Joshua would be a trial by fire—for both of them. It was pretty daunting.

He looked up from the little person in his arms to see Ali moving about the family room, gathering up her things and putting away her papers and the laptop computer she'd set up on the table.

"What are you doing?" he asked.

"Packing up and getting ready to go home."

"Why?"

"Because you're back now, that's why."

An unfamiliar sensation rippled through him. She was leaving him? With the baby? Alone?

"There's no need for you to rush off."

She paused in the middle of sliding her laptop into a vibrant pink leather case. "I thought you'd prefer to have some time alone with Joshua. Get to know one another a little better."

"Ali, I haven't the slightest idea what to do with this baby. Please stay. At least until the nannies start on Monday. I'll make it worth your while." He added the last as a final incentive in the hope it might sway her.

Ali felt her chest constrict. He had no idea what he was asking her to do. Over the past few days she'd been forced to face so many of her hopes and dreams that had always been tied up in having a baby of her own to love and care for. She'd thought she'd moved past those dreams when she learned they could never come true, but the longing was still there. It had been distressing to attempt to hold herself aloof from Joshua, and in the end, and to what she suspected would be her eternal cost, she'd crumbled, giving him her heart despite her best intentions to protect herself. She already fiercely loved this baby, who she'd known from the start she wouldn't be able to keep.

She'd looked forward to Ronin's return so she could leave—for selfish reasons, she admitted. Her job was done, she affirmed quietly, and now it was time to go. She needed to distance herself from them both. She could never be part of their family, and it was better to abandon the illusion now before she risked being hurt even more.

It had crucified her when her own husband, a man she'd loved since she was sixteen years old, fell out of love with her when they found she was the reason they couldn't have a baby of their own. Yes, they'd built the foundation of their future on their plans to have a family, and yes, it had been her fault that they couldn't have children of their own. But she had thought he loved *her* more than he loved his plans for their picture-perfect life together. She'd been wrong.

Himself a late surprise to older parents, as well as an only child, Richard had always joked about creating their own dynasty. When she'd suggested adoption he'd been strangely reluctant. When he'd come home one day and said he was leaving her to be with someone else, that he *loved* that someone else, it had shocked her to her core. She had still loved him, still wanted to make their marriage work. Thousands—hundreds of thousands—of couples were childless, either by choice or chance, and still lived long and happy lives together.

But he hadn't been prepared to give up his chance to have a family. It had devastated her. She wouldn't, no, *couldn't* put herself in the path of that freight train again. It had been hard enough to fight out of the misery and eventually put herself back together after Richard had left her. She doubted she'd find the strength to do it again.

That made it all the more important to protect herself now. To shore up the walls she needed around her heart before she lost herself to Ronin and Joshua completely.

Ronin sat there, holding the baby and looking at her. Obviously expecting an answer.

"It's not about the money," she said.

He kept looking at her with an expression in his eyes that she struggled to define. It was almost a challenge and yet there was a plea reflected there as well. Ali struggled for the right words to turn him down.

"Look," she sighed, "I can't work as effectively from here as I do in my office, and I really can't leave Deb managing all on her own for the rest of this week. It's not fair to her or to the rest of Best for Baby's clientele. I've already spent far too much time away from my office."

"I understand," he said. "But if I could arrange some assistance for Deb in the office, and take on some of Joshua's care myself to free you up a bit more during the day to work as you have been doing, would you reconsider?"

She watched him with the baby and realized that the bottle was now empty, and Joshua was still sucking furiously at it.

"You'll have to take the bottle from his mouth. He's just sucking air now."

Ronin tried to pull the bottle from the baby's mouth, but now Joshua was latched on he wasn't letting go. Ronin cast her a helpless look.

"Here," she said, moving to his side. "Slide the tip of your little finger into the corner of his mouth to break the suction. Then you'll need to burp him."

She took the bottle from Ronin. Turning to grab a soft towel from the stack folded on the table beside the chair, she lay it on his shoulder.

"Now, lift him to your shoulder and rub his back. He's okay with a firm touch. It'll help him bring up the wind."

Ronin did everything she said, and his expression when Joshua belched was a picture. Despite her desire to flee this man and child and the way they reminded her of all of her deficiencies, she still felt compelled to do as he asked—to stay.

"You really have no idea, do you?" she asked, her voice soft.

"None whatsoever. Mum was going to be in charge of helping me until the nannies started, but…" He shrugged helplessly, jiggling his tiny charge on his shoulder. The baby let out another burp.

Ali was torn. Ronin hadn't asked for this responsibility to land in his lap. All his plans had gone awry when his mother had collapsed. Even Neil, his father, had been fingers and thumbs with the baby the few times he'd come out to give Ali a hand.

This was going to destroy her, she just knew it. Every day she would fall more deeply in love with the baby, and, she recognized, very likely with Ronin, too—no matter how hard she fought it. She'd be setting herself up for hurt and failure when the time inevitably came to leave them behind—two things she'd already had more than her fair share of.

Logically, she knew, her job here was done, and she needed to run and run fast to avoid the pain that surely lingered on the horizon. She didn't want to fall in love again. It hurt too much. But, against her better judgment, the words formed in her mouth.

"Fine. I'll stay."

# Eight

Ronin rose with the baby in his arms and came toward her. Her first instinct was to fend them off. This was not what she'd anticipated when she'd taken on this job with him—not by any means.

She didn't want to think about how he was everything she'd ever wanted in a man. Strong and capable. The kind of guy who could take charge in any situation and make things happen. An amazing lover.

No! She slammed the door on that thought. That was a line she couldn't afford to cross again. If she did, she might as well just throw herself on a railroad track and wait for the next train. The effect would be the same.

And he came complete with a precious, adorable baby who already had her wrapped around his tiny little fingers. Again her heart tugged hard, but she took a step back, her action making Ronin halt in his tracks. A wary expression passed across his face.

"Thank you, Ali. I appreciate your staying. And I mean it about making it worth your while. I'll get Maeve, my P.A., to send someone from our office to help Deb out. I assume she'll need someone who can answer calls, take messages and do a bit of filing. Take care of the grunt work while she attends to the more important things?"

Ali grasped hold of his offer and went with it. "Yes, that would be fine. It'll only be for a couple of days, after all."

"I think I know just the person. She's not an office junior—far from it. In fact she's probably one of our most senior staff members, in terms of age and office experience. She'll be an excellent asset in assisting Deb."

"She sounds perfect," Ali replied woodenly.

And it should be great, except it meant she had no excuse to leave Ronin's home. Deb had already been to her apartment and packed enough clothing for her when Ronin had first gone overseas. She could claim she needed to run by her apartment and pick up some more things, but it would just be an excuse to give herself a little time away. She'd made the commitment to stay, and now she had to stick to it.

She looked at the man and the child only a meter in front of her and felt a physical ache deep inside her chest. It would be all too easy to just let go of that hard-earned control. To allow herself to follow where her instincts were trying so hard to lead. But it wouldn't end well. She might be able to keep them for a little while, but it wouldn't last for long. She was damaged goods. Richard had made that patently clear.

"Can I give you Joshua so I can call Maeve right away?"

Ali cast an eye over the baby, who appeared to have dozed off in his uncle's arms.

"Actually, now would be a good time to learn how to swaddle him and put him back down in his bassinet."

"Swaddle him? Sounds difficult."

She'd thought the same when she'd discovered Joshua would keep startling and waking himself in the night. Exhausted after two nights and two very full days of unsettled baby, she'd eventually called her mother for a suggestion on what to do. Her mum had described the way she'd wrapped and put her own babies to sleep. She'd ended with, "Don't you remember? Each of your sisters did the same with theirs, too."

She did remember and had kicked herself for not thinking of it. Her first attempts had been abysmal, but by the end of her third day she'd had it down pat.

"Bring him over here," she said to Ronin, who followed her to the bassinet. "I've used squares of muslin because they're what my sisters used and because his bed covers are warm enough and I don't want him to get overheated. I'll order some fitted wraps, though. They're a lot simpler to use."

She put down the fabric and told Ronin to put Joshua in the middle. Then she folded the bottom flap up and the edges over, wrapping him until he was secure.

"See?" she said. "It's quite straightforward."

"You're a natural," Ronin replied. "Have you never thought about having a child of your own?"

Ali closed her eyes briefly and swallowed. *Only every single day of my life until about five years ago,* she thought to herself. Ignoring his question, she unwrapped the baby and stepped back from the bassinet.

"It'll come easily to you, too, once you get in a bit of practice. There, you have a go," she encouraged.

He did as she had demonstrated. It wasn't perfect, but it was a whole lot better than her first attempts.

"Looks like you're a natural yourself," she said with a forced smile. "Now leave him on his back and tuck his covers around him. He'll be okay for hopefully the next couple of hours."

"That's it? That's all he does? Eat and sleep?"

"And poop, but that's a lesson for another time." Her smile was more relaxed this time.

"Shouldn't he be upstairs in his nursery, where it's quiet?"

"It's probably a good idea for him to learn to sleep in any environment. You're not always going to be able to ensure perfect sleeping conditions for him while you're out or visiting your parents."

"Good point," Ronin said, eyeing the wee bundle in the white cane bassinet. "I had no idea it would be like this. The responsibility, I mean. How can I be sure that I'm going to make the right decisions for him?"

His honesty struck a chord with her. On a smaller scale she'd felt like that from the moment she'd realized she was solely responsible for the baby's care until Ronin's return. "You just have to trust yourself. The way your sister and her husband trusted you when they named you Joshie's guardian."

And, she realized, she had to trust herself, too. Trust herself not to let her guard down and open her heart any further to the man and the child before her.

Ronin woke with a start as the sound of Joshua's cry disturbed his slumber—again. For a second he was disoriented, the night-shaded surrounding of his master bedroom momentarily unfamiliar to him. But then it all came crashing back, and he got to his feet, his bleary eyes registering the time—four thirty-two a.m.—on the bedside clock before he stumbled toward the nursery. He'd assured Ali he could cope with the night-time feeds and that she was to get a decent night's sleep but he'd had no idea just how fractured that would leave him. He rubbed his face wearily. He usually coped well on little sleep. It must be the jet lag catching up with him.

Ali's soothing voice came through the open nursery door as he approached.

"Hey," he said softly. "I'm sorry. I didn't mean for him to wake you."

"It's okay," she said, turning to him with a smile, the baby squalling in her arms. "I was already awake."

His eyes raked over her. Her tumbled dark curls, the faint crease on her cheek that must have come from her pillow. The shadows of her curves beneath her nightgown. His body reacted without a second thought, his senses coming to swift attention even as his ears continued to be filled with the baby's cries. This situation shouldn't be having this effect on him, he told himself, and yet he could barely tear his eyes from Ali.

He realized he was staring and forced himself to move. "Let me get his bottle, and then you can go back to bed."

His tongue thickened on the words. *Back to bed.* Three simple words and yet they opened a floodgate on his memories, filling his mind with images of what they'd shared. Of what he wanted to share with her again.

"Thanks," Ali said, turning to change Joshua's diaper.

He forced his feet in the direction of the kitchenette that formed part of the nanny suite. Forced his mind back to more mundane things. When he returned with the bottle she was settling into the rocking chair with the baby in her arms. The soft glow of the night-light bathed her in a golden wash of color. There was nothing mundane about Alison Carter in a nightgown. Nothing at all.

"I'll take him," he offered.

"It's okay. This shouldn't take too long. Besides, you look dead on your feet."

He handed her the bottle and leaned in the doorjamb watching as she fed his little nephew. Once Joshua was done, she wrapped him and put him back in his bassinette.

"You could have gone back to bed," she said gently as she closed the nursery door behind them.

"I was up, too."

She looked up at him, and her breath seemed to catch in her throat at what he knew was reflected in his eyes. Hunger. Desire. Need. Ali took a step away from him, and then another.

"I'll…um…I'll see you later in the morning, then," she said, turning away from him and back toward the nanny suite.

"Yeah, later."

He watched her go, tamping down the little voice in the back of his mind that urged him to follow her. To reach out and turn her to face him. To draw her into his arms and against his aching body and to do with her all the things his flesh clamored for.

"Ali?"

She hesitated a step, and then stopped.

"Yes?"

Words froze on the tip of his tongue.

"Ronin? Are you okay?"

No, he wasn't okay. He was jet-lagged and he was still staggering under the weight of his responsibilities—both old and new. He wanted more than anything in the world to lose himself in the oblivion he knew he'd find in her arms. But he knew he'd scare her away for good if he pressed her now.

"I'm glad you're here. Sweet dreams."

"Sweet dreams?" she answered, a quizzical look lifting one brow.

"Yeah."

*Walk back to me,* he silently begged her. Instead she gave him a sweet smile.

"You, too."

He stood there until he heard her bedroom door close, until he knew for certain that she wasn't going to change her mind and come to him. He returned to the master suite and threw himself down on his bed, his mind and his body too alert now for sleep to come back easily. She was resisting the attraction between them, but she felt it as strongly as he did. He knew it as well as he knew the stubbled reflection that greeted him in the bathroom mirror every morning. It didn't make sense. He thought back to the instant sizzle of awareness that had struck them back in Hawaii and how quickly they'd both given in to it.

The sizzle was still very definitely there, but she was fighting it. Was it because he now came with a child as part of the package, or was there something else that was holding her back? He didn't know right now but his specialty was solving puzzles. It would only be a matter of time before he solved hers, he promised himself as he rolled over onto his side and forced his eyes closed.

It was harder than she'd expected to fight the allure of the two males under the same roof as her over the next two days. There was something about seeing

Ronin with his nephew that plucked at her emotions until her attraction to him was near impossible to resist. Whether it was watching him bathe the baby, or use his large hands to scoop the wriggling wee tadpole from the bathwater and gently towel him dry, she couldn't help but be mesmerized.

She shifted a little in Ronin's chair and tried to focus on her laptop screen. He'd suggested she work in his office so she'd be less likely to be interrupted, but the entire time she was in there all she could think about was him. His office held an eclectic collection of things that reflected the type of man he was. A scale suspension bridge filled a table to one side of the desk—apparently a replica of a job in South America his firm was consulting on at the moment. When she'd asked if he needed to go there like he had to Vietnam recently, he'd shaken his head and informed her he didn't plan to do any overseas travel for at least the next six months.

His words had surprised her. From what she'd been able to glean so far, a big part of his work had included overseas travel, but now he seemed to have changed all that. The fact he was taking his duty to Joshua so seriously was just another facet to him that warmed her in places that had no business being warmed. Not when she was going to be leaving here, leaving them, first thing on Monday morning.

She thought about the past two days sharing the baby's care. They had fallen into an all-too-comfortable routine. Ronin would get up with the baby in the morning and leave her to catch up on email and make all necessary calls. By the time she was done, the baby was usually waking from his morning sleep and ready for another bottle. Now Joshie was getting the hang of things, he was turning into a voracious feeder—a fact which caused an equally vigorous output in other areas, which had horrified Ronin to no end. The rest of the day they shared his care around their own work commitments and even enjoyed some time with the three of them together.

For Ronin it had been simple—he'd delegated all but the most urgent of matters to his team. Even for Ali things had gone more smoothly than she'd imagined. In fact, Deb had even asked if they could keep the woman she referred to in her daily updates as Mrs. Fix-It.

When all was said and done, though, Ronin was coping well and, with the news that his mother would be released from hospital over the weekend, things were definitely improving. The agency had confirmed the nanny roster would begin, as originally planned, from Monday. Only two more nights, Ali assured herself, and she'd be able to get her life back on track. In fact, there really was no reason for her to continue to stay through to Monday. Ronin had slid into the role of Joshua's carer so competently he really didn't need her any more. Maybe she should talk to him about that, she mused, before dragging her attention back to her computer screen.

She hit Send on the email she'd just written to a new client and leaned back in her chair. Technically she shouldn't even be working on a Saturday. She looked outside. It was raining. It wasn't as if there was any motivation to head out for a brisk walk, which was a shame since she'd been neglecting her usual daily exercise while she'd been here. Maybe she'd ask Ronin if she could use his gym for an hour or so.

The door behind her opened.

"Coffee?" Ronin asked from behind her.

Ali could smell the brew and she swiveled the chair around to face him.

"Thank you."

She took the mug he offered, their fingers brushing as she did so. It didn't matter how often they touched, or how accidentally—the result was always the same. Her heart rate would speed up, her breath would quicken and the spot where they'd connected would tingle for a few seconds. It was growing harder and harder to resist him. Even her nights were filled with dreams about what they'd shared back in Hawaii. She'd lost count of the number of times she'd woken, her heart pounding and her body straining for a release that never came.

"Joshie's gone down for a sleep," he said, hitching his butt against the edge of the desk beside her.

The heat from his body reached out to her, filling the space between them. Enticing her. Daring her to move closer. Ali stood—or, more accurately, sat—her ground.

"That's early," she commented, before taking a long sip from the steaming mug warming her hands.

With the rain had come a bitter southerly wind, and temperatures had definitely dropped.

"Yeah, maybe it's the weather."

"Speaking of the weather, I had planned to go for a jog today, but with the rain, that's not going to happen. I was wondering if I could use your gym for a while."

"Of course. You don't need to ask. You have the run of the place."

"Great. It's just down the end of this hall, isn't it?"

"Yeah, let me show you," he said, putting his coffee mug down on the desk and heading for the door.

She followed him out of the office and down the hall. He opened the door to usher her into his multi-gym, complete with a leg press, a stand stacked with free weights, a treadmill and an elliptical trainer, all of which showed he was serious about fitness. Not that she didn't know that already. She'd examined almost every inch of his well-sculpted form once before. A girl didn't forget details like that.

"Are you familiar with all of this?" he asked.

"Most of it," she said, dragging her attention back to his question, "although I'll probably just use the treadmill for half an hour or so. It's been a while since I've done any proper exercise."

"Use whatever you want," he offered.

"Great, thanks. I'll go get changed."

It only took a few minutes to slip into her running gear and then she was back in the gym. To her surprise, Ronin had changed into a loose-fitting singlet and shorts, and was shifting an impressive set of weights on the leg press.

"I thought I'd follow your example and grab some exercise while I can," he said as she crossed the room to the treadmill. "I've brought the monitor in here with us."

"Oh, good idea," she said.

Her eyes danced over the muscles in his long legs as he worked through a series of repetitions. She flung him a distracted smile before mounting the treadmill and adjusting the settings to start a slow, steady run. She began to pound out the kilometers, trying to keep her gaze averted as Ronin went through a routine of weight training and exercises. But it was impossible to ignore the power in his shoulders as he did a set of lateral pull-downs. Power she'd felt beneath her fingertips.

A buzz started up in her body that had nothing to do with the endorphins that should be starting to build up about now. She forced her eyes away from him again and focused on her breathing. When that didn't work she increased the incline on the treadmill. Anything that would keep her attention on herself and away from the man working out only a couple of meters away from her.

A trickle of sweat worked its way down her spine, heightening her sensitivity. Still she pushed herself. Still to no avail. Ronin had moved to lay down on the bench press, his legs straddling the bench as he reached for the bar. Unbidden, an image of her straddling him, right here, right now, burned across her retinas.

A shaft of longing pierced her, so sharp and so swift she stumbled a little on the treadmill mat.

"You okay?" Ronin asked.

"Sure, I'm fine," she said breathlessly. "Just a bit out of condition."

"You look pretty fine from where I am," he teased with a smile.

She was anything but fine. Every cell in her body cried out for her to act on her fantasy. For her to strip herself of the tight-fitting Lycra top she wore and to press her heated skin against his. She pushed against the rise of desire that swelled through her, but it pushed back twice as hard.

This was hopeless. She'd have been better off running outside in the driving rain and chilling wind. She lowered the incline a notch and dialed back the speed a little. The sooner this was over the sooner she could get out of the room and head for a shower. A very cold one. By the time her half hour was up her legs felt like jelly, and it had nothing whatsoever to do with the run she'd just completed. Ronin, having finished his set, sat up to wipe his face with a towel. Sweat soaked his singlet, making it cling to the sculpted contours of his body.

Ali swallowed hard against the sudden dryness in her throat.

"There are water bottles in the little fridge over there in the corner," Ronin said, gesturing with a nod of his head.

"Uh, thanks."

She walked past, struck by the heat wave that flowed around him. Sweaty male had never been her thing—in fact, she'd never understood the appeal when friends had giggled over some guy or another at the gym—but she got it now, all right. Her inner muscles clenched with a primal response to the intensity and strength that emanated from him, and she felt her breasts grow heavy and begin to tingle.

Eager for any distraction, she opened the small fridge tucked in the corner and swiped two bottles from the door. She tossed one in Ronin's direction before opening hers and taking a long drink.

"Feeling better now?" Ronin asked.

"Better?"

"You're clearly used to exercising, and with looking after Joshua for me I guess you haven't been able to work out like you would normally. I know I get antsy when I can't work out."

That wasn't the only thing she hadn't done in a while. The thought pinged through her mind so strongly that for a moment she was worried she'd actually said it out loud. Ronin still looked at her, clearly awaiting her reply.

"Yeah, I know what you mean. It felt good to run."

"Ever tried mountain biking?"

She shook her head. "That's for people more intrepid than I," she said with a rueful smile.

Ronin laughed softly. "You should try it sometime. The Whitford forest runs behind the house and into the valley. It has some great trails."

"No, I don't think so. I like my bones intact."

She regretted her words the moment she'd said them, as they became a catalyst for Ronin to sweep his gaze over her body. She felt it physically—as if it were a long caress—and her body reacted instantly. Her breasts, already sensitive, felt almost painfully constricted beneath her sports bra, and a deep throb pulsed at the apex of her thighs. She took another sip of water, this time spilling some of the liquid, a droplet running off her chin and down her chest to the shadowed cleft at the neckline of her fitted top.

Ronin's eyes darkened as they followed the track of that single drop. Ali knew she should do something. Move. Anything. But she was held hostage to the look on his face, the burning hunger in his gaze. When he stood and took a step toward her, she felt a bolt of electricity zap through her. The heat she'd felt pouring off him before was nothing compared to the scorching temperature that sizzled between them now.

# Nine

Ronin slid the towel from around his neck and lifted it toward her.

"Here," he said, his voice thick, as though even words were too much at this point.

She watched his long strong fingers, tan against the white cotton of the towel, as he dabbed at the moisture on her chest. Then, whether by accident or design, his knuckle grazed against her skin. She dragged in a ragged breath at his touch. Again she reminded herself to move. To step away. To remove herself from the temptation that this man presented. Again she remained rooted to the spot.

The towel slid from his grasp and fell to the floor at their feet. He ignored it, instead tracing the swell of her breast with the backs of his fingers. Despite the heat that threatened to make her combust right here, goose bumps peppered her skin at his caress.

"You're so beautiful," he said, his voice a rumble from deep in his chest.

She couldn't respond. Her heart was pounding like a mad thing and it took all her concentration just to be able to breathe. When he bent his head toward her, it was pure instinct that responded. Not reason, not common sense—no, it was need, pure and simple. She was so desperate now for his touch, his heat. Her body ached.

His lips took hers hungrily, his tongue a welcome intrusion. She pressed against him and rocked against his arousal, earning a groan of torment from him in reply. It did nothing to relieve the demand that built deep inside her—it only served to stoke the flames that licked her body. When Ronin's hands went to the bottom edge of her top and began to peel it off, she lifted eager hands to assist him. Then, as his fingers deftly unsnapped the hooks of her sports bra, she pulled it from her shoulders, exposing her breasts to his hungry gaze and, even better, his hungry mouth.

A spear of need pierced her as he dragged one nipple into his mouth and sucked hard. Her legs weakened, but he held her upright as he feasted first on one breast, then the other. Ali's fingers tightened on his broad shoulders, her nails embedding a row of tiny crescents in his skin. Somewhere in the back of her mind she knew she should stop him, stop this before it went too far, but she craved him with a longing that went soul deep. She couldn't deny it, not anymore.

When he released her, she wobbled on her legs. For a second she was confused, not understanding, but then she felt his hands at the waistband of her running shorts—felt him pull them, together with her panties, down over her hips to tangle at her feet. Then he was on his knees before her, his breath a heated rush against the tender skin at the top of her thighs. His hands reached around her to splay across her buttocks, to tilt her closer to him. Her sex felt swollen, and the pulse that had built up before grew to a pounding beat.

He nuzzled her, making a shudder ripple in a giant wave through her body. She leaned back against the front rail of the treadmill, her arms reaching behind on either side, desperately searching for an anchor. With relief she found and gripped hold of the rail as Ronin's tongue swept across her. Spears of pleasure shot from her center. Ali could barely stand and she tried to ease her feet further apart but, manacled as they were by her shorts, she was captive to his whim.

She caught sight of her reflection in the mirrored wall opposite. Her cheeks were flushed, her breasts thrust forward by her grip on the equipment behind her. Her nipples were tight dark pink bullets, and every muscle in her torso was rigid. She looked lower, to the dark blond head, the strong neck and the broad shoulders that tapered to Ronin's narrow waist. The vision before her blurred as he stroked her again and again with his tongue, his hands kneading her buttocks in silent rhythm with his mouth, his stubbled jaw rasping against her inner thighs. And then he closed his lips around her most sensitive point, his teeth gently grazing the nub of exquisitely responsive nerve endings, and sucked hard.

Her orgasm swept through her, wave after escalating wave of pleasure swamping her senses. She let go of the rails and, with his guidance, sank to the floor, vaguely aware of him pulling her shoes and socks from her feet and untangling her clothing until she lay naked on the carpet before him. With swift, sure movements he tugged off his singlet and kicked off his footwear before carefully removing his shorts.

His erection jutted, thick and proud, from the nest of curls at his groin. Ali reached for him, her fingers closing around the silken length of his shaft, stroking him firmly. His eyes closed and he shook as she repeated the action. When he opened his eyes again they were burning blue flames, burning for her.

"I want you so badly," he said, through gritted teeth, "but if you don't want this, say it now."

In answer, Ali positioned him at her wet swollen entrance, her eyes locked on his. "I want this," she whispered, as she lifted her hips to feel the blunt tip of him nudging her slick folds. "I want *you*."

Without a second's hesitation Ronin surged forward, filling her completely and triggering a new raft of sensation deep inside. Ali gasped with the wonder of it all, her legs locking around his hips as he rocked against her. She was oblivious to the roughness of the carpet beneath her, her entire being focused solely on the man who surged above and within her, again and again until her body responded with renewed vigor and tumbled once more over the precipice and into the realms of delight.

Her hands gripped his shoulders, shoulders that were taut with tension, as he drove into her, seeking his own release. Suddenly he withdrew and groaned as his seed spilled across her belly. Beneath her hands she felt him shudder, felt his muscles begin to relax.

He reached for the towel he'd dropped—was it only minutes before? It felt like so much longer. Carefully, he wiped her clean.

"I'm sorry, I didn't think—" he started.

"It's okay," she interrupted. "We're safe."

Bowled over by their desire, neither of them had given a thought to contraception. She couldn't tell him that it wouldn't have made any difference. That no matter what method he'd used, pregnancy was not an option. The reminder hit her with a stinging cold dose of reality.

Ali eased away from him, unable to look him in the eye. As intimate as they'd been, right now she needed distance. Right on cue, a cry sounded from the baby monitor Ronin had placed on the shelf earlier. She hurried to her feet, grabbing her clothing from the floor and clutching it to her.

"I'll see to him," Ronin offered. "You go shower."

She gave him a nod of acceptance, relieved to be able to put some distance between them. Dressed, he'd always been a temptation. Naked, he was nigh on irresistible. But she couldn't afford to go there again. Couldn't lower her defenses. Not when she knew she would only prove to be a disappointment to him in the long run.

His words of only a few short weeks ago, that he'd always imagined he'd fill his house with a family, echoed in her mind. While she could give him everything that was within her, it would never be enough. Giving him a family was the one thing at which she would always fail.

Ronin pulled on his sweat-dampened clothing with a grimace and grabbed the monitor before leaving the gym. He should be buzzing with satisfaction right now and yes, physically he felt sated. But mentally he felt like Ali had taken several giant steps away from him, and he was at a complete loss as to why. Joshua's cries became more demanding. He could hear him in stereo now, Ronin realized as he neared the downstairs sitting room and turned down the monitor in his hand. Figuring out what had just gone wrong with Ali would have to wait for another time.

A few minutes later he eyed the baby's diaper with distaste.

"Gee, thanks, mate," he muttered to the little boy who, now diaperless, gleefully kicked his legs. "You couldn't have left this one for Ali?"

He quickly cleaned up the mess and rediapered the little guy before lifting him and propping him against his shoulder.

"I guess you're ready for some lunch, huh? Steak and eggs? Poached salmon and wilted spinach? No? How about a bottle then?"

He gently put his nephew in the baby bouncer and went to wash his hands and prepare Joshie's bottle. He went through the motions automatically, all the while trying to sort through the niggle of unease that still bothered him about Ali. She'd been a willing partner in what they'd just shared, he knew that for a fact. He'd given her an out, and not only had she refused it, she had given every indication of wanting him just as badly as he'd wanted her. How he'd ever found the presence of mind not to come inside her was nothing short of a miracle.

And what if he had? he wondered. To his surprise he couldn't push the idea of what might have happened next from his mind. In fact, a sense of warmth filled him at the idea of having children with Ali. He shook his head as Joshua squawked in protest at how long he was taking to ready the baby's feed. One step at a time, he thought as he scooped the little boy back up into his arms and offered him the bottle. One step at a time.

He was just burping the baby when Ali came into the kitchen. He didn't know whether she was attempting to keep him at bay or was genuinely feeling cold, but the jeans and loose-fitting turtleneck skivvy she wore shrieked "hands off."

"Everything okay?" she asked. "I tried to be as quick

as I could. I imagine you're starting to feel a bit cold dressed like that?"

Ronin hadn't even noticed the temperature, but now she mentioned it his damp gym gear did feel a bit uncomfortable. "It's okay."

"Here, do you want me to take him so you can go and get cleaned up?"

Even her voice sounded distant. At a time when they should have been closer than ever, she'd cloaked herself with the speed of the *U.S.S. Enterprise* anticipating a Klingon attack.

"Regrets?" he asked, determined to get to the point of her distance. He could fix this—he was sure of it—if she would just tell him what was wrong.

Her eyes flared wide at his question. She shook her head and looked down at the table, tracing an imaginary pattern on its surface as she allowed her hair to swing forward and block her expression from his view. She sighed.

"No," she finally answered, her voice small.

"Then what's the problem? We're two consenting adults, aren't we?"

She dragged in another ragged breath before answering. "Yes, last time I looked."

"Then there's *nothing* wrong."

"As long as we both agree it was just a pleasant interlude and no more," she said, lifting her head to look at him.

"What else could it be?" he asked, fighting back the urge to ask why she was so determined to dismiss the special connection they shared. For goodness sake, he was thirty-five years old. He'd been around the block a few times, certainly enough to know that the sparks they struck off one another were more than sheer luck.

Joshua chose that moment to belch loudly, showering Ronin's shoulder with a warm, wet dampness that told him that as much as he'd like to pursue this conversation with Ali a little further, now really wasn't the time.

"You're right," he said, handing over his wee charge. "I need to take a shower and get dressed."

She took the baby without a word and wandered over to the couch, where she sat down with him tucked into the crook of her arm. He watched as Ali picked up a baby book with her free hand and began thumbing through the pages, reading the story to Joshua as she went.

They'd just been as intimate as a couple could be, and still she was keeping her distance. Frustration unfurled within Ronin's mind. Why couldn't he get past her barriers? It was like trying to piece together a puzzle while blindfolded. No matter which way he turned or which angle he used to approach her, she continued to retreat. Should he just give up and let her walk away?

He turned and left the room and pounded up the stairs to his master suite. After he stripped off, he stepped into his voluminous shower stall and turned on the pulsating cascade of water. He braced his arms against the shower wall and bent his head beneath the stream, letting it rush over him and soak away the tension that had built so quickly. Life was so short, so precious. Losing his sister and her husband had proven that. That tragedy was making him reevaluate things on a daily basis. He thought again about the question he'd asked himself downstairs. *Should I just give up and let Ali walk away?*

The answer that echoed through his mind was a resounding *no.* He wasn't ready to give up yet.

# Ten

By Sunday morning the stormy weather had blown away to reveal a typical Auckland late-autumn blaze of sunshine. As Ali made her way downstairs to the kitchen for breakfast, she thanked her lucky stars that today marked her last full day here with Ronin. After yesterday's weakness, she doubted she'd be able to hold out against him much longer if he made overtures to her again.

Ronin was already downstairs with Joshua. She watched from the door for a while as he interacted with the baby, and it made her heart ache to see them. To see Joshie's blue eyes fix on Ronin as he held the baby in his arms and talked a barrel load of nonsense to him.

"Good sleep?" he asked, looking up at her when he realized she was standing there.

"Okay," she said, not prepared to admit just how disjointed her rest had been, filled as it was by reenactments of their gym encounter.

"I need to ask you for a favor today," Ronin continued, putting Joshua into his bouncer and jiggling the attached mobile. "Would you mind looking after this little man while I help Dad bring Mum home from the hospital?"

"Sure. How long do you think you'll be?"

Not that it mattered, because she'd promised she'd stay until the next day, anyway.

"A couple of hours with Mum and Dad, I guess, but then I have to go to CeeCee and R.J.'s house. I have to remove their personal effects so the other contents can be auctioned and the property can be listed for sale. Will you be okay?"

She nodded. Hadn't she single-handedly cared for the baby when he'd been released from hospital already?

"Sure, take however long you need. We'll be fine here."

He gave her a grateful smile. "Thanks, I really appreciate it. I'd have left Dad to mind Joshua but it'd be too much for him with Mum coming home as well. He's had enough on his plate."

*And what about you?* Ali asked silently. *Haven't you shouldered the responsibility for everyone, without question? Who's been there for you?* There'd only been her, and she was counting the minutes until she could leave. A pang of guilt struck her. Maybe she'd read too much into yesterday, thinking he was looking to start a relationship that she knew she couldn't handle. Maybe he'd just been seeking surcease in sensation. Maybe it wouldn't have made a difference if it had been her or some other woman he knew and was attracted to.

The second the thought came to her mind, an irrational wave of jealousy hit her. She groaned inwardly. This was ridiculous. Second-guessing herself all the time was one thing, second-guessing how Ronin's mind worked was a road she certainly didn't want to tread. Besides, she rationalized as she poured some cereal into a bowl and added milk, the nanny rotation started from tomorrow and everything would run like clockwork without her. He wouldn't need her at all.

"What time are you heading out?" she asked, fighting back the completely irrational twinge she'd felt at the fact he wouldn't need her.

"As soon as I can. I'll collect Dad on the way to the hospital."

"You do what you need to do. Joshua and I will manage perfectly," she said, a smile firmly pasted on her mouth.

And they did manage perfectly. Aside from a short-lived cranky episode in the late afternoon—a time Ali remembered her sisters referring to as Arsenic Hour—the day had gone well. But it was well dark before Ali heard the garage door roll open and then, after a few moments, heard Ronin's weary steps come down the hallway from the garage to the kitchen.

She looked up from the table where she'd been sitting with her laptop and was shocked to see how gray Ronin looked. Weariness had scored deep lines between his brows and his eyes, usually flashing with brilliance, looked dull and unhappy.

"Hi," she said, unsure of how to ask him how his day had gone. "You've just missed seeing Joshua. I put him down ten minutes ago."

"No doubt I'll see him during the night," Ronin said, with a weight in his voice she'd never heard before.

"I kept a meal for you. It's warming in the oven."

"Thanks," he said, turning to the oven and reaching for his plate.

"Look out—it's hot!" she warned, moving to her feet and across to the oven to pass him an oven mitt.

"Sorry. Wasn't thinking."

"That's okay. They're *your* fingers. Look, why don't you sit down and I'll bring this over to you?"

"I'm not helpless," he argued.

"I didn't say you were," she consoled. "Now, go. Sit."

She deftly slipped on the mitt and pulled his plate from the oven shelf and popped it on the bench. Once Ronin sat at the table, she lay out cutlery in front of him, then went to the bench and grabbed a half bottle of red wine he'd left there the night before and poured him a glass.

When she plunked the glass in front of him, he looked up with a crooked smile.

"Do I look like I need this?"

"Yes, you do. Frankly you look like you need hard liquor, but since I don't know where you keep your whiskey, this will have to suffice," she answered, and then went to peel the aluminum foil off his plate and deliver it to the table.

She poured herself a glass of wine, too, and joined him at the table. She watched as he used his fork to shift the braised lamb shank with kumara mash around on his plate.

"No good?" she asked. "I can put some mac and cheese together if you'd rather."

Mac and cheese had always been her mother's staple comfort offering, Ali remembered, when one of her girls had had a tough day. And Ronin looked as if he'd had a very tough day.

"No, it's fine. Better than fine," he said, and ate a few

mouthfuls before putting his fork down and pushing the plate away from him. "I'm sorry. I can't do it justice."

"That's okay."

Ali went to remove the plate, but Ronin reached out and caught her by the wrist.

"It's not you or your cooking," he said, his voice strained. "It's just been a hellish day."

"Is your mother okay?"

"She's fine. Tired, which is understandable, but glad to be home again. It was being at my sister's house that really hit me hard. I thought the funeral had given me closure, you know? That now, a few weeks down the track, I'd be ready for this. I didn't realize how difficult it would be to be in their house, to go through their things, or to discover how much I miss her."

His voice cracked and, with that sound, the hard shell around Ali's heart did, too. She knew what loss felt like. What it did to you when the world you knew ceased to turn on its axis anymore. When everything shattered and you were left with your life in pieces you had no idea how to put back together.

"I'm sorry," he continued, letting her go. "I shouldn't off-load onto you."

"It's okay," she said quietly. "And—trust me on this—if you don't off-load onto someone, eventually it will consume you."

He looked up from the table, his eyes bleak and empty. "I'm glad you're here, Ali."

Ronin stood and took his plate over to the kitchen bench. He scraped his uneaten food into the trash before stacking his plate and utensils in the dishwasher.

"Look, I'm beat. I think I'll take this—" he snagged his glass of wine "—and head off for an early night."

"Good idea," Ali said. "I'll see you in the morning."

She stayed downstairs a little longer, sipping her wine and looking out the French doors toward the lights that glittered in the distance like glow worms on a black canvas. This was her last night here. She should be positively gleeful at the prospect of returning to her world, her life, and yet somehow the edge had rubbed off her eagerness to leave. Why was that?

The answer came quite swiftly, and she rolled it round in the back of her mind before finishing her wine in a single gulp and putting her glass on the kitchen bench. She switched off the downstairs lights and headed for the stairs. At the top, she hesitated. Turn left toward her room, or turn right toward the master suite?

She turned right.

She'd never been into this part of the house before. Somehow, knowing it was Ronin's private domain had made it feel completely off-limits. Besides, she'd had no cause to come here. From the layout of the ground floor, she knew the master suite had to be large, but she hadn't realized it also included a very spacious sitting room. She took a deep breath and stepped through the double doors that opened into the sitting room. She could hear the sound of water running, then silence. Ali froze in her tracks. It wasn't too late to change her mind. She could leave now and he'd never know.

She turned, one hand on the door to retrace her steps, when across the sitting room a door opened. Ronin walked out, a white towel slung around his hips. A towel he'd barely used, judging by the droplets of moisture that still clung to his body.

Her eyes roamed his bare flesh, the damp matted scattering of hair at his chest, the trail that formed a line bisecting his lower belly.

"Ali?"

She dragged her gaze up to his face, to the confusion she saw there. Whatever she'd thought she could say to him fled her mind.

"Is Joshua okay?" Ronin asked, taking a few steps toward her.

She inhaled, readying herself to speak, but her senses were filled with the scent of him. With the cool sea air crispness of whatever soap he used blended together that that inimitable scent that was pure male, pure Ronin. "He—he's fine," she managed. "I just…I just wanted to make sure you're okay," Ali finished lamely.

Ronin's eyes darkened. "Okay?"

"Yeah, I…look, never mind."

She turned to leave, feeling ridiculous for having thought for a second she could go through with this. But then warm fingers caught at her hand and stopped her in her tracks. Slowly, ever so slowly, she turned back.

Ronin gave her a gentle tug toward him. Unresisting, she went, her hands flattening on the expanse of his chest.

"Ronin, I—"

She never managed to finish her sentence. The words she had been about to say fled. Her palms tingled and her fingers curled against his skin. She lifted her face to his and rose on tiptoe to capture his mouth with her own. Their kiss swept her away on a tide of longing. They were two wounded souls, each needing oblivion, a chance to forget.

When Ronin broke their embrace, a small cry of regret escaped her, but he took her by the hand and led her into the master bedroom. Soft lighting bathed the wide bed in a golden glow. Ronin tugged down the sheets with a few swift movements and then turned back to Ali.

"Here, let me," she said as his hands reached for her.

She quickly pulled off her sweater and unfastened her jeans before skimming them down her legs. She stepped out of her house shoes and the pooled denim at the same time and stood, dressed only in her apricot lace panties and bra.

Ronin reached for her again and she came into his arms, her skin warming instantly on contact with his. Her hands went to the towel at his waist, tugging firmly until it came loose, and she tossed it to one side. She gave him one brief, hard kiss and then pulled back.

"Sit," she commanded in a whisper. "No, lie down."

With a tiny smile pulling at his lips, he did as she said. Ali joined him on the bed, straddling his legs and placing her hands at his shoulders. Slowly she began to trace the outline of his muscles with her fingertips, working down his body—over the taut discs of his nipples, down his ribcage, lingering at his belly button. Beneath her touch his skin dotted with goose bumps. She followed each touch with a gentle swirl of the tip of her tongue until she heard him groan and felt his hands fist in her hair.

"Ali, stop. You don't have to do this," he gritted between clenched teeth.

"Let me be the judge of that," she said, looking up at him from beneath her lashes.

When his fingers relaxed a little, she continued on her path. He was fully aroused, his flesh a taut shaft against his lower belly. She traced the length of him, from base to tip with her fingers, and then with her tongue. His hips pushed upward, and beneath her legs she felt his thighs grow rigid. She teased the tip of her tongue around his swollen head before taking him into her mouth.

His sharply indrawn breath was his only acknowledgment as she pleasured him with her hands, her mouth, her tongue. As tension built in his body, she could feel him coiling tighter and tighter, determined to maintain control.

"I want to be inside you," he groaned. "Please, now."

She released him to fall wetly against his belly and rose to her knees.

"Condom," he said, reaching for a packet in his bedside drawer and tearing it open.

Ali took the sheath from him and took her own good time rolling it on. The entire time, he watched her, his eyes glittering like multifaceted sapphires. When he was covered, she raised herself over him and positioned him at her center. Slowly she took him into her body, relishing the tug and pull of flesh as he slid deeper and deeper again.

A ripple of pleasure rolled through her, making her clench her inner muscles around him and dragging another groan from his lips.

"Too much?" she asked with a half smile.

"Never," he declared, and reached for her hips, encouraging her to move.

As she slowly began to rock, Ronin thrust beneath her, his movements increasing the need that built and built until she felt him strain and push and cry out as his climax struck. She was so close, so close. She rocked against him, harder this time, faster, until she, too, felt the welcome swell of satisfaction swamp through her.

She lay down on his body, her head resting on his chest, and listened as his heart beat double time in her ear. Ronin traced lazy shapes on her back with his fingertips.

"Thank you," he said, his voice a rasp in the air.

"What for? You mean this?" she clenched around him again.

"No. For coming to me."

She lay there, silent for a while longer. Then she spoke. "You needed me."

And there it was. She'd admitted it to herself. He needed her, so she'd gone to him. She hadn't protected herself, her heart, as she'd promised she would. She'd put his needs above her own need to protect herself. And she couldn't bring herself to regret the choice, even though she knew she had just laid herself open for some serious trouble ahead. She wasn't the kind of woman who could just have sex with someone and walk away saying "Thanks for the memories."

Even in Hawaii she'd felt a link to Ronin that had led to her choice to sleep with him that first night—and that had left her feeling hurt and rejected when he'd vanished by the next morning. That link had grown stronger and deeper, and now it involved far more than just the two of them.

She hadn't wanted to love him, or even begin to love him, but she knew now that she was fighting a losing battle.

Ronin's hands splayed across her back, his palms warm and strong, and he rolled them both so they were lying side-by-side.

"I'll be right back. Don't move a muscle," he instructed as he slipped from the bed.

She should get up anyway, find her clothes and go back to her room. Except she didn't want to. Tonight she'd felt closer to Ronin than ever before. It was a terrifying prospect. She didn't have long to ponder—he was back within seconds. Had he sprinted the distance to and from the bathroom?

Back in bed, Ronin reached above him and hit a switch, plunging the room into darkness. Her eyes adjusted slightly, and she could almost make out his features in front of her.

"Stay," he said firmly, hooking one arm around her and pulling her to him. "Stay with me here. Don't go tomorrow. Please?"

It was the final word that broke her last barrier down. The knowledge that he needed her, wanted her. At least for now.

"Yes," she answered, placing a kiss on his chest, "I'll stay."

His arm tightened around her and she waited as his breathing slowed, as he drifted off into slumber. Her eyes burned in the dark. Leaving him, and she eventually would have to, would come soon enough. But for now, she'd take what she could and damn the consequences to her fragile heart.

# Eleven

There were times, Ali decided on Monday morning, when working with your best friend really wasn't the smartest of ideas.

"Ali, honey, are you sure you're doing the right thing? I mean, helping the guy out when he couldn't get a nanny is one thing—but moving in with him?"

Ali took in a long breath and counted to five. "No, I'm not sure I'm doing the right thing, but I can't see myself *not* doing it. I want to be with him, Deb."

She met Deb's concerned gaze and cringed inside as the concern turned to pity.

"Does he know?"

"That I can't have kids?" Ali shook her head. "It hasn't come up, and besides, it's too soon to throw that into the conversation. We're still really getting to know one another."

"Which is all the more reason why you should keep

your distance for now, don't you think? You know, do things the old-fashioned way. Actually get to know one another before you live together?"

"Sarcasm really isn't your best trait," Ali sniped in return, then sighed. "Look, I'm sorry. I shouldn't take it out on you."

"Too right you shouldn't. But it's okay. I understand. He's one hell of a hunk of man, isn't he? So, he must be pretty good between the sheets, huh?"

Ali's blush gave Deb all the reply she was going to get. Deb stood up from behind the reception desk and gave Ali a hug.

"Hey, if he makes you happy then I'm all for it. I just need to know you'll take care of yourself, buddy. I don't want to see you hurt again. Not like before. Promise?"

"Don't worry," Ali replied, putting on as brave a face as she could muster. "I know how to protect myself."

The thing was, she *did* know how to protect herself, and yet she'd chosen not to. Instead, she'd decided to embrace their budding relationship, for as long as it lasted.

Throughout the day Ali found her mind straying from her work and back out to Whitford—to Ronin, more specifically. She wondered how the meeting with the first nanny had gone, and how Joshua was adjusting to his new caregiver. A stupid pang of envy hit her straight in the solar plexus at the thought of someone other than herself or Ronin providing Joshua with care and attention. And love? Yes, and love. She pushed the thought away. She'd find out how Joshua's morning had gone later on today. After she'd been to her place to collect more clothes and a few personal effects, she'd be back out at the house and seeing the new nannies in action, all of them, over the next few weeks.

The idea sent a tiny thrill through her. She'd risen early this morning, remade the bed she'd been using in the nanny's suite and, at Ronin's suggestion, had shifted the things she already had with her into the second walk-in wardrobe in his room. Plonking her toothbrush into the holder on the marble bathroom vanity had given her an unreasonable sense of belonging. That said, she wasn't hurrying to let go of the lease on her apartment just yet. She knew full well how nothing was a sure thing in this life.

Her apartment was exactly as she'd left it just over a week before, albeit with a fine surface coating of dust in evidence. It didn't take her long to clean up and pack. She had a sparse wardrobe, preferring to buy select quality pieces she could mix and match for work and a handful of cheaper items for casual wear. Her suitcase was hardly bulging when she did up the zipper and hefted it onto the floor.

*Am I doing the right thing?* she asked herself as she locked the apartment door behind her and took the elevator down to the underground parking level. Only time would tell.

The week went quickly. Ali had forgotten how it felt to have something to look forward to at the end of the working day. Settling into a routine had come very naturally. When Ali pulled her car into her allotted bay in the garage on Friday night, she realized that the sensation that filled her now was genuine happiness. A feeling she hadn't felt in so long that she'd almost been unable to identify it at first. The connecting door to the house opened, and Ronin stood in the doorway, waiting to greet her.

Her heart swelled at the sight of him. His business

shirt was open at the throat, his tie seemingly long since discarded, and his shirtsleeves were rolled up, exposing strong forearms dusted with dark blond hair. She hurried from the car. Her briefcase and the quotes she needed to work on tonight would have to wait. Right now she had another priority.

"Good evening," she said with a smile as she slid her hands around Ronin's waist and lifted her face for his kiss.

"It is now," he murmured.

His lips were firm against hers, and Ali let herself revel in his caress, every fiber in her body firing to instant life at his touch. As much as they'd pleasured one another all the nights that she'd spent in his bed, she still wanted more. She thanked her lucky stars that Ronin felt the same way. Each day, each hour, each minute in his company had grown more precious than the last, and Ali had forced herself to admit that she was hopelessly and irrevocably in love.

Ronin pulled away and, taking her hand, led her through to the kitchen.

"Sit down," he said. "I'll pour you a glass of wine."

"You don't need to tell me twice," she said, walking through to the sitting room.

She sat on the sofa and slipped off her shoes before tucking her feet up underneath her. Ronin brought two glasses of red wine through and sat next to her, passing her one and then putting his arm around her shoulder to tug her closer. Outside, it started to rain. The northeasterly wind picked up and spattered droplets against the glass.

Ali snuggled against him, enjoying the solid feel of his strength and warmth at her side. It would be so easy to dream that this could be a forever thing. Despite the risk, she chose to ignore the fact that she was on borrowed time. Instead, she reveled in the here and now, savoring each precious memory and experience with Ronin, and with Joshie. She wasn't going to waste this moment, right here, right now.

"I saw my parents today," Ronin said, after taking a sip of wine. "They'd like to come out and visit on Sunday. You okay with that?"

"Sure, why wouldn't I be? How's your mum doing today? I'm amazed with her recovery."

Ronin had been in touch with his parents daily, visiting them at their home when he wasn't snowed under with work. His mother, Delia, had been making steady progress, which had been a great relief after all the family had been through. It reminded Ali again of how precious life was—of how you had to make the most of each moment, each opportunity presented to you, because it could be snatched away just as quickly as it had appeared.

"Going stir crazy stuck at home. Dad's doing his best, but I think they'd both benefit from an outing."

"Then let's plan a special lunch," Ali suggested.

"You sure you're okay with that?"

"Is there any reason I shouldn't be? I've met your father before and we got along okay." Another thought sprang to mind. "Are you worried your mum won't like me? Or that she'll disapprove? We haven't known each other long and she's bound to wonder about me living here."

Ronin squeezed her shoulders in response. "Not at all. She knows we're together. And for that, if nothing else, she'll love you."

\* \* \*

His words didn't prevent Ali from being hopelessly nervous when Ronin's parents' car pulled up outside the house at eleven thirty a.m. on Sunday. As it turned out, she needn't have worried. Both Delia and her husband, Neil, were warm and friendly. Delia had gone so far as to envelop Ali in her arms and whisper a fervent "thank you" to her for being there when they needed help.

"I was only too glad to be able to," Ali replied.

"We'll be forever in your debt," the older woman whispered fiercely, tears springing to her eyes. Delia dabbed at the moisture with a tissue. "Oh go on, look at me. This is a happy occasion. Now, where's my grandson?"

"He's in the sitting room, waiting to see you," Ronin said with a smile. As his mother went into the house he bent his head to Ali's. "See? I told you she'd love you."

Ali just smiled as they followed his parents through to where Joshua lay sleeping in his bassinet.

"Oh, my," Delia cooed, "hasn't he grown? He looks so much like you and your sister did at that age. Don't you think so, Neil?"

Neil's expression said he pretty much thought all babies looked the same at a month old, but he murmured something indistinct in response. Ali watched him as he observed his wife. So much love and devotion shone from his eyes—Delia could have said the moon was made of blue cheese and he would have agreed, if it made her happy.

It was lovely to see their enduring affection, but it made her a little envious, too. After her divorce, she'd convinced herself she would never be the recipient of such steadfastness. And, until recently, she'd managed to convince herself that it didn't matter. That she had her growing business, her family—really, what more did she need? But, as she watched Ronin with his parents and his nephew—three generations gathered together, like so many of her own family's gatherings—it made her realize that she wanted so much more. That she wanted what they had.

If only it were possible.

Joshua chose that moment to wake up, delighting his grandmother with the opportunity to spoil him with attention until it was time for their lunch at one. The nanny came to take him back upstairs and Delia reluctantly let him go. They sat at the kitchen table to dine and Ali very proudly served up the meal she'd concocted after several hours of research on the internet yesterday. She'd been determined to follow as heart-friendly a menu as she possibly could, and her hard work had paid off.

It was as they were enjoying a coffee in the sitting room after lunch that Delia suddenly rose from her seat.

"Oh, heavens, I can't believe I forgot!" she exclaimed.

"Forgot what, Mum?" Ronin asked, rising also.

"I was going out of my mind with boredom this week, so I decided to put something together for Joshie—an album with photos of CeeCee and R.J. I know he's still far too young to appreciate it, so I was going to hold on to it until he was a bit older, but I thought you might like to take a look. I brought it with us, but left it in the car."

"That sounds like a lovely idea," Ali said with a smile as she gathered up their cups and saucers and stacked them on a tray to take out to the kitchen.

"I'll go and get it. Honestly, I can't believe I didn't bring it in with me. My memory seems to have taken quite a hit with this operation of mine."

"Don't worry, dear," Neil said, rising from the table

and putting his hands on his wife's shoulders to encourage her to regain her seat. "I'll get it from the car. Don't you worry about a thing."

"He's such a good man," Delia said as her husband left the room. "He's been my rock through all of this. I don't know what I'd have done without him."

"Dad's been your rock, but remember that you've always been his, too," Ronin said, settling down on the sofa beside his mother. "He needs you just as much as you need him."

"I still can't believe it," she said with an audible sniff. "That they're gone."

"I know, but we have to stay strong for Joshua. To keep them in his life."

"Yes, that's why I want him to grow up with the album—so they're familiar to him. So he can love them as much as we do," Delia said, fighting to gather her emotions back under control.

Ali felt the sting of sympathetic tears in her own eyes as she watched Ronin comfort his mother. To distract herself, she picked up the tray to take it out to the kitchen.

"You okay with that?" Ronin asked, looking up at her.

"I'm fine," she said behind a forced smile.

In the kitchen she gave Delia and Ronin a moment's privacy and busied herself stacking the dirty crockery in the dishwasher. By the time she returned to the sitting room, Neil had returned with the album and Delia had it on her lap.

"There you are, dear. I didn't want to start without you. It's a shame you never got to meet our CeeCee, or her husband, R.J. He'd been married before, you know, but his first wife never wanted children. CeeCee said that when she met him he was dreadfully unhappy, but our girl made him smile again."

Before Ali could comment, Delia was opening the cover and turning to the main page. Ronin started to get up from his seat beside his mother, but Ali waved him back down and perched on the arm of the sofa next to him.

"This is my favorite of all their wedding photos. Don't they just look so happy?" Delia smiled in reminiscence. "CeeCee told me later she'd just whispered to R.J. that they were having a baby. He was completely over the moon."

Ali leaned over slightly to get a better look at the page and instantaneously wished she hadn't. She hadn't expected to recognize the couple smiling happily, with eyes only for one another, nor did she expect to feel the sudden pain that ripped through her chest—as if her heart was being rent in two.

"Didn't they just make the most beautiful couple?" Delia asked.

But Ali couldn't answer, couldn't breathe. Couldn't believe she was staring at her ex-husband and his interior decorator. The woman he'd left her for. The woman who had borne him a baby.

# Twelve

She must have murmured something in response to Delia's question, because Delia was now turning the pages—describing in detail why she'd chosen each picture for the scrapbook, lingering over the first ultrasound photo of Joshua, unwittingly driving a stake deeper and deeper into Ali's heart.

It wasn't that she still loved Richard—he'd destroyed that when he'd walked out on her for another woman—but she'd spent twelve years of her life with him. And he'd gone straight into the arms of a woman who'd been able to give him everything he'd ever wanted. Everything Ali had failed at. That little baby sleeping upstairs who she'd learned to love practically from the start was the son she'd never been able to give her husband. The son he'd had with another woman. The woman who, with Richard, had died only weeks ago. Ali couldn't believe he was dead. The awful finality of the word echoed in her mind. How could she not have known, not have heard somehow from anyone?

Delia finally closed the album. "And now little Joshie is the start of your family, Ronin. I'm so glad you're choosing to raise him yourself."

"It's what CeeCee and R.J. wanted," he said gruffly.

"But you'll be sure to give him brothers and sisters, won't you?" Delia pressed.

"All in good time, Mum. Let me come to grips with Joshua first," he laughed.

*All in good time.* Ronin's words signaled a death knell in Ali's mind to the relationship they'd just begun. Of course he'd want more children. She'd told herself that already. And they were the only thing she could never give him.

Ali operated on automatic for the balance of Neil and Delia's visit. She couldn't help but feel a deep sense of relief when Neil noticed his wife's energy levels were flagging and suggested they head home. After they'd waved them off, she and Ronin went back into the house.

"Are you okay?" Ronin asked. "You got really quiet there."

"A bit of a headache, that's all," Ali deflected.

"Why don't you put your feet up? I'll finish clearing up."

"It's all pretty much done," she answered. "But I think I might go and lie down for a bit."

His eyes narrowed in concern. "You're feeling that bad?"

Worse, she thought. But she couldn't tell him. Not now. Maybe not ever. He'd clearly adored his sister. How could she tell him that CeeCee had been the other woman in the breakup of her marriage?

"Do you need the doctor?" Ronin pressed.

"No, I'll be all right."

She went upstairs before he could say another word. In the master suite she walked through to the bathroom. She'd just closed the door behind her as the first sob fought its way out of her throat. Hard on its heels came another, and another. As she slid to the floor, the door at her back, she knew she wasn't mourning for her late ex-husband. She was mourning for what they'd never had—what she could never have with Ronin, what she'd been foolish to even attempt to reach for.

Delia's earlier words came back to haunt her. *His first wife had never wanted children.* How could Richard have said that? It was such a blatant untruth. She'd wanted to refute it, to scream that nothing had been further from the reality they'd shared. Why had Richard felt the need to lie about the reasons their marriage had failed? Was it perhaps because it had painted him and his relationship with CeeCee in a less than favorable light?

Whatever he'd been thinking, none of that mattered now. Richard was dead. Those three words repeated again and again in the back of her mind. And the bitter irony was that she now loved his son as if he were her own. The son of the woman who had inadvertently been the final chink in breaking apart the fragile armor of Ali's marriage. The pain that scored her now made her feel as if she was being betrayed all over again.

Richard. Married. Logically, Ali had known Richard had moved on with his life, but she'd made no effort to keep up with the details. Their friends had chosen sides, and she no longer kept in touch with anyone who was a significant part of Richard's life. There was no one to tell her about the wedding. But seeing those photos, seeing him happy in a way he hadn't been happy with her since the earliest days of their marriage, had been yet another blow. And it had made her current situation all the more clear.

Yes, Ronin was deeply attracted to her, and maybe he could even come to love her the way she knew she already loved him. But she knew that she couldn't count on that love to last, especially once her deficiency came to light. She didn't want to face that day, or watch what they'd started to build together be stripped away, layer by layer, until they had nothing left.

Ali buried her face in her knees and wrapped her arms tight around her lower legs, trying to make herself as small as possible. As if doing so could make the pain smaller, too. But it was useless. The pain kept on building until she knew there was only one thing left for her to do. She had to leave. She couldn't stay with the baby who was living proof of her shortcomings, or with the man she'd never be able to make lastingly happy. She had to stop this now before she gave Ronin false hopes. Before she set herself up for the silent recriminations that she'd already borne from another man.

She staggered to her feet and splashed some water on her face in an attempt to soothe the ravages of her misery, but the tears wouldn't stop coming. She grabbed a fistful of tissues from the vanity and walked through to the bedroom, throwing herself down on the bed and closing her eyes. Tomorrow. She'd leave tomorrow— that way she'd still have tonight. It would have to be a night to remember, because in her future, the memory would be all she had left.

Ronin moved quietly into the room. Ali lay asleep on the bed, still fully dressed and with her face turned in to her pillow. He grabbed a mohair blanket from the chest at the end of the bed and gently placed it over her before leaving the room again. Something was up. He knew it in his gut the same way he knew when something was going to go wrong with a contract. That was part of what made him so good at his job—being able to anticipate a problem before it became one. Having a working solution in his mind before it was required. Some people found his worst-case-scenario thinking to be downbeat, but he just called it risk management. Since he was totally risk averse, it had worked for him so far.

But with Ali, things had been different from the start. He had no worst-case scenarios worked out, no contingency plans in place. He'd gotten so swept up in her and the way she made him feel that all of his usual behavior had fallen by the wayside. Instead, he'd simply reveled in the sort of relationship he'd never expected to find in his tidy, orderly life. One that made him so simply and uncomplicatedly happy that he hadn't even considered that something could go wrong.

And that meant he had no idea how to fix things.

She wasn't something he could pick apart and peer through the layers to find out what was wrong. Even so, he racked his brain for what might have happened this afternoon to upset her, because despite her doing her best not to show it, he'd seen the pain reflected in her eyes and the tightness around her lips.

Was it something his mother had said? Was it the idea of having more children? No, it couldn't be that, he decided. It made no sense for her to be bothered by that. He'd seen Ali with Joshie. She loved him—it was there in every smile, every caress, every moment she spent with him. Her maternal instincts were right out there for anyone to see. Maybe it had been his quick rebuttal of his mother's suggestion that he give Joshie brothers and sisters in the near future? He tossed the thought around in his mind, examining it from every angle before putting it aside for now. Until he could get Ali to open up and tell him what she was thinking, anything else would merely be conjecture, and he knew that wouldn't get him where he needed to be.

He'd wait, keep an eye on her and figure out the problem. Then he'd fix it. Simple as that.

It was getting late when Ronin returned upstairs. The fact Ali still hadn't risen worried him. He'd made dinner and had waited for her to join him, putting her meal in the oven for her when she hadn't put in an appearance, then eventually wrapping it up and putting it away in the fridge. She'd even missed Joshua's evening bath and feed, something he knew she enjoyed sharing with him. Now the house was quiet.

He let himself into the master suite and checked on Ali. She was still in the same position she'd been when he'd left her. *That must have been some kind of headache.* With a faint sigh, he turned and went to the bathroom, stripping off his clothes as he went. He was standing at the vanity, contemplating a hot shower, when he saw a shadow of movement behind him in the mirror.

Ali. A sense of relief washed through him as her bare arms slid around his waist and he felt the heat of her body against his back. Relief quickly turned to something else as he realized she was, like him, naked.

"Feeling better?" he asked, searching her face in the mirror. There were still shadows in her eyes and she was a little pale, but she gave him a half smile. "You had me worried there," he continued.

"Nothing to worry about," she said simply.

"You missed dinner."

She pressed a kiss to the center of his spine that sent a bolt of longing straight to his groin. "I'm not hungry. Not for food, anyway."

She kissed a trail from between his shoulder blades to the small of his back. He turned around and pulled her up against him.

"Are you sure you're okay?"

"How about a bath?" she asked, avoiding his question. "I could do with a good soak."

He watched, slightly puzzled by her avoidance, as she sauntered to the raised steps that led to the marble spa bathtub he rarely used. Puzzlement fled as she bent over to turn on the faucet, adjusting the mixer until the water was at the right temperature. His body grew tight, his mind feeding his arousal with thoughts of how she'd look, slick with soap and lying in the warm water. Of how she'd feel beneath his hands.

He crossed the short distance between them and reached out to touch her, to cup the shape of her sweet buttocks and to run his hands down over her thighs as he pulled her back against his arousal.

"In a hurry?" she teased as she squirmed against him.

"For you, always," he replied, skimming his hands over her hips and her belly, and filling his palms with her breasts.

He rubbed his thumbs over her nipples, felt them shrink and grow tight under his touch. The bath filled with water and she reached for his wrists, gently easing his hands from her body and pulling him behind her up the steps to the bath. She let go of him as she entered, enticing him once again with the curve of her buttocks as she reached for a dish of bath salts and sprinkled them liberally through the water.

A spicy scent rose on the steam, which curled lazily

in the air around them. Ali sat down at one end of the bath and motioned for him to sit down in front of her. Game for whatever she suggested, he did exactly that.

Ali reached for the faucet and turned the water off, then pumped some liquid soap into her hands and began to wash his shoulders and his back. Her fingers slid over him. The touch felt exquisite, as always, but it wasn't nearly what he wanted. She reached around him with soapy hands and drew circles on his chest, drawing closer and closer to his nipples, pinching them gently between thumb and forefinger before sliding her hands deeper into the water.

Ronin's eyes slid shut as she closed her hand around his length, as she let her fingers clench and release as they worked their way to his tip and then back down again. He shuddered with the effort it took to hold back, to not give himself over to what she was doing, but he was determined to make sure she joined him on the same journey.

"Enough," he growled, mimicking her earlier action and grasping her gently by her wrists and pulling her hands away.

He was so hard, so ready, that it hurt. All he wanted to do was give in to his body's demand, but something still niggled at the back of his mind. Something that told him things weren't quite right.

"My turn," he said, shifting in the bath until he'd turned around and faced her.

Ronin pulled her forward, adjusting her legs so they bracketed his hips. Ali gripped the sides of the bath as he lathered up his hands and starting with her hands, began to work his way slowly up her arms. He took his time working the soap over her shoulders, along her collarbones, then down to her breasts, which rose, proud and full, just above the water line. He loved the feel of his hands on her skin, loved the sight of the contrast between his dark tan and her more golden hue. Again and again he circled his fingers closer to her nipples, and again and again he retreated.

A small frown appeared between her brows and her eyes narrowed as she looked at him.

"I never took you as a man who liked to torture a person," she said.

Despite the accusing words, her voice was thick with desire, music to his ears.

"I understand patience is a virtue," he teased, scooping up handfuls of warm water and allowing it to drizzle down over her chest, washing the bubbles away.

A tiny smile pulled at her lips. "So they say," she answered, her voice growing tight as he pumped more soap in his hands and began to wash her stomach. "I guess I'll just have to wait and find out."

"That you will," he promised, letting his hands drift lower, over the gentle swell of her belly to her hips, and then along the inside curve of her upper thighs.

She gasped as he stroked the tender skin on the inside of her legs, her body stiffening, waiting for his touch to become even more intimate. Ronin smiled and kept his eyes firmly on hers, locking her with his gaze, daring her to break it. He kept his touch light and teasing, watching as her pupils dilated, as her cheeks flushed pink with desire.

Seeing her response played havoc with his body. His erection strained between them, aching to be buried in that special place where his fingers tantalized and tangled. Ali's breaths grew shorter, her eyes now glazing, but still she held that connection between their gazes. When he firmed his touch, sliding first one, then a second finger inside her while stroking her clitoris with his thumb, her lips parted in a frantic pant. Still she looked into his eyes.

He'd never shared this depth of bond with another person. To have them laid open to him like this, trusting him implicitly. He curled his fingers and stroked her again, driving a deep moan from her. Encouraged, he repeated the action, and again and again until he saw the rise of color spread across her body, felt the contraction of her inner muscles against his fingers, saw her eyes slide shut. And watched as she dropped her head back and gave herself over to sensation.

Ronin gently withdrew his hand and rose in the water, reaching to scoop her up into his arms. Carefully he stepped from the bath and crossed to his bedroom, uncaring that they dripped water across the carpet as he put her, soaking wet, on the bedcovers. He quickly found a condom and tore it from its packet, covering himself with swift efficiency before positioning himself between her legs.

Ali lifted her hips to welcome him, her arms reaching for him and closing around his neck to hold him tight. He guided his erection inside her slowly, relishing the miracle of her slick and swollen flesh. *This,* he thought, giving himself over to the now primal demand of his body, *is where I want to be. Where I belong. With her. Forever.* When his climax hit, it hit hard and felt as if it would have no end.

# Thirteen

Ali woke an hour before dawn. She was curled up in Ronin's arms, sheltered by his strength. She inhaled, wanting to lock this moment, this memory, the very scent of his skin, in her heart forever.

Sometime during the night, Ronin had discarded the damp bedcovers and pulled the sheet and some extra blankets over them, but not before they'd made love again. In the darkness their joining had been so poignant it had brought tears to her eyes, and she'd been thankful for the mantle of shadows that night had given her, letting her hide her emotions from Ronin's sharp scrutiny.

She was afraid to move, to even draw a deep breath, in case it broke the spell that currently bound her. The spell that made her want to believe this could last forever. But she knew that, soon, any thought of forever would be gone, just as the darkness would fade into light as the sun rose on the new day.

He'd be leaving before her this morning. The helicopter was due to collect him at seven thirty to take him to a site near Rotorua for the day. She'd be packed and gone before his return.

A knife twisted in her chest. It was cowardly to sneak away without actually saying goodbye—but she hardened her heart against the shame. She'd leave a note—clichéd, true, but necessary in this case, because if she had to talk to him face-to-face she'd cave and tell him everything. The thought of having to explain her imperfections made her feel sick. No, she'd let herself take the coward's way out this time. She'd save her energy and her determination to face the days ahead. It was time to gather what was left of her strength around her like a carapace. To go on as she'd gone on before. Although this time she knew it would be more difficult than anything she'd ever done.

Ronin's alarm discreetly buzzed, and he flung out an arm to turn it off. Ali feigned sleep as he eased from their embrace and left the bed. She sensed him looking at her, but she focused on keeping her breathing even, her limbs relaxed. Words were useless to her right now, and the last thing she wanted to do was to meet his gaze. People always said that eyes were the window to the soul—if he looked into hers right now she doubted she could hide the sorrow and regret that lingered there.

When he left the room, she felt his absence like a physical pain. *Get used to it,* she told herself, burrowing her face into her pillow. *It's going to get a whole lot worse before it gets better.* If *it gets better.*

Twenty minutes later, a whiff of his cologne mingled with the fresh scent of mint as he leaned over her and pressed his lips to her shoulder. She mumbled something indistinct and felt him pull away. In the distance she could hear the whup-whup-whup of the helicopter rotors as it approached the house.

*Please go,* she chanted silently. *Please go so I don't have to say goodbye out loud.*

She heard a faint sigh, and felt the briefest touch on her back. Then he was gone. Only minutes later the helicopter departed.

Ali forced herself from the bed and to the wardrobe, where she'd stored her suitcase and her things. Packing didn't take long. She took a quick shower, dressed in a suit for work and automatically applied her makeup. Her hair was a tangled chaotic mess that she lacked the energy to fix, so she twisted it into a chignon of sorts and viciously pinned it into place.

Taking her case downstairs and putting it in her car only took a couple of minutes, which left just one more thing for Ali to do before she left the house. No, she corrected herself, two things. She had to say goodbye to Joshua and she had to write Ronin a note of farewell.

Right now she didn't know which was the lesser of two evils, and it wasn't like she could rock/paper/scissors with herself. What the hell, she thought, she was downstairs already. She'd write the note in Ronin's office and leave it on the kitchen table for when he returned. Then she'd find the courage she needed to say goodbye to the tiny human who had completely captured her heart and now held it hostage in his perfect little hands.

Choosing the right words to say to Ronin was more difficult than she'd expected, even though she'd had several hours to think about it. In the end, she kept the note short and sweet, thanking him for giving her the opportunity to create Joshua's nursery and for opening his home to her. She finished by saying she'd never forget him, but that in the long term she felt it was better if they parted. No reason. No excessive explanation. Before she could change her mind she shoved it into an envelope, sealed it and wrote his name across the front.

Once she'd put it on the kitchen table, she made herself return up the stairs to the nursery. She could hear Joshua already, his cries mingling with the nanny's soothing tones.

"Good morning," Ali said, forcing a smile to her face as she entered the nursery. "Someone sounds grumpy this morning."

"Nothing his morning bottle won't fix," the nanny said serenely as she changed Joshua's diaper and then lifted him from the changing table. "Would you like to hold him while I get his bottle?"

"I'd love to, and if you don't mind, I'll give him his bottle, too."

It would be the last time, she told herself. The very last.

"No problem. I'll be back in a moment." The nanny smiled, handing the baby into Ali's willing arms and leaving the nursery.

Ali cuddled Joshua close, but instead of settling as he usually did, he continued to cry. She studied his wrinkled face and tried to soothe him, but to no avail. Did he sense her unhappiness? she wondered, feeling her own tears prickling near the surface as his wails picked up in volume.

She tried to find any sign of her ex-husband in the baby's features—any reason, no matter how inane, not to feel this overwhelming love for the infant in her arms. She failed completely. Whether he'd grow to look like Richard, or his wife, or whether he'd be his own little person, it didn't matter. She loved him wholly from top to toe. Even so, she had to walk away.

"Hush, little man. Hush," she whispered, lifting him to her shoulder and rocking from side to side. "How can I say goodbye when you won't let me get a word in?"

She kissed the top of his little head and inhaled his sweet baby scent, knowing this had been a bad idea. She should simply have left. Why had she been determined to prolong the agony? Joshie was more than well cared for. He didn't need her anymore. And he certainly wouldn't know one way or another if she said goodbye.

The nanny came back into the room, bottle in hand.

"Here you are," she said, offering the bottle to Ali.

"I've just remembered I have an early appointment at the office. Do you mind terribly if I leave you to it?"

It was the coward's way out again, she knew, but right now it was the only thing she could manage to do. If she didn't leave this minute, she might never find the courage to go—at least until, maybe, she was forced to. And she couldn't bear that again. Far better to pre-empt it now than to open herself up for an even greater world of hurt.

"Not at all," the nanny said, with one of her calming smiles.

Ali gave Joshie one last kiss and passed him back to the nanny, then compelled her lips into a smile.

"I've left a note downstairs for Mr. Marshall. Could you see that he gets it?"

"Sure. I'm going off shift shortly but I'll make sure the new nanny coming on lets him know."

"That's great, thanks. Well, I'd better be off."

Despite her undeniable need to leave, to get away and put some distance between here and getting her life back together, she found herself reluctant to go.

"Have a nice day, Ms. Carter," the nanny said, offering the bottle to her charge and turning away.

She couldn't bring herself to answer. Nice days would be a thing of the past for quite a while. Possibly even forever. She waved a hand in response, and ignoring the crushing weight that built in her chest, went down the stairs and to her car. Her hand shook uncontrollably as she tried to put her key in the ignition and she forced herself to take several deep breaths before trying again.

"You can do this," she said out loud. "It's not the end of the world."

No, it might not be the end of the world, her inner voice reminded her. But it was the end of hope as she knew it.

As she headed down the long driveway she didn't look back. She had a busy day ahead, with no time to dwell on "might have beens" or "if onlys." She'd already had a bellyful of them the first time around. And she'd learned her lesson this time, at least. It didn't pay to fall in love. It only set you up for immeasurable loss.

Storming through the front entrance of Best for Baby felt more than a little like déjà vu, Ronin thought, and he had just about the same head of steam built up this time, too. A problem at the project yesterday, followed by a delay with the helicopter that had eventually seen him hire a car to drive home from Rotorua, had made him very late home last night. Too late to do anything about the ridiculous note he'd found waiting for him on the kitchen table when he'd finally gotten home, or the empty bed he'd been forced to toss and turn in.

Yesterday had been a crock from start to finish. He rubbed a hand across eyes that still felt scratchy from lack of sleep and looked around the reception area. Just like the last time, there was no one in attendance. He reached for the bell on the countertop just as Deb came through from what he assumed was a kitchenette, judging by the tray of coffee cups she carried.

"Oh!" she cried when she saw him, the cups rattling a little as she startled.

"Is Ali in? I need to see her."

"She's not expecting you," Deb stated firmly, as if that would be enough to make him turn tail and leave.

Ronin studied the other woman carefully. Did she really think she could stop him from seeing Ali if that's what he wanted to do? Something of his determination must have shown on his face, because she put the tray down on her desk and stepped in front of him, barring his access to Ali's door.

"Is she in her office?" he asked.

Deb's body language gave him all the response he needed.

"She's with clients and can't be disturbed," Deb replied implacably. "Look, now really isn't a good time."

Ronin cast a look at the tray Deb had been carrying. Yes, there were three cups and saucers there and a small plate of bite-sized servings of what looked like chocolate-and-caramel slice.

"I'll wait," he replied, settling himself on one of the two-seater sofas in the waiting area.

"Mr. Marsh—" Deb started, but he cut her off.

"I said, I'll wait."

He reached for the morning paper, still folded neatly on the coffee table in front of him, and, crossing his legs, began to read. Deb threw him a fulminating look. Clearly she knew that Ali had left him, and had been prepared to run interference, but she was no match for his purpose. He watched from behind the paper as she sniffed in his direction then picked up the tray and knocked on Ali's office door before going in. As she closed the door carefully behind her, he caught a glimpse of a couple seated opposite Ali's desk.

So, she had a consultation. It shouldn't take more than an hour, tops, surely. He settled himself more comfortably on the sofa, quite prepared to wait her out. The printed ink on the sheets in his hands blurred before his eyes as his mind wandered.

He'd known there was something up with Ali on Sunday night. Even when they'd made love, she'd been different. Although she'd been no less involved in what they were doing than usual, there'd been a degree of desperation about her he'd found hard to define. For the life of him he couldn't understand why, or even *when*, things had changed. Everything had been going so well. They'd been happy, hadn't they? So what the hell had gone so terribly wrong?

His phone buzzed in his pocket and he checked the screen, diverting the incoming call to his voice mail. There was only one matter he was prepared to deal with right now, and that involved the person sitting in the office on the other side of that wall.

Deb came out of Ali's office and closed the door behind her again, then flung him another look that told him in no uncertain terms that she wasn't happy about him being there. Well, she could be unhappy about it. This was too important for him to be ruffled by her behavior.

It was coming up on forty minutes when he heard Ali's door open again, followed by her voice thanking the couple for choosing Best for Baby. He knew the precise moment she realized he was here. Her face suddenly paled, and the smile that had been on her face disappeared. She appeared to quickly gather herself together, but he discerned a faint tremor in the hand she offered her clients as she said goodbye.

"I'll leave Deb to get your full contact details and we'll forward you a proposal for your baby's nursery by the end of the week. Have a great rest of your day," Ali said to the glowingly pregnant woman and her slightly distracted-looking husband.

Ronin waited to see what she'd do next. He expected her to come toward him, but instead she turned on her very high heel and went back into her office. Before she could shut the door, he was there.

"You don't want me to make a scene in front of your new clients, do you?" he said, his voice pitched only for her hearing.

For a second he swore she was considering it, but then she held the door wide and said, "Come in." As she closed it, she continued, "This had better be quick. I have an onsite appointment I need to head out to very shortly."

He studied her carefully, noting the strain around her eyes and the continued lack of color in her cheeks. Quick? She wanted quick? He wasn't going anywhere until this was sorted out. Fury and frustration vied for equal dominance as he shoved his hand in his suit pocket and dragged out her note. He held it up between them.

"*This* was your idea of saying goodbye?" he demanded. "I think we both know I deserved more than that."

"Not used to being turned down?" she answered glibly, moving behind her desk as if the expanse of wood and paper could protect her from his questions.

"It has nothing to do with that and you know it," he persisted. "You don't spend a night together like we had and then simply up and leave the next morning with this pathetic piece of—"

"Please," she hissed, interrupting him before he could tell her what he really thought of her note. "Keep your voice down."

"Then tell me why, Ali? Why did you leave?"

"Look, isn't it enough for me to say that I feel we can't see each other anymore? We rushed into things. It was all just too much."

Too much? It had felt just right to him, and he'd have wagered his very substantial salary that it had felt pretty damn good to her, too. Confusion over her choice of words clouded his thoughts, feeding the anger and frustration that had been building in him since he'd read her short, cold note. He didn't like feeling this way. It was foreign to him. He fixed things. He was organized and logical. He liked life clear-cut, and this was anything but.

The only thing Ronin knew for certain was that he wanted her back. It was the solution to a problem he couldn't even fully define. From the day he met Ali he'd been acting out of character. He'd reached for things with her that he'd never dreamed of sharing with anyone else. But even acting out of character had felt right, with her.

She'd literally rocked his world and made it a better place after everything around him had gone to hell in a handbasket. Mentally, he'd committed to her. Physically, he'd committed to her. Surely she could see that.

When he remained silent, fighting with the thoughts that swirled uncharacteristically in his normally linear mind, she continued.

"Ronin, I have an appointment. I have to go. Please respect my wishes. I don't want to see you again."

Her lips had moved and the words had come out, but he remained unconvinced that she meant them. It was time to regroup, he decided, to give her some space and sort out his next steps. He needed to get his own head straight rather than going off at her half-cocked.

"This isn't over yet, Ali," he said as he turned to leave.

"It has to be," she answered, a quaver in her voice.

He couldn't bring himself to reply, but he did as she'd bade him and left her office. Ignoring Deb, who jumped from her seat as if she'd been given an electric shock, he exited the offices. All the while, he felt himself forming a new resolve. He'd get to the bottom of what had scared her away. It was what he did. He had always solved the most intricate of problems, eventually.

And he would again, because—in this matter, even more than anything else he'd achieved in his life to date—failure was simply not an option.

# Fourteen

Ali headed for home with a heavy heart. This week had been a tough one. It had been busy, which was fantastic for business, but it had been lonely, too. Every aspect of her job had her dealing with happy couples, who just reminded her every day of what she'd walked away from with Ronin. Now, it was Friday evening and she had an entire empty weekend to look forward to. She couldn't even visit family, as her sisters and their husbands and children had headed away on a Pacific Island cruise with her parents.

She had, of course, been invited to join them on the cruise, but she'd had to decline. She'd already booked her non-refundable tickets to Hawaii before her family had found out about the special price promotion, and she couldn't justify the cost of the cruise or the time away from the office when she'd just gotten back from her own holiday. She wished now she'd found some way to make it work to go with them. She'd known their trip was coming up, but she hadn't expected to feel so alone when they left.

Deb, too, had plans for the weekend. A lovely romantic retreat with her husband. An unreasonable pang of envy hit Ali in the stomach. Everyone, it seemed, was happy but her. "Get over yourself," she grumbled aloud as she parked her car and then took the stairs to her second-story apartment. The bottle of wine she had in a grocery bag would go a long way toward making up for company tonight, she decided, along with the magazine, the antipasto selection and the half loaf of French bread she'd picked up at the same time. Tomorrow, and the rest of the weekend? Well, she'd tackle each hour, each minute, as it came.

She began to ferret around in her handbag for her front door key, her head bent and not looking where she was going, when a deep male voice arrested her in her task.

"Can I take those for you?"

Ronin! What was he doing here? Since his visit to her office on Tuesday she'd all but convinced herself that her plea had finally sunk in with him and that he'd accepted she didn't want to see him anymore. Her body called her a liar on that score the instant she lifted her head. His hair was spikier than usual, as if he'd been running his fingers through it repeatedly, and the stubble on his jaw was longer than she was accustomed to seeing. Her skin tingled as she remembered just how it had felt when those whiskers had rasped along her inner thigh or over her breasts.

She slammed the door closed on her wayward thoughts. She'd turned her back on that part of her life. On him. What the hell was he doing here?

"I thought I made myself clear," she said, still juggling her shopping bag in her attempt to find her house key.

In response, Ronin relieved her of her groceries as she finally wrapped her fingers around the missing keychain.

"You did. I'd like to talk. That's all."

Every nerve, every cell in her body tensed at his words. Talk? When had they really just talked? Perhaps the last time had been when they'd had that lunch on Waiheke Island. Before he'd gone to Vietnam. Before Joshie had come home. At the thought of the infant boy her insides twisted sharply. Her arms ached with the need to hold him again—but he wasn't hers to hold, she'd told herself that. Convinced herself she'd get over it. If Ronin would only leave her alone, maybe she'd actually begin to believe it, too.

She sighed. "Fine. Come in, then."

Ali flipped on the overhead light only to have the bulb blow out. Muttering under her breath, she used the light from her cell phone to guide her to the other side of the room, where she flicked on an occasional lamp. With its burnished shade, it cast a warm and cozy glow about the room. Too cozy. All they needed were some candles and, with her wine, the scene would be set for seduction. Except she didn't need to seduce Ronin. Though he was clearly upset with her, she could feel the chemistry between them hadn't diminished one bit. She knew he was hers for the taking if she was willing to put in a little effort, but she didn't want him.

*Liar.* The voice inside her head slithered from her mind's darkest recesses. The same voice that clearly held sway with the part of her brain that created the dreams that had found her waking, several times each night, wracked with frustration and sorrow combined.

"Can I offer you something to drink?" she forced herself to ask. "Some wine perhaps?"

"Sure, a glass of wine would be nice. Thank you."

He handed her the grocery bag and sat down on a sofa she'd found at a bargain price at the local thrift store. It was comfortable, even if the color, a virulent chartreuse green, was a little hard on the eyes.

Ali busied herself in the kitchen, pouring each of them a glass of the imported Australian Shiraz she'd bought. She eyed the antipasto and French bread. *What the heck,* she thought, and quickly sliced some bread and laid all the ingredients on a long ceramic platter. She had to eat anyway. Might as well be a good hostess at the same time.

She brought the items through to the small sitting room and, once she'd offered him his wine and something to eat, sat down opposite Ronin.

"You said you want to talk," she started. "So talk."

Ronin leaned forward and put his wine on the coffee table untouched. He rested his elbows on his knees and clasped his hands loosely together. Ali waited for him to start, but when he remained silent she felt the atmosphere between them thicken and become awkward. Eventually he spoke.

"I've been trying to make sense of why you left."

"Ronin, we've been through this—"

"No, we haven't. All that's happened is that you wrote a note and said you were leaving, then when I came to see you, you told me you didn't want to see me again. Why?"

Ali closed her eyes and shook her head slightly. She didn't want to go through this. Couldn't he just accept that things were over? People broke up all the time. They moved on. Period. Why wouldn't he let her go?

*Maybe because he loves you?* The idea came out of the blue. Her lungs squeezed closed and she struggled to draw in a breath. She didn't want him to love her. He couldn't, or at least he wouldn't when he knew she wasn't what he really wanted. But could she bring herself to tell him?

"Ali?" he prompted.

She opened her eyes. "Ronin, sometimes things just don't work out. We have to accept that and move on."

"Don't work out? What part of *us* wasn't working out? Were you unhappy with me, with Joshua? From what I could tell everything was fine until my parents came around on Sunday afternoon. Even then everything was great..." He hesitated a moment, as if working something out in his mind. "Right up until Mum showed you the album. Was that what it was? Was there something in there that upset you?"

Everything in her wanted to tell him to get up and leave right now. She didn't want to discuss this. Didn't want to strip herself totally bare and admit the truth to him. But if she didn't do it now, she realized, he would keep chipping away at her until he unraveled the ball of knots that was her past, her pain.

"Ali, I want to fix this. How can I make it right for you if you won't tell me what's wrong?" he said, more gently than she'd ever heard him speak before.

Oh how she wished it could be that simple. That she could just tell him and have him wipe every slate clean so they could start anew. But over the past few years, she'd learned to be a realist. Some things were simply unfixable. She cupped her wineglass in her hands and took a deep breath.

"It's nothing you can fix. It's me."

"C'mon, Ali. At least give me a chance."

She looked at him, at the intensity and integrity reflected back at her in his eyes. He really believed that he could make a difference? She hated to burst his bubble of confidence. But maybe that was what it would take for him to take that step back and release her to her solitude.

"I guess I should start at the beginning, then," she said with a deep sigh. "I first met Richard, my ex-husband, in high school—we were both sixteen. We were pretty much inseparable right from the start. He was so different to the other guys. He wasn't about the here and now, he always had his future clearly in his sights. Part of that future was to have a big family. He was an only child and his parents were in their forties when he came along. His arrival had come as a bit of a shock, I think. I got the sense that it was a fairly lonely childhood for him, though his parents loved him very much. Anyway, he had a plan already mapped out, even when he was sixteen. He knew exactly what he wanted from life and nothing would deter him from his course."

"He sounds focused," Ronin commented.

"Oh, he was. Very much so. I liked that, especially since our goals were so similar. I'm the youngest of four girls and my older sisters were already marrying and starting families when Richard and I started dating. Being a wife and mother was all I ever wanted, really. I didn't want to be a highflier in business. I wanted to create a world filled with the kind of warmth and love that my parents had given to us girls. The kind of world my sisters were creating with their partners for their families. Anyway, once Richard graduated from university he got work as a business analyst and he was very good at it. We married and started trying for a family straightaway."

Ali paused and took a long sip of her wine. This was harder than she'd thought it would be. Relating the bare bones of what had been both the happiest and the most devastating time of her life without injecting it with the emotions that bubbled so close to the surface was enough to have her heart racing with the strain.

She looked across at Ronin, who had leaned back against the back of the sofa and was watching her carefully, his relaxed pose encouraging her to continue.

"Anyway, long story short, we had trouble conceiving and Richard was frustrated that his plans, *our* plans, had stalled. When we discovered the reason why we were having trouble, he changed. He began to withdraw from me, refusing to talk about what the news meant for us as a couple. I thought he just needed time to get his head around the fact that his grand life plan had to be reevaluated, but that we'd be able to go forward on a new track after that. I thought he loved me enough to see us weather through it all."

Her voice cracked on the last few words, and she struggled to pull herself together. She thought she'd learned to control the hurt and sense of betrayal that had remained as the legacy of her marriage, but hard on the heels of her discovery last Sunday—on seeing that gloriously happy photo of Richard with his new bride—she'd realized any control she'd thought she'd had was merely a front. The hurt still cut like a razor, still made her bleed inside.

She shook her head as if to clear her thoughts and continued. "Anyway, one day he came home from work and said he loved someone else who had made him happy again, and he wanted a divorce. In her he saw a new chance to live his dream, to create the future and the world he wanted more than he wanted me. I was blindsided. God, I was such a fool.

"For months he'd been having an affair with a woman he'd hired to redecorate his offices at work. He'd been falling in love with her and out of love with me. I should have realized. I knew how focused he was, how determined he'd always been to reach his goals. I should have realized that once he saw I couldn't give him what he dreamed of, he'd want out."

Ali looked at Ronin again and could see him processing what she'd told him. She could pinpoint the moment when the pieces fell together to make a whole.

"Richard was R.J.?" he asked.

She nodded. "I had no idea he'd remarried, no idea he'd been about to become a father. I hadn't even heard he was dead."

The thought that he'd been on the verge of realizing his greatest goal in life, only to have it snatched cruelly away, made her feel an ironic sense of loss on his behalf.

"I'm so sorry you had to find out that way. No wonder you weren't yourself after seeing the album. And I think I understand why you were so angry when you thought I was married, but—" he shoved a hand through his hair "—I still don't understand why you ran. We could have talked about this. Yes, the situation is unusual, and I understand if it changes the way you view Joshua and me, but we can hardly be held accountable for what R.J. did. You're feeling hurt now, but once the initial shock has passed, I'm sure we can work through it."

"You don't understand," Ali replied, putting her glass down on the table and twisting her hands together.

"Then tell me, so I can do something about it."

"There's nothing you can do, Ronin. It's not just that

my husband cheated on me with your sister. It's not just that together they created a baby, or even that I ended up looking after that baby when he came home from hospital. None of that really matters now."

"No, you're right. We matter. Working out a solution to what's keeping us apart is what matters most."

"You're not listening to me. There is no solution. Tell me if I'm wrong, but I'm sure that when I came out to see you after Hawaii, you said you'd always imagined filling your house with kids, yes?"

"Y-es," Ronin answered carefully, his gaze not budging from her face for a second.

"And didn't you imply to your mother that you planned to give Joshie brothers and sisters in the future?"

"I did, but I'm not in a hurry for that, Ali. We can wait."

She gritted her teeth. Did she have to spell it out in foot-high letters? "Ronin, you won't ever have that with me. I can't have children. Ever."

His eyes dulled a little, but only for a second. Before she knew it they'd fired up again, deepening and glittering in the soft light of her sitting room.

"We'll have Joshua. That's fine. You love him—I saw it with my own eyes. Surely you don't love him any less now because of who his parents were? We can make this work, trust me. If I have no other children than him, I can live with that."

She swallowed against the lump in her throat and gave a humorless laugh. "*Live with that?* For now, maybe. But what about a year from now, or five years from now? What about when your friends have children? When you see families down at the beach or playing in the park? What then? Can you honestly tell me you won't regret not having had more children of your own?"

His silence gave her all the answer she needed.

"And what about me?" she continued, pressing her advantage. "How do you think I'll feel, seeing those families, knowing I'm the reason you can't have one? How can I feel like anything other than a failure as a woman when I'm often reminded of what I can't give you? When our only child is, quite literally, the son I could never give my husband?"

She stood up from her seat, her legs unstable and weak beneath her. As much as she loved him, there was no way she'd put either of them through the hell that she knew would come. Even if he thought he loved her now, she knew regrets would eventually peel away their affection for one another until all that was left was resentment and reproach.

"I'd like you to leave now," she said, as levelly as she was able.

She walked to the front door and held it open, leaving him no other choice but to go.

When Ronin drew level with her, he stopped. "You've got it all wrong, Ali. We can make this work. I know we can."

"You forget, Ronin. I've been through all of that, and it hurt. In fact it hurt so badly that I'm never going to put myself in that position again."

# Fifteen

For the duration of his forty-minute drive back home, Ronin turned over every word Ali had said during their meeting. For the first time in his life he was up against a problem that refused to be solved.

And despite what she seemed to think, her infertility was *not* the problem. So what if she couldn't have children? That wasn't the be-all and end-all of his existence. He loved *her*. Not her ability to procreate, and not her instinctive skill as a mother. Her. The problem was her refusal to believe that she could be enough— that he loved her far more than any vague dreams of having a big family.

He groaned out loud. And had he told her that? Had he reassured her that he didn't just look at her as a baby-making machine? Had he so much as hinted at the fact that even if they didn't have Joshua in their lives that she would be enough for him, for all time?

And he thought that he was so clever. That he was Mr. Organized. That the right decision could always be reached with sound deductive reasoning. There was nothing reasonable about the cards life had dealt to Ali. No clear-cut guidelines existed to show a person how to handle successive blows like that. Life didn't come with a handbook, and after the number that R.J. had done on her it was no wonder she felt so insecure about herself.

A part of him wanted to turn his car around and head straight back to her tiny apartment and make his claim on her heart. To tell her he loved her and that he would make everything all right. But the other part, the logical part that ruled his life and governed his decisions, could see that not even a declaration of love would convince Ali that he meant what he said.

But there had to be something. One way or another, he'd nail down a resolution to her fears. He just had to.

A week later, Ronin walked the hallway between the nursery and his master suite with Joshua on his shoulder. The baby simply would not settle down for his afternoon sleep. He'd been fussy and cranky as all get-out for nearly two weeks now, and had failed to make any significant weight gain since Ali had left. Could it be that he missed her as much as Ronin did? Or was this just one of so many different facets of raising a child?

"Would you like me to take him, Mr. Marshall?" the day nanny asked as she came upstairs with a bundle of Joshie's laundry.

It was remarkable the amount of work one tiny baby created, Ronin thought. He wondered anew how single parents who couldn't afford professional childcare coped with the responsibility and the workload. With the doubts about whether you were doing the right thing, and the fears of what might happen if you didn't. It reminded him that he hadn't shown Ali anywhere near sufficient appreciation for what she'd done caring for the fretting child in his arms on her own, as she had when he'd first gotten out of the hospital.

"It's okay," Ronin replied. "He'll settle, eventually."

He didn't want to simply hand Joshua off to the nearest set of willing hands. He'd taken his sister's baby on with all that had entailed. And if that meant walking him up and down this hallway until he wore a track in the carpet, then that's exactly what he'd do. It wasn't easy, though, and a man could go deaf with the noise reverberating in his ear.

Ronin took his guardianship seriously, as he did any project he accepted. Except this was different in so many ways. He'd never been as emotionally invested in his work projects as he was in this tiny individual. And while he loved his work, it certainly didn't hold a candle to how he'd felt when, a couple of days ago, Joshie had beamed a gummy smile in his direction.

But the baby wasn't smiling now. Another ten minutes felt like sixty. Ronin was suddenly reminded of how quickly Joshua had settled when he'd held him in the hospital. What had they called it again? Kangaroo cuddles. Anything was worth a shot. He went into the nursery and put Joshua on the change table while he quickly pulled off his T-shirt, then eased the baby's onesie off as well. Clad only in his jeans and with Joshie in just a diaper, he sat down in the rocker and slung a blanket around them both to keep them warm.

The baby headbutted him a few times, still voicing his discontent, but as Ronin set the chair to move gently back and forth, Joshie finally calmed and dropped off to sleep. Ronin's first instinct was to put the baby back in his bassinet and leave him to it, but as he looked down at his nephew a new sense of wonderment stole over him. He'd forgotten how special it felt to hold the baby to his heart. To feel his little sigh of release as he let go of wakefulness and slid into slumber.

Only six weeks old and Joshua had already changed so much from the helpless scrap Ronin had first seen in the newborn intensive care unit. Ronin wasn't the kind of man who gave his heart easily, but when he did, he went all the way, and he knew without doubt that he'd cross shark-infested waters if Joshua needed him on the other side. He'd do anything to protect Joshie—to make sure he was safe and happy.

So what did that really mean? What would it take to give Joshie the life that he deserved? Ronin had been convinced that the rotation of nannies would be enough to see to the baby's care, freeing him up to lend a hand when possible and mostly just oversee it all. But the past two weeks had proven that that wasn't enough. Joshie needed something more—something that Ronin seemingly couldn't give the baby, no matter how much he loved him. In fact, it was *because* he loved his nephew so much that he had to come to terms with the truth.

He'd followed his sister's wishes by stepping up to raise her son, but had he really done what was best? Was his certainty that he could handle the challenges of being a parent well-founded, or was it just arrogant? Was he overconfident in his abilities to complete any task he laid out for himself? Had his pride, and his certainty in his own abilities, blinded him to what the baby really needed?

He thought back to CeeCee and R.J.'s funeral, to his cousin Julia's offer to take the baby and raise him with her family. Should he have done that? Given Joshie a mum and a dad? Would it have been the best thing for Joshie in the long run? He couldn't say one way or the other, but he knew it was an idea he'd have to seriously consider. Joshie's future was at stake, and he couldn't afford to make the wrong choice. Nor would he forgive himself if he denied the baby the chance to have a loving mother's care—care that he was obviously missing since Ali had left.

But as he weighed his decision over in his mind another thought butted in from left field. He turned the idea this way and that, examining it from all angles. It would be risky, he thought, and he couldn't go at it halfheartedly—it was something to which he had to be prepared to commit fully. Could he do it?

He looked down at the sleeping baby nestled against him. Love and devotion filled him in equal proportion. Of course he could do it if he had to, no matter how much it contradicted his every instinct to hold on. He'd do whatever was best for Joshua, always.

Carefully, Ronin rose from the rocker and tucked the baby into his bassinet, making sure his bedcovers were snugly tucked around him. Ronin tugged his shirt back on and exited the nursery, bumping into the day nanny as he did so.

"Success?" she said softly, with a conspiratorial smile.

"Yes. It was a bit of a battle of wills, but we got there in the end."

"He's lucky to have you."

"I think I'm lucky to have him," Ronin replied before making his way downstairs to his office.

He *was* lucky to have Joshua, which made what he was about to do all the more important. And he had to do it right—for everyone's sakes.

* * *

By Monday morning everything was in place. Ronin secured Joshua in his car seat in the car and headed toward Best for Baby. Joshua, thankfully, slept through the morning rush hour traffic that kept them bound in gridlock on the Southern Motorway, stirring only briefly when Ronin pulled into the visitor parking at Ali's office. He didn't see her car there, which promised a potential wrinkle in his plans, but he knew he wouldn't be that easily deterred. He'd find out when she was due in and adjust accordingly.

With the car seat hooked over his arm, he entered the office. Deb looked up from the reception desk with a smile as he pushed open the doors. A smile that froze, then faded, as she recognized him.

"Can I help you?" she asked, in an arctic tone.

"I'd like to see Ali. It's important."

"She's not here. In fact, I don't expect her in all day."

The woman looked uncomfortable, almost pitying, as she imparted the information.

"As I said, it's important." He hefted Joshie's carrier onto the reception desk and saw Deb's eyes soften as she looked upon his, currently, angelic face.

"He's doing well, now, is he?" she asked, looking up briefly at Ronin.

"Not so great these past couple of weeks. Neither of us are."

She got his point immediately.

"He misses Ali?"

"I've taken him to his pediatrician and she confirmed there's nothing physically wrong with him, so yes, I believe so."

Deb reached out, and with the back of one finger stroked Joshua's round little cheek.

"It's a crime that she can't have babies, you know that."

"It is," he agreed vehemently.

"But the worst crime is the way it makes her feel about herself—as if she doesn't hold value as a woman without the ability to bear children. I don't want to speak ill of the dead, but Richard crushed her sense of self-worth when he left the way that he did. For a while her family and I didn't expect her to recover, but after the divorce was finalized, she rallied. That's when she poured everything she had into this place. All her longing, all her love, it goes into every contract we make, every family she helps."

Ronin didn't speak—a tactic he'd learned many years ago that usually led him to exactly the information he wanted. Most people were uncomfortable with a vacuum of silence. It appeared Deb was no different from the rest.

"If I tell you where she is, will you promise not to hurt her? If you do, I *will* have to hurt you."

He looked at the diminutive figure seated behind the reception desk. Based on her build he doubted the woman could hurt a fly, but given the look in her eyes, Ronin chose his words carefully. "It isn't, and has never been, my intention to hurt her."

Deb gave him a hard look. "I'd like to ask you your intentions, but I have a feeling you'd probably tell me they're none of my business."

He couldn't help it—he smiled at her perceptiveness. "You're probably right."

She smiled in return and grabbed a small sheet of paper, on which she scrawled an address.

"The tenant above her had a water leak and it flooded Ali's apartment. She's staying a few nights at her par-

ents' house while her landlord makes the necessary re-
pairs and dries her place out. She's working from there
today. And her family's away, just in case you were
wondering."

"Thank you," he said, studying the address and then
slipping the paper into his pocket.

Knowing her parents weren't around was a relief.
While he was prepared to do this with an audience if
he had to, he vastly preferred to keep this just between
the three of them.

"Mr. Marshall, I meant what I said about hurting
her."

"And I meant what I said, too."

She nodded, accepting that would have to suffice.

"As long as we're clear on that."

"Crystal," he replied, reaching for the carrier.

As he neared the door, Deb caught his attention once
more.

"Mr. Marshall?"

He turned around.

"For what it's worth, she's missed you, too. Both of
you. Good luck."

He smiled in response. He needed all the luck he
could get. Everything hinged on this going as he'd
hoped. Everything.

Ali's parents' house was a simple weatherboard bungalow in one of the older parts of town. A bed of tired-
looking standard roses stood in a circular garden in the
middle of the front lawn. He walked up the narrow con-
crete front path with a now wide-awake Joshua in the
car seat. The baby startled when Ronin rapped on the
multipaned rippled glass front door, but he didn't cry.

Ronin spied Ali coming up a hallway toward the

door. She hesitated when she figured out it was him, but then she eventually lifted an arm and warily opened the door.

"What do I have to say to you, Ronin? I told you I don't want to see you anymore."

Dressed simply in jeans and a long-sleeved T-shirt, she'd never looked so appealing. His hands itched to reach out and touch her. To trace the signs of tiredness that were drawn on her face. To kiss the firm set of her lips into a softer, more welcoming state. He swallowed and drew in a breath. This wasn't going to be easy, but then again, he certainly didn't expect it to be.

"I thought you might like to say goodbye to Joshua before he leaves."

She paled, her gaze flicking from the baby to him. "L-leaves? Why?"

He used the silence tactic, determinedly holding her gaze.

Ali sighed and opened the door a little wider. "You'd better come in."

She led him into a simply furnished sitting room. He looked around, seeing the everyday things that made up a family's life. The photos on the display cabinet, the clumsy school project crafts and sculptures that took pride of place within it, peppered in between fine china cups and saucers that probably never so much as saw a drop of tea or a cookie unless "company" came to visit. He put Joshua's carrier on a floral-covered couch and stepped over to look at the photo frames on the cabinet.

So many of them, he thought, and all of them family. He picked Ali out immediately in a picture of four little girls, arrayed from left to right, oldest to youngest. He felt his heart tug. She'd grown up surrounded by family. A family that had expanded as her sisters, who he recognized in newer photos, had children of their own. He felt a jolt of shock as he recognized R.J. in a frame shoved to the back—or, more particularly, R.J. and Ali on their wedding day.

Her dress was simple and she had such a look of optimism and devotion on her face as she looked up at her new husband. So much hope, so many dreams. Could Ronin even begin to hope that one day he might see that look on her face when it was turned to him? There was only one way to find out.

"Well?" Ali demanded from behind him. "What did you mean about Joshua leaving?"

He turned to face her, noting how her regard kept drifting toward Joshie, recognized the longing there. Despite what he'd told Deb, he knew what he was about to say was going to hurt. But sometimes, he knew, you had to be cruel to be kind. You just had to rip the bandage off in one hard swipe to allow true healing to begin.

"I'm giving him up."

# Sixteen

"W-what?" He had her full attention now. "What do you mean you're giving him up? You're his guardian. You can't just *give him up!*"

"I mean I can't do it—I can't raise him on my own. He deserves more than I can give him. I've tried and I've looked at this from every angle. Yes, I can look after his basic needs. He's fed and cared for, he's got shelter and, yes, he's loved. But I know what my sister wanted for him—what any parent wants for their child, and what Joshie himself has been suffering without. He deserves people who are totally invested in him. He deserves a complete family—a mother and a father. Even with his rotation of nannies, I can't do that on my own."

"But you do love him, don't you?"

"Of course I love him. But this isn't about me. It's about him, and that's why I have to do what's right by Joshua."

"So, what? You're just going to put him up for adoption? Just like that? What if they're not right for him? What if they don't love him like you do?"

Ronin began to feel something ease a little inside him. She was fighting. Fighting for Joshie. It was a start.

"I'm not letting him go to just anyone. A cousin of mine offered to raise him when CeeCee died. Julia and her husband already have a couple of kids and they want him. Really want him. It's a win-win. He'll stay in the family, and my parents will still have full access to him. Even better, he'll be with people who love him and who will care for him."

"How can you say it's a win-win when you're letting him go?" she asked in confusion. "You're not winning. I don't understand how you can do that…how you can say it's what's best for him. I've seen you with Joshie. I've seen how much you love him. He deserves to stay with you. It's what your sister and—" she paused and took a shuddering breath "—Richard wanted."

Ronin shoved his hands in his trouser pockets and fought to find the right words.

"When they made their wills, I'm sure they didn't expect me to ever actually have to take responsibility for their child or children."

"No one intends to die, but people make contingency plans. They named you as their preferred guardian. You were their first choice. Surely if they wanted your cousin to raise Joshie they'd have mentioned her in their wills."

Ronin's fingers ached, his fists were so tight. It hurt to say this, but he had to.

"And I'm equally sure they always imagined that one day I'd be married and have someone at my side to help me. To love and raise Joshua with me."

"And you will, one day."

He shook his head. "No, I won't."

She looked at him incredulously. "Don't be ridiculous. Of course you will. Let's face it, you're highly eligible."

"Thank you," he acceded wryly. "But eligibility aside, I am not marrying. Not when I can't be with the only woman I want."

Ali backed up until the back of her legs hit the chair behind her. "I beg your pardon?" she said, her voice small and baffled.

"Ali, if I can't have you, I don't want anybody else. You seem to have this misguided notion that I'd want something more than you, or that I'm going to change my mind about my feelings for you. That my first priority is to have more children in my life. It's not. Sure, if you agreed to be with me, and you wanted more kids, I'd be happy to look into adoption. God knows we have the capacity for more kids and more love in the house. But it's not something that's vital to me. You are. Without you, children aren't in the picture anyway, because I won't have them with anyone else. And I won't have Joshie, either, because he deserves to have a loving mother, and the only one I want filling that role in my home is you."

"You can't be serious," she gasped.

"I've never been more serious about anything in my life. I'm not the kind of guy to say things I don't mean, and I'm not the kind of guy who pretends to feel things I don't feel. I've got to do what's right for me—and that means being with you or being alone. If I'm alone, then I can't be the right parent for Joshie. I'm not denying this is going to hurt. It's going to kill me inside. But I can't do everything, or be everyone, that Joshua needs. I have to do what's right for *him*." He paused. "And what's right for *you*. And I can't help thinking that nothing could be better for you than to be with the man who wants to devote his life to making you happy. I love you, Ali, completely, utterly and totally, with everything I am."

Ali stared at him in disbelief then shook her head as if she could shake free the things he'd just said. "It's easy for you to say that now. But I know you'll regret it."

"The only thing I'll ever regret is not being able to convince you that what I'm saying is true."

"You don't want me, Ronin. You couldn't possibly."

All the pain of the past five years swelled within her. All her feelings of inadequacy, and lack of self-worth. She was flawed, incomplete. A reject.

"I'm not Richard. Can't you understand that? I'm not going to stop loving you just because you can't have a baby. That's not why I want to be with you. I'd rather have a childless life than an eternity without you."

"How can you love me?" she cried. "We've known each other just over six weeks. People don't make plans for the rest of their lives based on that."

Even as she said the words she argued with herself. She and Richard had known each other nearly six years when they'd married, but it hadn't changed the outcome. Love didn't have any sort of set time line, and there were no guarantees. She couldn't have known that Richard wouldn't love her forever…but where his love had failed, Ronin's might last. Maybe. Possibly. Could Ronin be telling her the truth? Did he really love her so much that he was prepared to ignore the life he'd always imagined for a life with her? She wanted to believe it was possible, that she was worthy of such a love, but it went against everything she felt, everything she'd learned, when her marriage had folded into nothing.

"Do you love me?" he demanded, breaking into her thoughts.

She lifted her face to meet his gaze. What she saw reflected back at her made the words clogging her throat so much easier to say.

"Of course I love you," she whispered, barely able to let the truth out. Doing so made her vulnerable, opened her to more harm. But at her words, she could see the tension begin to ease from his face, his body.

"Then know this," Ronin replied earnestly. "I'm not normally the kind of man who rushes into things. The only time in my life I have ever done so was with you. But one thing remains constant for me. When I commit to something, or someone, I follow through—all the way. I want to commit to you, Ali, for a lifetime if you'll let me. I won't lie to you. What you see is what you get. I'm not perfect. I can be overly analytical and set in my ways, and I don't embrace change easily, but I want you in my life. Every day. Every night. Forever, if you'll have me."

"What about Joshua?" she asked.

Ronin looked at the little boy who sat, uncharacteristically quiet for a change, in his car seat. Grief struck him anew. For Joshua, for his dead parents and for the sacrifice he was prepared to make to win Ali back.

"He's Richard's son and always will be. I know how much that must distress you. I fully understand if you can't raise Joshua with me. He'll have a good home, I promise you. I won't deny that I'll miss him, but I *will* let him go if it means having you back, Ali. I don't want you to hurt anymore."

Ali looked from him to the baby and back again. She hardly dared to believe his words, but his actions bore him out. He was willing to give up Joshua, despite his love for him, to ensure that both she and Joshua could have happy lives. She couldn't let him do it.

"No," Ali replied shakily.

The tension that had painted his face into stark lines before was back, this time even worse.

"No?" he repeated, his voice hoarse.

"You can't let him go."

That much was patently clear. He loved Joshua as if he were his own child. She'd seen that with her very own eyes. With the baby's parents gone, no one else would, or could, be a better dad for him than Ronin. Ali could see the struggle he went through to hold on to his normally formidable control as her words began to sink in.

"I can't?" His voice was flat, devoid of emotion.

Ali took a deep breath, and then another. She had to make a decision, to either take a leap of faith or to become a victim of all the suffering that had defined her life since Richard had walked out on her. Ronin was offering her a future. One filled with love, with passion, with a family. It was all she'd ever wanted and yet it remained a terrifying prospect. Was she brave enough, woman enough, to take that leap?

"You can't let him go, because I couldn't come to you unless you included Joshie, as well. I love you both too much to lose either one of you again."

Ronin's features lightened. "You won't regret it, Ali. Every day I'll make sure you won't regret it."

"I know," she answered simply.

"Then what are you doing standing over there when you could be here?" he said, opening his arms.

She flew across the room and buried her face in his chest, relishing the sensation of his arms closing around her—holding her safe within the love and assurance he offered. He squeezed her close and a tremor rocked through him, as if he was afraid that if he let go, she'd leave. It made her realize that she hadn't stopped once to consider his feelings in all of this. She'd left him with no real explanation, and when he'd come after her she'd turned him away more than once. All because she'd been too afraid to love again. Too afraid to trust again.

Both concepts still terrified her, she admitted, but deep down she knew that Ronin would help her through her fears. The last couple of weeks without him had been miserable, and she'd mourned both him and little Joshie with an ache that had been as much physical as it was emotional.

"You had me worried there for a while," Ronin admitted. "More than worried. I thought I was happy with my life until you came into it. I enjoyed—no, relished— my rather solitary existence and the challenges of my work. I leapt at the opportunity to troubleshoot problems that arose all over the world, and had the greatest sense of fulfillment when the job was done. But nothing, absolutely nothing, has matched the satisfaction I feel when I'm with you."

She squeezed him tight, the lump in her throat not allowing her to speak.

He continued. "I never realized it was possible to open up to another person without weakening or diminishing myself. I had no idea how loving someone as much as I love you would enrich me—how much it would strengthen me. I never knew, until I met you, that a vital piece was missing from my life."

Any last vestige of doubt that Ali might have harbored disappeared as he spoke, and when he cupped her face and tilted it upward she willingly met his lips, kissing him with a fierceness that told of her love for him, of her need and her desire to never let go of him again.

He lifted his head. "You complete me, Ali Carter. Will you marry me and adopt Joshie with me so we can create our family and our future together?"

"I would be honored to," she said, through happy tears that coursed unchecked down her cheeks. "I love you with all my heart, and I can't believe I could be so lucky as to have you in my life. Both of you."

And as Ronin kissed her again she realized that finally she had everything she ever wanted. A man who loved her unreservedly, and a family to fill her heart for a lifetime.

\* \* \* \* \*

**Phillip Beaumont stood and looked over the top of the limo, all blond hair and gleaming smile.**

His gaze settled on her. As their eyes met across the drive, Jo felt…disoriented. Looking at Phillip Beaumont was one thing, but apparently being looked at by Phillip Beaumont?

Something else entirely.

Heat flushed her face as the corner of his mouth curved up into a smile. She couldn't pull away from his gaze. He looked like he was glad to see her—which she knew wasn't possible. He had no idea who she was and couldn't have been expecting her. Besides, compared to his traveling companions, no one in their right mind would even notice her.

But that look…

Happy and hungry and relieved. Like he'd come all this way just to see her, and now that she was here, the world would be right again.

No one had looked at her like that. Ever.

\* \* \*

**Tempted by a Cowboy**
is part of The Beaumont Heirs trilogy:
One Colorado family, limitless scandal!

# TEMPTED BY A COWBOY

BY
SARAH M. ANDERSON

Published in Great Britain 2014
by Mills & Boon, an imprint of Harlequin (UK) Limited,
Eton House, 18-24 Paradise Road, Richmond, Surrey, TW9 1SR

© 2014 Sarah M. Anderson

ISBN: 978-0-263-91482-5

51-1014

Harlequin (UK) Limited's policy is to use papers that are natural, renewable and recyclable products and made from wood grown in sustainable forests. The logging and manufacturing processes conform to the legal environmental regulations of the country of origin.

Printed and bound in Spain
by Blackprint CPI, Barcelona

Award-winning author **Sarah M. Anderson** may live east of the Mississippi River, but her heart lies out West on the Great Plains. With a lifelong love of horses and two history teachers for parents, she had plenty of encouragement to learn everything she could about the tribes of the Great Plains.

When she started writing, it wasn't long before her characters found themselves out in South Dakota among the Lakota Sioux. She loves to put people from two different worlds into new situations and to see how their backgrounds and cultures take them someplace they never thought they'd go.

Sarah's book *A Man of Privilege* won the *RT Book Reviews* 2012 Reviewers' Choice Best Book Awards Series: Harlequin Desire.

When not helping out at her son's school or walking her rescue dogs, Sarah spends her days having conversations with imaginary cowboys and American Indians, all of which is surprisingly well-tolerated by her wonderful husband. Readers can find out more about Sarah's love of cowboys and Indians at www.sarahmanderson.com.

To Phil Chu, who kept his promise and got me on
television—that's what friends are for, right?
I can't believe we've been friends for twenty years!
Here's your book, Phil!

# One

Jo got out of the truck and stretched. Man, it'd been a long drive from Kentucky to Denver.

But she'd made it to Beaumont Farms.

Getting this job was a major accomplishment—a vote of confidence that came with the weight of the Beaumont family name behind it.

This wouldn't be just a huge paycheck—the kind that could cover a down payment on a ranch of her own. This was proof that she was a respected horse trainer and her nontraditional methods worked.

A bowlegged man came out of the barn, slapping a pair of gloves against his leg as he walked. Maybe fifty, he had the lined face of a man who'd spent most of his years outside.

He was *not* Phillip Beaumont, the handsome face of the Beaumont Brewery and the man who owned this farm. Even though she shouldn't be, Jo was disappointed.

It was for the best. A man as sinfully good-looking as

Phillip would be...tempting. And she absolutely could not afford to be tempted. Professional horse trainers did not fawn over the people paying their bills—especially when those people were known for their partying ways. Jo did *not* party, not anymore. She was here to do a job and that was that.

"Mr. Telwep?"

"Sure am," the man said, nodding politely. "You the horse whisperer?"

"Trainer," Jo snapped, unable to help herself. She detested being labeled a "whisperer." Damn that book that had made that a thing. "I don't *whisper.* I *train.*"

Richard's bushy eyebrows shot up at her tone. She winced. So much for *that* first impression. But she was so used to having to defend her reputation that the reaction was automatic. She put on a friendly smile and tried again. "I'm Jo Spears."

Thankfully, the older man didn't seem too fazed by her lack of social graces. "Miz Spears, call me Richard," he said, coming over to give her a firm handshake.

"Jo," she replied. She liked men like Richard. They'd spent their lives caring for animals. As long as he and his hired hands treated her like a professional, then this would work. "What do you have for me?"

"It's a—well, better to show you."

"Not a Percheron?" The Beaumont Brewery was world-famous for the teams of Percherons that had pulled their wagons in all their commercials for—well, for forever. A stuffed Beaumont Percheron had held a place of honor in the middle of her bed when she'd been growing up.

"Not this time. Even rarer."

Rarer? Not that Percheron horses were rare, but they weren't terribly common in the United States. The massive draft horses had fallen out of fashion now that people weren't using them to pull plows anymore.

"One moment." She couldn't leave Betty in the truck. Not if she didn't want her front seat destroyed, anyway.

Jo opened the door and unhooked Betty's traveling harness. The donkey's ears quivered in anticipation. "Ready to get out?"

Jo scooped Betty up and set her on the ground. Betty let off a serious round of kicks as Richard said, "I heard you traveled with a—well, what the heck is *that?*" with a note of amusement in his voice.

"That," Jo replied, "is Itty Bitty Betty. She's a mini donkey." This was a conversation she'd had many a time. "She's a companion animal."

By this time, Betty had settled down and had begun investigating the grass around her. Barely three feet tall, she was indeed mini. At her size and weight, she was closer to a medium sized dog than a donkey—and acted like it, too. Jo had trained Betty, of course, but the little donkey had been Jo's companion ever since Granny bought Betty for Jo almost ten years ago. Betty had helped Jo crawl out of the darkness. For that, Jo would be forever grateful.

Richard scratched his head in befuddlement at the sight of the pint-size animal. "Danged if I've ever seen a donkey that small. I don't think you'll be wanting to put her in with Sun just yet." He turned and began walking.

Jo perked up. "Sun?" She fell in step with Richard and whistled over her shoulder. Betty came trotting.

"Danged if I've ever," Richard repeated.

"Sun?" she said.

"Kandar's Golden Sun." Richard blew out hard, the frustration obvious. "You ever heard of an Akhal-Teke?"

The name rang a bell. "Isn't that the breed that sired the Arabian?"

"Yup. From Turkmenistan. Only about five thousand in the world." He led the way around the barn to a paddock off to one side, partially shaded by trees.

In the middle of the paddock was a horse that probably *was* golden, as the name implied. But sweat matted his coat and foam dripped from his mouth and neck, giving him a dull, dirty look. The horse was running and bucking in wild circles and had worked himself up to a lather.

"Yup," Richard said, the disappointment obvious in his voice. "That's Kandar's Golden Sun, all right."

Jo watched the horse run. "Why's he so worked up?"

"We moved him from his stall to the paddock. Three hours ago." Jo looked at the older man, but he shrugged. "Took three men. We try to be gentle, but the damn thing takes one look at us and goes ballistic."

*Three hours* this horse had been bucking and running? Jesus, it was a miracle he hadn't collapsed in a heap. Jo had dealt with her share of terrified horses but sooner or later, they all wore themselves out.

"What happened?"

"That's the thing. No one knows. Mr. Beaumont flew to Turkmenistan himself to look at Sun. He understands horses," Richard added in explanation.

Heat flooded her cheeks. "I'm aware of his reputation."

How could anyone *not* be aware of Phillip Beaumont's reputation? He'd made the *People Magazine* "Most Beautiful" list more than a few years in a row. He had the sort of blond hair that always looked as if he'd walked off a beach, a strong chin and the kind of jaw that could cut stone. He did the Beaumont Brewery commercials but also made headlines on gossip websites and tabloid magazines for some of the stunts he pulled at clubs in Vegas and L.A. Like the time he'd driven a Ferrari into a pool. At the top of a hotel.

No doubt about it, Phillip was a hard-partying playboy. Except…except when he wasn't. In preparing for this job, she'd found an interview he'd done with *Western Horseman* magazine. In that interview—and the accompanying photos—he hadn't been a jaded playboy but an honest-to-God cowboy. He'd talked about horses and herd management and certainly looked like the real McCoy in his boots, jeans, flannel shirt and cowboy hat. He'd said he was building Beaumont Farms as a preeminent stable in the West. Considering the Beaumont family name and its billions in the bank—it wasn't some lofty goal. It was within his reach.

Which one was he? The playboy too sinfully handsome to resist or the hard-working cowboy who wasn't afraid to get dirt on his boots?

No matter which one he was, she was not interested. She couldn't *afford* to be interested in a playboy, especially one who was going to sign her checks. Yes, she'd been training horses for years now, but most wealthy owners of the valuable horses didn't want to take a chance on her nontraditional methods. She'd taken every odd job in every out-of-the-way ranch and farm in the lower forty-eight states to build her clientele. The call from Beaumont Farms was her first major contract with people who bought horses not for thousands of dollars, but for *millions*. If she could save this horse, her reputation would be set.

Besides, the odds of even meeting Phillip Beaumont were slim. Richard was the man she'd be working with. She pulled her thoughts away from the unattainable and focused on why she was here—the horse.

Richard snorted. "We don't deal too much with the partying out here. We just work horses." He waved a hand at Sun, who obliged by rearing on to his back legs and whinnying in panic. "Best we can figure is that maybe something happened on the plane ride? But there were no marks, no wounds. No crashes—not even a rough landing, according to the pilots."

"Just a horse that went off the rails," she said, watching as Sun pawed at the dirt as if he were killing a snake.

"Yup." Richard hung his head. "The horse ain't right but Mr. Beaumont's convinced he can be fixed—a horse to build a stable on, he keeps saying. Spent some ungodly sum of money on him—he'd hate to lose his investment. Personally, I can't stand to see an animal suffer like that. But Mr. Beaumont won't let me put Sun out of his misery. I hired three other trainers before you and none of them lasted a week. You're the horse's last chance. You can't fix him, he'll have to be put down."

This had to be why Richard hadn't gone into specifics over email. He was afraid he'd scare Jo off. "Who'd you hire?"

The older man dug the tip of his boot into the grass. "Lansing, Hoffmire and Callet."

Jo snorted. Lansing was a fraud. Hoffmire was a former farm manager, respected in horse circles. Callet was old-school—and an asshole. He'd tracked her down once to tell her to stay the hell away from his clientele.

She would take particular joy in saving a horse he couldn't.

Moving slowly, she walked to the paddock gate, Betty trotting to keep up. She unhooked the latch on the gate and let it swing open about a foot and a half.

Sun stopped and watched her. Then he *really* began to pitch a fit. His legs flailed as he bucked and reared and slammed his hooves into the ground so hard she felt the shock waves through the dirt. *Hours of this*, Jo thought. *And no one knows why.*

She patted her leg, which was the signal for Betty to stay close. Then Jo stepped into the paddock.

"Miss—" Richard called out, terror in his voice when he realized what she was doing. "Logan, get the tranq gun!"

"Quiet, please." It came out gentle because she was doing her best to project calm.

She heard footsteps—probably Logan and the other

hands, ready to ride to her rescue. She held up a hand, motioning them to stop, and then closed the gate behind her and Betty.

The horse went absolutely wild. It hurt to see an animal so lost in its own hell that there didn't seem to be any way out.

She knew the feeling. It was a hard thing to see, harder to remember the years she'd lost to her own hell.

She'd found her way out. She'd hit bottom so hard it'd almost killed her but through the grace of God, Granny and Itty Bitty Betty, she'd fought her way back out.

She'd made it her life's work to help animals do the same. Even lost causes like Sun could be saved—*not* fixed, because there was no erasing the damage that had already been done. Scars were forever. But moving forward meant accepting the scars. It was that simple. She'd accepted hers.

Jo could stand here for hours listening to the world move, if that was what it took.

It didn't. After what was probably close to forty-five minutes, Sun stopped his frantic pacing. First, he stopped kicking, then he slowed from a run to a trot, then to a walk. Finally, he stood in the middle of the paddock, sides heaving and head down. For the first time, the horse was still.

She could almost hear him say, *I give up.*

It was a low place to be, when living hurt that much.

She understood. She couldn't fix this horse. No one could. But she could save him.

She patted her leg again and turned to walk out of the paddock. A group of seven men stood watching the show Sun had put on for her. Richard had a tranq gun in the hand he was resting on a bar of the paddock.

They were silent. No one shouted about her safety as she turned her back on Sun, no one talked about how the horse must be possessed. They watched her walk to the gate, open it, walk out, and shut it as if they were witnessing a miracle.

"I'll take the job."

Relief so intense it almost knocked her back a step broke over the ranch manager's face. The hired hands all grinned, obviously thankful that Sun was someone else's problem now.

"Provided," she went on, "my conditions are met."

Richard tried to look stern, but he didn't quite make it. "Yeah?"

"I need an on-site hookup for my trailer. That way, if Sun has a problem in the middle of the night, I'm here to deal with it."

"We've got the electric. I'll have Jerry rig up something for the sewer."

"Second, no one else deals with Sun. I feed him, I groom him, I move him. The rest of you stay clear."

"Done," Richard agreed without hesitation. The hands all nodded.

So far, so good. "We do this my way or we don't do it at all. No second-guessing from you, the hired hands or the owners. I won't rush the horse and I expect the same treatment. *And* I expect to be left alone. I don't date or hook up. Clear?"

She hated having to throw that out there because she knew it made her sound as if she thought men would be fighting over her. But she'd done enough harm by hooking up before. Even if she was sober this time, she couldn't risk another life.

Plus, she was a single woman, traveling alone in a trailer with a bed. Some men thought that was enough. Things worked better if everything was cut-and-dried up front.

Richard looked around at his crew. Some were blushing, a few looked bummed—but most of them were just happy that they wouldn't have to deal with Sun anymore.

Then Richard looked across the fields. A long, black limousine was heading toward them.

"Damn," one of the hands said, "the boss."

Everyone but Jo and Richard made themselves scarce. Sun found his second wind and began a full-fledged fit.

"This isn't going to be a problem, is it?" Jo asked Richard, who was busy dusting off his jeans and straightening his shirt.

"Shouldn't be." He did not sound convincing. "Mr. Beaumont wants the best for Sun."

The *but* on the end of that statement was as loud as if Richard had actually said the word. *But* Phillip Beaumont was a known womanizer who made headlines around the world for his conquests.

Richard turned his attention back to her. "You're hired. I'll do my level-best to make sure that Mr. Beaumont stays clear of you."

In other words, Richard had absolutely no control of the situation. A fact that became more apparent as the limo got closer. The older man stood at attention as the vehicle rolled to a stop in front of the barn.

Phillip Beaumont didn't scare her. Or intimidate her. She'd dealt with handsome, entitled men before and none of them had ever tempted her to fall back into her old ways. None of them made her forget the scars. This wouldn't be any different. She was just here for the job.

The limo door opened. A bare, female leg emerged from the limo at the same time as giggling filled the air. Behind her, Jo heard Sun kick it up a notch.

The first leg was followed by a second. Jo wasn't that surprised when a second set of female legs followed the first. By that time, the first woman had stepped clear of the limo's door and Jo could see that, while she was wearing clothing, the dress consisted of little more than a bikini's worth of black sequined material. The second woman stood up and pulled the red velvet material of her skirt down around her hips.

Beside her, Richard made a sound that was stuck somewhere between a sigh and a groan. Jo took that to mean that this wasn't the first time Phillip had shown up with women dressed like hookers.

Betty nickered in boredom and went back to cropping grass. Jo pretty much felt the same way. Of course this was how Phillip Beaumont rolled. Those headlines hadn't lied. The thing that had been less honest had been that interview in *Western Horseman*. That had probably been more about rehabilitating his brand image than about his actual love and respect for horses.

But on the bright side, if he'd brought his own entertainment to the ranch, he'd leave her to her work. That's what was important here—she had to save Sun, cement her reputation as a horse trainer and add this paycheck to the fund that she'd use to buy her own ranch. Adding Beaumont Farms to her résumé was worth putting up with the hassle of, well, *this*.

Then another set of legs appeared. Unlike the first sets, these legs were clad in what looked like expensive Italian leather shoes and fine-cut wool trousers. Phillip Beaumont himself stood and looked at his farm over the top of the limo, all blond hair and gleaming smile. He wore an odd look on his face. He almost looked *relieved*.

His gaze settled on her. As their eyes met across the drive, Jo felt…disoriented. Looking at Phillip Beaumont was one thing, but apparently being looked at by Phillip Beaumont?

Something else entirely.

Heat flushed her face as the corner of his mouth curved up into a smile, grabbed hold of her and refused to let her go. She couldn't pull away from his gaze—and she wasn't sure she wanted to. He looked as if he was glad to see her—which she knew wasn't possible. He had no idea who she was and couldn't have been expecting her. Besides, compared to his traveling companions, no one in their right mind would even notice her.

But that look.... Happy and hungry and *relieved*. Like he'd come all this way just to see her and now that she was here, the world would be right again.

No one had looked at her like that. *Ever*. Before, when she'd been a party girl, men looked at her with a wolfish hunger that had very little to do with her as a woman and everything to do with them wanting to get laid. And since the accident? Well, she wore her hair like this and dressed like she did specifically so she wouldn't invite people to look at her.

He saw right through her.

The women lost their balance and nearly tumbled to the ground, but Phillip caught them in his arms. He pulled them apart and settled one on his left side, the other on his right. The women giggled, as if this were nothing but hilarious.

It hurt to see them, like ghosts of her past come back to haunt her.

"Mr. Beaumont," Richard began in a warm, if desperate, tone as he went to meet his boss. "We weren't expecting you today."

"Dick," Phillip said, which caused his traveling companions to break out into renewed giggles. "I wanted to show my new friends—" He looked down at Blonde Number One.

"Katylynn," Number One giggled. Of course.

"Sailor," Number Two helpfully added.

Phillip's head swung up in a careful arc, another disarming smile already in place as he gave the girls a squeeze. "I wanted to show Sun to Katylynn and Sailor."

"Mr. Beaumont," Richard began again. Jo heard more anger in his voice this time. "Sun is not—"

"Wha's wrong with that horse?" Sailor took a step away from Phillip and pointed at Sun.

They all turned to look. Sun was now bucking with renewed vigor. *Damn stamina*, Jo thought as she watched him.

"Wha's making him do that?" Katylynn asked.

"You are," Jo informed the trio.

The women glared at her. "Who are you?" Sailor asked in a haughty tone.

"Yes, who are you?" Phillip Beaumont spoke slowly—carefully—as his eyes focused on her again.

Again, her face prickled with unfamiliar heat. *Get ahold of yourself*, she thought, forcibly breaking the eye contact. She wasn't the kind of woman who got drunk and got lost in a man's eyes. Not anymore. She'd left that life behind and no one—not even someone as handsome and rich as Phillip Beaumont—would tempt her back to it.

"Mr. Beaumont, this here is Jo Spears. She's the horse…" She almost heard *whisperer* sneak out through his teeth. "Trainer. The new trainer for Sun."

She gave Richard an appreciative smile. A quick study, that one.

Phillip detached himself from his companions, which led to them making whimpering noises of protest.

As Phillip closed the distance between him and Jo, that half-smile took hold of his mouth again. He stopped with two feet still between them. "You're the new trainer?"

She stared at his eyes. They were pale green with flecks of gold around the edges. *Nice eyes*.

Nice eyes that bounced. It wasn't a big movement, but Phillip's eyes were definitely moving of their own accord. She knew the signs of intoxication and that one was a dead giveaway. He was drunk.

She had to admire his control, though. Nothing else in his mannerisms or behaviors gave away that he was three sheets to the wind. Which really only meant one thing.

Being this drunk wasn't something new for him. He'd gotten very good at masking his state. That was something that took years of practice.

She'd gotten good at it, too—but it was so exhausting to keep up that false front of competency, to act normal when she wasn't. She'd hated being that person. She wasn't anymore.

She let this realization push down on the other part of her brain that was still admiring his lovely eyes. Phillip Beaumont represented every single one of her triggers wrapped up in one extremely attractive package. Everything she could never be again if she wanted to be a respected horse trainer, not an out-of-control alcoholic.

She *needed* this job, needed the prestige of retraining a horse like Sun on her résumé and the paycheck that went with it. She absolutely could not allow a handsome man who could hold his liquor to tempt her back into a life she'd long since given up.

She did not hook up. Not even with the likes of Phillip Beaumont.

"I'm just here for the horse," she told him.

He tilted his head in what looked like acknowledgement without breaking eye contact and without losing that smile.

Man, this was unnerving. Men who looked at her usually saw the bluntly cut, shoulder-length hair and the flannel shirts and the jeans and dismissed her out of hand. That was how she wanted it. It kept a safe distance between her and the rest of the world. That was just the way it had to be.

But this look was doing some very unusual things to her. Things she didn't like. Her cheeks got hot—was she blushing?—and a strange prickling started at the base of her neck and raced down her back.

She gritted her teeth but thankfully, he was the one who broke the eye contact first. He looked down at Betty, still blissfully cropping grass. "And who is this?"

Jo braced herself. "This is Itty Bitty Betty, my companion mini donkey."

Instead of the lame joke or snorting laughter, Phillip leaned down, held his hand out palm up and let Betty sniff his hand. "Well hello, Little Bitty Betty. Aren't you a good girl?"

Jo decided not to correct him on her name. It wasn't worth it. What was worth it, though, was the way Betty snuffled at his hand and then let him rub her ears.

That weird prickling sensation only got stronger as she watched Phillip Beaumont make friends with her donkey. "We've got nice grass," he told her, sounding for all the world as if he was talking to a toddler. "You'll like it here."

Jo realized she was staring at Phillip with her mouth open, which she quickly corrected. The people who hired her usually made a joke about Betty or stated they weren't paying extra for a donkey of any size. But Phillip?

Wearing a smile that bordered on cute he looked up at Jo as Betty went back to the grass. "She's a good companion, I can tell."

She couldn't help herself. "Can you?"

Richard had said his boss was a good judge of horses. He'd certainly sounded as if were true it in that interview. She wanted him to be a good judge of horses, to be a real person and not just a shallow, beer-peddling facade of a man. Even though she had no right to want that from him, she did.

His smile went from adorable to wicked in a heartbeat and damned if other parts of her body didn't start prickling at the sight. "I'm an *excellent* judge of character."

Right then, the party girls decided to speak up. "Philly, we want to go home," one cooed.

"With you," the other one added.

"Yes," Jo told him, casting a glare back at the women. "I can see that."

Sun made an unholy noise behind them. Richard shouted and the blondes screamed.

*Jesus*, Jo thought as Sun pawed at the ground and then charged the paddock fence, snot streaming out of his nose. If he hit the fence at that speed, there wouldn't be anything left to save.

Everyone else dove out of the way. Jo turned and ran toward the horse, throwing her hands up and shouting "Hi-yahh!" at the top of her lungs.

It worked with feet to spare. Sun spooked hard to the left and only hit the paddock fence with his hindquarters—which might be enough to bruise him but wouldn't do any other damage.

"Jesus," she said out loud as the horse returned to his bucking. Her chest heaved as the adrenaline pumped through her body.

"I'll tranq him," Richard said beside her, leveling the gun at Sun.

"No." She pushed the muzzle away before he could squeeze the trigger. "Leave him be. He started this, he's got to finish it."

Richard gave her a hell of a doubtful look. "We'll have to tranq him to get him back to his stall. I can't afford anymore workman's comp because of this horse."

She turned to give the ranch manager her meanest look. "We do this my way or we don't do it at all. That was the deal. I say you don't shoot him. Leave him in this paddock. Set out hay and water. No one else touches this horse. Do I make myself clear?"

"Do what she says," Phillip said behind her.

Jo turned back to the paddock to make sure that Sun hadn't decided to exit on the other side. Nope. Just more bucking circles. It'd almost been a horse's version of *shut the hell up*. She grinned at him. On that point, she had to agree.

She could feel her connection with Sun start to grow, which was a good thing. The more she could understand what he was thinking, the easier it would be to help him.

"Philly, we want to go," one of the blondes demanded with a full-on whine.

"Fine," Phillip snapped. "Ortiz, make sure the ladies get back to their homes."

A different male voice—probably the limo driver—said, "Yes sir, Mr. Beaumont." This announcement was met with cries of protest, which quickly turned to howls of fury.

Jo didn't watch. She kept her eye on Sun, who was still freaking out at all the commotion. If he made another bolt for the fence, she might have to let Richard tranq him and she really didn't want that to happen. Shots fired now would only make her job that much harder in the long run.

Finally, the limo doors shut and she heard the car drive off. Thank God. With the women gone, the odds that Sun would settle down were a lot better.

She heard footsteps behind her and tensed. She didn't want Phillip to touch her. She'd meant what she'd said to the hired hands earlier—she didn't hook up with anyone. Especially not men like Phillip Beaumont. She couldn't afford to have her professional reputation compromised, not when she'd finally gotten a top-tier client—and a horse no one else could save. She needed this job far more than she needed Phillip Beaumont to smile at her.

He came level with her and stopped. He was too close—more than close enough to touch.

She panicked. "I don't sleep with clients," she announced into the silence—and immediately felt stupid.

She was letting a little thing like prickling heat undermine her authority here. She was a horse trainer. That was all.

"I'll be sure to take that into consideration." He looked down at her and turned on the most seductive smile she'd ever seen.

Oh, what a smile. She struggled for a moment to remember why, exactly, she didn't need that smile in her life. How long had it been since she'd let herself smile back at a man? How long had it been since she'd allowed herself even a little bit of fun?

Years. But then the skin on the back of her neck pulled and she remembered the hospital and the pain. The scars. She hadn't gotten this job because she smiled at attractive men. She'd gotten this job because she was a horse trainer who could save a broken horse.

She was a professional, by God. When she'd made her announcement to the hired hands earlier, they'd all nodded and agreed. But Phillip?

He looked as if she'd issued a personal challenge. One that he was up to meeting.

Heat flushed her face as she fluttered—honest-to-God fluttered. One little smile—that wouldn't cost her too much, would it?

*No.*

She pushed back against whatever insanity was gripping her. She no longer fluttered. She did not fall for party boys. She did not sleep with men at the drop of a hat because they were cute or bought her drinks. She did not look for a human connection in a bar because the connections she'd always made there were never very human.

She would not be tempted by Phillip Beaumont. It didn't matter how tempting he was. She would not smile back because one smile would lead to another and she couldn't let that happen.

He notched up one eyebrow as if he were acknowledging how much he'd flustered her. But instead of saying something else, he walked past her and leaned heavily against the paddock fence, staring at Sun. His body language pulled at her in ways she didn't like. So few of the people who hired her to train horses actually cared about their animals. They looked at the horse and saw dollars—either in money spent, money yet to be made, or insurance payments. That's why she didn't get involved with her clients. She could count the exceptions on one hand, like Whitney Maddox, a horse breeder she'd stayed with a few months last winter. But those cases were few and far between and never involved men with reputations like Phillip Beaumont.

But the way Phillip was looking at his horse… There was a pain in his face that seemed to mirror what the horse was feeling. It was a hard thing to see.

No. She was not going to feel sorry for this poor little rich boy. She'd come from nothing, managed to nearly destroy her own life and actually managed to make good all by herself.

"He's a good horse—I know he is." Phillip didn't even glance in her direction. He sounded different now that the ladies were gone. It was almost as if she could see his mask slip. What was left was a man who was tired and worried. "I know Richard thinks he should be put out of his misery, but I can't do it. I can't—I can't give up on him. If he could just…" He scrubbed a hand through his hair, which, damn it, only made it look better. He turned to her. "Can you fix him?"

"No," she told him. What was left of his playboy mask fell completely away at this pronouncement.

In that moment, Jo saw something else in Phillip Beaumont's eyes—something that she didn't just recognize, but that she understood.

He was *so* lost. Just like she'd been once.

"I can't fix him—but I can save him."

He looked at her. "There's a difference?"

"Trust me—all the difference in the world."

Jo looked back at Sun, who was quickly working through his energy. Soon, he'd calm down. Maybe he'd even drink some water and sleep. That'd be good. She wanted to save him in a way that went beyond the satisfaction of a job well done or the fees that Phillip Beaumont could afford to pay her.

She wanted to save this horse because once, she'd hurt as much as he did right now. And no one—no horse—should hurt that much. Not when she could make it better.

She wasn't here for Phillip Beaumont. He might be a scarred man in a tempting package, but she'd avoided temptation before and she'd do it again.

"Don't give up on him," he said in a voice that she wasn't sure was meant for her.

"Don't worry," she told the horse as much as she told Phillip. "I won't."

She would *not* give up on the horse.

She wasn't sure she had such high hopes for the man.

# Two

Light. Too much light.

God, his head.

Phillip rolled away from the sunlight but moving his head did not improve the situation. In fact, it only made things worse.

Finally, he sat up, which had the benefit of getting the light out of his face but also made his stomach roll. He managed to get his eyes cracked open. He wasn't in his downtown apartment and he wasn't in his bedroom at the Beaumont Mansion.

The walls of the room were rough-cut logs, the fireplace was stone and a massive painting showing a pair of Percherons pulling a covered wagon across the prairie hung over the mantle.

Ah. He was at the farm. Immediately, his stomach unclenched. There were a lot worse places to wake up. He knew that from experience. Back when his grandfather had built it, it'd been little more than a cabin set far away from the world of beer. John Beaumont hadn't wasted money on opulence where no one would see it. That's why the Beaumont Mansion was a work of art and the farm was…not.

Phillip liked it out here. Over the years, the original cabin had been expanded, but always with the rough-hewn logs. His room was a part he'd added himself, mostly because he wanted a view and a deck to look at it from. The hot tub outside didn't hurt, either, but unlike the hot tub at his bachelor pad, this one was mostly for soaking.

Mostly. He was Phillip Beaumont, after all.

Phillip sat in bed for a while, rubbing his temples and trying to sift through the random memories from the last few days. He knew he'd had an event in Las Vegas on… Thursday. That'd been a hell of a night.

He was pretty sure he'd had a club party in L.A. on Friday, hadn't he? No, that wasn't right. Beaumont Brewery had a big party tent at a music festival and Phillip had been there for the Friday festivities. Lots of music people. *Lots* of beer.

And Saturday…he'd been back in Denver for a private party for some guy's twenty-first birthday. But, no matter how hard he tried to remember the party, his brain wouldn't supply any details.

So, did that mean today was Sunday or Monday? Hell, he didn't know. That was the downside of his job. Phillip was vice president of Marketing in charge of special events for Beaumont Brewery, which loosely translated into making sure everyone had a good time at a Beaumont-sponsored event and talked about it on social media.

Phillip was very good at his job.

He found the clock. It was 11:49. He needed to get up. The sun was only getting brighter. Why didn't he have room-darkening blinds in here?

Oh, yeah. Because the windows opened up on to a beautiful vista, full of lush grass, tall trees and his horses. Damn his aesthetic demands.

He got his feet swung over the bed and under him. Each movement was like being hit with a meat cleaver right between the eyes. Yeah, that must have been one *hell* of a party.

He navigated a flight of stairs and two hallways to the kitchen, which was in the original building. He got the coffee going and then dug a sports drink out of the fridge. He popped some Tylenol and guzzled the sports drink.

Almost immediately, his head felt better. He finished the first bottle and cracked open a second. Food. He needed food. But he needed a shower first.

Phillip headed back to his bathroom. That was the other reason he'd built his own addition—the other bathroom held the antique claw-foot tub that couldn't hope to contain all six of his feet.

His bathroom had a walk-in shower, a separate tub big enough for two and a double sink that stretched out for over eight feet. He could sprawl out all over the place and still have room to spare.

He soaked his head in cool water, which got his blood pumping again. He'd always had a quick recovery time from a good party—today was no different.

Finally, he got dressed in his work clothes and went back to the kitchen. He made some eggs, which helped his stomach. The coffee was done, so he filled up a thermal mug and added a shot of whiskey. Hair of the dog.

Finally, food in his stomach and coffee in his hand, he found his phone and scrolled through it.

Ah. It was Monday. Which meant he had no recollection of Sunday. Damn.

He didn't dwell on that. Instead, he scrolled through his contacts list. Lots of new numbers. Not too many pictures. One he'd apparently already posted to Instagram of him and Drake on stage together? Cool. That was a dream-come-true kind of moment right there. He was thrilled someone had gotten a photo of it.

He scanned some of the gossip sites. There were mentions of the clubs, the festival—but nothing terrible. Mostly just who's-who tallies and some wild speculation about who went to bed with whom.

Phillip heaved a sigh of relief. He'd done his job well. He always did. People had a good time, drank a lot of Beaumont Beer and talked the company up to their friends. And they did that because Phillip brought all the elements together for them—the beer, the party, the celebrities.

It was just that sometimes, people talked about things that gave the PR department fits. No matter how many times Phillip tried to tell those suits who worked for his brother Chadwick that there was no such thing as bad PR, every time he made headlines for what they considered the "wrong" reasons, Chadwick felt the need to have a coming-to-Jesus moment with Phillip about how his behavior was damaging the brand name and costing the company money and blah, blah, blah.

Frankly, Phillip could do with less Chadwick in his life.

That wasn't going to happen this week, thank God. The initial summaries looked good—the Klout Score was up, the hits were high and on Saturday, the Beaumont party tent had been trending for about four hours on Twitter.

Phillip shut off his phone with a smile. That was a job well done in his book.

He felt human again. His head was clearing and the food in his stomach was working. *Hair of the dog always does the trick*, he thought as he refilled his mug and put on his boots. He felt good.

He was happy to be back on the farm in a way he couldn't quite put into words. He missed his horses—especially Sun. He hadn't seen Sun in what felt like weeks.

The last he knew, Richard had hired some trainer who'd promised to fix the horse. But that was a while ago. Maybe a month?

There it was again—that uneasy feeling that had nothing to do with the hangover or the breakfast. He didn't like that feeling, so he took an extra big swig of coffee to wash it away.

He had some time before the next round of events kicked off. There was a lull between now and Spring Break. That was fine by Phillip. He would get caught up with Richard, evaluate his horses, go for some long rides—hopefully on Sun—and ignore the world for a while. Then, by the time he was due to head south to help ensure that Beaumont Beers were the leading choice of college kids everywhere, he'd be good to go. Brand loyalty couldn't start early enough.

He grabbed his hat off the peg by the door and headed down to the barn. The half-mile walk did wonders for his head. The whole place was turning green as the last of the winter gave way to spring. Daffodils popped up in random spots and the pastures were so bright they hurt his eyes.

It felt good to be home. He needed a week or two to recover, that was all.

As he rounded the bend in the road that connected the house to the main barn, he saw that Sun was out in a paddock. That was a good sign. As best he could recall, Richard had said they couldn't move the horse out of his stall without risking life and limb. Phillip had nearly had his own head taken off by a flying hoof the one time he'd tried to put a halter on his own horse—something that Sun had let him do when they were at the stables in Turkmenistan.

God, he wished he knew where things had gone wrong. Sun had been a handful, that was for sure—but at his old stables, he'd been manageable. Phillip had even inquired into bringing his former owner out to the farm to see if the old man who spoke no English would be able to settle Sun down. The man had refused.

But if that last trainer had worked wonders, then Phillip could get on with his plan. The trainer's services had cost a fortune, but if he'd gotten Sun back on track, it was worth it. The horse's bloodlines could be traced back on paper to the 1880s and the former owner had transcribed an oral bloodline that went back to the 1600s. True, an oral bloodline didn't count much, but Philip knew Sun was a special horse. His ancestors had taken home gold, the Grand Prix de Dressage and too many long-distance races to count.

He needed to highlight Sun's confirmation and stamina—that was what would sell his lineage as a stud. Sun's line would live on for a long time to come. That stamina—and his name—was what breeders would pay top dollar for. But beyond that, there was something noble about the whole thing. The Akhal-Tekes were an ancient breed of horse—the founder of the modern lines of the Arabians and Thoroughbreds. It seemed a shame that almost no one had ever heard of them. They were amazing animals—almost unbreakable, especially compared to the delicate racing Thoroughbreds whose legs seemed to shatter with increasing frequency on the racetrack. A horse like Sun could reinvigorate lines—leading to stronger, faster racehorses.

Phillip felt lighter than he had in a while. Sun was a damned fine horse—the kind of stud upon which to found a line. He must be getting old because as fun as the parties obviously were—photos didn't lie—he was getting to the point where he just wanted to train his horses.

Of course he knew he couldn't hide out here forever. He had a job to do. Not that he needed the money, but working for the Beaumont Brewery wasn't just a family tradition. It was also a damned good way to keep Chadwick off his back. No matter what his older brother said, Phillip wasn't wasting the family fortune on horses and women. He was an important part of the Beaumont brand name—that *more* than offset his occasional forays into horses.

Phillip saw a massive trailer parked off to the side of the barn with what looked like a garden hose and—was that an extension cord?—running from the barn to the trailer. Odd. Had he invited someone out to the farm? Usually, when he had guests, they stayed at the house.

He took a swig of coffee. He didn't like that unsettling feeling of not knowing what was going on.

As he got closer, he saw that Sun wasn't grazing. He was running. That wasn't a good sign.

Sun wasn't better. He was the same. God, what a depressing thought.

Then Phillip saw her. It was obvious she was a *her*— tall, clad in snug jeans and a close-fit flannel shirt, he could see the curve of her hips at three hundred yards. Longish hair hung underneath a brown hat. She sure as hell didn't look like the kind of woman he brought home with him— not even to the farm. So what was she doing here?

Standing in the middle of the paddock while Sun ran in wild circles, that's what.

Phillip shook his head. This had to be a post-hangover hallucination. If Sun weren't better, why would *anyone* be in a paddock with him? The horse was too far gone. It wasn't safe. The horse had knocked a few of the hired hands out of commission for a while. The medical bills were another thing Chadwick rode his ass about.

Not only did the vision of this woman not disperse, but Phillip noticed something else that couldn't be real. Was that a donkey in there with her? He was pretty sure he'd remember buying a donkey that small.

He looked the woman over again, hoping for some sign of recognition. Nothing. He was sure he'd remember thighs and a backside like that. Maybe she'd look different up close.

He walked the rest of the way down to the paddock, his gaze never leaving her. No, she wasn't his type, but variety was the spice of life, wasn't it?

"Good morning," he said in a cheerful voice as he leaned against the fence.

Her back stiffened but she gave no other sign that she'd heard him. The small donkey craned its neck around to give him a look that could only be described as *doleful* as Sun went from a bucking trot to a rearing, snorting mess in seconds.

Jesus, that horse could kill her. But he tried not to let the panic creep into his voice. "Miss, I don't think it's safe to be in there right now." Sun made a sound that was closer to a scream than a whinny. Phillip winced at the noise.

The woman's head dropped in what looked like resignation. Then she patted the side of her leg as she turned and began a slow walk back to the gate. Betty followed close on her heels.

The donkey's name was Betty. How did he know that?

Oh, crap—he *did* know her. Had she been at the party? Had they slept together? He didn't remember seeing any signs of a female in his room or in the house.

He watched as she walked toward him. She was a cowgirl, that much was certain—and not one of those fake ones whose hats were covered in rhinestones and whose jeans had never seen a saddle. The brown hat fit low on her forehead, the flannel shirt was tucked in under a worn leather belt that had absolutely no adornment and her chest—

Phillip was positive he'd remember spending a little quality time with that chest. Despite the nearly unisex clothing, the flannel shirt did nothing to hide the generous breasts that swelled outward, begging him to notice them. Which he did, of course. But he could control his baser urges to ogle a woman. So, after a quick glance at what had to be perfection in breast form, he snapped his eyes up to her face. The movement made his head swim.

It'd be *so* nice if he could remember her, because she was certainly a memorable woman. Her face wasn't made up or altered. She had tanned skin, a light dusting of freckles and a nose that looked as if it might have been broken once. It should have made her look awkward, but he decided it was fitting. There was a certain beauty in the imperfect.

Then she raised her eyes to his and he felt rooted to the spot. Her eyes were clear and bright, a soft hazel. He could get lost in eyes like that.

Not that he got the chance. She scowled at him. The shock of someone other than Chadwick looking so displeased with him put Phillip on the defensive. Still, she was a woman and women were his specialty. So he waited until she'd made it out of the gate and closed it behind Betty.

Once the gate clicked, she didn't head for where he stood. Instead, she went back to ignoring him entirely as she propped a booted foot up on the gate and watched the show Sun was putting on for them.

What. The. Hell.

He was going to have to amend his previous statement—*most* women were his specialty.

Time to get back to basics. One compliment, coming right up. "I don't think I've ever seen anyone wear a pair of jeans like you do." That should do the trick.

Or it would have for any other woman. Instead, she dropped her forehead onto the top bar of the gate—a similar motion to the one she'd made out in the paddock moments ago. Then she turned her face to him. "Was it worth it?"

His generous smile faltered. "Was what worth it?"

Her soft eyes didn't seem so soft anymore. "The black-out. Was it worth it?"

"I have no idea what you're talking about."

That got a smirk out of her, just a small curve of her lips. It was gone in a flash. "That's the definition of a blackout, isn't it? You have no idea who I am or what I'm doing here, do you?"

Sun made that unholy noise again. Phillip tensed. The woman he didn't know looked at the horse and shook her head as if the screaming beast was a disappointment to her. Then she looked at Phillip and shook her head again.

Unfamiliar anger coursed through him, bringing a new clarity to his thoughts. Who the hell was this woman, any-way? "I know you shouldn't be climbing into the paddock with Sun. He's dangerous."

Another smirk. Was she challenging him?

"But he wasn't when you bought him, was he?"

How did she know about that? An idea began to take shape in his mind like a Polaroid developing. He shook his head, hoping the image would get clearer—fast. It didn't. "No."

She stared at him a moment longer. It shouldn't bother him that she knew who he was. Everyone knew who he was. That went with being the face of the Beaumont Brew-ery.

But she didn't look at him like everyone else did—with that gleam of delight that went with meeting a celebrity in the flesh. Instead, she just looked disappointed.

Well, she could just keep on looking disappointed. He turned his attention to the most receptive being here—the donkey. "How are you this morning, Betty?"

When the woman didn't correct him, he grinned. He'd gotten that part right, at least.

He rubbed the donkey behind the ears, which resulted

in her leaning against his legs and groaning in satisfaction. "Good girl, aren't you?" he whispered.

Maybe he'd have to get a little donkey like this. If Betty wasn't his already.

Maybe, a quiet voice in the back of his head whispered, that blackout *wasn't* worth it.

He took another swig of coffee.

He looked back at the woman. Her posture hadn't changed, but everything about her face had. Instead of a smirk, she was smiling at him—him and the donkey.

The donkey was hers, he realized. And since he already knew the donkey's name, he must have met the woman, too.

Double damn.

That's when he realized he was smiling back at her. What had been superior about her had softened into something that looked closer to delight.

He forgot about not knowing who she was, how she got here or what she was doing with his prize stallion. All he could think was that *now* things were about to get interesting. This was a dance he could do with his eyes closed—a beautiful woman, a welcoming smile—a good time soon to be had by all.

Genuine compliment, take two. "She's a real sweetie, isn't she? I've never seen a donkey this well-behaved." He took a risk. "You did an amazing job training her."

Oh, yeah, that worked much better than the jeans comment had. Her smile deepened as she tilted her head to one side. Soft morning light warmed her face and suddenly, she looked like a woman who wanted to be kissed.

Whoever she was, this woman was unlike anyone he'd ever met before. Different could be good. Hell, different could be great. She wasn't a woman who belonged at the clubs but then, he wasn't at the clubs. He was at his farm and this woman clearly fit in this world.

Maybe he'd enjoy this break from big-city living more than he'd thought he would. After all, his bed was more than large enough to accommodate two people. So was the hot tub.

Yes, the week was suddenly looking up.

But she still hadn't told him who the hell she was and that was becoming a problem. Kissing an anonymous woman in a dark club? No problem. Kissing a cowgirl who was inexplicably on his ranch in broad daylight?

Problem.

He had to bite the bullet and admit he didn't remember her name. So, still rubbing Betty's ears, he stuck out a hand. "We got off to a rough beginning." He could only assume that was true, as she'd opened with a blackout comment. "Let's start over. I'm Phillip Beaumont. And you are?"

Some of her softness faded, but she shook his hand with the kind of grip that made it clear she was used to working with her hands. "Jo Spears."

That didn't ring a single damned bell in his head.

It was only after she'd let go of his hand that she added, with a grin that bordered on cruel, "I'm here to retrain Sun."

# Three

"*You're* the new trainer?"

Jo fought hard to keep the grin off her face. She wasn't entirely sure she succeeded. Even yesterday, when he'd been toasted, she hadn't been able to surprise Phillip Beaumont. But she'd caught him off guard this morning.

How bad was his hangover? It had to be killer. She could smell whiskey from where she stood. But she would have never guessed it just by looking at him. Hell, his eyes weren't even bloodshot. He had a three-day-old scruff on his cheeks that should have looked messy but, on him, made him look better—like a man who worked with his hands.

Other than that…she let her eyes drift over his body. The jeans weren't the fancy kind that he'd spent hundreds of dollars to make look old and broken in—they looked like the kind he'd broken in himself. The denim work shirt was much the same. Yes, his brown boots had probably cost a pretty penny once—but they were scuffed and scratched, not polished to a high shine. These were his work clothes and he was clearly comfortable in them.

The suit he'd had on yesterday had been the outfit of the Phillip Beaumont who went to parties and did commercials. But the Phillip Beaumont who was petting Betty's ears today?

This was a cowboy. A real one.

Heat flooded her body. She forced herself to ignore it. She would not develop a crush or an infatuation or even an *admiration* for Phillip Beaumont just because he looked good in jeans.

She'd been right about him. He had no memory of yesterday and he'd spiked his coffee this morning. He was everything she couldn't allow herself, all wrapped up in one attractive package. She had a job to do. And if she did it well, a reference from Phillip Beaumont would be worth its weight in gold. It'd be worth that smile of his.

"I believe," she said with a pointed tone that let him know he wasn't fooling anyone, "that we established our identities yesterday afternoon."

The change was impressive. It only took a matter of seconds for his confusion to be buried beneath a warm smile. "Forgive me." He managed to look appropriately contrite while also adding a bit of smolder to his eyes. The effect was almost heady. She was *not* falling for this. Not at all. "I'm just a little surprised. The other trainers have been..."

"Older? Male? Richard told me about his previous attempts." She turned her attention back to the horse to hide her confusion. She could not flutter. Too much was at risk here.

Sun did seem to be calming down. Which meant he hadn't made that screaming noise in a couple of minutes. He was still racing as if his life depended on it, though. "I think it's clear that Sun needs something else."

"And that's you?" He kept his tone light and conversational, but she could hear the doubt lurking below the surface.

The other three men had all been crusty old farts, men who'd been around horses their whole lives. Not like her. "Yup. That's me."

Phillip leaned against the paddock fence. Jo did not like how aware of his body she was. He kicked a foot up on the lowest railing and draped his arms over the top of the fence. It was all very casual—and close enough to touch.

"So what's your plan to fix him?"

She sighed. "As I told you yesterday, I don't fix horses. No one can fix him."

She managed to keep the crack about whether or not he'd remember this conversation tomorrow to herself. She was already pushing her luck with him and she knew it. He was still paying her and, given how big a mess Sun was, she might have enough to put a down payment on her own ranch after this.

Wouldn't that be the ultimate dream? A piece of land to call her own, where the Phillip Beaumonts of the world would bring her their messed-up horses. She wouldn't have to spend days driving across country and showering in a trailer. Betty could run wild and free on her own grass. Her own ranch would be safety and security and she wouldn't have to deal with people at all. Just horses. That's what this job could give to her.

That's why she needed to work extra hard on keeping her distance from the man who was *still* close enough to touch.

He ignored the first part of the statement. "Then what do you do?"

There was no way to sum up what she did. So she didn't. "Save him."

Because she was so aware of Phillip's body, she felt the

tension take hold of him. She turned her head just enough
to look at him out of the corner of her eye. Phillip's gaze
was trained on the half-crazed horse in the paddock. He
looked stricken, as if her words had sliced right through
all his charm and left nothing but a raw, broken man who
owned a raw, broken horse.

Then he looked at her. His eyes—God, there was so
much going on under the surface. She felt herself start
to get lost in them, but Sun whinnied, pulling her back
to herself.

She could not get lost in Phillip Beaumont. To do so
would be to take that first slippery step back down the
slope to lost nights and mornings in strangers' beds. And
there would be no coming back from that this time.

So she said, in a low voice, "I *only* save horses."

"I don't need to be saved, thank you very much."

Again, the change was impressive. The warm smile
that bordered on teasing snapped back onto his face and
the honest pain she'd seen in his eyes was gone beneath a
wink and twinkle.

She couldn't help it. She looked at his coffee mug. "If
you say so."

His grip tightened on the handle, but that was the only
sign he'd gotten her meaning. He probably thought the
smell of the coffee masked the whiskey. Maybe it did for
regular folks, but not for her.

"How are you going to *save* my horse then?" It came out
in the same voice he might use to ask a woman on a date.

It was time to end this conversation before things went
completely off the rails. "One day at a time."

*Let's see if he catches that*, she thought as she opened
the gate and slowly walked back into the paddock, Betty
trailing at her heels.

As she closed the gate behind her, she heard Richard
come out of the barn. "Mr. Beaumont—you're up!"

Good. She wanted more time with Sun alone. The horse had almost calmed down before Phillip showed up. If she could get the animal to stay at a trot...

That wasn't happening now. Sun clearly did not like Richard, probably because the older man had been the one to tranquilize him and move him around the most. She was encouraged that, although the horse did freak out any time Phillip showed up, he had sort of settled down this morning as she and Phillip had talked in conversational tones. Sun didn't have any negative associations with Phillip—he just didn't like change. That was a good thing to know.

"Just getting to know the new trainer," Phillip said behind her. She had to give him credit, he managed not to make it sound dismissive.

"If you two are going to talk," she said in a low voice that carried a great distance, "please do so elsewhere. You're freaking out the horse."

There was a pause and she got the feeling that both men were looking at her. Then Richard said, "Now that you're here, I'd like you to see the new Percheron foals." That was followed by the sounds of footsteps leading away from the paddock.

But they weren't far away when she heard Phillip say, "Are you sure about her?"

Jo tensed.

Richard, bless his crusty old heart, came to her defense. As his voice trailed off, she heard him reply, "She came highly recommended. If anyone can fix Sun... She's our last chance."

She couldn't fix this horse. She couldn't fix the man, either, but she had no interest in trying. She would not be swayed by handsome faces, broken-in jeans or kind words for Betty.

She was just here for the horse.

She needed to remember that.

* * *

Phillip woke up early the next day and he knew why. He was hoping there'd be a woman with an attitude standing in a paddock this morning.

Jo Spears. She was not his type—not physically, not socially. Not even close. He sure as hell remembered her today. How could he have forgotten meeting her the day before? That didn't matter. What mattered now was that he was dying to see if she was still in that arena, just standing there.

He hurried through his shower while the coffee brewed. He added a shot of whiskey to keep the headache away and then got a mug for her. While he was at it, he grabbed a couple of carrots from the fridge for the donkey.

Would Jo still be standing in the middle of that paddock, watching Sun do whatever the hell it was Sun did? Because that's what she'd done all day yesterday—just stand there. Richard had gotten him up to speed on the farm's business and he'd spent some time haltering and walking the Percheron foals but he'd always been aware of the woman in the paddock.

She hadn't been watching him, which was a weird feeling. Women were always aware of what he was doing, waiting for their opportunity to strike up a conversation. He could make eye contact with a woman when he walked into a club and know that, six hours later, she'd be going back to his hotel with him. All he had to do was wait for the right time for her to make her move. She would come to him. Not the other way around.

But this horse trainer? He'd caught the way her hard glare had softened and she'd tilted her head when he'd complimented her little donkey. That was the kind of look a woman gave him when she was interested—when she was going to be in his bed later.

Not the kind of look a woman gave him when she proceeded to ignore him for the rest of the day. And night.

Phillip Beaumont was not used to being ignored. He was the life of the party. People not only paid attention to what he was doing, who he was doing it with, what he was wearing—hell, who he was tweeting about—but they paid good money to do all of that with him. It was his job, for God's sake. People always noticed him.

Except for her.

He should have been insulted yesterday. But he'd been so surprised by her attitude that he hadn't given a whole lot of thought to his wounded pride.

She was something else. A woman apart from others.

*Variety is the spice of life*, he thought as he strolled down to the barn. That had to be why he was so damned glad to see her and that donkey in the middle of the paddock again, Sun still doing laps around them both. But, Phillip noted, the horse was only trotting and making a few small bucks with his hind legs. Phillip wasn't sure he'd seen Sun this calm since...well, since Asia.

For a moment, he allowed himself to be hopeful. So three other trainers had failed. This Jo Spears might actually work. She might save his horse.

But then he had to go and ruin Sun's progress by saying, "Good morning."

At the sound of Phillip's voice, Sun lost it. He reared back, kicking his forelegs and whinnying with such terror that Phillip's hope immediately crumbled to dust. Betty looked at him and he swore the tiny thing rolled her eyes.

But almost immediately, Sun calmed down—or at least stopped making that God-awful noise and started running.

"You got that part right today," Jo said in that low voice of hers.

"It's good?" He looked her over—her legs spread shoulder-width apart, fingers hooked into her belt loops. Everything about her was relaxed but strong. He could imagine those legs and that backside riding high in the saddle.

And then, because he was Phillip Beaumont, he imagined those legs and that backside riding high in his bed.

Oh, yeah—it could be good. Might even be great.

"It's morning." She glanced over her shoulder at him and he saw the corner of her mouth curve up into a smile. "Yesterday when you said that, it was technically afternoon."

He couldn't help but grin at her. Boy, she was tough. When was the last time someone had tried to make him toe the line? Hell, when was the last time there'd even *been* a line?

And there was that smile. Okay, *half* a smile but still. Jo didn't strike him as the kind of woman who smiled at a man if she didn't actually want to. That smile told Phillip that she was interested in him. Or, at the very least, attracted to him. Wasn't that the same thing?

"Back at it again?"

She nodded.

Sun looped around the whole paddock, blowing past Phillip with a snort. His instinct was to step back from the fence, but he didn't want to project anything resembling fear—especially when she was actually inside the fence and he wasn't.

She pivoted, her eyes following the horse as he made another lap. Then, when he went back to running along the far side of the paddock again, she made that slow walk over to where Phillip stood.

Watching her walk was almost a holy experience. Instead of a practiced wiggle, Jo moved with a coiled grace that projected the same strength he'd felt in her handshake yesterday.

Did she give as good as she got? Obviously, in conversation the answer was *yes*. But did that apply to other areas?

She opened the gate and, Betty on her heels, walked out. When the gate closed behind her, she didn't come to him. She didn't even turn her head in his direction.

What would it take to get her to look at him? He could say something witty and crude. That would definitely get her attention. But instead of being scandalous and funny—which was how such comments went over when everyone was happily sloshed at a bar—he had a feeling that Jo might hit him for being an asshole.

Still, he was interested in that image of her riding him. He was the kind of man who was used to having female company every night. And he hadn't had any since he'd woken up at the farm.

He would enjoy spending time in Jo's company. He couldn't say why he liked the idea so much—she wouldn't make anything easy on him.

But that didn't bother him. In fact, he felt as if it was a personal challenge—one he was capable of meeting.

When was the last time he'd chased a woman? He tried to scroll through the jumbled memories but he wasn't coming up with anyone except…Suzie. Susanna Whaley, British socialite. She'd come from vulgar money—which was to say, by British definition, someone whose family had only gotten rich in the last century. She didn't care that Phillip was wealthy. She had enough money of her own. And she didn't care that he'd been famous. Before they'd met, she'd been dating some European prince. Phillip had been forced to work overtime just to get her phone number.

Something about that had been…well, it'd been *good*. He'd liked chasing her and she'd liked being chased. They'd dated internationally for almost a year. He'd looked at rings. He'd been twenty-six and convinced that *this* marriage would be different from his parents' marriage.

Then his father had died. Suzie had accompanied him to the funeral and met the entire Beaumont clan—his father's ex-wives, Phillip's half-siblings. All the bitter fighting and acrimonious drama that Phillip had tried so hard to get free of had been on full display. The police had gotten involved. Lawsuits had been filed.

So much for the Beaumont name.

The relationship had ended fairly quickly after that. He'd been upset, of course but deep down, he'd agreed with Suzie. His family—and, by extension, he himself—were too screwed up to have a shot at a happily-ever-after. They'd parted ways, she'd married that European prince and Phillip had gone right back to his womanizing ways. It was easier than thinking about what he'd almost had—and what he'd lost.

Still, he'd liked the chase. It'd been…different. Proof that it wasn't just his name or his money or even his famous face that a woman wanted. He'd had to prove his worth. That wasn't a bad thing.

Jo Spears clearly wasn't swayed by his name or his money. If she was as good a trainer as she claimed to be, she'd probably spent plenty of time in barns owned by equally rich, equally famous men and women. He didn't spend a lot of time with people who didn't want a piece of his name, his fortune—of him. The feeling was…odd.

He could stay out here for a few weeks. And he wouldn't mind having a little company.

He could chase Jo. It'd be fun.

"Coffee?" A thoughtful gesture was always a good place to begin.

She looked at the mugs in his hands and sniffed. "I don't drink."

He was going to have to switch brands of whiskey. Apparently Jack had a stronger smell than he remembered.

"Just coffee." When she gave him a look that could have peeled paint, he was forced to add, "In yours."

She took the mug, sniffed it several times and then took a tentative sip. "Thanks."

He stood there, feeling awkward, which was not normal. He wasn't awkward or unsure, not when it came to women. But every time he deployed one of his tried-and-true techniques on her, it backfired.

Oh yeah, this was going to be a challenge.

"How's it going?" he asked. Always good to focus on the basics.

That worked. She tilted her head in his direction, an appreciative smile on her face. "Not bad."

"I noticed," he continued, trying not to stare at that smile, "that you spend a lot of time standing in the paddock. With a donkey."

Her eyebrow curved up. "I do."

"Can I ask why, or are the mysteries of the horse whisperer secret?"

Damn, he lost her. Her warm smile went ice-cold in a heartbeat. "I do not *whisper*. I *train*."

Seducing her was going to prove harder than hell if he couldn't stop pissing her off. "Sensitive about that?"

Oh, that was a vicious look, one that let him know she'd loaded up both barrels and was about to open fire. "I'd explain my rules to you again, but what guarantee do I have that you'll remember them *this* time?"

*Ouch*. But he wasn't going to let her know how close to the quick she'd cut. He wouldn't back up in fear from his horse and he sure as hell wouldn't do it from a woman. He gave her his wicked smile, one that always worked. "I can be taught."

"I doubt it." Her posture changed. Instead of leaning toward him, she'd pulled away, her upper body angled in the direction of the barn.

Okay, he needed a different approach here, one that didn't leave his flank open to attack. Yesterday, when he hadn't remembered meeting her, she'd warmed up while he'd patted Betty. Time to put this theory to the test.

"Come here, girl," he said, crouching down and pulling the baggie of carrots out of his back pocket. "Do you like carrots?"

Betty came plodding over to him and snatched the carrot out of his hand. "That's a good girl."

"Did you bring one for Sun?"

"I did." He hadn't, but he'd brought enough. "But I don't think he likes me enough to let me give him one."

Then he looked up at her. Her light brown eyes were focused on his face with such intensity that it seemed she was seeing into him.

He fished another carrot out and looked at the horse that was still going in pointless circles around the paddock. Yeah, no getting close to *that* without getting trampled. "Like I said, I don't think he likes me."

"He doesn't *not* like you, though." She kept her gaze on the horse.

"How do you figure?" Betty snuffled at his hand, so he gave her the carrot he was holding. He still had two left. "Every time he sees me, he goes ballistic."

Jo sighed, which did some impressive things with her chest. "No, every time he sees you, it's something different. He doesn't like the different part. It has nothing to do with you. If you want to see what he does when he actively hates someone, you can call Richard out here."

"He hates Richard?" Although, now that he thought about it, Sun often did seem more agitated when the farm manager was around.

She nodded. "Richard and your hands are the ones who've shot him with the tranq gun, lassoed him in his stall and, from Sun's point of view, generally terrorized him. You don't have those negative associations in Sun's mind."

Everything she said made sense. He palmed another carrot, wondering if he should give it to the donkey or if he should try to walk into the paddock and give it to his horse. He'd be risking death, but it might be a positive thing the horse could associate with him. "He just doesn't like change?"

"Nope." She looked at his hand, then nodded to where there was a water bucket and a feed bucket hanging on the side of the paddock. "Put it in his bucket. But go slow."

"Okay." So it felt a little ridiculous to move at a snail's pace around the fence. But he noticed that Sun slowed to a trot and watched him.

Phillip held up the remaining two carrots so that Sun could see them and then dropped them over the fence and into the bucket. Then Phillip slowly worked his way back to where Jo was standing.

The approval on her face was something new. Something good. Wow, she could be pretty when she smiled.

"How was that?" He felt a little like a puppy begging for approval, but, for some reason, it was important to him.

Her smile deepened. "You *can* be taught."

"I'm a very quick study." He didn't walk over to her or run his hand down her arm—all things that worked wonders in a club—but he didn't need to. The blush that graced her cheeks was more than good enough to know that, no matter how icy or judgmental she could be, she was also a flesh-and-blood woman who responded to him.

Oh, yeah—the chase was *on*.

She looked away first. Aside from the blush and the smile, she gave no other sign of interest. She didn't lean in his direction, she didn't compliment him again. All she said was, "Watch," as she looked at Sun.

The horse was still trotting, but Phillip realized that each pass brought him closer to the buckets. Within a few minutes, he was making small loops back and forth right in front of the carrots.

He could probably smell them. Phillip hoped the horse would realize they were treats.

Sun slowed down enough that he was moving at a fast walk. He dipped his long nose into the bucket but before Phillip could allow himself to be hopeful, the horse knocked the whole thing off the fence, spilling the carrots and leftover grain on the ground. Then he was off again, running and bucking and throwing a hell of a fit.

"Damn."

"It's not you," Jo said again. "It's different. He's got to get used to someone leaving him a treat."

"And in the meantime?"

She shrugged. "We wait."

"Wait for what?"

"Wait for him to get tired."

He looked at her. "*This* is your grand plan to save him? Wait for him to get bored?" At his words, Sun began to rear up.

Jo sighed. "Don't you ever get tired?"

"Excuse me?"

"*Tired.*" She spoke the word carefully, as if she were pronouncing it for someone who didn't speak English. "Don't you get tired of the days and the nights blending together with no beginning and no end? Of waking up and not knowing who you are or where you are or most importantly of all, *what* you've done? Tired of realizing that you've done something horrible, something there's no good way to move on from, so you angle for that blackout again so you don't have to think about what you've become?"

She turned her face to him. Nothing about her was particularly lovely at this moment, but there was something in her eyes that wouldn't let him go.

"Doesn't it ever just wear you out?"

He did something he didn't usually allow himself to do—he glared at her. She couldn't know what she was talking about and, as far as he was concerned, she was not talking about him.

Still, her words cut into him like small, sharp knives and although it made no sense—she was wrong about him and that was *final*—he wanted to drink the rest of his coffee and let the whiskey in it take the edge off the inexplicable pain he felt, but she was watching him. Waiting to see if he'd buckle.

Well, she could just keep right on waiting. "I have no idea what you're talking about." His voice came out quieter than he'd meant it to. He almost sounded shaky to his own ears. He didn't like that. He didn't betray weakness, not to his family, not to anyone.

A shadow of sadness flickered across her face, but it was gone as she turned back to the paddock. "If that's what gets you through the night." She didn't wait for him to deny it. "Sun's been in this paddock for three straight days now. Sooner or later, he's going to get tired of doing the same thing over and over again. He'll want to do something different. Anything different, really, as long as it's not going mad. That's when I'll get him."

Going mad. Was that how she thought of the horse? Of him?

He needed to get the conversation onto firmer ground. Thus far, she'd responded best when he'd actively engaged her about horses and donkeys—not when the focus had been on him. "If he gets bored, won't he start cribbing or something? We've got collars that keep him from doing that, but I don't want to try and put one on him at this stage."

Cribbing happened when horses got bored. They bit down on the wood in their stalls or their rubber buckets and sucked in air. It seemed harmless at first, but it could lead to colic. And colic could be deadly.

Jo pivoted—not a sideways glance, but her whole body turned to him. He kept his eyes above her neck, and saw how she looked at him—confused, yes. But there was more to it than that.

"Really." The way she said it, it wasn't a question. More a wonderment.

He kept his voice casual. "You may not believe this, but I actually know a great deal about horses. My father had a racehorse back in 1987 that died of colic when the former farm manager hadn't realized the mare was cribbing. Yet another stumbling block in my father's eternal quest to win a Triple Crown."

That had been a bad year. Hardwick Beaumont had fired the entire staff at the farm and some of his employees at the Brewery and had been so unbearable to be around that he'd probably hastened his second divorce by at least two years.

Needless to say, it hadn't been much fun for Phillip. Even back then, the farm had been a sanctuary of sorts— a place to get away from half-siblings and step-parents. A place where Hardwick realized he *had* a second son, where they did things together. Even if those things were just leaning on a pasture fence and watching the trainers work the horses.

Hardwick had talked to Phillip during those times. Not Chadwick, not his new babies with his new wife. Just Phillip. The rest of the time, Hardwick had always been too busy running the Beaumont Brewery and having affairs to pay any attention to Phillip. But on the farm…

Phillip had cried that day. He'd cried for Maggie May, the horse who'd died, and he'd cried when the farm staff— the same grizzled old cowboys who'd always been happy to saddle up Phillip's pony and let him ride around the property—had been kicked out. Up until that day, he'd always thought the farm was a place safe from the real world, but all it had taken was one prize-winning mare's death to rip the veil from his eyes.

"Maggie May—that was the mare's name, right?"

Phillip snapped his attention back to the woman standing four feet from him. She was looking at Sun, who'd calmed down to an almost-mellow trot, but there was a sadness about her that, for once, didn't carry the weight of disappointment. It was almost as if she felt bad for the horse.

"You know about that?"

This time, she did give him the side-eye. "I'm also a quick study."

Electricity sparked between them. He felt it. She had to have felt it—why else did that pretty blush grace her cheeks again? "What else do you know about me?"

It was unusual to ask, more unusual to not know the answer. But she'd confounded him at every single turn thus far and, he realized, it was because she knew far more about him that he was anticipating.

She shrugged. "I always do my homework before I take a job. You're an easy man to find online."

But Maggie May—that horse wouldn't pop up in the first twenty pages of a web search. That sort of detail would be buried deep underneath an avalanche of Tumblr feeds and press releases. That was the sort of detail someone would really have to dig to come up with.

"Are you always this thorough, then?"

She didn't hesitate. "Always." Her blush deepened. "But how can I be sure that your reported horse sense is on the level?" She tried to give him a cutting look, but didn't quite make it.

So she was aware of the magnitude of his reputation. That certainly explained her disapproval of his high-flying lifestyle. But there was something underneath that, something deeper.

Something interested.

He recalled doing an interview in *Western Horseman*. He'd had a particularly bad month of headlines. Chadwick had been ready to kill him, so his half-brother Matthew had suggested setting up the interview to show people that there was more to Phillip Beaumont than just scandals.

The reporter had spent three days on the farm with Phillip, following him around as he evaluated his horses, worked with Richard, and generally projected a sane, in-control appearance. The write-up had been so well received that Chadwick had been almost charitable to him for months after that.

That had to be what she was talking about. She'd probably assumed that one main article about him being a real cowboy was a PR plant. And she hadn't been half wrong.

Except he was a real cowboy—at least, he was when he was on the farm. This was the only place where he fit—where he could be Phillip instead of Hardwick's forgotten second son. The horses never cared who he was. They just cared that he was a good man who looked out for them.

Was that what she needed—to know that the horses came first for him? "I guess I'll have to prove myself to you."

"I guess you will," she agreed.

Oh, yeah—the chase was *on*. Jo was unlike any woman he'd ever pursued before. Instead of being a turn-off, he was more and more intrigued by her. She refused to cut him a single bit of slack, but all the signals were there.

Maybe she was a good girl who was intrigued by his bad boy antics. Maybe she'd like a little walk on the wild side. But the things that got her attention weren't the bad boy things. She noticed his interactions with the horses more.

Bad boy with a healthy dash of cowboy—*that* was something he could pull off. If she needed to know that his horse sense, as she called it, was on the level, then he'd have no problem showing her exactly how much he really understood about horses.

Starting now. "I need to get to the foals," he said, leaning toward her just a tad. She didn't pull back. "I'll stop by later and see if Sun ate his carrots."

She did not turn those pretty eyes in his direction, but her grin was broad enough that he knew he'd said the right thing. "I'd like that," she said in a low voice. Then she seemed to remember herself. Her cheeks shot bright red. "I mean, that'd be good. For Sun." Then, before he could say anything else, she opened the gate and walked into the paddock, the tiny donkey at her heels.

Interesting. She might try to act as if she were a tough-as-nails woman, but underneath was someone softer—someone who was enjoying the chase.

Oh, yeah—it'd be good, all right.

Might even be great.

# Four

What the hell was she doing?

Jo stood in the middle of the paddock as Sun wore down. At least he was finally wearing down after three days. He kept looping closer to where the carrots lay in the dirt near his bucket.

The horse was calming down, but Jo? She was beginning to spiral out of control.

She had absolutely no business flirting with Phillip Beaumont. None. The list of reasons why started and ended with whiskey. And vodka. And tequila. She'd always been partial to tequila—she thought. She couldn't really remember.

And that was exactly why she had no business encouraging him. *Really, Jo? Really? It'd be good if he stopped by later?*

She didn't want to look forward to seeing him again. She was not the least bit curious to know if he'd bring her more coffee or Betty and Sun some carrots. She didn't even want to know what he was doing with the Percheron foals.

She was not here for Phillip Beaumont.

Now if she could get that through her thick skull.

It was hard, though. No one brought her coffee. Everyone took her at her word when she said she didn't hook up and left her alone. Which was how she liked it.

Well, maybe she didn't like it. It was a lonely life, never letting herself get close to people.

She'd made friends with Whitney Maddox last winter because Whitney...understood. Whitney had been down the same path, after all. It was easy to be friends with someone else who only trusted animals.

But Phillip? Not only did he *not* leave her alone, he kept coming back for more. It was almost as if he enjoyed her refusal to kowtow to him.

She started to wonder why that was but stopped. She didn't care if he thought she was a hoot or a breath of fresh air or if he was silently mocking her every single move. She *didn't* care.

Not much, anyway.

She rubbed Betty's ears and focused on Sun. Her thoughts didn't often get away from her like this, not anymore. And when they did...

No. She wasn't going to have a bad night. She wasn't even going to have a bad day. She forced herself to breathe regularly. Just because Phillip Beaumont was handsome and tempting and got this smile on his face when he looked at her....

Right. Not happening.

His reputation preceded him. He probably looked at every woman as if she were the one person he'd been waiting for. This had nothing to do with her and everything to do with the fact that she was the only woman on the ranch.

She knew all these things. The sheer logic of the situation should have defused her baser instincts. That's how it'd always worked before.

So why was she thinking about that smile? Or the way his hands would feel on her body? Or what his body would feel like against hers?

Jesus, this was getting out of control. She'd left men in her past with the tequila and the nights she couldn't remember. She would not be tempted by a man who was every one of her triggers wearing a pair of work jeans.

Work jeans that fit him really well.

*Damn.*

Betty leaned against her, anchoring Jo to reality. She let herself rub the back of her neck, her fingers tracing the scar tissue that she'd earned the hard way. This was not the first time she'd been tempted by a man. The first job she'd taken off her parents' ranch had featured a hot young cowboy named Cade who liked to raise hell on a Friday night. Yes, it'd been a year since the accident at that point, but Jo had healed. She'd been flattered to know that she hadn't managed to totally destroy her looks and, truthfully, she *had* been tempted.

Cade had been her idea of a good time for years. It would have been so easy to take him up on his offer for a little fun. So damned easy to get into his truck, not knowing where they were going and not knowing if she'd remember it in the morning.

But she was tired of not remembering. So she'd passed on Cade's offer and never forgotten him. Funny how that worked out.

Sun was calmer today. That was good. The carrots had provided him something to focus on.

Finally, after Jo spent an hour and a half trying not to think about Phillip's smile or his jeans while she waited for Sun to get tired, the horse slowed down to what looked like an angry walk, as if he'd only stopped running as a favor to her. He continued to pace near the carrots.

Jo waited. Would the horse actually eat one? That would be making more progress than she'd hoped for. And if Sun improved faster, the sooner she could pack up Betty into the trailer and be on her way to the next job, far away from the temptation named Phillip Beaumont.

Sun dipped his nose into the water bucket and took a couple of deep drinks, then leaned down to sniff the carrots.

And pawed them into mush.

*Close*, she thought with a weary sigh.

She tried to focus on the positive here. Sun was, in fact, getting bored with being out-of-control. Something as innocent as carrots hadn't sent him into spasms of panic. He hadn't even destroyed them outright. He'd been curious—so much so that his curiosity had distracted him from his regularly scheduled pacing. This was all good news.

She heard hoofbeats coming up the drive. Sun heard them too and, with a whinny that sounded closer to a horse than a demon, resumed trotting and kicking.

Moving slowly, Jo turned to see a beautiful pair of Percherons hitched to a wagon loaded with hay and driven by none other than Phillip Beaumont, who was sitting high on a narrow bench. His coffee mug was nowhere in sight. The wagon looked as though it was a hundred years old—wooden wheels painted red and gray. The whole thing was a scaled down version of the Beaumont Beer wagon that the Percherons pulled in parades and commercials.

Phillip put both reins in one hand and honest-to-God tipped his hat to her. Heat flushed her face.

"Did he eat the carrots?"

"He pulverized them." She pointed to the orange-colored dirt.

"Damn." He looked a little disappointed, but not as if the world had ended. "I'll try again tomorrow."

He seemed so sincere about it—a man who was concerned about his horse.

She'd be lying if she said she didn't find it endearing. "That'd be good."

She was pretty sure this was flirting. Maybe she was being the ridiculous one, reading intent where there was none.

Her face got hotter.

"I can't help but notice," Phillip went on as if she weren't slowly turning into a tomato, "that you've spent at least two days standing in the middle of a paddock."

"This is true."

He jiggled the reins. "There's more to this farm than just that patch of dirt." The invitation sounded pretty casual, but then he turned that smile in her direction. That was a smile that promised all kinds of wicked fun. "Want to go for a ride?"

*That* was flirting. It had to be.

And she had no idea how to respond.

After a moment's pause, Phillip went on. "I'm getting Marge and Homer here used to pulling the wagon. I'm headed out to the other side of the ranch, where I keep the Appaloosas. Have you seen them?"

"No." She hadn't even really seen the Percherons—but she wanted to. Could she accept this ride at face value—a chance to see the rest of the storied Beaumont Farm and the collection of horses it contained? "You named your horses after *The Simpsons?*"

"Doesn't everyone?" Good lord, that grin was going to be her undoing. "I'd love to get your professional opinion on them and the Appaloosas."

There—now did that qualify as flirting or not? Dang it, she was *so* out of practice.

He must have sensed her hesitation. "I'm just going to drop off the hay. Twenty, thirty minutes tops."

Wait—a multi-millionaire like Phillip Beaumont moved his own hay? This she had to see for herself. "One condition—I want to drive."

For a moment, the good-time grin on his face cracked, but she was serious. Drunk driving—whether it was a team of Percherons or a Porsche—was a non-starter for her.

Then the grin was back. "Can you handle a team?" His voice had dropped a notch and was in danger of smoldering. If she hadn't seen the crack in his mask before, she might not have noticed it this time. He hid it well.

"I can see how you'd question my skills, what with me being an equestrian professional." He notched an eyebrow at her and she almost felt bad for being a smart-ass. So she added, "I was raised on a ranch. I can drive a team."

"Ever driven Percherons?"

"There's a first for everything."

*That* was flirting—for her, anyway. Phillip took it that way, too. "Then come on."

He waited while she exited the paddock, her donkey on her heels. "What about Betty?" she asked after she got the gate closed.

She couldn't leave Betty alone with Sun. But she didn't want Betty wandering around the farm. She was small enough that, if she really put her mind to it, she could fall down a hole or get stuck in a gap in the fences.

"I thought she might like to try out a new pasture, meet some of the not-crazy horses we have here," he replied, pointing to a gate about two hundred yards up the drive. Clearly, he'd been anticipating this question. There was a certain measure of thoughtfulness about him that was, she had to admit, appealing. "The grass is always greener on the other side."

She grinned up at him. "So it is. I'll follow the wagon up."

She gave Sun a final look. The horse was actually standing still, watching them with the kind of look that seemed to say that he was taking in everything they did and said. Would he freak out as they left him alone or would he watch them go?

Phillip gave her one of those old-fashioned nods of his head and clucked to his team. The wagon started and she followed, Betty on her heels.

This was just some professional consideration, right? Phillip was a noted horseman and she was an increasingly noted horse trainer. His asking her to look at other horses on the farm had nothing to do with any real or imagined interest on his part and everything to do with getting the most out of what he was paying her.

When they got to the gate at the pasture across the road, Phillip surprised her again by hopping down off the wagon and opening the gate for Betty. "There you go, girl. Enjoy the grass—we'll be back."

Betty gave him one of her looks as she plodded past him into the pasture. Phillip latched the gate behind her. "Have fun!" He turned to Jo, the goofiest grin she'd ever seen on his face.

"What?"

"I like Betty. Everything about her is hilarious. Here, let me help you."

Now, Jo was perfectly capable of climbing up onto the narrow seat of a rack wagon all by herself, but Phillip moved to her side and placed a hand on the small of her back. "Just step up on the wheel there...."

His touch sent licking flames of heat up and down her back. His hand was strong and confident against her. How long had it been since a man had touched her? Since...

Bad. Bad, bad, *bad*. She slammed the breaks on that line of thinking and shook him off before she did something insane like pretend to stumble so he'd be forced to catch her. "I have done this before, you know."

She didn't catch the double entendre until he said, "Have you, now?" low and close to her ear. His breath was warm and didn't smell like whiskey.

It had been a long time. Really long. Could she indulge herself, just this once, and not slide back down to rock bottom? She had needs. It'd be nice to have someone else help her meet them.

She looked over her shoulder at Phillip, who was less than two feet away, an expectant look on his face. But he didn't press the issue or find some excuse to keep touching her. He just waited for her response.

She swallowed and hefted herself into the seat. This was starting to look like a bad idea—all of it. She tried to refocus her thinking. She was at the Beaumont Farms because this job would make her reputation as a trainer. Phillip Beaumont was not just an attractive, attentive man with a reputation as one of the better lovers in the world, he was the client who'd hired her to save his horse.

And getting in the wagon to see the farm and his other horses was…was…a wise business decision. He might have another horse who needed retraining, which would mean more money for her, a better reference.

That was a stretch and she knew it, especially when Phillip swung up into the seat and managed to make it look smooth. He settled onto the bench next to her, their thighs touching, and handed her the reins. "Marge likes to go fast, Homer likes to go slow. Try to keep them together." Then he leaned back, slung one arm behind her on the bench and said, "Show me what you can do."

He wasn't touching her but she swore she could feel the heat from his arm anyway. She gathered the reins and flicked them. "Up!"

Phillip chuckled as the horses began to walk. "Up?"

"It's what we said at home. And," she couldn't help but point out, "it worked. What do you say?"

"I'm partial to 'Let's Go.' So you were raised on a ranch?"

She adjusted the reins in her hands until she had more tension on Marge's. "Yup." She felt as if she should say more, but small talk was not one of her strengths. Never had been. Maybe that's why parties had always been easier with a beer in her hand.

"Where's home?"

"Middle of nowhere, South Dakota. Nothing to do but stare at the grass."

"Oh? So you've been training horses your whole life?"

She shrugged. She didn't like talking about herself. She especially didn't like talking about the six or so years that were a total blur. So she skipped it entirely.

"Not like this. But I'd come back to the ranch after college—" That was the most diplomatic way to put it. "—and a neighbor's barn caught fire. He lost four horses, but one survived. Oaty was his name. That horse was a mess. The vet almost put him down twice but…"

"But you couldn't let him do that." Phillip's tone was more than sympathetic. He understood.

"Nope. I just watched him. For days. And the longer I watched him, the more I could understand him. He was terrified and I couldn't blame him."

"You waited for him to get bored?"

"More like to calm down. Took about a month before I could get close enough to brush him. He was scarred and his coat never did grow back right on his flank, but he's still out on my parents' ranch, munching grass and hanging out with the donkeys."

The day she'd saddled old Oaty up and ridden him across the ranch had been one of the best days of her life. For so long she'd felt lost and confused and hadn't known why, but saving Oaty had been saving herself. She hadn't given up on Oaty and she wouldn't give up on herself.

She was good at something—saving horses no one else could. She'd stayed on her parents' ranch for a few more years, driving around the state to other semi-local ranches to work with their horses, and as her successes had mounted, so had the demand for her services.

Besides, a woman could only live with her parents for so long. So she'd bought her trailer and hit the road, Betty in tow, determined to make a name for herself. It'd taken years, but she'd finally made it to a place like Beaumont Farms—the kind of place where money was no object.

"That must have been huge for you."

"Oaty was a tough case. Probably the toughest I've had up until now."

Phillip chuckled. "I'm honored to be the toughest case."

She couldn't help it. She turned to look at him. "It's not really an honor."

Their gazes met. There was something raw in his eyes, something…honest.

She did not fix people. She did not sleep with people. She didn't do anything involving alcohol anymore. She'd been clean and sober for ten years and had never crossed back over to the dark side. Apart from a long-ago cowboy named Cade, she'd never once been tempted by a man.

Until now.

She shouldn't be attracted to Phillip and most certainly not interested in him.

But she was. Against all known logic and common sense, she was.

"Here," she said, thrusting the reins at him. "You drive."

# Five

"You really haul your own hay?" Jo asked as she watched him grab a bale.

The question struck him as funny, considering the woman was holding a bale at mid-chest without breaking a sweat.

"Of course. This is a working farm, after all."

"But *you* work?"

He shot her a smarmy look, but it felt differently on his face than it normally did. He picked up a bale, aware of how she was looking at his arms. "I work." Then he flexed.

She could be quite lovely when she blushed—as she was doing right now. She wasn't a traditionally beautiful woman, what with her strong jaw, dark hair that brushed her shoulders and her flannel shirt with only one button undone, but underneath that...

She wasn't his type. But he was having trouble remembering what he liked so much about all the women he normally kept company with. Compared to Jo, they all looked…the same.

"This way," he said, leading her back to the hay room.

Working in silence, they got the hay unloaded in a matter of minutes. He carried in the final bale and turned to get out of her way. But he didn't walk back out to the wagon. He stood there for a moment in the dim room, watching her heft her final bale on top of his. Then she turned and caught him staring at her.

A ripple of tension moved across her shoulders and he thought she was going to blow past him and rush for the open air. After all, they could do things in this hay room and no one would be the wiser. But she'd made her position pretty damned clear. If she stormed out of here, he wouldn't be the least bit surprised.

She didn't. Instead, she hooked her thumbs in her belt, leaned back against the hay bales and looked at him as if she was waiting for him to make his move. No overt come-on, no suggestive posturing. Just standing there, watching him watch her.

He knew what he wanted to do. He wanted to press her back against the bale and find out if she liked things soft and sweet and pretty like her blush or if she wanted it rough and tough.

But, as she stood there and waited, he *didn't* want to. Which didn't make any sense. Of course he wanted to kiss her, to touch her. But…

Something stopped him.

She was starting to unnerve him. Suddenly, he realized this must be what his horse felt like. She could stand here all day and wait for him to get bored.

So he did something. Something that bordered on being out of character for him. He did not ask her to dinner and he did not ask her if she'd like to soak in his hot tub with a view. "Would you like to see the Appaloosas?"

The corner of her mouth moved up into what might have been a pleased smile on someone else. It was almost as if that had been the thing she'd hoped he'd say. It was weird how good that little half-smile of approval made him feel. "I would."

He walked her through the barn to the nearby pasture where his Appaloosas were grazing. "I've got four breeding mares," he told her, pointing the spotted horses out to her. "We usually get two foals a year out of them. We have between six and nine on site at any given time."

"What do you do with them?"

"Sell them. They're good workhorses, but I sell a lot to Hollywood. I focus on the blanket-with-spots coloring, which is what producers want." He pointed to the nearest mare. "See? Black in the front, white flank with spots in the back."

She gave him that look again, the one that said he was making a fool of himself. "I know what a blanket Appaloosa is, you know."

He grinned at her. She did *not* cut him any slack. Why did he like it so much? "Sorry. The women I normally hang out with don't know much about horses."

"I'm not like other women."

He couldn't help it. He leaned toward where she was, his voice dropping an octave. "A fact I've become more aware of every day."

She let him wait a whole minute before she acknowledged what he'd said. "Are you hitting on me?"

"No." Even though she wasn't looking at him, he still saw the way her face twisted in disagreement, so he added, "By all agreed-upon Dude Law, this barely breaks the threshold for flirting."

She snorted in what he hoped was amusement. "Do you have an Appaloosa stallion?"

"No. I use different stock to keep the genetics clean."

"Smart," she said in the kind of voice that made it clear she hadn't expected a smart answer.

"I told you, I know a great deal about horses." He pointed out the yearling. "That's Snowflake. I've got a breeder who's interested in him out in New York if his coat fills in right."

"Why do you breed them?"

"I like them. They've got history. The story is that my great-grandfather, Phillipe Beaumont, drove a team of Percherons he'd brought over from France across the Great Plains after the Civil War and then traded one with the Nez Perce for one of their Appaloosas—he considered that a fair trade."

She looked at him again, those soft hazel eyes almost level with his. If this were any other woman in the world, he'd touch her. He was thinking about doing it anyway, but he didn't want to push his luck.

He'd basically promised that they were just here to look at the horses, so that's all they were going to do. He'd given his word. He wanted the woman, but he wanted her to want him, too.

And she just might, given the way she was looking at him, her full lips slightly parted and her head tilted to one side as if she really wouldn't mind a kiss. "You keep Appaloosas because your great-grandfather bought one a hundred and fifty years ago?"

"More like a hundred and thirty years. Of course, he only got the one Appaloosa, so my mares don't go back that far. But the Percherons do."

Man, he could get lost in her eyes. He could only guess at what she was thinking right now.

Because she didn't seem to be thinking about horses. "You spend a lot of time out here with them?"

"Always have. The farm is a more pleasant place to be than the Beaumont Mansion."

That was the understatement of the year. Growing up a Beaumont in the shadow of Hardwick's chosen son, Chadwick, had been an experience in privileged neglect. No one had paid a bit of attention to Phillip. His mother had divorced his father when he was five, but Hardwick had retained full custody of the boys for reasons that, as far as Phillip could tell, could only be called spiteful.

Hardwick had devoted all of his attention to Chadwick, grooming him to run the Beaumont Brewery. Phillip?

No one had cared. When his mother had lost the lengthy custody battles, she acted as if Phillip had purposefully chosen Hardwick just to punish her. Then Hardwick had gotten married again—and again, and again—and always paid more attention to his new wife and his new children. Because there were always new wives and new children.

Phillip had been all but invisible in his own home. He could come and go and do as he pleased and it just didn't matter. The freedom was heady. What had grades mattered to him? They hadn't. Teachers didn't dare make him toe the line because of his father's reputation. He'd discovered that, although no one cared a bit for him at home, people out in the world cared about his name a great deal—so much so that he could break every rule in the book and no one would stop him.

By the time he'd gotten to college, he had his pick of women. He had a well-deserved reputation as a man who would satisfy. Women were complicated. They liked to feel sexy and desirable and wanted. Most of them wanted to feel swept away, but some liked to call the shots. He'd learned that early.

Not much had changed since then. His reputation always preceded him. Women came to him, not the other way around. And his brother Chadwick only cared what he did when he thought Phillip had made a spectacle of the Beaumont name. Chadwick was the only person who ever tried to make Phillip toe the line, and Phillip made him pay for it.

No one stopped Phillip Beaumont. Except possibly a horse trainer named Jo Spears.

"That surprises me," she said in her quiet tone. "You seem more like a big-city kind of man."

That's what she said. What he heard was 'party guy.' And he couldn't blame her. Beaumont Farms wasn't exactly the social center of the world.

"The big city has its advantages, it's true. But sometimes it's good to take a break from the hustle and bustle and slow down."

He'd always come out to the farm to get away from the tension that was his family. Here, there were rules. If he wanted to ride his pony, he had to brush that pony and clean the stall. If he wanted to drive the team with a wagon, he had to learn how to hook up the harness. And if he wanted to gentle the foals and get them used to being haltered, he had to be able to hold on to a rearing animal.

When he'd been a kid, this had been the only place in his life where there were consequences for his actions. If he screwed up or only half-assed something, then he fell off the horse because the girth wasn't tight enough or got kicked for startling a horse from behind.

But it'd also been the place where he'd done things right and gotten rewarded for it. When he got his pony saddled all by himself, he'd gotten to go for a ride with his father. When he'd learned how to walk around horses without scaring them, he'd gotten to spend more time working with them. And when he learned how to ask a horse to do something the right way, he'd gotten to race and jump and have a hell of a good time.

He'd gotten the attention of his father. Hardwick Beaumont had been a horseman through and through. It came with the Beaumont name and Hardwick had lived up to it.

His horse obsessions had followed all the usual paths—expensive Thoroughbred horses in an attempt to win the Triple Crown, lavish show horses designed to win gold and the Percherons, of course.

Phillip had been too big to be a jockey, so he couldn't ride for the Crown. He'd been a good rider, but never great. But he could talk horses and help with the Percherons. When it'd been just the two of them out on the farm, his father had not only noticed him, but approved of him. He'd never won the Triple Crown, but his jockeys and trainers had won the Preakness three times and Churchill Downs twice.

Horses had been the only thing that had set Phillip apart from Chadwick. Phillip was good with horses. He understood the consequences—never understood it better than when Maggie May had died. Horses were valuable and, as the second son, it was his duty to keep that part of the Beaumont legacy alive.

The only time he missed his father was when he was on the farm.

"So, you work," Jo repeated, calling him back to himself.

She wasn't looking at him, but he felt as if he had her full attention. "Yes."

"Do you clean tack?"

The question would have been odd coming from any other woman. Somehow, he wasn't surprised she'd asked it. "I have on occasion."

He could only see half her face, but he didn't miss the quick smile. "Can you be in the paddock around eight tomorrow morning?" Then she angled her face in his direction. "Or is that too early for you?"

Hell, yeah it was early. But he wasn't going to let her know that. "I'll bring the coffee." Doubt—he recognized it now—flashed over her face. "You take yours black, right?"

She held his gaze for another long moment. Finally, she said, "Yup," and let it drop.

"You want to drive the team back to the barn?"

She brightened. "They're beautiful animals. I've never worked with them before."

He felt himself relax. He could talk horses, after all. As long as they came back to the horses, she wouldn't look at him as if she was disappointed in him. "Well, you've come to the right place. Have you seen any of the foals?"

Her eyes lit up. She really was striking. So very tough but underneath that... "Foals?" Then she sighed. "I need to get back to Sun."

"Maybe tomorrow afternoon?"

She dropped her chin and looked up at him through thick lashes. "I guess that depends on how well you clean tack."

There was that challenge again, writ large in both words and actions. Everything about her was a bet—one that he wanted to take. "I guess it does."

He could prove himself in the morning cleaning tack. It didn't matter why. He would show her that he knew his stuff and that he was good with his hands.

And then? He'd get out his carriage, the one with the roomy padded seat and the bonnet that provided a modicum of privacy. It was a big farm. Plenty of shady lanes hidden behind old-growth trees where a couple could have a picnic in private.

She was a challenge, all right. But he'd bet that he could win her over, even if he had to clean tack to do it.

# Six

Phillip strolled up to the paddock at 7:58, two mugs in hand. "Good morning," he called out. "What are you doing?"

"Waiting for you," she replied, setting the cutter saddle down on the blanket she'd laid out in the middle of the paddock. Betty was nibbling the untrampled grass near the gate, but she looked up as Phillip approached and went to meet him.

Behind Jo, Sun whinnied. She turned in time to see him trot past his buckets. Checking for carrots? That was a good sign.

"I'm on time *and* under budget." His tone—light and teasing and promising good things—made her look up. Even though the dawning light of morning was just casting the farm in pinks and yellows, Phillip's smile was warm and bright. He reached through the gate to rub Betty's little head. "I even brought carrots."

*Oh.* He'd shaved today. The four-day growth he'd been

working on was gone and suddenly he looked more like the man in the commercials—the one to whom women flocked.

No flocking. She would not flock. This exercise in tack was not about spending time with Phillip Beaumont. This was about the fact that Phillip was Sun's owner. She was just encouraging the relationship between the horse and the man.

"Grab the saddle," she said, nodding toward the Trilogy English jumping saddle she'd set on top of the fence. The cutter saddle was by far the more complicated of the two saddles. Cleaning it would take her hours. If Phillip knew what he was doing, the jumping saddle would take him forty-five minutes. An hour, tops. And if he didn't know what he was doing...

Why did she want him to be able to clean a saddle so badly? It was just tack. True, both saddles were high-end. She felt bad about using them, but there hadn't been a lower-end option. She took some comfort in the fact that this wouldn't be a hardship for someone with the Beaumont name.

Phillip's brows jumped up. "And?"

"And open the gate, walk in slowly, and have a seat." She motioned to the blanket on the ground.

"What about the carrots?"

"Hang on to them. We might need them later."

"Okay." He grabbed the saddle and opened the gate.

Sun stopped trotting, stood still and watched Phillip— at least, until the gate was latched. Then he went into a round of bucking that would have won him first prize at any rodeo.

Phillip froze, just two steps inside the fence. Jo turned to watch Sun throw his fit. He'd been calming down for her quite nicely, but she couldn't say this was a surprise.

He didn't like change and another person in the paddock was a big change. Even if it was the person with the carrots.

"Should I leave?" Phillip asked. She had to admire the fact that he didn't sound as though he was quaking in his boots. If he could keep calm, Sun would chill out faster.

"Nope. Just walk toward me. Slowly."

She kept her eyes on Sun as Phillip made the long walk. Sun wasn't bucking as high as he had during the first days and he certainly wasn't working himself into a lather.

Phillip made it to the blanket, handed her a thermal mug and set the saddle down at his feet. Betty sniffed the saddle while Jo sniffed the coffee. "Thanks." Black, with no secret ingredients. Had he spiked his coffee again this morning? If so, he'd gone light. She didn't catch a hint of whiskey about him.

Instead, he smelled like…she leaned closer. Bay rum spice, warm and clean and tempting.

When he said, "Now what?" she almost jumped out of her skin.

Right. She had a job here, one that required her full attention. They couldn't sit down while Sun was bucking. The risk that he might charge was too great. But she was going to stop standing in this paddock today, by God. She could feel it. "We wait. Welcome to standing."

So they stood. Betty wandered back over to where the grass was greener, completely unconcerned with either Sun's antics or what the people were doing.

How long could Phillip do this? Thus far, he had not struck her as a man of inaction. Which was admirable, but there was something to be said for just watching. She was thinking he'd only last about five minutes before he started to get twitchy. Seven at the most.

After about ten minutes, Phillip asked, "How long is this going to take?"

She tried not to smile. *Not bad.* "As long as it takes."

Another five minutes passed. "Maybe I should give him the carrots? Would that help?"

"Nope."

"Why not?" Phillip was starting to sound exasperated. She wondered which one would crack first—the horse or the man.

"Because," she explained, "if you give him the carrots now, he'll associate carrots with temper tantrums. Wait until he's managed to be calm for at least ten minutes."

"Oh. Right."

They were silent for another five minutes as Sun continued to go through the motions.

"We're really just going to stand here?"

She couldn't help giving him a look. "Do you have a problem with silence?"

"No," he defended a little quicker than was necessary. Which was almost the same as a yes. "This just seems pointless."

This was not going how she'd thought it would. Yesterday, he'd seemed like a man who would understand what it took to retrain a horse. "Do you have something else you'd rather do than train your multi-million-dollar horse?"

That made him look a little more sheepish, which had the unfortunate side effect of making him look positively adorable. "No."

Sun reared up, which drew their attention. "See? He's a smart horse," she told Phillip. "He's picking up on your impatience. Just *be*, okay?"

"Okay."

She didn't think he could do it. Hell, the only reason she could do it was because she'd been in traction for a few months, physically incapable of doing anything but be still and quiet and painfully aware of her surroundings.

Months in traction, then almost another year out on her parents' ranch just sitting around while her body healed, watching the world. God, she'd been so bored in the beginning. She'd hurt and couldn't take any of the good painkillers and none of the nurses would bring her a beer. She'd tried watching television, but that had only made things worse.

Then her granny, Lina Throws Spears, had come to sit with her. Sometimes, Lina had told her old Lakota stories about trickster coyotes and spiders, but most of the time she'd just sat, looking out the window at the parking lot.

It'd almost driven Jo insane. Lina had always been weird, burning sage and drinking tea. But then Jo had started to actually see the world around her. People came with balloons and hopeful smiles for new babies. People left with tissues in their hands and tears in their eyes when someone died. They fought and sometimes met for quickies in the back of the parking lot. Some smoked. Some drank. Some talked on cell phones.

They did things for reasons. And, if you paid attention, those reasons weren't that hard to figure out.

When she'd finally been discharged and went home, she hadn't been good for much. So she sat on her parents' porch and watched the ranch.

It'd always been such a boring place—or so she'd thought. But then she'd actually sat still and paid attention.

She'd noticed things that she'd never seen before, like the snake that lived under the porch and the starlings that lived in the barn. The barn cat napped in the sun until the sun moved and then he went mousing.

There'd been something peaceful about it. She watched the wind blow through the pastures and storms blow in. She watched her dad saddle the horses and her mom bake pies.

The world had felt…okay. She'd felt okay in it. She'd never been able to say that before. And then, when Oaty had survived that fire, she'd watched him and figured out what he'd been trying to say.

But getting to the point where she could understand a horse as messed up as Oaty had taken her well over a year. It was ridiculous to think that a man like Phillip Beaumont—known for his wild ways—would be able to just stand here and pay attention because she asked him to half an hour ago.

And he couldn't. He was trying, that she could see, but within fifteen minutes, his fingers were tapping against his legs, beating out a staccato rhythm of impatience.

Not surprisingly, Sun picked up on this. His hoofbeats against the ground nearly matched Phillip's rhythm.

"Stop," she said, reaching over and pulling his hand away from his leg.

Which meant she was now holding his hand.

His fingers wrapped around hers. "Sorry." He didn't sound particularly sorry.

She stood *very* still. Aside from handshakes, she hadn't touched a man in so long. The feeling of something as simple as holding hands was...

It was a lot. Heat bloomed from where his skin touched hers, which set off a chain reaction across her body. Her nipples tightened. They went hard in a way she'd forgotten about. Her heart rate picked up and she knew she was blushing but she couldn't help it.

*Skin on skin.* It was only a light touch, but for the first time in a very long time, desire coursed through her.

Oh, no—this was bad.

She couldn't pull her hand away. The sensations flooding her body—the weight growing heavy between her legs, the heat clouding her thinking—left her unable to do anything but stand there and *keep* touching him.

As she spun out of control, both Phillip and Sun seemed

to be calming down. Instead of drumming his fingers against his leg, he went to...

To rubbing his thumb against her skin.

Jo's head swam as desire hit her hard. One of the most attractive, wealthy, available men in the country was stroking the back of her hand.

Once, it'd taken far less than this—coffee in the morning, horses in the afternoon, a light touch—to get her back to a room. Or into a car. Or even just up against a wall. Once, all a guy would have had to do was buy her a drink and maybe tell her she was hot. *Maybe*. That'd been all the reason she needed to go off with another man she didn't know, to wake up in a place she couldn't remember.

How was Phillip doing this to her? He hadn't pinned her against a wall or bitten her in that space between her neck and her shoulder or anything. He was just holding her hand! It shouldn't make her think of being pinned against walls and being bitten or touched. It just shouldn't.

In her confusion, she made the mistake of looking at him. He turned his head at almost the same time and smiled. That was it. Nothing but a nice, sexy, hot smile. For her.

Ten long years of no touching and no smiling caught up to Jo in milliseconds. She *wanted* him to pin her against the wall and bite that place on her neck. And a few other things. She wanted to feel his hands on a whole bunch of places. She wanted to know exactly how good this cowboy was.

This—this was exactly why she'd abstained from men. Something as small as a single touch having this much effect on her—it was like an alcoholic saying he could have one sip and be just fine.

Men, like drinking, were an all-or-nothing proposition for her. That's just the way it was. She was not going to fall off the wagon because Phillip Beaumont was gorgeous, thoughtful, rich and worried about his horse. She'd worked too hard to be the person she was now.

The look in his eyes got deeper. *Warmer*. And damn it all if it didn't make him look even hotter.

He was close enough that Jo could lean forward and kiss him.

Thank God, Sun saved her. He came to a halt in front of them, clearly trying to figure out what new thing the humans were doing.

Which made Phillip turn those beautiful eyes away from her. "Hey," he said in a quiet, strong voice that sent shivers racing down the back of her neck. "He stopped."

What's more than that, the horse didn't start back up when Phillip spoke. He just stood there. Then he *walked* over to where the buckets were. He stuck his nose into the food bucket and then looked back at Phillip. It was an amazing development.

"He wants a carrot," she told Phillip.

"Should I give him one?"

"Go ahead and put one in the bucket, but make sure he sees you've got more. After all, he did calm down and ask politely. He's earned a reward."

At this observation, Phillip turned a dazzling smile in her direction. "Do I get a reward, too?" he said in that same strong voice as the pad of his thumb moved over her hand again.

This time, the shivers were stronger.

His mouth settled from the dazzling smile into the grin that was so wicked she couldn't help but think about him scraping his teeth against her bare flesh as he pulled the snaps of her shirt apart....

"No," she gritted out, hoping she didn't sound as if she was about to start swooning.

She wasn't fooling him. She wasn't even fooling herself. He leaned forward, the air between them crystalizing into something so sharp it almost cut her. His grip on her hand tightened as he tried to pull her toward him. "Why not? I calmed down. I asked politely."

"You didn't do it on your own." She was desperate to stop touching him and completely unable to do so. "You have to earn a reward."

"And how do I do that?" Somehow, he managed to make it sound innocent and sensual all at the same time.

"Carrots for the horse. Then tack. Done right."

She jerked her hand out of his grasp, desperate.

He leaned forward, the air between them growing hot. He was going to kiss her and she was going to let him and if that happened, would she be able to control herself? Or would she be gone? Again?

His gaze searched hers. God, she probably looked like a deer in the headlights—blinded by his sheer sex appeal.

"One condition—I get to choose my own reward." His voice dropped to a dangerous level—silky and sensual and promising all sorts of good things. "I don't like carrots." Then he turned and began to walk to the bucket. Slowly.

Sun removed himself to the far side of the paddock and paced slowly. Jo knew she should be thrilled at this progress. The horse and the man were actually communicating.

So why did she feel so terrible? No, not terrible. *Weird.* Her skin felt hot and her knees had yet to stop shaking and her heart was pounding fast.

Then Phillip was walking back toward her.

Oh, God. She wasn't sure she was strong enough for this. She'd spent the last ten years convincing herself that she could get through the nights without a drink or a man or a man holding a drink.

Phillip Beaumont was going to be her undoing.

"So," he said when he reached her again. He waved at the saddles. "What are we doing with the tack?"

"Cleaning it."

Instead of looking as if he had her right where he wanted her, he looked more off-balance. Good. She shouldn't be the only one off-balance here. "It's...not dirty."

"Do you want to ride?" His eyes widened in surprise and she realized what she'd said. "I mean, the horse. Do you want to ride the horse? *Sun*."

Sweet merciful heavens, she could not be embarrassing herself more if she tried.

"Yes." But the way Phillip said it left the question of which kind of riding he was interested in doing wide open.

"Then you clean tack."

# Seven

What did he want for a reward?

Phillip knew. He wanted to open his door tonight with a bottle of wine chilling on the table and then skip dinner entirely and head straight to the hot tub. He'd love to see how Jo's body filled out a bikini—or nothing at all. Nude was always fashionable.

He'd love his reward to go on for most of the evening. It'd been close to a week since he'd first woken up alone in his own bed and he missed having a woman to spend the evening with.

But that wasn't necessarily the reward he'd ask for.

He might ask for a kiss. That was a pretty big *might*. Her hand—warm and gentle but firm in his—had seemed to say that she was interested in a kiss. Combined with the entirely feminine blush that had pinked her cheeks? Yeah, a kiss would be good.

But he had to earn it first—by cleaning saddles, of all things. When was the last time he'd had to work so hard for something as simple as a kiss? He shouldn't be having fun. He should be frustrated that she was being so damned stubborn or insulted that his considerable charms were falling on mostly deaf ears.

But he wasn't. It struck him as beyond strange that he was actually enjoying the slow process of seducing Jo Spears.

So he cleaned a not-dirty saddle.

Normally, Phillip did not enjoy cleaning tack. It was his second least-favorite job on the farm, after shoveling stalls, the one he'd always had to do when he messed up.

But instead of feeling like a punishment, sitting on a blanket in the middle of a paddock taking apart a saddle and wiping it down—next to Jo—wasn't awful. In fact, it bordered on pleasant. The weather was beautifully sunny, with a bright breeze that ruffled the leaves on the trees.

As Phillip cleaned his saddle, he kept half an eye on the horse as he moved around the paddock. Sometimes he walked, sometimes he trotted, but he didn't race or buck or generally act like a horse that was out of control. That made Phillip feel pretty good.

But what made him feel better was the woman sitting next to him.

He had been patient and waited for her to touch him first. True, he hadn't been expecting her to grab his hand. He hadn't realized his hand had actually been moving. He'd been focused on not spooking Sun and trying to be still like she was. It'd taken a lot more energy than he'd anticipated. Who knew that standing still would be so hard?

Until she'd taken his hand. He realized she hadn't meant it as a come-on—but the way she'd reacted to his touch? The wall between them had busted wide open. She was attracted to him. He was interested in her.

Things were moving along nicely.

He kept cleaning the saddle until his feet started to fall

asleep. Boots were good for many things, but sitting on the ground wasn't one of them. "How long do we have to keep doing this?"

She leaned over to appraise his work. "Nice job."

"I had several years of practice."

"Really?" She stretched out her legs, which looked even longer and more muscular at this angle. What would it feel like to have legs that strong wrapped around his back? And how many saddles would he have to clean to find out? "How come?"

"Every time I did something wrong, I had to either clean tack or muck stalls. And when you're a hyper kid who's never had to follow rules before..." He shrugged. It was the truth, of course, but...he had never admitted that to another person.

He cleared his throat. "I cleaned a lot of tack. But it was good. I can harness the entire team of Percherons to the wagon myself."

She turned to look at him, an odd half-smile on her face. "What?"

"It's just that none of this," she replied, looking at the pile of polished leather they'd worked through, "fits with your public persona."

"There's more to me than just parties."

She grinned at him—a grin he was starting to recognize. She was about to give him some crap and she was going to enjoy doing it. He braced himself for the worst, but oddly, the fact that she was having fun made it not so bad.

"What would your lady friends say if they saw you sitting in the dirt?"

That's what she said. What he heard was superiority mixed in with a healthy dose of jealousy.

Jealous because she was interested.

*Excellent.* But he needed to move carefully here.

"I doubt they'd understand. Which is why they're not here." Only her. Before she could reload, he took control of the conversation. "Tell me about Betty."

Jo looked up, finding where her small donkey was now drinking from the bucket set at her height. "What do you want to know?"

"How long have you had her?" Yes, this was part of showing Jo there was more to him than a good time at a party or a family fortune. But he had to admit, he was curious.

"About ten years."

He supposed he shouldn't have been surprised by the short answer, but something in her tone indicated that perhaps not too many people had asked. "Where'd you get her?"

"My granny gave her to me." Jo sighed, as if the conversation were unavoidable and yet still painful. "I had...a rough patch. Granny thought I needed someone to keep me company. Most people would have gotten a puppy, but not Lina Throws Spears. She showed up with a donkey foal that only weighed twenty pounds." She grinned at the memory. "Itty Bitty Betty. We've been together ever since."

Phillip let that information sink in. There was a lot of it. How old was Jo? Given the faint lines around her eyes, he'd guess she wasn't in her twenties anymore.

What sort of rough patch had she had? Had someone broken her heart? That would certainly explain why she worked so hard at keeping that wall up between her and everyone else.

Letting Suzie go had hurt more than he'd expected—and that was before he'd read about her engagement to that prince. But to have a true broken heart, a man had to be in love.

After watching his parents and all of his stepparents and every horrid thing they did to each other in the name of love, Phillip would never do something as stupid as give his heart to anyone. Falling in love meant giving someone power to hurt you.

No love, no hurt. Just a long list of one-night stands that satisfied his needs quite well. Love was for the delusional. Lust was something honest and real and easily solved without risking hearts or family fortunes.

Also, what kind of name was Lina Throws Spears? Jo didn't look like an Indian—not like the ones in the movies, anyway. Her skin was tanned, but he'd always assumed that was because of the time she spent in the sun. She had a dusting of freckles across her nose and cheeks. Her hair was medium brown, not jet black.

Then there were her eyes. They were a pretty hazel color, light and soft in a woman who otherwise could appear hard.

On the other hand, there was that whole communing-with-the-animals thing she did. That certainly fit with his preconceived notions of American Indians.

"Yes?"

He quickly looked away. "What?"

Jo sighed again. "Go on. You know you're dying to ask."

"Throws Spears?"

"Granny—and my dad—are full-blooded Lakota Sioux. My mom's white. Any other questions?"

"You shortened your name?"

"My dad did."

Her tone brooked no warmth. Right. The topic of family was off-limits. He got that. His own family tree was so complicated that instead of a sturdy, upright oak it resembled a banyan tree that grew new trunks everywhere.

It was time to change the subject. "Where does Betty sleep?"

"If it's nice out, she stays in a pasture, but she's house trained," she said, nodding to the trailer.

"Really?"

That was a nice smile. "Really. I made a harness for her when we're driving. She sits up front. Likes to stick her nose out the window."

This bordered on the most ridiculous thing he had ever heard. "And you're sure she's a donkey and not a dog in disguise?"

"Very sure." She shot him a look that seemed to be the opposite of the hard tone she'd had when discussing her family. "Tomorrow, I'll saddle her up."

He looked at the small, fuzzy donkey. He couldn't quite imagine Betty with a saddle. "*Really?*" When Jo nodded, he added, "I...I look forward to seeing that."

She grinned. "Everyone does. Come on." Jo leaned back and stood, stretching her back. Which thrust out her chest.

From his angle, the view was amazing. His body responded with enthusiasm. Damn. This was going to make standing up even more difficult. "Where are we going?" It'd be nice if hot tubs or beds were the answer but somehow he knew it wouldn't be.

He managed to get to his feet, then leaned back down to grab his saddle. He'd spent close to an hour and a half getting the damned thing polished to a high shine.

"Leave it," Jo instructed.

"But I *cleaned* it."

"Leave it," she repeated in that no-nonsense tone. Then she began to walk to the gate.

"Better be a damn good reward," he muttered as he left all his hard work behind. He had a bad feeling about this.

Jo held the gate open for him, which meant it wasn't his fault that he had to pass close enough to her that he could count the freckles on her nose. She swung the gate behind him, but didn't step away. He didn't either. Close enough to touch, they both leaned against the now-closed gate. "Explain to me why we left the saddles in there? You know Sun is probably going to destroy them. Do you have any idea how much they cost?"

"You're already showing him you're not going to shoot him with a tranq gun or do anything else scary. Now you're going to show him that saddles and bridles are also not scary."

"But—"

"Shh." She had her eyes trained on the horse. "Just watch."

*A damn good reward*, he thought as he tried to rein in his irritation.

He watched. Trotting in looping circles, Sun looked at them, at the saddles and then at the bucket where Phillip had left the carrots.

Suddenly, Jo's fingers closed around his. "Be still," she said in that low voice again.

He hadn't realized he was moving, but did it matter? No, not with her fingers curling around his. Her touch did things to him—things that had nothing to do with being still and had everything to do with wanting to keep on moving—moving his lips over her fingers, her neck, her lips, his body moving over hers, with hers.

She must have felt it, too, because she turned her head toward him and favored him with one of those half-smiles.

He turned his hand over without letting go of her so they were palm-to-palm. He interlaced their fingers without looking away from Sun. After a moment, her hand relaxed into his.

It took everything he had to *not* lift her hand and press it to his lips, but he didn't. She'd made the first move and he'd countered with his own. Now it was her turn. If he skipped a turn, she might stop playing the game.

Then her fingers tightened on his. No mistaking it. They were holding hands in a way that had only the smallest of connections to what was happening in the paddock.

Not that the paddock wasn't interesting. Sun's loops were getting tighter and slower as he closed in on the bucket and carrots. Just when Phillip thought he would eat them, Sun spun and made straight for the saddles.

*Oh, no.* The horse hit the saddles with everything he had—and, considering he hadn't been bucking for hours on end, that was a lot. Phillip winced as Sun ground the saddles into the dirt.

The whole thing took less than five minutes. Betty stood off to the side, watching with an air of boredom. Then, head held high, Sun pranced over to the bucket and ate his carrots as if he'd planned it like that from the beginning.

"Some reward," Phillip muttered. He'd been upset about Sun before, but this was the first time he was out-and-out furious with the beast. That was an expensive saddle—and the one she'd been cleaning wasn't cheap, either. If his brother Chadwick knew that the horse trainer was letting Sun destroy several thousands of dollars of tack, he'd have her thrown off the premises. And possibly him, too.

"Stupid horse."

"Smart horse." Jo squeezed his hand, but that smile? That was for the horse.

"Why are you smiling? He ruined those saddles. *And* ate my carrots."

She notched an eyebrow as she cast him a sideways glance. The sudden burst of realization made him feel as if he'd been conned. "You *knew* he was going to do that?"

"Everyone's got to start somewhere," she replied, sounding lighthearted.

All that work for nothing. "Next time, he doesn't get carrots until he can behave himself." Even as he said the words, he knew they sounded ridiculous. Was he talking about a horse or a toddler? He glared at his multi-million dollar animal. "No rewards for that kind of attitude and that's final."

"Ah." Her voice—soft and, if he wasn't mistaken, nervous—snapped his attention back to where they were still palm-to-palm.

He had something coming to him, all the more so because she'd made him do all that work. He stroked his thumb along the length of her finger. He felt a light tremor, but she didn't pull away.

"Do I get my reward now? That saddle was very clean, right before it wasn't."

She tilted her head away, as if she were debating the merits of his argument. But he couldn't miss the way her lips were quirked into a barely contained smile.

"And I didn't even kill that horse when he trashed my tack," he reminded her as he leaned in.

She didn't lean away. "True." Her voice took on a sultry note, one that invited much more than holding hands. The pupils of her eyes widened; her gaze darted down to his lips. "Is this flirting?"

She was expecting him to kiss her, but something told him not to. Not yet. The longer he defied her expectations of him, the better the odds he'd wake up with her in his bed.

"It might be." He held her hand to his lips. A simple touch, skin against skin. Even though it about killed him not to take everything she was offering, he didn't.

Without breaking the contact between them, he raised his eyes to see Jo looking at him, her eyes wide with surprise and—he hoped—desire.

Raw need pumped through his blood. He almost threw his plans out the window and swept her into his arms. She was his, waiting for him to make his move....

She dropped her gaze. "What did you want for your reward?" The question could have been coy, but there was something else in her expression.

"All I wanted," he replied, not taking his eyes off her face, "was to see that beautiful blush on you."

Of course, that wasn't all he wanted. But it'd do for now. Then, to prove his point, he let her go and stepped back.

"That's...all?" The confusion that registered on her face was so worth it.

Clearly, not a lot of people had told her she was beautiful. What a crying shame. She had a striking look that was all her own. If that wasn't beautiful, he didn't know what was.

"Well..." He looked as innocent as he could. "I was supposed to clean a saddle. The saddle is, at this moment, quite dirty so I didn't really complete my task."

She blinked, managing to pull off coy in a cowboy hat. "Funny thing about that."

"What's funny?"

It shouldn't be right to find that little look of victory—one corner of her mouth quirked up into a smile, one eyebrow raised in challenge—so damned sexy, but he did. "Tomorrow morning—you, me and some saddles."

Phillip tried to stifle a groan, but he didn't manage it. "No."

"Yes." She paused, suddenly looking unsure of herself. "If you do a good job..."

He grinned on the inside but he kept his face calm. Oh, yeah—he had her right where he wanted her.

Almost, anyway.

Behind them, someone cleared his throat. Jo stiffened, a hard look wiping away anything sultry about her. She turned away and focused on Sun.

Phillip looked past her to see Richard standing a few feet away, hat in hands and an odd look on his face.

Damn. How long had he been standing there? Had he seen Phillip kiss her hand? It'd been easy to pretend that he and Jo were alone on the farm. The other hands steered well clear of her—probably because she'd told them to—and everyone more or less left him alone. The farm operated well enough without him.

But he and Jo weren't alone.

"I've got a farm to run," he said in a voice that was pitched just loud enough for Richard to hear. "I'll stop by later to see how you're getting on with Sun."

She nodded, looking as uninterested as physically possible.

She could hide the truth from Richard, but not from him.

# Eight

Jo sat at the dinette table in her trailer that night, not seeing her email. She was supposed to be replying to horse owners who were looking for a miracle, but that's not what she was doing.

Phillip Beaumont had kissed her hand. And nothing more.

If that were her only problem, it would have been enough. But it wasn't. She wasn't sure how much Richard had seen.

For the first time in a very long time, Jo was...unsure of herself. One man who, by all accounts, was a spoiled party boy with more money than sense and she had apparently lost her damned mind.

She did not fool around with clients. Under any circumstances. Beyond being a temptation back into her old ways, it was bad for business. If word got around that she was open to affairs, people might stop hiring her.

What a mess. If flirting with Phillip Beaumont was

causing such a problem for her, why on God's green Earth was she letting it go on?

Because she'd seen the look on his face when she'd hinted that if he cleaned another saddle tomorrow morning, he'd get another reward.

She should have jerked her hand out of his when he kissed it. Hell, she shouldn't have touched him at all. She should have followed her own rules—rules she had in place for a variety of exceptionally good reasons—and steered well clear of Phillip Beaumont and his reputation.

If she didn't feel such a duty to Sun, she'd pack up and drive off to another, less tempting job tomorrow. Yes, it'd be a blow to her reputation to lose Beaumont Farms as a reference, but three other trainers had already failed. Bailing on this job wouldn't end her aspirations, not like having an affair with Phillip could.

But she wouldn't abandon the horse, not when they were making such progress. Richard had told her that if she couldn't save the horse, he'd have to be put down. True, Sun might have calmed to the point where another trainer could come in and finish the job, but she didn't know if she wanted to hope for the best and never look back. That's what the old her would have done. That's not what the woman she was now did.

Her only consolation was that she had rediscovered her restraint this afternoon when Phillip had driven past the paddock with a wagon full of hay to ask if she wanted to see his Thoroughbreds. Then he'd held the reins out to her.

She'd passed on his offer, saying she needed to keep an eye on Sun.

This would be so much easier if Phillip were a jerk. Some of the men—and women—who'd hired her were, in fact, total jerks. That's why she had that upfront policy of not hooking up or dating. That's why she kept her trailer door locked.

But Phillip wasn't a jerk. At least, not once he'd sobered up.

He cleaned tack because she asked him to. He tried to be still because it was important to Sun, even if he didn't totally succeed. He let her drive his Percheron team. Hell, he brought her coffee.

That wasn't jerkiness. That was thoughtfulness.

She had no idea how to respond to it.

Crap, she was in so much trouble.

This was a sign of how far she'd come. The old Jo would have embraced the trouble she was in and gone looking for more. She shouldn't beat herself up for encouraging Phillip, not really. She should be proud of the fact that she'd resisted his considerable charms and good looks thus far.

Now she just had to keep doing that.

In the midst of losing to herself in a debate, she heard something that sounded suspiciously like shouting. Loud, but muffled, shouting.

She scowled at the clock. That wasn't right. It was close to ten in the evening. The hired hands had all gone home before five. The whole farm was usually quiet at night, with the exception of the guards who checked the barns every other hour.

Not this evening. The shouting was louder now. She could make out two different voices.

*Betty*, she thought in a panic. The weather was supposed to be clear, so Jo had left the little donkey out in the pasture across the drive from Sun's paddock.

Moving fast, she slipped her jeans back on and shoved her feet into her boots. Thankfully, she hadn't taken her shirt off yet, so she didn't have to mess with the buttons. She left the trailer and grabbed her pistol from the glove box, tucking it into the back of her waistband. If someone was trying to take Betty or Sun or any other horse on this property, she wanted to catch them in the act. Then she could hold them until the guards came back around. She'd interrupted attempted robberies before. She knew how to handle her weapon.

She slipped along the side of her trailer and peeked out. A pair of headlights pointed into Sun's paddock and the horse was going nuts.

Two men were arguing in front of the headlights. She realized with a start that one of the men was Phillip. The other was slightly taller, slightly broader and had a slightly deeper voice but otherwise, he could have been Phillip's twin.

Chadwick Beaumont? Who else could it be?

Keeping to the shadows, she edged closer. They weren't trying to be quiet but she was having trouble making out what they were arguing about.

"...be insane!" Phillip yelled as he paced away then spun back to face his brother.

"The company—and, I might add, the family—cannot afford to keep standing idle while you throw good money after bad and you know it." Chadwick's voice was level, bordering on cruel. This was not a man who could be easily moved.

Phillip was anything but level. "The Percherons are not throwing money away," he shouted, flinging his hands around as if he were throwing money around. "They're our brand name!"

"Are they?" Chadwick sneered. "I thought *you* were our brand name. The face of Beaumont Beer. God knows you stick that face out enough."

Behind them, Sun made a noise that was closer to a scream than a whinny. Jo winced. How long would it take for the horse to calm down after this?

But the men didn't notice the horse. They were too lost in their argument.

Phillip threw up his hands. "Do you know what it'll do

to our public goodwill if we get rid of the Percherons? Do you have *any* idea?"

"This farm costs millions of dollars to operate," Chadwick countered so smoothly that Jo didn't have any doubt he'd anticipated this defense. "And all your pet projects cost several million more." At this, he threw a glance toward Sun, who was flat-out racing, just like he'd been the day Jo had shown up. The way Chadwick looked at the horse made Jo think that, if he'd been in charge, he would have let Richard put the animal down without hesitation. "To say nothing of all your little 'escapades.'"

As he paced, Phillip groaned. It was the sort of noise a man might make if he'd been punched in the kidneys. "Do you understand nothing about marketing? For God's sake, Chadwick—even Matthew—could explain how this works! People love the Percherons. *Love* them. And you want to just throw that all away?"

"Love," Chadwick intoned, "doesn't run a company."

Phillip whipped back to his brother, his fists balled. Jo flinched. If they started to brawl, she'd have to break them up. "You got that right, you heartless bastard. Can your bean-counting brain wrap itself around the damage you'll cost us with consumers? The Percherons are a part of this company, Chadwick. You can't sell them off any more than you can sell the company."

The silence that fell between the two men was so cold that Jo shivered.

"I already sold the company."

Jo's mouth dropped open, just as Phillip's had. "You… *what?*" Jo wasn't sure she'd ever heard Phillip sound so wounded. She couldn't blame him.

"I'm not going to work myself into an early grave so that I can pay for your failed horses or Frances's failed art or even Byron's failed romances," Chadwick said in a voice as hard as iron. "I've worked for ten years to keep the Beaumont family going and I'm sick of it. AllBev made an offer. The board accepted it. It's *done*. We'll announce when the lawyers give us the go-ahead."

Phillip gaped at him. "But…you…Dad…the company!"

"Hardwick Beaumont is dead, Phillip. He's been dead for years. I don't have to prove myself to him anymore and neither do you." Something in Chadwick's tone changed. For a moment, he sounded…kind. It was at such odds with the hard man she'd been listening to that Jo had to shake her head to make sure the same person was speaking. "I'm getting married."

"You're *what*? Aren't you already married?"

"My ex-wife is now just that—my ex. I'm starting over, Phillip. I'm going to be happy. You should do the same. Figure out who you are if you aren't Hardwick's second son."

Phillip's mouth open, closed, then opened again. "You can't sell the farm. You can't, Chadwick. Please. I need this place. I need the horses. Without them…"

Chadwick was unmoved. Anything that might have been understanding or brotherly was gone. "The new owners of the Brewery have no desire to take on the sinking money pit that is this farm. They do not want the Percherons and I can't afford them. I can't afford *you*."

Jo must have gasped or stepped on a twig or something because suddenly both men spun.

"Who's there?" they demanded in unison.

She stepped into the edge of the light. "It's me. Jo."

Phillip gave her something that might have been a smile. Chadwick only glared. "Who?" He turned his attention to Phillip. "Who's she?"

Phillip's shoulders slumped in defeat. "Jo Spears. The horse trainer who's saving Sun."

Jo nodded her head in appreciation. He'd gotten the saving part right.

Chadwick was not impressed. "Now you're keeping women on the farm?" He made a noise of disgust. "And how much is this costing?"

Jo bristled. Clearly, Chadwick Beaumont did not have his brother's way with words *or* women.

When Phillip didn't answer, Chadwick shook his head in disgust. He said, "I only came out here to warn you because we're family. If I were you, I'd start getting rid of the *excess*—" he looked at Sun, then at Jo "—as soon as possible on your own terms. Save yourself the embarrassment of a public auction." He walked back to his car. "If you don't, I will."

Then Chadwick Beaumont slammed the door shut, put the shiny little sports car in reverse, and peeled out.

Phillip dropped his head.

And stood absolutely still.

Chadwick was going to sell the horses. All of them. Not just Sun or the Appaloosas or even the Thoroughbreds, but *all* of them. The Beaumont Percherons—a self-sustaining herd of about a hundred horses that went back a hundred and twenty-three years—would be gone. The farm would be gone. The farmhouse that his great-grandfather had built as a refuge from the rest of the world—gone. And what would Phillip have once the horses and the farm were gone?

Nothing. Not a damned thing.

God, he needed a drink.

Sun made that unholy noise again, but Phillip couldn't even look. It was so tempting to blame Sun for this. The horse had cost seven million dollars. He'd never seen his brother so mad as when Phillip had told Chadwick about the horse. If only Sun hadn't cost so much....

But that was a cop-out and he knew it. Phillip was the one who'd bought the horse. And all the other horses. And the tack, the wagons, the carriages. He was the one who'd hired the farm hands. And Jo.

*Jo.*

Almost as if he'd called her, she came to stand next to him. Her hand slipped into his and her fingers intertwined with his. She felt…smaller than she had this afternoon.

He felt smaller.

"Come on," she said in that low voice that brooked no arguments. She gave his hand a gentle tug and he stumbled after her.

She led him to her trailer. Any other time, Phillip would have been excited about this development. But he couldn't even think about sex right now. Not when he was on the verge of losing everything he'd worked for.

She basically pulled him up the narrow trailer steps and then pushed him toward a small dinette table. "Have a seat."

He sat. Heavily. *Jesus.* He knew that the company was in trouble. But he had no idea that Chadwick would do this. That he'd even been considering selling the Brewery, much less the farm. He'd thought…Chadwick would win. That's what Chadwick did. He'd fight off the acquisition and save the company and everything would continue on as it had before.

But Chadwick hadn't. Wouldn't. He was going to get rid of the farm. Of Phillip.

This was…this was his home. Not the Beaumont family mansion, not the apartment in the city. The farm was where he'd always felt the most normal. *Been* the most normal. He'd been able to do something that had made him proud. Had made his father proud of him. Hardwick Beaumont had never had a second look for his second son out in the real world. But here, talking horses, his father had noticed him. Told him he'd done a good job. Been so proud of him.

And now it was going to be taken away from him.

Jo made some noise. Phillip looked up to see her filling an electric kettle, a small handgun set on the counter next to her. "What?"

"Making tea," she said in that same low and calming and ridiculously self-assured voice—the one she used when she was working with Sun.

He laughed, even though there was nothing funny about tea. "Got any whiskey to go with that? I could use a drink."

She paused while reaching into a cabinet. The pause lasted only a moment, but he felt the disapproval anyway.

He didn't care. He needed a drink. Several drinks. Maybe a fifth of drinks. He couldn't deal with losing the farm. With his horses. With Sun. Everything.

"I don't have any whiskey."

"I'll settle for vodka."

"I don't have anything but tea and a couple of cans of soda."

He laughed again. The universe seemed hell-bent on torturing him.

The kettle whistled—a noise that seemed to drive straight into his temple. Everything was too much right now—too much noise, too much light. Too much Jo sliding into the seat opposite him, looking at him with those big, pretty eyes of hers. His hands started to shake.

"Here." She slid a steaming mug toward him.

He looked at the tea. Insult to injury, that's what this was. It wasn't enough that he was about to lose everything he held dear. He had to have a horse trainer rub his nose in it.

The anger that peaked above the despair felt good. Well, not good—but better than the horrible darkness that was trying to swallow him inside out. "I've got whiskey at the house, you know. You're not stopping me from drinking."

She held her mug in her hands and blew on the tea, her

gaze never leaving his face. "No," she agreed, sounding too damned even, "I'm not."

"And I'm not some damned horse, either, so stop doing that whole calm-and-still bullshit," he snapped.

If she was offended, she didn't show it. Instead, she sipped the tea. "Does that help?"

"Jesus, you're doing it again. Does *what* help?"

"The blackout. Does that help?"

"It's a hell of a lot better than *this*." Logically, he knew he wasn't mad at her. She hadn't done anything but the job he'd hired her for.

But his world was ending and Chadwick was gone. Someone had to pay. And Jo was here.

"Don't you ever get tired of it?"

"You think you know me?" he said. Except it came out louder than he meant it to. "You don't know anything about me, so you can stop acting superior. You have no idea what my life is like."

"Any more than you have an idea of mine?"

He glared at her. "Fine. Just get it off your chest. Go ahead and tell me that I'm throwing my life away one drink at a time and alcohol never solved anything and blah, blah, blah."

She shrugged.

"I can stop whenever I want," he snapped.

"You just don't want to."

"I *want* a damn drink." Water pricked at his eyes. "You wouldn't understand."

"Yes," she said and this time he heard something different in her voice. "I would."

He looked up at her. She met his gaze without blinking and without deflecting. Her nose, he noticed again. It'd been broken. Without the shadows cast by her hat, it was easier to see the bump on the bridge that didn't match the rest of her.

She was beautiful. If she wasn't going to get him some whiskey, she could still sleep with him. Sex was always fine with him. He'd been chasing her for a week now with nothing more than a kiss on the hand to show for it. He could lose himself in this woman and it might make him feel better. At least for a little while.

She turned her head in one direction, then the other, giving him a better look at her nose. "I stopped."

The compliment he'd loaded up came to a screeching halt. "Stopped what?"

She set her mug down and slid out of her seat. "There was never a good reason. My parents are normal, happily married. No abuse, no alcoholism. I wasn't shy or awkward or even that rebellious." She stood and undid the top button on her shirt.

As her fingers undid the second button, his pulse began to pound. What the hell? He hadn't even busted out the compliment and she was undressing? All his hard work was paying off. He was about to get lucky. Thank God. Then he wouldn't have to think.

Except…this wasn't right. First off, there was far too much talking. But beyond that, Jo—just stripping? Jesus, he must be so messed up right now, because this wasn't how he wanted her. He didn't want her to give it up just to make him feel better. He wanted her to want him as much as he wanted her.

He didn't get the chance to tell her to wait. She went on, "Dad's Lakota, so I had my fair share of people who called me a half-breed, but doesn't everyone get teased for something?" Another button popped open.

Why was she telling him this? Even if she was trying to seduce him, this didn't seem like the proper way to go about it. But he could just see the swell of her breasts peek over the top of the shirt.

She undid another button. Unlike her nose, her breasts

were perfect. He opened his mouth to tell her just that, to try and get this seduction back on track, but he didn't get any further.

"I had my first drink in seventh grade at a Fourth of July party. A wine cooler I snagged. I opened it up and poured it into a cup and told everyone it was pink lemonade. It was good. I liked it. So I had another. And another."

She undid the last button and stood there. The curves of her breasts were tantalizingly at eye level, but she didn't move toward him, didn't shimmy or shake or anything a normal woman might have done. He leaned forward. If he could touch her, fill his hands with her soft skin and softer body, they could get to the part where they were both naked and he wasn't thinking about anything but sex. About her. That's what he wanted, wasn't it?

She turned her back to him. "By the time I was in high school, I was the resident party girl. I don't know how I graduated and I don't know how I didn't get pregnant. I have no idea how I got into college, but I did. I don't know if I ever went to a class sober. I don't remember going to that many classes."

The shirt began to slide down.

Phillip began to sweat. He tried to focus on what she was saying and not the body she was unwrapping for him, but it was a damned hard thing to attempt—a fact that was directly connected with other damned hard things happening to him right now.

"I'd wake up and not know where I was, who I was with. College guys, older guys—men I didn't know. I couldn't remember meeting them or going home with them." She shrugged, a bare shoulder going up and down. The movement pushed the shirt down even farther. "Couldn't remember the sex—couldn't remember if I wanted it or not."

Phillip tensed, torn between despair, desire and sheer confusion. Confusion won. Instead of a swath of smooth skin, Jo was revealing a back covered in puckers and ripples.

"I'd stumble back to my room and scan my phone for pictures or messages. For the memories, I told myself, but there were things I'd done..." She paused, but it was only the barest hint of emotion. "Facing them—no. It was easier to find another party and tell myself I was having a good time than it was to accept what I'd done. What I'd become."

The shirt fell off her right arm, revealing the true extent of the damage. Most of her back was scarred—horrible marks that went below the waistband of her pants. She tilted her head to the left and lifted her shoulder-length hair. Even her hairline was messed up—rough and uneven where the scars stole farther up. "The only reason I know his name is because my granny saved the article. Tony Holmes. He ran a red light, got T-boned so hard by a big SUV that it flipped the car. He wasn't buckled in. I was."

She tilted her body so he could see the contours of her back. Hidden among the mass of twisted skin were other scars—long, neat ones that looked surgical. "The car caught fire, but they got me out in time."

"Tony?"

For the first time in this dry recitation of facts, she seemed to feel something. "He wouldn't have felt the flames anyway."

Jesus. His stomach turned. This wasn't some crazy, "let's get in touch with our feelings" kind of talk. This was serious—life and death.

He didn't want to believe her—he'd never wanted to believe anything less in his life—but there was no arguing with the scars.

*It could have been me*, he thought. The realization made him dizzy. It *could* have been him—the wild party he didn't remember, the strange person buckled in next to him that he wouldn't have remembered, either. There was only one reason something like that hadn't happened. He wished to God that reason was because he was a responsible man.

But it wasn't. No, Ortiz—his driver—was the reason. His brothers Chadwick and Matthew had decreed that Phillip would have a driver whenever he was at a company-sponsored event. It was company policy.

A company policy that no one else in the company had to follow.

"My back was broken in two places. I shouldn't be able to walk. I shouldn't even be alive." She turned to the side to grab the shirt from where it hung off her left arm. Phillip caught a glimpse of her breast, full and heavy and his dick responded to the sight of her bare breast before she got ahold of her shirt and snapped the buttons back together.

But all he felt was cold and shaky. His head was pounding as if he had a hangover. He still wanted a drink. He dug the heels of his hands into his eyes, trying to block out the images she'd put there on purpose—images of her waking up with strangers, never really knowing what had happened. Of her trapped in a burning car next to a dead man. "I'm not like that."

"Because you don't drive?"

He nodded. He'd never been with anyone who'd died after a good party. He never did anything with anyone who didn't want it.

He felt the dinette shift as she sat back down at the table. It'd be safe to look at her. But he couldn't. He couldn't move.

"Between the back surgeries and the burn care, I was in traction in the hospital for months," she went on, as if he needed more torture. "It was a year before I could move without pain. And because I *am* an alcoholic, I never even got the good painkillers. I had to feel it all. Everything I'd done. Everything I was. I couldn't hide from it."

"How do you stand it?" Why did he have to sound as

though she was twisting the knife in his gut a quarter-turn at a time?

Because that's what she was doing. Twisting.

Except she wasn't, not really. More like she was holding up a mirror so he could see the knife he was twisting himself.

"I stopped. Stopped drinking, stopped sleeping around, stopped fighting it."

"What if…" He swallowed. *What if he couldn't stop*?

He heard the seat rustle as she leaned back. "Did you spike your coffee this morning?"

"No." But he was really wishing he had. Anything to numb the pain.

"What about yesterday?"

He shook his head. He'd thought he felt hopeless after Chadwick had driven off. But now?

He didn't know if he was coming or going.

"It's now…10:53. Another hour and seven minutes and you'll have made it through two days." She had the nerve to sound optimistic about this fact. "That's as good a place to start as any."

"Is this the part where I'm supposed to say 'One day at a time' and we sing 'Kumbaya' and then we talk about steps?"

"Nope."

"Good. Because I don't want to hear it."

"Our kind never does."

"We are not the same kind, Jo." But even as he said it, he knew it was a lie. The only difference was that she'd stopped and he hadn't.

"No," she agreed. "I have the scars to prove it."

"Does it…does it still hurt?" He didn't know if he was asking about the scars on her back or the other kind of scars.

"Not really. I have Betty now. She helps. It's only when…"

Something in her voice—something longing and wistful—made him pull his hands away from his face.

Jo was looking at him. That wasn't a surprise. The trailer was small and they were talking. But it was *how* she was looking at him. Gone was the unnatural calm.

Sitting across from him was a woman who wanted something that she would never allow herself to have.

Him.

She looked away first. "He wants you to give up," she told him as she studied the bottom of her mug.

Phillip was still trying to figure out that look, so her words took him completely off guard. "What?"

"Your brother. He expects you to run off and get so drunk that he can do whatever he wants with *your* farm and *your* animals and you won't be able to put up a fight." When she looked back up again, whatever longing he'd seen in her eyes was gone.

"What should I do?"

"That's not my place." She gave him a tight smile. "You have to decide for yourself. Fight or give up, it doesn't matter to me."

"It doesn't?" It hurt to hear that, but he wasn't sure why. "Not even a little?"

She gave him a long look. He got the feeling she wanted to say something else, but she didn't.

Finally, she said, "Can you live with yourself if you let the farm go without a fight?"

Phillip dropped his head into his hands again. This was the only place he'd ever been happy—where he was still happy, even though his father was dead and gone.

He didn't know who he was without the farm to come back to. The Phillip Beaumont that put on suits and went to parties—he didn't remember half of what that Phillip did.

He'd been telling himself that not remembering was the sign of a good time for how long? Years.

Decades.

Even if he fought for the farm, as she said, he wasn't sure he could live with himself.

"I need this place."

"Then fight for it."

He nodded, letting the words roll around in his head. They bounced off memories of Dad lifting him onto the back of a Percheron named Sally and leading him down the drive. Of piping up as Dad and his trainer argued over a Thoroughbred to say that Daddy should buy the horse because he ran fast—and having Dad pat him on the head with a smile as he said, "My Phillip's got a good head for horses."

Memories of buying his first Thoroughbred and watching it win its first race in the owner's box with Dad.

Of buying the Appaloosas over Dad's objections, then overhearing Dad tell the farm manager that the horses were better than he expected, but he should have known because Phillip always did have a good head for horses.

Of harnessing up the Percheron team himself for Dad's funeral and driving the team of ten in the procession over the objections of every single member of his family because that was how he chose to honor his father.

When he wasn't on the farm…he had nothing. Vague snippets of dancing and drinking and having sex with nameless, faceless women. Headaches and blackouts and checking his phone in a panic the next morning to see what he'd done.

"If I go back to the house, I'll get the whiskey."

Just saying it out loud was an admission of failure. It was also the truth. He didn't know which was worse.

He heard Jo take a deep breath. "If I make up a bed for

you, you understand that's not an invitation?" She exhaled. "It's not that I'm not…" her voice trailed off.

*Interested.*

She was interested. Here, in the safety of her trailer, with all their cards on the table, she wasn't going to hide it. "It has to be this way," she went on, sounding as hopeless as he'd ever heard her. "I gave up men when I gave up drinking."

He nodded even though he couldn't remember spending the night with a woman that didn't involve sex. "You'd let me stay? Why?"

The smile she gave him was sadder than anything he'd ever seen on her face. "Because," she said, leaning forward and placing her hand on top of his. "No one's past saving. Not even you."

But as quick as she'd touched him, she pulled away and was standing up. "I'll be right back."

He blinked up at her. "Where are you going?"

Jo stood. He didn't miss that she grabbed the gun off the counter and shoved it into her waistband. "I need to check on Sun and get Betty. She's good for nights like this."

He managed a small smile. "I'll be here."

No one was past saving. Not even him.

He didn't know if he should laugh or cry at that.

Jo stopped halfway down the steps and shot him that side-eye look. "Good," was all she said.

Then she was out the door.

# Nine

Jo did not sleep.

She lay in her bed, listening to the sounds of Phillip also not sleeping. She could tell he wasn't sleeping by the way the trailer creaked with every toss and turn and also by the way that Betty would occasionally shake her head and exhale heavily.

Even without Betty's added exasperation, Jo would have been aware of every single one of Phillip's movements. She hadn't been this close to a man in, well…since before the accident.

She felt as if she'd walked into a bar and bellied up to the counter, only to nurse a Sprite. How was she supposed to make it through the night without falling back into her old ways?

Around two in the morning, Phillip shifted again. That noise was followed by the distinctive sound of the floors squeaking as he walked. Jo tensed. It wasn't a huge trailer. Where was he going?

Not here. Not to her. If he opened the sliding door and told her he couldn't get through the night and he needed her, she didn't think she'd be strong enough to direct him back to the dinette table that had converted into a too-small bed.

The footsteps stopped in the middle of the trailer, then she heard the fridge open up. Then the fridge door shut and his steps went back to the front of the trailer. She heard the cushions sag as he sat, then heard Betty shake her head.

She could see him sitting there, rubbing Betty's ears as he struggled. How many nights had she done the same thing?

She remembered when she'd finally been cleared to drive by herself. She'd made up some excuse to run to the grocery store, only to have her dad say, "Don't forget, Joey." Her mom had met her at the front door, car keys in hand. But instead of stopping her or announcing she was coming along, Mom had just wrapped Jo in a hug and said, "Don't forget, sweetie."

They hadn't stopped her. If they had, who knows— she might have tried harder to go around them. But they didn't. They made it clear it was her choice and hers alone.

So she'd stood there in the booze aisle at the convenience store and stared at the bottles of amber liquid. It would have been so easy to buy one can, slam it in the car and throw the can away. No one would have known.

Except…she would have known.

Jo had gone home empty-handed to find her granny, Lina, sitting on the front porch with a twenty-pound donkey on her lap. Lina had pulled Jo into a strong hug, taken a deep breath—to check for the smell of booze, no doubt— and asked, "Did you remember what you were looking for?"

"Yeah." She'd expected a greater sense of accomplishment. She'd stopped. She'd walked away. She was a stronger, better person now.

But all she'd felt was drained. How was she going to make the same choice every day for the rest of her life? She didn't think she could do it.

"This here is Itty Bitty Betty," Lina had said, plopping the donkey into Jo's lap. "She needs someone to look after her."

Jo sighed, doing some tossing and turning of her own. Betty was mellower now, less prone to taking corners too fast and crashing into walls. But she still had the same soft ears, the same understanding eyes. She kept Jo grounded.

Except that Betty was out there with Phillip—and Phillip was still not sleeping. Jo couldn't sleep if he didn't sleep.

She could open up the sliding screen that separated her bedroom from the rest of the camper and sit with him. She could wrap her hand around his and then he'd be still.

But she didn't. She didn't fix people and she couldn't save them and she sure as hell wasn't going to put herself in a position where she might kiss him because if she kissed him, she wasn't sure she could stop at just one kiss. She'd never been able to stop at just one.

And if she didn't stop at one kiss, what was to say she'd be able to stop at a couple of kisses? Or that she'd not run her hands over his body? That she wouldn't lean into his groan and tilt her head back, encouraging him to kiss her on that spot where her neck met her shoulders?

She kept the door firmly shut. And did not sleep.

At six, she heard him get up again. Groggy from lack of sleep, she wondered if she should make coffee for him. But before she could get her feet on the floor, the door opened and shut and the trailer was still.

Phillip was gone.

Somehow, she knew she'd be cleaning tack alone today.

* * *

Phillip was waiting at the door when Matthew drove up. "Took you long enough."

Matthew gave him a tired smile. "Something came up at work. I need a drink."

"Uh…"

Matthew turned. "Problem?"

"I don't have any alcohol in the house."

Matthew studied him, taking in everything from the boots to the jeans before finally staring him in the eye. "Either you drank everything you already had or…"

It wasn't the observation that hurt so much as the fact that it could have been true. "I had Richard come get all my booze and give it to the hands."

"You did?"

Phillip nodded. "I, uh, I'm trying to drink less. Or not at all."

"Is that so." It wasn't a question.

"Yeah…." Although a drink would be nice right now. When had it gotten so hard to talk to his brother? "A friend helped me realize if I wanted to keep the farm, I had to be sober to do it."

Matthew rubbed his eyes. "And when did this start?"

"Yesterday." Phillip swallowed.

"Good start." He almost sounded sincere. "I can't wait to meet this 'friend' of yours."

"She's down at the barn. With Sun."

Matthew rubbed his temples. "The seven-million dollar horse?"

"Yes."

There was a long pause. Phillip's stomach caved in. This was too much—he couldn't deal. What the hell had he been thinking? He couldn't even handle Matthew. He had to have been out of his mind to think he could confront Chadwick.

*"She?"*

Phillip nodded.

"You're going to screw up Chadwick's deal because you're trying to get *laid?*"

"I'm trying to save my farm," Phillip shot back. "Besides, correct me if I'm wrong, but aren't you about to lose your job if his deal goes through? I can't imagine that new owners would want a Beaumont vice president of whatever it is you do."

"Public relations," Matthew snapped, glaring at Phillip. "Which means I get to manage you whenever you go off the rails. Lucky freaking *me*."

"I didn't go off the rails," Phillip promised. "Chadwick showed up here and said he was going to sell all my horses, the whole farm—what was I supposed to do? Go drink myself into oblivion? This is my life, Matthew. This is…" His voice caught. "This is the only part of me that's *real*. And you know it. I can't let it go."

"You're serious, aren't you?"

"Of course I'm serious. I need your help. Chadwick won't listen to me. I doubt he'll even listen to a poll with the tens of thousands of votes to keep the Percherons. You're the only one of us he trusts."

That was the right thing to say. Sure, Matthew raised an eyebrow as if he was certain Phillip were feeding him a line of bull, but the pissed-off look softened. "You really don't have anything to drink in the house?"

"I had my cleaning service go through my apartment, too."

Matthew nodded. "Okay. Tell me your plan. You do have one, right?"

Phillip took a deep breath. "I want to buy the farm from the company."

The hours he'd had to wait for Matthew had been filled

with frantic planning. Because if the farm stayed with the company, he'd still lose it. That was unacceptable.

But if he bought the farm, well, he could *lease* the Percherons back to the Brewery. The company would have all the marketing benefits of the Percheron team without having to carry the expense of the farm on the balance sheet.

It could work. Except for two little details. Matthew was staring at him, mouth open. Finally, he got himself under control. "Do you know how much that will cost? The land alone is probably worth five, ten million dollars."

"Eight. Eight million for three hundred acres, seven barns, twelve outbuildings and one house."

Matthew eyed him suspiciously. "And the horses?"

"About fifteen to twenty thousand a piece, just for the Percherons. I've got a hundred, so that's another one to two million. The total value of all the horses on the farm, including Kandar's Golden Sun and the Thoroughbreds, is between fifteen and twenty million. The hitches, tractors and other things are maybe another million, plus the ongoing cost of hired help, grain, and other overhead."

Phillip cleared his throat. So it wasn't such a little detail. "To buy the whole thing outright would be thirty million. To buy it piecemeal at auction might push it as high as fifty million. People would want a part of the Beaumont name."

For once in his life, Matthew did not have a snarky comeback to that. He shook his head before finally speaking. "You've done your homework. That worries me."

A sense of pride warmed the cockles of Phillip's heart. He'd managed to impress his younger brother. "The farm is mostly self-sustaining," he went on. "I sell a lot of horses. If I leased the Percherons back to the company, maybe started charging a nominal fee for parade appearances, that'd cover a lot of the cost. And Sun...well, the stud fees alone are going to earn back his purchase price."

That was all true. With some judicious management

and perhaps selling off some additional horses, the farm could break even.

Which still left one little problem.

"Do you have thirty million?" Matthew asked.

"Not exactly. I hoped Chadwick might cut me a deal, seeing as we're family."

Matthew gave him a look that didn't put much stock in brotherly love. "How much do you have?"

That little sticking point was stuck all right—in Phillip's throat. "I'd sell the apartment in the city and live here full time. Downsize my wardrobe, cars—everything. That'd bring in a million, maybe two."

"How much," Matthew said, carefully enunciating each word, "do you have?"

"Plus, I'd get my share of the company sale, right? I have executive benefits. How much is that worth?"

Matthew gave him a look better suited to their father. "You *might* get fifteen million. That's sixteen, seventeen million tops. I don't know if 'brotherly love' would cover the other twelve."

Phillip forced himself to breathe as Matthew scowled. "It's the best I can do."

"That's it?" Matthew said it in the kind of dismissive tone that made it sound as if they were talking about hundreds, not millions. "That's all you've got? You don't have any other assets? Stocks?"

Phillip shook his head.

"Property?" When Phillip shook his head again, Matthew groaned. "Nothing?"

"I drank it all."

His brother rubbed his temples again, as if that would provide the solution. "You realize Chadwick's still bitter about the seven-million-dollar horse?"

"Yeah, I realize."

"He's going to make you pay him back for that horse. You're aware of that."

"Yeah." This is what defeat tasted like. Bitter.

But, really, did he deserve any less? He'd spent most of a lifetime being a pain in Chadwick's ass.

When it came to horses, Phillip could finally beat his older brother. For a few hours a month, he was Hardwick's golden son. He'd done everything in his power to make sure that Chadwick never forgot it.

Even bought a horse named Kandar's Golden Sun. Just because he could. Because that's what Hardwick would have done.

But their father was dead and gone. Had been for years. Why had it only been in the last six days that Phillip had tried to figure out who he was if he wasn't Hardwick Beaumont's second son?

It'd been because of Jo, because she hadn't seen Hardwick's forgotten second child. She'd seen a man who had a good head for horses—a man who could be weak and stupid, yes, a man who drank too much and remembered too little. She hadn't seen a man she could fix.

She'd seen a man worth saving.

"Matthew," Phillip said, suddenly unsure of what he was going to say. "I'm sorry."

Matthew glared at him. "You should be. This is one hell of a mess."

"No," Phillip went on, trying to find some steel for his resolve. "I'm *not* sorry about trying to save the farm. I'll do anything to save this place. I'm...I'm sorry about everything else. I'm sorry your job is managing me when I go off the rails. I'm sorry I go off the rails sometimes—" Matthew shot him a mean look. "All the time. I'm sorry I don't remember half the stuff I've done because I blacked out."

"Phillip," Matthew said, sounding uncharacteristically nervous.

"No, let me finish." Finishing was suddenly important. Phillip had been so mad at Chadwick, he'd never taken the time to understand why the man was so mad at him. But he could see it now, cleared of the haze of drinking. "I'm sorry you were always in between me and Chadwick. *Are* always in between us. I'm—I'm sorry I hated you when you were a kid."

Matthew stared at him. "What?"

"I'm a terrible brother. I blamed you for my mother going away but you were just a kid. It wasn't your fault and it wasn't fair of me to blame you."

They stood there, staring at each other as Phillip's words settled around them. He felt as if he should say something else but he didn't know what. Of course, he hadn't known he was going to say that, either.

"Why are you saying all of this?"

Phillip shrugged. Truthfully, he didn't know. Only... he needed to. He couldn't live with himself if he didn't.

"I don't want to be the kind of guy who has to have someone else clean up his messes anymore. I want to manage myself, my own life from here on out." He swallowed again. "I'm sorry it took me this long to figure that out."

"You..." Matthew cleared his throat and straightened his shoulders. "You were just a kid, too. It wasn't your fault."

Phillip shook his head. "Maybe when we were six, but we're not anymore. We're grown men and I've been—well, I've been an asshole and I'm sorry."

Matthew walked away from him. He didn't go far, maybe five paces before he stopped and dropped his head, but in that moment, Phillip felt hopelessness clawing at him. It'd seemed like a good idea. A *necessary* one. But....

"You can't hide out here forever. You're still contractually obligated to represent Beaumont Breweries at events. If you have any hope of convincing Chadwick to go along with your plan, you've got to hold up your end of the bargain. You're still the—what was it? The 'handsome face of the Beaumont Brewery'."

"I know." That was the other little detail that wasn't little. He knew that if he stayed out here on the farm where he could work with Sun, talk to Jo and pet Betty's ears, he could stay sober. It wasn't that hard.

Hell. He'd already asked Matthew to make the long drive down because he didn't trust himself to go into Denver and not hit a liquor store or a club. If he *had* to go to a club and spend several hours surrounded by alcohol and party people—how was he going to Just Say No? He'd wanted to crack open a fifth about three times in the last twenty minutes. And that was just talking to Matthew.

"That's why I need your help, Matthew. I don't know how to do this myself and you're the only one of us who Chadwick listens to."

"You're not just doing this for a woman?"

"She's not like that."

He needed Matthew's organization, his contacts, his ability to pacify Chadwick. Especially that.

Matthew sighed deeply. "I shouldn't."

"But you will?"

Matthew shot him a snarky look over his shoulder. "I must be nuts."

"Nope," Phillip said, unable to stop himself from grinning. He'd convinced Matthew. No matter what, that was a victory. One he knew he'd remember in the morning. "You're just a Beaumont."

# Ten

Jo cleaned saddles, then Sun trashed them. The process repeated itself several times over the next three days. The only change of pace was when she paused to saddle up Betty. She'd clean a saddle again, wait for Sun to grind it into the dirt and then unsaddle Betty.

She never left Betty's saddle where Sun could get to it.

Jo felt awful and she wasn't sure why. She was not responsible for Phillip Beaumont. Never had been. She could not be the reason he drank or didn't drink. She couldn't fix him and it wasn't her responsibility to save him. Anything he did—*everything* he did—had to be a choice he made of his own free will.

However, all of that fine logic was subsumed beneath a gnawing sense of guilt. He'd been in a world of hurt and she couldn't help but feel as if she hadn't done enough. After all, she'd had a medical staff monitoring her for a couple of months. She'd moved back in with her parents and grandmother. She'd had Betty.

The fight to sobriety might have felt lonely, but she hadn't been alone.

Not like Phillip was. She didn't know what his relationship was like with the rest of his family, but she didn't think she was wrong about his brother waiting for Phillip to drink himself out of the picture.

She'd loaned him Betty for the night. And then he'd left.

She shouldn't care. Her guilt had nothing to do with the way he'd brought her coffee in the morning or kissed her hand after she made him clean saddles. It had nothing to do with how he'd looked at her as if she was the boat he could cling to in a storm.

But it did.

Jo focused on her work. What else could she do? If Phillip had given up, Sun would be sold. It hurt her to even think of that—the change would erase all the progress they'd made. But she had an obligation to make sure he was as manageable as possible, no matter who owned him.

She had a duty to herself, too—her reputation as a world-class trainer, and the reference she'd get from this job. That's where her focus had to be.

On the third day of cleaning saddles, Sun wandered over to where she'd left the jumping saddle and gave it a few half-hearted paws before he went to check on his bucket.

She didn't have any carrots. But Phillip would have.

She walked over to the saddle, dusted the hoof prints off of it, and walked away. Sun sniffed the saddle a few minutes later, but didn't trash it.

*Finally*, she thought. He'd gotten bored with this game they were playing. They could move on to the next phase—getting the clean saddle on the horse.

She didn't have any illusions that saddling Sun would be something she could accomplish in an afternoon. The process might take weeks—weeks she didn't know if she had.

She needed a break. For the first time, she was tired of standing in a paddock. Impatience pulled at her mind.

She gathered up the saddle and her cleaning supplies and slung them over the paddock fence. She'd leave them there so Sun would see them. Maybe Richard wouldn't mind if she borrowed one of the horses and went for a long ride. She'd love to give the Appaloosas a go.

She could call Granny. Just to check in, see how she was doing. Or she could go see a movie. Or something. Anything, really, as long as it didn't involve Beaumont Farms.

She unsaddled Betty and left the saddle next to Sun's. Jo didn't trust Sun enough yet to leave Betty alone with him, but the two animals had been co-existing better than she'd hoped. The little donkey was doing quite well in the pasture across the drive. That was another encouraging sign that should have put her in a good mood but didn't.

She was walking out of the paddock when she heard it—the sound of a car. She looked up to see a long, black limousine driving toward them.

*Phillip.* She glanced back at the barn, but Richard hadn't popped his head out yet.

Suddenly, Jo was nervous. One of the nice side effects of not getting involved with her clients' personal lives was that she never had to wonder how to act around them because she always acted the same—reserved. Concerned about the horses and not with their messy lives.

What if he was drunk, like he'd been the first time? It would mean he'd given up. She'd load up Betty and be gone by tonight. She wouldn't have to call Granny—she could just go home for a bit and get right with the world again.

Then she could keep doing what she'd done—traveling from ranch to farm, saving broken horses, building her business and never getting involved. She'd never have to see Phillip Beaumont again.

But what if…

The limo pulled up in front of her. Instead of the expensive Italian leather shoes and fine-cut wool trousers that he'd been wearing the first time she'd seen him get out of that limo, a pair of polished ostrich cowboy boots and artfully distressed jeans exited the vehicle.

Then Phillip stood and smiled at her over the door.

*Oh God—Phillip.*

Even at this distance she could see his eyes were clear and bright. His jaw was freshly shaven, his hair artfully messy.

She blinked at him as he leaned forward and thanked his driver. Then he shut the door and the limo drove off, leaving Phillip in the middle of the drive.

In addition to the jeans, he was wearing the kind of western shirt that hipsters wore—black with faint pinstripes and a whole lot of detailed embroidery on the shoulders and cuffs. He even had a rugged-looking leather-and-silver cuff on his arm.

Her breath caught as he walked toward her. He shouldn't—couldn't—look that good. She watched for his tells—the extra-slow, extra-careful movements, the jumping eyes—but found nothing.

Phillip Beaumont strode toward her with purpose. God, he looked *so* good. Better than she remembered. Although, to be fair, he had looked like hell the last time she'd seen him. He certainly didn't look like hell at the moment. In fact, she couldn't remember him looking as confident, as capable—as *sexy*—as he did right now.

Behind her, Sun snorted. Jo heard his hoofbeats, but they weren't frantic. Sun was just trotting around. His lack of overreaction might mean he not only recognized Phillip, but was also glad to see him.

As though she was glad to see him. "You're back."

"I am." He stopped less than two feet from her—more than far enough away to be considered a respectable distance but close enough that Jo could reach out and touch him if she wanted to.

Oh, how she wanted to. The man standing before her was a hybrid of the slick, handsome playboy in commercials and the cowboy who'd worked by her side for over a week.

A man should not look this good, she decided. It wasn't fair to everyone else. It wasn't fair to her.

She forced herself to breathe regularly. No gasping allowed. "What have you been up to?"

"Did you watch *Denver This Morning* this morning?"

She gave him a look. "No."

"Or *Good Morning America* yesterday?"

"No."

"No," he said with the kind of grin that did a variety of very interesting things to her. "I didn't figure you had."

She couldn't help herself. She leaned forward and took a deep breath, just as Granny had done once to her. Coffee, subtly blended with bay rum spice. Not a hint of alcohol on him.

"I've had a lot of coffee in the last five and a half days." He smelled warm and clean and tempting. Oh so tempting. "It's a good place to start, I've heard."

"As good as any," she agreed. Why was breathing so hard right now? She shouldn't care that he'd been sober for five days. She shouldn't care that he'd come back to the farm looking better than any man had a right to look.

"I hired a sober coach," he went on. "Big guy named Fred. He'll help me stay on the straight and narrow. I'm meeting with him tomorrow morning and he'll be accompanying me to all my required club appearances."

"You did...*what?*" She couldn't have heard him right.

"Sober coach. To help me stay sober. So I can save my farm." He lowered his head to look at her. "I wanted to thank you."

She blinked at him. Why was he telling her this? "For what?"

Before he could answer, Betty wandered over and leaned into his leg, demanding to be petted. "Hey, girl," he said in a bemused tone as he rubbed her head. "Been keeping an eye on Jo for me?"

He'd been thinking of her. "She missed you," Jo managed to say.

Phillip notched an eyebrow at her. Yeah, she wasn't fooling him any. How could she hope to fool herself?

*You gave up men when you gave up drinking*, she reminded herself as he pulled a device out of his back pocket. *You don't get to have this. Him.*

Phillip tapped on the screen a few times. "Here," he said, handing it to her.

The sun chose that moment to break through the clouds. The glare off the screen made it impossible to watch what he'd called up, but she heard a perky voice say, "...with us this morning is the handsome face of the Beaumont Brewery, Phillip Beaumont himself."

"I can't see," she told him.

"You need to get out of the sun."

She glanced back at her trailer. Suddenly, the distance of a couple hundred feet felt way too close and also too far away at the same time. "We could go to my trailer."

The moment she said it, she knew she'd meant something other than to just watch a video.

She turned her head back to Phillip. Her mind was swimming. Fifteen minutes ago, she'd written him off as a drunk who wasn't interested in saving himself. But now?

Their eyes met and a spark of something so intense it almost wasn't recognizable passed between them. She recognized it anyway. Sheer, unadulterated lust coursed through her, suddenly as vital as the blood that pounded through her heart.

This was the moment.

She could invite Phillip back to her trailer and pin him against the wall and kiss him as a reward for having had nothing but coffee for almost a week and no one would ever know.

Except she would.

And so would he.

"We could," Phillip said, his voice dropping down to something that would have been a whisper if the tone hadn't been so deep. "If that's what you want."

She wanted. She wanted the Phillip who wasn't afraid to grab a hay bale or clean a saddle, the Phillip who knew how to harness and drive a team. The Phillip who made her blush.

She wanted to kiss him.

Unable to come up with any words at all, she simply turned and walked to her trailer.

She opened the door and stepped up. But she didn't make a move toward the bed. She stopped at the top of the steps and turned.

Phillip stopped, too—one foot on the lowest step. He wasn't inside, but he wasn't out either.

"Here," he said, leaning forward to tap the screen a few more times. "Watch."

The video restarted. "Welcome back to *Good Morning, America*," a perky woman who looked vaguely familiar beamed into the camera. "With us this morning is the handsome face of the Beaumont Brewery, Phillip Beaumont himself."

The camera panned to Phillip sitting on a couch. His leg was crossed and his hands rested on his shin. He seemed quite comfortable on camera. He looked so good in his fancy western shirt—different than the one he was wearing now—and boots that were probably eel. He grinned at the perky woman—the same grin he'd given Jo the first time they'd met.

"The Beaumont Brewery is home to the world-famous Beaumont Percherons," the woman went on. "But there could be some changes underway and Phillip is here today with the details. Phillip?"

Phillip turned his attention to the camera. There he was, the sophisticated man-about-town. "Thanks, Julie. The Percherons have been a part of the Beaumont Brewery since 1868."

The screen cut away to a black-and-white commercial with the Percherons leading a wagon of beer. Phillip's voice over explained the history of the Brewery's Percheron team from the Colorado Territory to the present as decades of commercials played.

Besides the quality of the video, very little changed across the years. The horses were all nearly identical, the wagon the same—years of Beaumont Percherons anchoring the company to the public consciousness.

The camera refocused on Phillip and the woman. "Those are some classic commercials," the woman announced.

"They are," Phillip agreed. "But now the Beaumont Brewery is trying to decide whether to branch out from the Percherons or stick with tradition. So we've set up a poll for people to vote—should Beaumont Brewery keep the Percherons or not?"

"Fascinating," the woman said as she nodded eagerly. "How can people vote?"

"Visit the Facebook page we've set up for the poll," Phillip said as the web address popped up at the bottom of the screen. "We encourage people to leave a comment telling us what the Percherons mean to them."

Phillip and the woman engaged in a little more light banter before the segment ended.

Jo blinked at the screen. "You did that?"

"I'd show you the one from *Denver This Morning*, but it was basically the same thing," he said. Then he set his other foot on the step.

"We?" Because that interview had been a lot of *we—we* set up the poll, *we* made a Facebook page.

"My brother Matthew helped me," he corrected. "But they didn't know that Chadwick hadn't exactly signed off on this particular line of publicity." He smiled the wicked smile of a man who does whatever he wants and gets away with it. "We've already had over sixty thousand votes to keep the Percherons and four thousand comments in less than forty-eight hours. I dare Chadwick to ignore that—and I doubt the new Brewery owners will be able to ignore it, either."

"You," she whispered, staring at the screen as if it held all the answers.

He wasn't going to give up on Sun or the Percherons. Or himself. He wasn't going down without a damned good fight.

He lifted her hat off her head and set it in the seat next to the door. He wasn't touching her, not really, but licking flames danced over her skin, setting her on fire. "I did a lot of thinking that night," he said, low and close. So close she could kiss him. "About who I was and what I wanted. Who I wanted to be."

"I know you didn't sleep," she admitted. "Neither did I."

"I decided I needed to make some changes, so I called my cleaning service the next morning," he went on, brushing his fingertips over her cheek and pushing her hair back. "I had them get rid of all the alcohol in my apartment in the city. I also told Richard to get everything out of the house and give it to the hands. I talked to Matthew and hired a sober coach."

"You did all that?" Amazing, yes—but why? Because

no matter how impressive of a step it was, she couldn't be the reason. "Did you do this for me?"

He climbed the second step. The door swung shut behind him, closing them off from the rest of the world. They were the same height now, close enough she could feel the heat from his chest radiating through his shirt. He brought his other hand up, cupping her face. "If you were any other woman in the world, I'd say yes." He searched her eyes. "But…"

"But?" It was the most important *but* she'd ever said.

"But," he went on, a small, soft grin taking hold of his lips, "I didn't. Not really."

"Who did you do it for?"

"I did it for Sun and Marge and Homer and Snowflake and all the horses. I even did it for Richard, the old goat, because he's a good farm manager and he's too damn old to be unemployed."

"Yeah?" She couldn't help herself. She dropped the device on top of her hat and slid her arms around his waist. He was solid and warm and quite possibly the best thing she'd ever held.

"I did it for me," he told her.

It should have sounded like a selfish announcement from one of the most selfish men in the world, but it didn't. His voice was low and steady and he looked at her with such heated fervor that she knew the touch of his lips would scorch her and there'd be no turning back.

"Because I couldn't live with myself if I let it go."

"Oh," was all she could say. It seemed inadequate. So she surrendered to the pull he had on her and kissed him. She couldn't fight her attraction to him any longer and she was tired of trying.

It was a simple touch of her lips to his, but he sighed into her with such contentment that it demolished her reserves. *Skin on skin.* Desire burned through her. Her nipples went tight—so tight it almost hurt. Only his touch could ease the pain.

She was kissing Phillip Beaumont, really kissing him. She tilted her head for better access. He responded by opening his mouth for her. When she swept her tongue in to touch his, he groaned, "Jo." Then he kissed her back.

Any sense she had left evaporated. She ran her fingers up his back, feeling each muscle before she laced her fingers through his hair. Everything about her felt...odd. Different. Warm and hot and shivery all at the same time.

She wanted to see the body that was doing things to her—pooling heat low in her belly that demanded attention *right now*. The weight between her legs got so heavy so fast that she was suddenly having trouble standing.

And thinking? Yeah, that wasn't happening either. All she could think was how long it'd been. Years. Over a decade she'd denied that she needed this—to feel a man's arms around hers, to feel desirable.

She grabbed the front of his shirt. Snaps, not buttons. *Done.* The shirt gave and Phillip's chest was laid bare for her.

She had to look—had to—so she broke the kiss and let her fingertips trace the outline of his chest.

*Carved* of stone, that's what his muscles were. Smooth and hard but warm—almost hot to the touch. Or maybe that was just her. "Wow," she breathed as she traced his six-pack.

"Mmm," he said, pushing the hair away from the left side of her neck—the smooth side—and...and...

Years of pent-up sexual frustration unleashed themselves on her when he bit down on the space between her shoulder and her neck. Her hips tilted toward him, desperate for a release of the tightness that felt like a rubber band about to snap back on her. "*Phillip.*"

"Too hard?" He kissed the spot he'd bitten. It was all the more tender compared to his bite.

This was it—the last possible moment she could back away from the edge before she went spiraling out of control.

Except she didn't want to back away. She wanted to throw herself forward without a look back.

"No," she said, grabbing at his belt buckle. The damned thing was far more complicated than the shirt had been. "Not hard enough."

He growled against her skin. "Bed?"

"Bed." Although she didn't exactly care at this moment where they wound up. Just so long as he kept doing what he was doing.

Then, to her surprise, Phillip picked her up. He held her against his chest as he mounted the last step. One arm around her waist, one under her bottom. The hand under her bottom squeezed her hard, making her squirm.

"You like it a little hard?" he asked.

"A little rough." Or, at least, she thought she did. A wave of insecurity almost froze her. "It's been so long...." Not only that, but she'd never done this with the scars. Even though the blinds were down, enough daylight suffused the bedroom that there was no way to hide.

He set her down and cupped her face again. "Then we better make sure it's worth the wait." As he kissed her, he unsnapped her shirt. "You about killed me the other night," he murmured against her skin before biting her shoulder as he pushed off her shirt.

She swallowed. "I did?"

The shirt hit the ground and then his fingers were tracing the swells of her breasts, barely contained by her bra. "Just a glimpse of you...." Then his mouth was moving lower as his hands went around her back. Over her scars. "I wanted a taste."

The bra gave and mercifully he brought his hands up to cup her breasts again. "Amazing," he whispered as his tongue lapped against her rock-hard nipple. "Simply amazing."

"I..."

He scraped his teeth down the side of her breast as he pulled her nipple into his mouth. "Yes?"

There was no mistaking the bulge in his jeans. "More," she gasped as he sucked hard.

"I love a woman who knows what she wants," he replied, smoothly undoing her belt and then her jeans.

He sat her down on the bed, where she kicked off her boots and jeans. Then she was in nothing but her panties.

Her pulse was racing so hard that she was having trouble focusing.

Which, admittedly, became a whole lot easier when Phillip undid his stubborn belt and shucked his jeans. His erection strained against the boxer-briefs he wore—red, of course—and those were gone, too.

Jo began to breathe so fast she was in danger of panting. She felt as if she should say something, but the problem was, she didn't know what. She was no shy, retiring virgin—but she had been celibate for the last decade.

She didn't know what she was doing.

Phillip stepped toward her. Jo sat up. Maybe he expected her to start with a little oral? Although—honestly—there wasn't much that was "little" about it.

He was, for lack of a better word, *huge*. She took him in hand, her fingers barely meeting as she encircled him. Once, twice, she moved her hand up and down.

"Jo," he groaned as his hands tangled in her hair.

When she leaned forward to take him in her mouth, he stopped her. "Wait."

"Wait?"

He pushed her back with enough force that she had to

lean on her elbows. She watched as he took a deep breath—a man struggling to remain in control. Then he opened his eyes—the green much darker with desire. "Saving the farm," he said, the strain in his voice unmistakable, "isn't about you."

Phillip crouched down to the ground and pulled a condom out of his back pocket. "But this," he said, dropping the condom on the bed next to her, "this *is*."

Before she could process that, he'd kneeled between her legs and was pulling her panties down. "It's really been ten years?"

She couldn't even talk as his fingertips slid down her thighs, over her knees, down her ankles. She bit her lip and tried to nod, but her head felt as if it was in danger of floating away.

His hands skimmed up her calves, flushing her with heat as he sat on his heels and looked her over. For a moment, she panicked. He was used to other kinds of women—women with perfect bodies and flat stomachs and smooth, soft skin. She hadn't even shaved her bikini line recently. She hadn't planned on things getting this far, this fast.

For a horrific moment, she wished she had a drink. A shot of liquid courage to help her get out of her own head and into the perfect man between her legs. And the moment she thought that, she almost told him to stop.

Like alcohol, men were a drug she'd already quit once.

Phillip leaned down and kissed…her knee. "Do you want to remember this?"

"What?"

He kissed her other knee. "You said you didn't remember the sex before. Didn't remember if you wanted it or not."

Good to know he'd been paying attention and all, but she was pretty sure this wasn't a normal seduction.

He shifted to place a kiss on her hip bone. It shouldn't have felt good—just a regular old hip bone—but the tender way he was touching her focused her thoughts. Where would he kiss her next?

"Well?" Another kiss on the top of her thigh.

"I want to remember," she told him, knowing it was the truth. "I want to remember *you*."

# Eleven

*Yes.* "That's what I want, too."

He leaned forward, letting his erection brush against her as he kissed the spot where he'd lost his head and bit down earlier. "Do you still want it a little rough? Or a little gentle?" Then he flicked his tongue over her earlobe.

She squirmed underneath him, which about drove him insane. "Both? Is that even an answer?" She tried to laugh it off as a joke, but he heard something else.

She was nervous. Well, he couldn't blame her. Ten years was a long time.

He grabbed her hands and pinned her down. Much more of her body moving under his and they wouldn't even make it to the memorable sex.

His arms began to shake under the strain of not plunging into her warm body. But he had to do this right for her.

"Both it is." Soft and tough—just like she was.

He bit down on the spot that had nearly broken her earlier. She sucked in a hot breath against his ear, her hips thrusting up against him. *Yes*, he thought again.

He moved to the other side—the side where she wore her scars like tattoos. She tried to tilt her head to hide herself but he had her pinned.

He kissed down her shoulder until he switched to her breast—full and heavy.

He licked her nipple, blowing air on the wet skin to see it tighten up. Her hips shimmied beneath his. Not yet. Too soon. He had to kneel back to break the contact.

He kissed the space between her breasts and then used his teeth to leave a mark on the inside of the left one. She sucked air again as her body strained against his hands. "Okay?" he asked, just to be sure.

"Yes." She nodded, but her eyes were closed.

"Then look at me," he ordered. When she didn't immediately open her eyes, he bit her again, his teeth skimming her nipple. "*Jo*. Look at what I'm doing to you."

Then he fastened onto her nipple and sucked hard until her eyes flew open. There—the anxiety that had lurked there earlier was gone, leaving nothing but need and want in its place.

He let his teeth scrape over her, putting a hint of pressure on her skin. Not enough to hurt her, but more than enough that she wouldn't forget this.

"Oh—Phillip," she gasped out, tilting her hips up—begging for his touch.

He didn't let go of her hands as he moved his mouth lower and lower. He pulled her with him until she was nearly sitting up. No way he was going to let her lie back.

"Keep your eyes open," he told her before he pressed a kiss against her sex.

"Why," she ground out through clenched teeth as he licked her, "why do you get to do this to me and I didn't get to do it to you?"

It was a fair enough question. "You've been a very good girl," he told her, keeping his mouth against her so she'd feel his voice more than she heard it. It worked, given the way she bucked against him, her body asking for more even if her mouth couldn't. He looked up the length of her body—she was watching him. *Good.* "You deserve a reward."

He filled his mouth with her, savoring her taste the way he'd savor a fine wine. Nothing was clouded by the haze of a wild night. This was just him and her and *nothing* in between them.

He was not gentle. It paid off. After only a few agonizing minutes of teasing her, Jo's back arched off the bed. She made a high-pitched noise in the back of her throat before collapsing back against the bed, panting hard.

He kissed her inner thigh, then turned his head and bit the other one. His dick throbbed, but in a good way. "Memorable?"

"Unforgettable," she said and this time, there was no hesitation in her voice at all. Nothing but a dreamy tone that spoke volumes about satisfaction.

"Good." He swallowed, the taste of her desire still on his lips. "Now roll over."

Jo froze. "What?"

She couldn't roll over. She absolutely could not have sex with a man—especially a man as physically perfect at Phillip Beaumont—where the only thing he could see would be the burn marks on her back.

He covered her body with his, the weight of his erection pressing hard against her. Her mind was in a state of confusion, but her body? Nothing confused there. That first orgasm had primed her pump, just as she knew it would. She needed more. She couldn't get enough of him.

He leaned over her and placed his teeth against her

neck. His hips flexed, putting him right against her. "Do you want this?"

She nodded.

He moved to the other side of her neck. The side with the scars that usually hid behind the collar of her shirts and her hair.

But she couldn't hide from him now. He wouldn't allow it.

"You can have it if you roll over," he whispered against her skin. He flexed again, his tip pushing against her. "Roll over for me, Jo. Don't hide who you really are."

"But I'm—it's—so ugly."

"Not to me." He let go of her and propped himself up on his hands so he could look her fully in the eyes. "It wasn't ugly when you stripped for me the other night. It was real and honest and true. That's what you are to me, Jo—the truth. No one else gives me a hard time like you do. No one else expects me to do anything—*be* anything. But you expect better of me. You make me want to be a better man."

They weren't the words of seduction, not even close. But that didn't change the fact that it was the sweetest thing anyone had ever said to her.

She took his face in her hands. "I can't be the reason." She wasn't fooling herself. When Sun was manageable, she and Betty would be gone and Phillip would be on his own again. The changes in his life couldn't be because of her.

That wicked grin would be her undoing. "You can be one of them. And a far more beautiful one than Richard's wrinkly old mug."

He leaned down to kiss her. The taste of coffee gone now; nothing but her and him mingled together. Her skin burned in the best possible way where he'd left marks on her body—pulling her into the here and now by brute force.

He flexed again, insistent in his need. "Let me see you, Jo. All of you."

She rolled, careful not to kick him.

Then she was exposed. Totally, utterly exposed to him. It left her feeling raw.

She didn't realize how tense she was until the first touch came. When his hands traced her shoulders, she jumped. "Sorry."

"Don't be." He smoothed her hair away and kissed the scar. His hands moved over her ribs, his fingertips tracing the sides of her breasts.

Then he was moving lower—kissing the surgical scars that ran alongside where her back had been broken. She'd been so broken.

She didn't feel broken right now. How could she, with Phillip lavishing such tender caresses on her?

He kissed the base of her back, just above her bottom. "You are so beautiful," he groaned—and then bit one of her cheeks.

Jo started against the bed. It felt good. It felt…as though she was alive. She grabbed the sheets and closed her eyes, letting her skin feel what she couldn't see—Phillip. She memorized every touch.

His hand grabbed her other cheek and squeezed, then a finger slipped inside of her. She clenched down. "More." She needed all of him.

His warmth left her. She turned her head to see him ripping open the condom wrapper, then rolling on the protection. Then he grabbed her hips, pulling her back to him with anything but gentleness.

*Both*. She'd asked for both because she didn't know what she wanted, not anymore. Just him.

*Make it worth ten years of waiting*, she thought.

He touched her again. "You're so ready for me." His tone was almost reverent. Then he was against her and, with a thrust, buried inside of her.

Jo's back arched as she groaned. "Oh, yes, *please*."

But he didn't. He stopped. The seconds dragged on for years before he grabbed her by the hips again, tilting her backside up. Then he grabbed her hair and wrapped it around his fist. "If this pulls at your back, you tell me, okay?"

Then he tugged her head back. Her neck lengthened and suddenly, his mouth was on her throat, biting at just the right spot.

Then he thrust. All Jo could do was groan at the wonderful agony of it all.

"Okay?"

"More." He tugged at her hair, popping her head up. "More, *please*."

He fell into a rhythm—long, steady strokes punctuated only by his teeth against her skin. Every bite, every thrust kept her in the here and now. Just her and Phillip.

It was freeing. She was free.

Jo came with a cry that she muffled against the mattress. Leaning back, Phillip let go of her hair and dug his fingertips into the flesh of her bottom, thrusting harder and harder until he let go with a low roar of pure satisfaction. Then he fell forward on her.

"Jo," he whispered in her ear in a voice that made him sound vulnerable.

She rolled again—not to hide her skin from him, but to face him.

Phillip smoothed her hair away from her cheeks and kissed her softly. "Beautiful," he sighed against her lips before he pulled her into a strong hug.

This was so much better than waking up with a sense of horror at feeling used and alone and knowing it was her own damned fault.

Her skin was still warm from Phillip's touch, her body weak from the orgasms. She wouldn't forget this. She wouldn't forget him.

And now that she had this moment, how was she supposed to not want it more? Already, she wanted him again.

*Oh, no.*

She couldn't believe she'd done this. She'd thrown away ten years of sticking to the straight and narrow and for what? For thirty minutes of sweet, heady freedom with Phillip Beaumont, a world-renowned womanizer with all of five days of sobriety under his belt?

How could she have been so stupid?

Then his phone rang.

# Twelve

"Is that…the Darth Vader theme music?"

Phillip tensed at the sound of Chadwick's ring tone. "The 'Imperial March,' yes."

He pulled Jo into his arms and kissed her forehead. He didn't want to get up. He wanted to stay here and explore Jo some more. Yeah, he'd wanted to make that memorable but the truth was, he wasn't going to forget her.

It was a weird feeling to realize that he couldn't remember the face, much less the name, of the last woman he'd been with. It all ran together.

Everything about Jo stood out. The way her body had closed around his, the way she'd responded to his touch, his commands—he wanted to do that again, just to make sure it hadn't been some one-off fluke.

But Chadwick was calling. He'd gotten wind of what Phillip had been up to.

This was about to get ugly.

He forced himself to let go of her and sat up. "I need to leave."

"Oh."

He didn't like her quiet note. But before he could say anything else, his phone started singing again. He grabbed his pants off the floor.

She tried to slip past him, but he hadn't forgotten that vulnerable *Oh*. "Tonight," he said as he grabbed her arm.

"Tonight?" Anything vulnerable about her was gone and the tough cowgirl was back in place.

"Have dinner with me." His phone stopped marching, only to pick up the beat two seconds later. "Come up to the house."

She tilted her head toward him and waited. The power had shifted between them. She'd given him control over the sex, but she'd taken that back now.

"Please," he added as he curled his arm around her waist. He put his lips against the curve of her neck and whispered, "Please," against her skin.

She pulled away from him. "No."

Then she was gone, striding down the hall and out the trailer before he could process what she'd just said. *No?*

He stared at the empty hallway, then the bed they'd only just vacated. What happened? One minute they were having electric sex—her pleading for more, for the release he knew she couldn't have been faking. The best sex he could remember. And the next, she was *done* with him?

He started after her, but his damned phone began to march again. *Son of a...*

"What?" he demanded as he slammed the trailer door shut after him. Jo already had Betty and was shutting the paddock gate behind them both.

She couldn't have been clearer—she didn't want to talk to him.

"Have you lost your mind?" Chadwick thundered on the other end.

"And hello to you, too," Phillip said as he tried to figure out where he'd gone wrong. She'd wanted it both soft and rough. Hadn't he delivered?

"You are single-handedly jeopardizing this *entire* deal," Chadwick yelled in his ear. "Even by your standards, you've screwed this up."

"I've done nothing of the sort," Phillip replied, forcing himself to remain calm. Mostly because he knew he wouldn't win a shouting match with his older brother, but also because he knew it'd drive the jerk crazy. "I've merely reminded the future owners of our brewery that we mean more to our vast customer base than just a nice, cold beer."

Jo stood with her back to him as she haltered Betty. Sun was aware of him, though. The horse was making short strides back and forth in front of her, his head never pointing away from where Phillip was pacing.

"...pissed off Harper and the entire board," Chadwick was yelling. "Do you know what that man will do to us if this deal falls through?"

"To hell with Harper," Phillip said, only half paying attention. Maybe he should have asked Jo if he could come back to her trailer instead of inviting her up to the house? "I can't stand the guy. And he hates us."

"I always thought you had a brain somewhere in that head of yours and that you *chose* not to use it," Chadwick fumed. "I can see now that I was wrong. For your information, Phillip, Harper will sue us into last *century*. And any hope that you're keeping the farm with this PR gambit will go down the drain in legal fees."

"Oh," Phillip said, Chadwick's words registering for the first time. "I hadn't thought about that."

"What a surprise—you didn't think something through. You *never* think things through, do you?" Chadwick made a noise of disgust in the back of his throat. "All you care about is where the next party is."

"That's not true," Phillip snapped. His head began to throb. This would be the time in his conversation with Chadwick where he'd normally tuck the phone under his chin and start opening cabinets to see if he had any whiskey. He hated it when his older brother talked down to him.

Even though Phillip knew he wasn't going to drink, the habit had him looking around for a cabinet.

Damn, this was going to be harder than he thought.

"Isn't it?" Chadwick's tone made it clear that he was sneering. "The next party, the next drink, the next woman. You've never cared for anything else in your entire, selfish life."

Phillip's pride stung, mostly because it was a somewhat accurate statement. But not entirely, and he clung to that *not* with everything he had.

If Chadwick wanted to hit below the belt, fine. Phillip would just hit right back. "You know who you sound like right now?" he said in his most calm voice, "Dad."

There was a hideous screeching noise and then the call ended. If he had to guess, Phillip would say Chadwick had thrown his phone at a wall. Good. That meant the asshole wouldn't be calling back anytime soon.

He glared at the phone, then the silent woman who, not twenty feet away from him, was leading Betty around the paddock. She might as well have been on a different continent. Any good buzz he'd had earlier from his media coup and seduction of Jo was dead.

He'd had a plan—show Chadwick and the new Brewery owners that the Percherons were too valuable to auction off.

That plan wasn't dead, he realized. He'd just finished Phase One. Now he needed to start Phase Two—getting control of this farm away from Chadwick.

Which meant he needed a new plan.

He looked at the paddock again. The cold shoulder from Jo was about to give him frostbite.

One-night stands were his specialty. He loved them when they were there, forgot about them when they were gone. So what if Jo was ignoring him? No big deal, right? He'd had his fun, just as he always did. Now was as good a time as any to move on.

But he didn't want to move on.

It must be the chase. She was exceptionally hard to get—that had to be what still called to him.

Fine. She wanted to be chased? He'd chase.

Time for Phase Two.

# Thirteen

Jo needed to go in. A breeze had picked up as dusk approached and, given the clouds that were scuttling across the spring sky, they were in for some rain. She hoped it was a gentle rain and not Mother Nature throwing a fit, but she wasn't going to hold her breath.

Besides, her legs ached. Okay, so it wasn't the standing and walking that had them aching. That was more to do with the *unusual* strain of the afternoon.

She shoved back that thought and focused on the tasks at hand. If it was going to rain, she wanted to brush Betty before the donkey could track any more dirt into the trailer. And Sun—a gentle rain wouldn't kill the horse, but a storm with crashing thunder and lightning might push him over the edge. She couldn't risk him trying to bust through the fences. She needed to get him haltered and into the barn.

She needed not to get killed doing it. There wasn't anyone else around at this point—everyone else had driven off about half an hour ago.

She was not going to ask Phillip for help. She didn't need it. She wouldn't need *him*.

Jo was so focused on her work that the effort was physically exhausting. But it was still better than thinking about what she'd just done. With Phillip.

So she didn't think about it. She thought about the horse.

Sun was, by all reasonable measurements, quite calm. She haltered Betty again and led the patient donkey around the paddock again. This time, she walked within five feet of Sun. The horse didn't skitter away.

No, she was not thinking about the way Phillip had picked her up and carried her back to bed. She was also not thinking about the way he'd made her watch as he went down on her. And she was certainly not thinking about the way every molecule in her body had been pulling her into his arms when he'd whispered "Please" against her skin.

How she'd wanted to say *yes*. Just…let herself be at his beck and call. Be in his bed when he wanted, how he wanted. Let him mark her skin and fill her body and make her come so hard. It'd be easy—for as long as she was here, she could have him.

He could have her.

But then what? She was going to throw herself at him—because, God, she *wanted* to throw herself at him—and then quit him cold turkey in a week, or two weeks or however long she had left to train Sun?

And if she went to his house, went to his bed—word would get out. People would notice. People would *talk*. Her reputation as a professional horse trainer who could take on the toughest cases would be shot to hell and back. People would think she'd gotten this job because she was sleeping with Phillip.

She knew what kind of man he was. He'd move on, just as he always did.

Just as she used to do. One man was the same as another, after all.

But he'd made her remember what she liked about men in the first place. The warm bodies, soft and hard at the same time. The way orgasms felt different in someone else's arms compared to when she did them herself. The feeling, for a fleeting moment, of being complete.

That was the part she'd blindly run after. She'd always confused being *wanted* with being *had*, though. But now she knew. Wanting and having were not the same.

She'd wanted Phillip. Now she'd had him. But, unlike all those men from long ago, she wanted him again. Not just *a* man, but Phillip.

God, she was so mad at herself. She knew she couldn't have him and just let him go any more than she could have one drink and not have any more. She *knew* that. What had she been thinking?

That was the problem. She didn't know what to think anymore.

So she un-haltered Betty. And re-haltered her. Again.

This time, she walked up to Sun and stopped right in front of him. The horse's head popped up and he stared at her, his ears pointed at her as he chewed grass.

This was good. She wished she felt more excited about the victory.

"See?" she said in a soft voice. Sun's head jerked back, but he didn't bolt. "It's not so bad. Betty doesn't mind it, do you girl?"

She rubbed Betty's head between her ears. *It's not so bad*, she silently repeated to herself. She'd had Phillip once. She could back away from the brink of self-destruction again. She'd already said no to him a second time, right? Right. *Not so bad.*

Out of the corner of her eye, she saw movement. Then, unexpectedly, Sun's nose touched Betty's. It was a brief thing, lasting only two seconds, tops. Then Sun backed up and trotted off, looking as if he'd just won the horse lottery.

Jo grinned at his retreating form as she un-haltered Betty. So her mental state was all out of whack. The horse, however, was doing fine and dandy. She watched as Betty trotted after Sun. It looked like a little sister chasing after her big brother. Jo could almost hear Betty saying, "*Wait for me!*"

Jo walked back over to the gate and picked up Sun's halter and lead rope. Maybe… "Betty," she called. "Come on."

Betty exhaled in what was clearly donkey frustration. She only had so much patience for non-stop haltering. But after a moment, she plodded toward Jo.

Sun followed.

Jo moved slowly, demonstrating on Betty how the halter went over the nose and then the ears, then how the lead rope clipped on. She knew he'd been haltered before, but a refresher never hurt anyone.

She held the halter up for Sun to sniff just as a distant rumble echoed from the clouds. Sun whipped his head around, trying to find the source of the noise—then he took off at a jumpy trot. Crap. This whole process needed to happen sooner rather than later. She didn't want to spend a night standing in a downpour just to make sure Sun didn't accidentally kill himself.

Just then, Sun's ears whipped back and he blew past her to rush to the edge of the paddock. Seconds later, she heard it, too—the sound of whistling.

Yes, she was mad at herself and yes, she knew that it wasn't healthy to take her anger out on anyone else but *damn* it was tempting to light into Phillip. Everything had been going fine until he'd arrived on the farm. She'd been a well-respected horse trainer that never, ever gave in to temptation, no matter how long or lonely the nights were.

She wanted to go back to being in control, removed from the messy lives of her clients.

She also wanted to stomp over to that gate, throw it open and demand to know what the hell he was thinking, but she didn't get that far.

Phillip came forward, looking at the halter in her hands. "Any luck?"

Then he had the damned nerve to wink at her.

She wanted to tell him to shove his luck where the sun didn't shine but she didn't. "I *was* making progress. A storm's coming in. I need to move him to the barn without setting him off again."

Phillip looked at her with such intensity that it made her sweat. "I know what he needs," he replied in a voice that was too casual to be anything *but* a double entendre.

She glared at him. She was not going to lose her head again. She was not going to give in to her addictions. One and done. That was final.

He reached into his shirt pocket and pulled out a small baggie of carrots. "Oh," she said, feeling stupid. "Okay."

Phillip opened the gate and walked in. He took out a carrot and stood remarkably still, the carrot held out on the flat of his palm.

Betty came up to him, her lead rope trailing behind her as she snuffled for the treat. "Go ahead," Jo said when Phillip looked to her for approval.

Sun looped around the paddock a few times, each circle tightening on where Phillip stood, another carrot at the ready. This wasn't how she wanted to do this. They were forcing something that she normally would have worked on for a week, maybe more.

But the sky was starting to roil as the clouds built and moved. So she stood next to Phillip, ready to halter a horse.

They waited. For once, Phillip had all the patience in the

paddock. Jo was the one who kept glancing at the menacing clouds as if she could keep them at bay by sheer will.

"Come on, Sun," Phillip said in a low voice that sent a tremor down Jo's back. "It'll be okay, you'll see."

Miraculously, Sun came. Head down, he walked toward them as if he agreed to be haltered every day.

Jo held her breath as the horse sniffed the carrot in the man's palm. Then Sun's big teeth scraped the carrot off Phillip's hand.

"Good, huh?" Phillip said, lifting his hand to rub Sun's nose. "I have more if you let Jo put the halter on you."

Sun shook his head and walked away. But he didn't go far.

A few days ago, Phillip might have whined about how long this was taking. But not today. He merely got another carrot out and waited.

Betty leaned against his legs, so he broke the carrot in half and gave her the smaller part. That got Sun's attention, fast. He came back over to Phillip.

"Carrots," Phillip said, letting Sun take the remaining half, "are *that* good, aren't they?"

He started to fish out another carrot—and Sun was waiting for it—but Jo stopped him. "Let me try to get the halter on, then give him another one if he cooperates."

Sun gave her a baleful look. Clearly, he was too smart for his own good.

"You heard the lady," Phillip said in a teasing tone to his horse. "No more without the halter."

Sun shook his head again. Thunder rumbled again, closer this time.

"You don't want to spend the night in the rain, do you?" Sun blew snot on the ground. "No," Phillip went on, "I didn't think so." He held out another carrot so Sun could smell it.

Jo stepped forward as quickly as she could and slipped

the halter over Sun's nose. He shook her off and reached for the carrot, but Phillip pulled back. "No halter, no carrot."

Sun dropped his head in resignation. Jo slipped the lead rope over his neck and handed the ends to Phillip. Then she leaned forward and slipped the halter over his nose, then over his ears. She clipped the throat latch.

*Victory.* She knew it, Phillip knew it—hell, even Betty seemed to know it. She clipped the lead rope on the halter. Phillip gave Sun another carrot.

"Now we have to get him to the barn," she said. "Can you lead him?"

Phillip gave her the kind of smile that didn't so much chip away at her defenses as blow them up. Nope. Not working on her today. Or any other day.

She was not that girl anymore. She would not throw herself at a man. Not even Phillip Beaumont.

"I can honestly say I've done this before. Plus," he added with that grin, "I'm the one with the carrots."

She steeled her resolve. Sun hadn't been indoors in almost two weeks. This could go south on them. Maybe she should leave Betty in the stall next to Sun for the night? It couldn't hurt. "Fine. Betty and I will lead the way."

Why did she have a sinking feeling that things were about to get interesting?

Phillip had a death grip on the lead rope. The odds that Sun would freak out were maybe 50/50. He couldn't do anything about bucking except stay out of the way, but if Sun tried to bolt, he'd have to spin the horse in a small, tight circle before he could build up a head of steam. And if he reared…

Damn, Phillip wished he had on some gloves. If Sun reared, Phillip just might get rope burn on both palms. He tightened his grip.

He followed Jo and Betty into the barn. The lights came

on overhead, which made Sun start, but he didn't bolt. Jo led her donkey past Sun's stall and then paused. "This stall is empty," she said in a gentle voice. "I'll put Betty in."

"Okay." The situation made him nervous. Leading a mostly-calm Sun down a wide hallway was one thing. Being in a stall with him was a whole different thing.

"Easy does it," Jo said. For the first time since she'd walked away from him that afternoon, he heard something soft in her voice.

Phillip nodded as he walked into the stall with Sun. Then Jo was standing next to him, unclipping the throat latch and sliding the halter from Sun's head.

The three of them stood there for a moment, humans and horse, wondering if they'd just accomplished that without shouting, ropes or guns. Sun shook his head and pawed at the ground, but didn't freak out. Hell, he didn't do anything even remotely Sun-like. He just stood there.

"Carrot?" Jo said in her quiet voice.

"Carrot," Phillip agreed, fishing the rest out of his pocket and holding them out to the horse.

*His* horse.

The wind gusted. He gave Jo a sideways smile that was absolutely not working. "It's going to storm."

"I know."

"We're under a tornado watch until eleven p.m.," he told her. "You should come up to the house—the trailer may not be safe."

Of all the sneaky, underhanded things… "I'll sleep in the barn with the horses."

"*Jo.*" He was forced to shout as the wind gusted up. "Come to the house, damn it. This isn't about seduction, this is about safety."

She hesitated. "I'm not sleeping with you tonight."

He stared at her. "First off, I have a fully stocked guest room. Second off..." He stepped toward her. "I'm sorry."

"For what?"

He ducked his head, looking sheepish. "Well, that's part of the problem. I'm not sure for what. But I've clearly done something you didn't like and it's put me in an odd position."

She stared at him as he studied the tips of his toes. Was this actual sincerity? "What position is that?"

"I want to make it up to you, but I don't have the first idea how. I mean, normally, I wouldn't even care if I'd been a jerk and if I did, I'd throw some roses or diamonds at the problem and be done with it. But I know that won't work. And I don't want to be done with it. With you."

Oh, God. This was sincerity. She considered bolting from the barn, but there was no guarantee he wouldn't follow her. "What do you want from me, Phillip?"

"I want..." He turned away as he ran his hands through his hair. "I want to understand what it is about you that makes me want to do...things. Stay home on the farm. Stay sober. Not—" He paused.

Jo leaned forward, suddenly very interested in that *not*. "Yes?"

He let out a short, sharp laugh. "Is it always this hard?"

"No. Sometimes it's harder." Although, frankly, this was pretty damned hard. She hadn't been faced with this level of emotion—involvement—in so long. She didn't know what to do.

It'd be easy to think he was feeding her a line of bull.

She watched as the muscles in his jaw twitched. He really thought he'd screwed up. Damn.

"If I say it's not you, it's me—will you laugh?" she asked.

That got her a rueful grin. "I haven't heard that line in a long time."

"I had given up men, remember?" She wanted to touch him, but she didn't want to. Life was so much simpler when she followed her own rules.

But there'd been that moment in his arms, watching him bring her to orgasm....

Simpler was not always better.

"You said that."

"I always mixed up the two. Men and alcohol. There was no way to separate them in my mind. They were two wagons that were hitched together and I couldn't fall off of one without falling off the other."

He nodded. "I can see that."

"Then you come along and you're...all my triggers wrapped up in one gorgeous smile. And I—" Jo swallowed, wishing this were easier. But it wasn't. It wouldn't ever be. "I wasn't strong enough to say no to you. Not the first time."

Phillip spun to face her fully. She could see him trying to understand, trying to make the connection. "You think that sleeping with me will lead to drinking?"

She nodded. "Don't get me wrong. The sex—you were amazing. I'd...I'd forgotten how good it could be. How much I liked it."

"That's a relief." He grinned, but instead of his normal, confident grin, this one seemed a little more unsure. "I thought I'd done something you didn't like."

"Yeah, no—*amazing*." She shuddered at the memory of his teeth moving against her skin. "But in my mind, I'd fallen off one wagon. I can't afford to fall off the other. What if I lose control? Because then I'll lose everything I've worked for. *Everything*."

"I understand. Weirdly enough."

She looked at him in surprise. "You do?"

"Look, my six days isn't much on your decade, but... this is *so* much harder than I thought."

She knew that feeling—that the mountain was insurmountable and failure was guaranteed. "*This*," she said, unable to keep the grin off her face, "is the part where I say 'one day at a time.'"

"I don't have to sing 'Kumbaya,' do I?"

She laughed. "God, no."

He came to her then, his arms slipping around her waist. She hugged him back. She couldn't fight this attraction. "Stay with me, Jo. Wake up with me."

"For how long? Sun's getting better. He won't need me much longer."

Phillip stroked his thumb over her cheek. "For as long as you want. Betty loves it here. And I have other horses, if you're worried about missing a job."

*A* job? No, she wasn't worried about that. She set her own schedule and that schedule could be rearranged. But would she still *get* jobs, if word got around? "I don't want people to know about this. About us. No tweeting or press releases or pictures."

His eyebrows shot up. She kept going before she lost her nerve. "I am a professional. I can't have this compromise my reputation as a trainer."

He nodded. "This has nothing to do with Sun. You've done an amazing job with him. This is between us and us alone."

She swallowed. "What about your club appearances?"

"That's why I hired Fred. He'll be with me any time I have to leave the farm." He stroked the edge of his thumb over her cheek.

They were standing on the edge again, but it felt less like falling off a cliff and more like...falling in love. Which was ridiculous. She'd never been in love. She had no plans to start now. "I thought you weren't seducing me."

He brushed his lips across her forehead. "You can stay in the guest room tonight if you want."

She gave him a look then pulled away from him so she could get her thoughts in order. "I can't put myself at risk for you. If you want to be with me, you have to stay sober." She cupped his face in her hands. "I *cannot* kiss you and taste whiskey. I just can't. It's a deal breaker."

His eyes searched hers. Gone was the haunted, raw pain she'd seen a few days ago. His eyes were clear and bright and filled with a different kind of need. "I'm *done* drinking, Jo."

He kissed her then, rough and gentle at the same time.

She'd already fallen off the man wagon. But that didn't have to mean she'd fall right back into drinking. As long as she kept a hard line between her time with Phillip and alcohol—and they kept a hard wall between what happened in the paddock and what happened in the bedroom—she could indulge in some great safe sex and enjoy herself without repercussions.

She hoped.

Thunder cracked around them. Sun whinnied, but he didn't freak out. "Come up to the house," Phillip murmured as his teeth scraped over the skin where her neck and shoulder joined. "Wake up with me."

Her remaining resolve crumbled. How could she say no to that?

She couldn't.

So she didn't.

# Fourteen

The next three weeks were something far outside of Jo's experience. Suddenly, she was living with Phillip Beaumont. She'd never lived with anyone besides her parents and a few unfortunate college roommates.

But this? Waking up with Phillip's arms wrapped around her waist? Making sweet love in the morning, then having breakfast together? Spending the day working with Sun—sometimes with Phillip, sometimes without—then heading back up to the house after the hired help had gone home for the night to have dinner with him? Falling into bed with him at night where he was both rough and gentle in the best possible ways?

It was easy. What's more, it was good. Well, of course the sex was good. But her time with Phillip went well beyond that. Yes, they had sex at least once a day—usually twice. But she got up the next morning, kissed Phillip, and did what she always did—worked with Sun.

After a week, he would come to her to be haltered. After

two, he consented to be tied to the fence so she could brush him. He really was golden, a shimmering color that she'd never seen on a horse before.

She even had Richard walk by a few times while Jo led the horse around the paddock. Sun wasn't happy, but he also wasn't insane with fear.

A new sense of calm filled her. After ten damned long years, she'd managed to unhook the men wagon from the drinking wagon. The realization that she could enjoy Phillip and still be the same woman was—well, it was freeing.

Phillip left the farm after a week and a half. His sober coach showed up at the farm the afternoon Phillip was to leave. Jo stayed with Sun, but she knew that Phillip, Fred and Ortiz were discussing ways they would keep Phillip in control. No drinking, no hook-ups—Phillip had promised—and no blackouts. That was the plan.

Phillip would text her at regular intervals. She could also follow along at home via Twitter, where he'd be posting to his account.

Jo stayed in her trailer, Betty bedded down next to her as she toggled between texts and Twitter, where Phillip shared his Instagram photos. "Can't believe how stupid some people are drunk," he texted her with a photo of a public sex act between two women and one guy.

She smiled at her phone. "Doing okay?"

"Miss you & Betty," was the response. "Home soon."

Later that night, her phone buzzed her out of a dream. It was a photo of Fred in one of two double beds in a hotel room. "Not alone tonight," the text read. "Just me & Fred. He's no Betty, but he'll do. J Miss you."

"Miss you too." She was shocked by how much.

Phillip was back in the paddock by four Sunday afternoon. He'd made it through three events in two days without a drop of liquor. They'd been doing really well about not displaying their affection in front of the hired help, but she didn't stop him when he kissed her for what felt like a good five minutes. When the kiss broke, they realized Sun was watching them.

"Later," she'd giggled. Actually giggled.

"You can bet on it."

"Later" couldn't come fast enough but finally they made it to the bedroom without even eating dinner. After amazing sex where Phillip held her down and left bite marks on her breasts, he said, "I did it," as he lay in her arms, both of them panting and satisfied.

She knew he wasn't talking about the two orgasms that had her body humming. "You did. I knew you could."

He propped himself up on his elbows to look down at her. "You did?"

"No one's past saving."

He lowered himself down onto her. "Who knew being saved could be so good?"

She didn't get a chance to reply.

Phillip was home for another week before he had to go again. This time, he headed to a music festival where Beaumont Brewery had sponsored a party tent. Jo was nervous for him—this wasn't a few hours at a party, but a solid weekend of temptation. But he had Fred and he knew he could do it. So she sent him off with a kiss and the reminder, "Don't forget." She wanted to say more. But she didn't.

"I won't," he promised her. And she believed him.

That Saturday, she had to fight the temptation to check her phone constantly. She'd made it a policy not to check her phone while she was in the paddock with Sun—the horse was smart enough to know when her focus was elsewhere. Distractions were how trainers got hurt. So she left her phone in the trailer. That way, it wouldn't tempt her.

She checked her messages at lunch. Only one text that

read, "Gonna be a long day. Wish I was home with you," that he'd sent at ten that morning. Nothing since.

She swallowed, feeling a kind of anxiety she hadn't felt in a long time—a futility that she couldn't change things so why bother? That'd been the way she used to think when she'd wake up and be confronted with what she'd done. Changing seemed so hard, so impossible—why even try?

Expecting Phillip to change, just like that?

No, wait. No need to jump to conclusions. Phillip had just realized that she'd be working in the paddock all day, that was all. And he was busy doing…party things.

She sent a text—"I know you can do this, babe." Then, she sent another—"Don't forget."

*Don't forget me*, she wanted to add, but didn't. Instead, she took a quick photo of Sun and sent it.

She didn't get a reply.

What could she do? Nothing. It was not as if she could go to him. He was in Texas. This was up to him. She couldn't make the choice for him, any more than her parents could have kept her from driving to that convenience store.

So she pushed her worry from her mind. She wanted to try and saddle Sun and that required her full attention. But the work didn't stop her from praying that Phillip remembered. Or, at the very least, that Fred forcibly reminded Phillip what was on the line.

Because what was on the line was the farm. The horses. This was about Sun and the Appaloosas and all the Percherons—Beaumont Farms. Not her. What she needed to remember was that she was here for the reference, the paycheck—the prestige of having saved a horse no one else could.

She had to keep up the wall between what happened in the paddock and the bedroom.

But he'd promised her. And she so desperately wanted him to keep that promise.

She didn't get Sun saddled. The horse must have picked up on her nerves because he refused to stand still long enough for her to brush him. She did get him back into his stall. She left Betty in the stall next to him—hopefully that would help him mellow out more.

Then, dread building in her stomach, she went to her trailer and got her phone. No new text messages.

She sat there, her fingers on the buttons. She shouldn't be afraid to look, right? He had Fred. He had a clear head. He wouldn't forget. He wouldn't forget *her*. She was making a mountain out of a molehill. He was working, no doubt. She needed to get a grip.

Fortified by these completely logical thoughts, she toggled over to Twitter—and her stomach immediately fell in. Oh, *no*. He'd posted pictures almost every half hour of him with famous people she recognized and a lot of people she didn't. A lot of women.

The women were concerning—but not nearly as worrisome as the look in Phillip's eyes. As she scrolled through the feed, his eyes got blearier. Each smile stayed the same—infectious and fun-loving—but his eyes? They were flatter and flatter.

What had he done?

Then she saw it. The bottle of Beaumont Beer in his hand, almost hidden behind the waist of a curvaceous redhead. Open.

The next photo, the bottle was less hidden. She needed to stop scrolling, but she couldn't help herself. How far had he fallen? How much had he forgotten?

Everything. The women in the pictures got more outrageous, more hands-on. The beer got more obvious. And the look in Phillip's eyes? He wouldn't remember any of this.

And she knew that she'd never forget it.

Each picture after that was worse until she got to the photos he'd posted about an hour ago. She knew the guys in the photo were some famous band, but she didn't know which one. All she knew was that they were surrounding Phillip on stage and they were toasting with their beer bottles. Phillip toasted with them.

After that, she shut her phone off and sat there, staring at the dinette tabletop. This *feeling* of hopelessness, helplessness—this was exactly why she'd held herself back. She'd always told herself it was to keep people safe, like Tony, the guy who'd died in a car next to her. She couldn't get involved with people because it would end badly for them. And there was no question that this would end badly for Phillip.

But he'd made his choice. He could drink away his pain.

She couldn't. That hard wall she'd demanded between men and alcohol—between Phillip and whiskey—she had to cling to that wall.

She never should have slept with him. Cared about him. Fallen for him.

Because now she was going to hurt. And just like the pain she'd had to feel when she'd been coming out of surgeries and physical therapy, she'd have to feel all of this.

She didn't want to. God, she didn't want to hurt, to know she'd broken her own rules and now she was going to pay the price for it.

Her mind spun, trying to find something that would allow her to sidestep around the heartache. Okay, Phillip had fallen off the wagon. Everyone did, right? Obviously, there'd been a problem with the sober coach because he hadn't been in any of the pictures. Fred had screwed up. They'd fire Fred, wherever he was, and hire another sober coach. Someone who wouldn't bail on Phillip in high-pressure situations. This could be fixed. This could be...

Against her will, she picked up her phone. A new picture popped up. Phillip, with his arms around two women who could have been the same two he'd brought to the ranch a month ago. He had a bottle in each hand. His lips were pressed against the cheek of one of the women.

No, it couldn't be fixed. She was making excuses for him and she knew it. They'd had a deal. She couldn't be with him if he wasn't sober. She couldn't kiss him and taste whiskey.

Whatever Fred did or did not do, it still came down to Phillip. It was his call. He'd gone to this event just like she'd driven herself to that gas station all those years ago. He'd been faced with a beer tent, just like she'd stood in front of the walls of cans.

She'd walked away from beer. She'd stayed on the wagon.

He hadn't.

Phillip was an alcoholic. And he was, at this very moment, drunk and probably getting drunker. She'd told him she couldn't be the reason he chose to stay sober. She'd meant it every single time she'd said it.

It shouldn't have hurt so much. But it did. God, it did.

She couldn't save Phillip if he didn't want her to. And to stay around him when he had whiskey on his breath.... He'd tempt her.

Could she really stop kissing him? Could she really stop loving him?

She couldn't. It was all or nothing with her. Always had been. And once she tasted that whiskey...

She rubbed at the skin on the back of her neck. The deal was broken. In so many ways.

What did that leave her with? Besides a broken heart?

It was time to go. She'd done her job. Sun could be haltered, moved and brushed without causing harm to himself or anyone else. The horse, at least, was on the road to recovery.

She *had* to leave before Phillip took her down with him.

She'd left jobs before. Leaving shouldn't be the hard part. Except…she'd started to think of the Beaumont Farms as home. Betty loved it here. Betty and Sun were friends.

She just…she needed another job. Something new to focus on. Something to remind her who she was and what she wanted. She was a horse trainer. One of the best. She didn't need friends or…love.

It just caused pain and since she was an alcoholic, she couldn't ever take anything to numb it. The high wasn't worth it. It wasn't worth *this*.

The only thing she had was her work and her rules. Rules she wouldn't bend, much less break, ever again.

She opened her laptop and blindly scrolled through emails about damaged horses, only to find herself typing a message to her parents. "*Coming home,*" she wrote. "*I didn't forget.*"

It was only then that she realized she was crying.

# Fifteen

Everything moved, including Phillip's stomach. *Urgh*.

*Jo*. He needed Jo. Jo would make this better.

He was moving. Why was he moving? He tried to open his eyes, but it didn't work, so he patted around with his hands.

God, his head. Why did it hurt so badly? Combined with the moving…his stomach was going to make him pay.

He hit something cool and round and long. A bottle. Why was there a bottle next to him on the seat?

Everything shifted to the right and the bottle rolled away. It made the dull clanking noise of glass bouncing off glass. The noise did horrible things to his head.

But he managed to get his eyes open. He was in his limo. He thought. Except…there were bottles everywhere. His fingers closed around something soft and lacy. He held up a scrap of fabric and stared at it for a minute before he realized that it was a pair of red panties. Not the kind Jo wore.

Oh, *shit*. He dropped them as if they were poison and stared around the limo. There were beer bottles all over the place and a few other scraps of clothing. And a woman's shoe. And some questionable stains. God, the *smell*. What had happened?

Oh, no. *No.*

He needed fresh air right now. He fumbled for the knobs on the door. His window went down, which let in way too much light. What time was it?

When was it?

He didn't know. He didn't know where he was or where Jo was and he didn't know what he'd done. But the limo—the limo was full of answers. The wrong ones.

That realization made him want to throw up.

He reached for his phone, but it wasn't there. He tried the knobs again and this time, the divider between the front and the back of the limo slid down.

"Mr. Beaumont? Is everything all right?"

"Uh…" He tried to think, but damn his head. "Ortiz?"

"Yes, Mr. Beaumont?"

"Where are we?"

"We'll be at the farm in ten minutes, Mr. Beaumont."

The farm. Jo. He needed her. Oh, God, she was going to be so mad. "What…time is it?"

"Four. In the afternoon," Ortiz helpfully added.

"Sunday?"

"Sunday."

That meant he hadn't missed that day. Just…Phillip rubbed his head, which did not help. Did he remember Saturday?

"What happened to Fred?"

"He was arrested."

That sounded bad. "Why?"

"He punched Pitbull—you know, the rapper?" Ortiz waited for some sign of recognition, but Phillip had nothing. Ortiz sighed. "There was a fight and Fred got arrested."

"I don't…" *I don't remember.* But that was probably obvious at this point. "Is he still in jail?"

Ortiz shook his head, which somehow made Phillip dizzy. "Your brother Mr. Matthew Beaumont bailed him out."

"Oh." That wasn't his fault, was it? If Fred got arrested and left him all alone, that wasn't his doing, right? He needed to send a message to Jo. He needed to tell her he hadn't done it on purpose. Any of it. It'd just been…it'd been a mistake. Everyone made them. He patted his pocket for his phone, but it still wasn't there. "Where's my phone?"

"It got…flushed. At least, that's what you told me." Ortiz looked at him in the rearview mirror.

"Oh. Right. I remember," he lied. Bad. Very bad.

He really was going to be sick.

Just then, they drove through the massive gates at the edge of Beaumont Farms. His heart tried to feel light—he loved coming back to this place—but there was no lightness in his soul.

He'd messed up. The blackout wasn't worth it.

But it wasn't his fault! Fred was supposed to be his sober coach and he'd gotten in a fight with a rapper and gotten hauled off to jail.

He just had to explain it to Jo, that was all. This was an accident.

He hadn't meant to drink. Bits and pieces filtered back into his consciousness. Fred had disappeared. Phillip had been onstage. Someone had put a beer in his hand. But he wasn't going to drink it. He remembered that clearly now. He wasn't going to drink that beer. He'd promised. He'd hold it, because that was his job. He wanted everyone else to drink Beaumont Beer and have fun. He did a good job. He always did.

But the beer…it'd smelled good. And some woman had kissed him, rubbing her body against his. Because he was Phillip Beaumont and that's what women did. And he *knew* that the picture would wind up online. And that Jo would see it. She'd see this strange woman who meant nothing to him kissing him and the beer bottle in his hand and Jo would think he'd failed her. She'd leave him.

Suddenly, he'd felt the same way he'd felt when Chadwick had said he was selling the farm and the horses—hopeless. He'd been good for three weeks, with Jo, but the moment things went wrong, he wound up with a beer in his hand and woman in his arms. Because it would never change. He would never change.

And the woman tasted like beer and he'd liked it. *Needed* it. Needed not to think about how Jo would look at him, the disappointment all over her.

There'd been a bottle in his hand….

And he'd stopped thinking. Stopped feeling.

"Mr. Beaumont, you want to go to the house?"

What had he done? He *needed* Jo. He needed that silly little donkey. He needed someone to tell him that it would be okay, that he could sleep it off and tomorrow they'd go back to normal. The farm. The horses. Sun. Tomorrow, this would all be a bad dream.

He needed to see her and know that she forgave him. That he hadn't disappointed her. That he hadn't forgotten her, not really.

"The white barn." Yeah, he probably looked like hell and smelled worse, but he had to talk to Jo *now*.

They drove through the perfect pastures. His horses trotted in the fields. It was perfect.

Except for the big trailer hitched to a truck out front. No, no, *no*. He'd gotten here just in time. She couldn't leave. She couldn't leave *him*.

Ortiz pulled off a few feet opposite the trailer. Phillip

tried to open the door but he missed the handle the first time. Then the door swung open and Ortiz was hauling him out. "You sure you want to do this, boss?"

Phillip winced at the sound. "Gotta talk to her." He tried to pull free, but the world started rolling, so he let Ortiz hold him up.

They awkwardly started toward her trailer. He didn't need Ortiz. He could walk. He stopped and straightened up, but his feet wouldn't cooperate. He stumbled and went down to one knee.

"Mr. Beaumont," Ortiz said. "Please."

Phillip heard noises but he couldn't make out what they were. Then he was on his feet again. His head rolled to one side and he saw that Richard was under his left side. "Dick?"

"Don't know if you realize this, sir, but you only call me Dick when you're drunk."

"Wasn't my fault," Phillip tried.

"Sure it wasn't. Let's get you to the house."

"No—need Jo. Betty?"

"*Sir,*" Richard said in a voice that was too loud for everything. Then they started moving. Away from the barn. Away from the trailer.

"Wait," came a different voice. A female voice.

*Jo.*

Somehow, Phillip got himself turned around and found himself facing Jo. This turned out not to be a good thing.

The woman he'd spent weeks chasing? Gone. The chase was over. He could see it in her eyes—hard and cold.

Next to her stood Betty, her small body wrapped up in something that had to be a harness.

"No." It came out shaky. Weak. He tried to clear his throat and start again. "Don't go. I'm sorry."

"Sun," Jo said, "is manageable. He can be haltered and

walked from the stall to the paddock. He can be brushed. He's doing much better."

That statement hung in the air. Phillip was pretty sure he heard someone else whisper "unlike you" but every time he tried to move his head, he had to fight off nausea.

"I didn't—Fred—*Jo*," he begged. Why weren't the words there? Why couldn't he say the right things to make her stay? "Don't go. I'm sorry. I'll do better. I'll *be* better. For you."

Jo looked at the men on either side of Phillip. Both of them stepped back and, miracle of miracles, Phillip's legs held. He stood before her. It was all he could do.

"No. Not *for* me." She took a step toward him. "We had a deal, you and I." This time, her voice was softer. Sadder.

"It won't happen again. Don't leave me. I can't do this without you."

She reached up, her palm warm and soft against his cheek. He leaned into her touch so much he almost lost his balance.

"I can't kiss you and taste whiskey. I can't be the reason you drink or don't drink. I never could. I can't…" She swallowed then, closing her eyes as if she was digging deep for something. "I can't love you more than you love the bottle. So I won't."

*Love.* That was a good word. The best one he had. "I love you, Jo. Don't go."

Her smile wasn't one, not really. Not when tears spilled down her cheeks. "I won't forget our time together, Phillip." She leaned in close, her breath warming his cheek. "I won't forget you. I just wish…I wish you could say the same."

He tried to put his arms around her and hold onto her until she stopped saying she was leaving, but she was gone—away from him, picking up Betty off the ground and cradling her in her arms.

"No," he tried, but his voice didn't seem to be working so well. "Don't." He tried to chase after her, but he tripped and went down to his knees again. *"Don't."*

Then people were holding him back—or up, or both—he didn't know. All he knew was that she walked away from him.

She carried Betty to her truck. She got in. The door shut. She drove away.

After that, he didn't remember anything else.

He didn't want to.

# Sixteen

Jo dusted off her chaps as she climbed back to her feet. Precious was not in the mood to run barrels right now. Jo sighed. If a horse could be passive aggressive, Precious was. She'd let Jo saddle her and mount up as if they were old friends and then *boom*. Jo was on the ground and Precious was on the other side of the paddock, munching grass.

Jo glared as she walked over to the horse. "Here's the bad news," she said as she grabbed the reins and wiped the sweat from her eyes. Late summer sun beat down on her head. Not for the first time, she missed the cool greenness of Beaumont Farms, even as she tried to tell herself that it was summer there, too. "That worked for about twelve seconds. Now we're going to do it again and again until you get tired of it."

Precious shook her head and tried to back up.

Oh, no—Jo wasn't having any of that. She swung into the saddle before the horse could get very far. This time, Jo was ready for her and managed to stay in the saddle when Precious went sideways. "Ha!" she said as she guided the horse around the makeshift barrel run she'd set up in her parents' paddock. "Again."

They ran the barrels several more times, Precious trying to buck her off at the same spot each time. Jo held on. The less fun the horse could have bucking her off, the more likely she'd stop doing it.

In the two months since she'd come home, Jo had continued to train horses. She'd given up the road—for the time being, at least. She was back in her room and her mom was back to grumbling about a donkey sliding around on the hallway rugs.

It'd taken a few days, but Jo had finally told her granny what had happened as they'd rocked on the porch swing.

"Be thankful for the rain," Lina had said after Jo had cried on her shoulder. Which was a very Lina thing to say. "Nothing grows, nothing moves forward without a little rain now and then."

Which was all well and good, except Jo didn't feel as if she'd grown much at all. She was still living with her parents, though that was her choice. She'd billed Beaumont Farms for the time she'd spent with Sun and received a check signed by Matthew Beaumont.

The check alone was enough for a down payment on a piece of land. She could have her pick of properties anywhere she wanted to stake her claim.

But she hadn't pulled the trigger on anything yet. It'd been a relief to come home, to be surrounded by people who loved her no matter what. People who didn't think she'd done the stupid thing by walking away from Phillip Beaumont, but the smart thing.

Plus, after a few months at Beaumont Farms, nothing seemed quite good enough.

She told herself that she was just taking some time off,

but that wasn't true, either. She'd had five horses delivered to her on the ranch, including Precious.

At least she was still getting jobs. Because Phillip had so spectacularly come apart, her leaving the job as she did—crying—had not come back to bite her on the butt. She didn't know what people might be saying about her and Phillip, but it hadn't impacted her work. She was still, first and foremost, a horse trainer who used "nontraditional" methods. Desperate horse owners still wanted her to save their horses. That was a good thing. It paid the bills.

She could be back on the road anytime she wanted to go. And now, she knew she would not have moments of weakness, moments of need. The walls she'd built up—for her own good—would stay up. No more Phillip. No more men. She'd gotten used to it once. She'd get used to it again.

She needed to get used to waking up alone, to going to sleep the same way. To frustrated sexual desire that she was having trouble burying like she used to.

She'd made it years without a man. It'd just take a little while to work Phillip out of her system, that was all. Once she was sure she could do fine on her own again, she'd load up her trailer and hit the road. She'd start looking for a place then.

She spent another hour with Precious, managing to stay in the saddle the whole time. Jo was about to call it a day when she saw a plume of dust kicking up down the road.

She looked back at the house. No one had mentioned they were expecting company today and Precious's owner wasn't due back until this weekend. Who would be driving this far out to the middle of nowhere?

As the car got closer, she saw it was an extended-cab, dual-wheeled truck—a lot like the one she used to haul her trailer. Must be a fellow rancher coming to talk to Dad, she reasoned as she pulled the saddle off Precious and began rubbing the horse down.

She heard the truck stop behind her, heard boots on gravel. "Dad's in the house," she called over her shoulder.

Then she heard Betty braying in the way she did when she was excited about something.

"Hey, Betty—you remember me? That's a good girl."

Jo froze, brush hovering over Precious's back. She knew that voice.

*Phillip.*

She turned slowly. Phillip Beaumont stood halfway between the truck and the paddock. He was wearing broken-in jeans and a button up shirt that walked the fine line between cowboy and hipster. The tips of brown boots were barely visible in the dirt.

He was rubbing Betty's ears. The donkey leaned into his legs as if the two of them had never been apart.

Something in Jo's chest clenched. He was here. It'd been almost two months, but he was here *now*.

Then he looked up at her. His eyes were brighter, the green in them greener. He looked good. Better than good. He looked right, like the true version of himself.

She was *so* glad to see him. She didn't want to be— she was getting him out of her system—but she was. God, she was.

Behind him, a small man wearing wire-rim glasses stepped out from the other side of the truck.

Phillip nodded his head to the man. "This is Dale," he said with no other introduction. "He's been my sober companion since I got out of rehab."

She should not be this glad to see him. It didn't matter to her one way or the other what he did or why he did it. But still… "You were in rehab?"

"Twenty-eight days in Malibu. I've been sober for fifty-three days now." He gave her a crooked grin, as if this statistic was something that he was both proud of and embarrassed by.

"You have?" She stared at him—and got hip-checked by Precious. She stumbled forward and turned to glare at the horse. "One second," she told Phillip and Dale.

She untied Precious's lead from the fence and opened the paddock gate. It didn't take longer than a minute or two to lead the horse to a pasture, but it felt as if it took a week. She felt Phillip's eyes on her the entire time and, just as it had that first time, it made her want to flutter.

She wanted to throw herself in his arms and tell him how damn much she'd missed him—missed working horses with him, missed waking up with him.

Things she couldn't miss. Things she *wouldn't* miss.

He was just a temptation, that was all. And she'd gotten very good at resisting temptations. Was this any different than standing in front of the beer coolers in a convenience store?

No. She was strong enough to resist.

Once the horse was turned loose, she faced Phillip again. "You finished rehab and have been sober for almost two months?"

"I knew you might not believe me." But instead of being put out by her doubt, Phillip's eyes focused on hers as if no one else in the world existed. "That's why I brought Dale. He can vouch for me."

She looked at Dale, who nodded. "He's followed his plan perfectly."

"You have a plan?" They'd had a plan before and that hadn't worked out so well. "What happened?"

Phillip took a step toward her. The confident grin was gone and he looked earnest. She wanted to believe him. Oh, how she wanted to believe him.

"I believe the correct phrase is 'hit bottom.' Matthew took me to rehab three days after you left. It wasn't exactly fun, but after my head cleared, I knew I could do it because I'd already done it with you."

Three days was a long time to bounce around at rock bottom. "And after that? Did you lose the farm?"

He took another step toward her. She wanted to reach out and touch him, to know that he was really here and whole and sober.

"The Beaumont Brewery has been sold. The deal closed. I was able to buy the horses with my share of the sale."

"Just the horses? But the farm…" The farm was his home.

For such a short time, the farm had felt like *her* home.

Another step forward. "Chadwick kept it."

"Oh."

Another step closer. He reached out and brushed his thumb over her cheek. "I no longer work for Beaumont Brewery," Phillip said, cupping her cheek in his hand. "After that last festival, well, we mutually agreed to part company. I have a new job."

"Doing what?"

This step brought him close enough that she could wrap her arms around his waist and hold on to him. She almost did, too. But she couldn't. She *wouldn't*.

"I'm the head of Beaumont Farms."

She blinked up at him. "You're *what?*"

"It turns out that the new owners of the Beaumont Brewery have decided that the Percheron draft team is too valuable to the brand to give up. They're leasing the Percherons from the Beaumont family. Chadwick got them to sign a ten-year non-exclusive contract."

"It worked? Going on the morning shows? The Facebook poll?"

He nodded. "It did. Plus, it turns out that Chadwick is keeping the Percheron Drafts craft beer brand for himself—he's going to use the Percherons, too. The Brewery had exclusive use of the Beaumont wagons and harnesses, but I've been working with Chadwick and Matthew on a marketing plan that will make the best use of the horses while differentiating between the companies."

"Wow. But—Percheron Drafts is still a beer company."

"I don't work for Percheron Drafts. I work for Beaumont Farms. Chadwick incorporated the land as a separate entity. Right now, I *choose* not to visit the new brewery. Chadwick and Matthew have been coming out to the farmhouse for our meetings. They're being extremely supportive."

"Even Chadwick?"

His smile—God, that was going to be her undoing. "Even Chadwick. It turns out that we get along a lot better when I'm not drunk and he's not a jerk."

He leaned down closer—too close. She pulled back, away from his sure hands and intent gaze. "That's really good. I'm happy for you. But why are you here?"

The space she'd put between them wasn't enough to stop the corner of his mouth from curving into a smile that wasn't quite predatory but came damned close. "Because I learned the hard way the blackouts weren't worth it. They weren't worth losing the farm and the horses and they most especially weren't worth losing you. I had a good month where you showed me that my life could be what I wanted it to be. I almost threw it all away. The choice was mine and so was the blame."

She shook her head. He was saying all the right things, all the things she needed to hear. But…

"I can't be the reason, Phillip."

For the first time, she saw doubt in his eyes. "I know. But it turns out, I couldn't live with myself for letting you go."

"You couldn't?"

"No." He took a deep breath. "I'm sorry that I broke my promise to you. I know I hurt you."

"You did. And worse, you made me doubt myself." He

nodded. No lame excuses, no blaming others. He took full responsibility. "But," she went on, "you also showed me that I was stronger than I gave myself credit for."

"Got your wagons unhitched now?"

She couldn't help herself. She smiled at him and was rewarded with a smile of his own. It wasn't fair for a man to look that good. It just wasn't. "Yup."

"Let me make it up to you, Jo. I want to make things right between us."

She eyed him. "How?"

There was that grin again—sharp and confident, a man who always got what he wanted. Even if he had to go through rehab to get it.

"As the manager of Beaumont Farms, I'm looking for ways to make Beaumont the premiere name in the horse world. I happen to have a well-trained stallion that's going to command huge stud fees, but I want to branch out."

Was he calling Sun well-trained? Her face grew hot. "Yeah?"

He nodded, warming to his subject. "I decided having a professional on-site trainer, someone who specializes in rehabilitating broken horses, would add a lot of validity to the brand."

Her mouth dropped open in shock. "You decided *that?*"

He cupped her face in his hands. "Come home to the farm, Jo. I want you. I don't want to lose you again. And I don't want to stay sober *because* of you. I want to do it *for* you. To show you that I'm the man who's not perfect, but perfect for you. Because with you, I'm the man I always wanted to be."

"I can't be with you if you drink. I can't kiss you and taste whiskey. Not now, not ever."

He leaned down, his lips brushing over hers. She was powerless to stop him, powerless to do anything but wrap her arms around his waist and pull him in tight.

"I will never drink again, Jo—because more than the horses, more than the land, I can't lose you. You make me chase you. You never pull your punches with me. I'm not a Beaumont when I'm with you. I'm just Phillip."

"You've always been more than a Beaumont to me," she told him. Her voice came out shaky, but she didn't care.

"I don't want to forget you," he whispered. "I *never* want to forget you."

She crushed her lips against his. His teeth scraped over her lip—rough, but gentle. Just the way she wanted it. Just the way she wanted *him*.

He rested his forehead against hers. Her hat fell off, but she didn't care.

"Don't give up on us. I can't fix what I did, but what we have is worth saving. Marry me, Jo. Come home."

*Home*. With Phillip. A piece of land she could call her own—*their* own. Everything she'd ever wanted.

"I couldn't forget you, either. I tried. I kept telling myself I just had to get you out of my system, but…"

He grinned, satisfied and hungry all at the same time. One of his fingers traced the spot where her neck met her shoulder. Her body ached for his touch, his bite. "Marry me. We'll remember the days—*and* the nights—together."

How could she say no to that?

She couldn't.

So she didn't.

\* \* \* \* \*

# MILLS & BOON®

**Power, passion and irresistible temptation!**

The Modern™ series lets you step into a world of sophistication and glamour, where sinfully seductive heroes await you in luxurious international locations. Visit the Mills & Boon website today and type **Mod15** in at the checkout to receive

## 15% OFF

your next Modern purchase.

Visit **www.millsandboon.co.uk/mod15**

# MILLS & BOON®

## Why not subscribe?
Never miss a title and save money too!

Here's what's available to you if you join the exclusive **Mills & Boon Book Club** today:

✦ *Titles up to a month ahead of the shops*
✦ *Amazing discounts*
✦ *Free P&P*
✦ *Earn Bonus Book points that can be redeemed against other titles and gifts*
✦ *Choose from monthly or pre-paid plans*

### Still want more?
Well, if you join today we'll even give you
***50% OFF your first parcel!***

So visit **www.millsandboon.co.uk/subs**
**or call Customer Relations on 020 8288 2888**
to be a part of this exclusive Book Club!

## Snow, sleigh bells and a hint of seduction

Find your perfect Christmas reads at
**millsandboon.co.uk/Christmas**

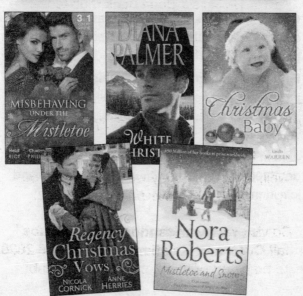